Praise for *The Queen of Last Hopes*

"From the moment King Henry appears in *The Queen of Last Hopes*, I was captivated. With elegantly simple brushstrokes, Susan Higginbotham reveals the disarming innocence and sweetness of Henry, and the tender affection between him and his young bride, Margaret of Anjou. And then at once we are swept along with them into the maelstrom of political intrigue that destroys them. Step by inexorable step we endure with them the betrayals, the humiliations, the horrific deaths of their supporters, all visited upon them by those who saw them as a fool and his sorceress, intent on destroying the glory of England—the king's powerful cousins who took advantage of his descent into madness. In the end, Margaret of Anjou's fury is ours. Higginbotham's portrayal of Henry and his fiercely loyal queen never sinks into melodrama."
—Emma Campion, author of *The King's Mistress*

"A beautiful blending of turbulent history and deeply felt fiction, Susan Higginbotham's *The Queen of Last Hopes* brings alive an amazing woman often overlooked or slandered by historians. Fast-paced and sweeping, this novel of the little-known English queen, Margaret of Anjou, pulls the readers into the heads and hearts of the movers and shakers during the devastating Wars of the Roses. Higginbo ven readers of historical fiction a gift to
—Karen Harper, *New York Times* author of *The Irish Prince*

D0710859

"*The Queen of Last Hopes* is an inspiring novel of a woman who, in the face of betrayal and loss, would not surrender. Susan Higginbotham brings Margaret of Anjou to life and tells the story of the Frenchwoman who was one of the strongest queens England has ever known."
—Christy English, author of *The Queen's Pawn* and *To Be Queen*

"A compelling, fast paced, and well-written saga that is destined to both entertain and educate anyone interested in the spirited and fascinating Margaret of Anjou for generations to come!"
—D. L. Bogdan, author of *Secrets of the Tudor Court*

THE
QUEEN
OF LAST
HOPES

THE QUEEN OF LAST HOPES

The Story of Margaret of Anjou

Susan Higginbotham

The Book of the Love-Smitten Heart, trans. Stephanie Gibbs/Kathryn Karczewska.
Copyright 2001 by Taylor & Francis Group LLC—Books. Reproduced with permission of Taylor & Francis Group LLC—Books via Copyright Clearance Center.

Published by Sourcebooks Landmark, an imprint of Sourcebooks, Inc.
P.O. Box 4410, Naperville, Illinois 60567-4410
(630) 961-3900
Fax: (630) 961-2168
www.sourcebooks.com

Library of Congress Cataloging-in-Publication Data

Higginbotham, Susan.
 The queen of last hopes : the story of Margaret of Anjou / by Susan Higginbotham.
   p. cm.
 1. Margaret, of Anjou, Queen, consort of Henry VI, King of England,
1430-1482--Fiction. 2. Queens--Great Britain--Fiction. 3. Great Britain--
History--Henry VI, 1422-1461--Fiction. 4. Great Britain--History--Edward
IV, 1461-1483--Fiction. 5. Great Britain--Kings and rulers--Fiction. I. Title.
 PS3608.I364Q44 2011
 813'.6--dc22
                          2010039641

Printed and bound in the United States of America.
 VP 10 9 8 7 6 5 4 3 2 1

Also by Susan Higginbotham

The Traitor's Wife

Hugh and Bess

The Stolen Crown

Characters

ALL OF THE NAMED CHARACTERS IN THIS NOVEL ARE BASED ON HISTORICAL figures. I have included all those who have extended or recurring speaking parts, those who are mentioned frequently by other characters, and those who are important to understanding the relationships between the characters.

The House of Lancaster

Henry VI, King of England. Son of Henry V and Katherine of Valois.
Margaret of Anjou (sometimes called "Marguerite"), his queen.
Edward of Lancaster, Prince of Wales, their son.
Humphrey, Duke of Gloucester, uncle of Henry VI.

The House of York

Richard, Duke of York.
Cecily Neville, his wife, Duchess of York.
Edward ("Ned"), Earl of March, later Edward IV, their son. Married to Elizabeth Woodville.
Edmund, Earl of Rutland, their son.
Margaret, Duchess of Burgundy, their daughter.
George, Duke of Clarence, their son.
Richard, Duke of Gloucester, their son, later Richard III.

The Nevilles

Richard Neville, Earl of Warwick.

Anne Beauchamp, Countess of Warwick, his wife.

Isabel Neville, Duchess of Clarence, their daughter.

Anne Neville, Princess of Wales, their daughter. Married to Edward of Lancaster.

John Neville, Lord Montagu, later Earl of Northumberland, later Marquess of Montagu, brother to Richard Neville, Earl of Warwick.

Richard Neville, Earl of Salisbury, father to Richard Neville, Earl of Warwick, and John Neville.

The Beauforts

Edmund Beaufort, Marquess of Dorset and Earl of Somerset, later Duke of Somerset (died 1455).

Eleanor Beauchamp, his wife.

Henry ("Hal") Beaufort, their first son, Earl of Dorset, later Duke of Somerset (died 1464).

Edmund Beaufort, their second son, styled Duke of Somerset after 1464 (died 1471).

John Beaufort, their third son (died 1471).

Margaret Beaufort, Countess of Richmond. Cousin to Henry, Edmund, and John Beaufort. Mother to Henry Tudor, later Henry VII.

The Tudors

Owen Tudor, stepfather to Henry VI and husband of Katherine of Valois, Henry V's widow.

Edmund Tudor, Earl of Richmond, son of Owen Tudor and Katherine of Valois and half brother to Henry VI. Married to Margaret Beaufort, Countess of Richmond.

Henry Tudor, son of Edward Tudor and Margaret Beaufort. Later Henry VII.

Jasper Tudor, Earl of Pembroke, son of Owen Tudor and Katherine of Valois and half brother to Henry VI.

The French Royal Family

Charles VII, uncle to Margaret of Anjou.

Louis XI, his son, cousin to Margaret of Anjou.

The House of Anjou

René of Anjou, father to Margaret of Anjou.
Isabelle, mother to Margaret of Anjou.
Jeanne de Laval, stepmother to Margaret of Anjou.

The Scottish Royal Family

Mary of Gueldres, dowager queen and regent of Scotland, widow of James II.
James III, King of Scotland.

Dukes of Burgundy

Phillip, Duke of Burgundy.
Charles, his son, Count of Charolais, later Duke of Burgundy.

Others

Bertrand de Beauvau, Seigneur de Précigny.
Black Jack, a thief.
Pierre de Brézé, friend of Margaret of Anjou.
John Cleger, groom to Edward of Lancaster.
Thomas Courtenay, Earl of Devon (died 1461).
Marie, Countess of Devon, his wife, cousin of and lady in waiting to Margaret of Anjou.
John Courtenay, Earl of Devon (died 1471), brother of Thomas Courtenay.
John Dudley, Constable of the Tower of London.
Lorenzo de Florencia, subordinate to Bishop of Terni.
John Fortescue, tutor to Edward of Lancaster.
William, Lord Hastings, chamberlain to Edward IV.
Joan Hill, mistress to Henry Beaufort, Duke of Somerset.
Henry Holland, Duke of Exeter.
James Kennedy, Bishop of St. Andrews.
John Morton, administrator.
Katherine Peniston, later Katherine Vaux. Lady-in-waiting to Margaret of Anjou.
William de la Pole, Earl of Suffolk. Later Marquess of Suffolk, later Duke of Suffolk.
Alice de la Pole (Chaucer), his wife.

XII   SUSAN HIGGINBOTHAM

Thomas ("Tom"), Lord Ros. Older half brother of Henry, Edmund, and John Beaufort.

Emma Scales, lady in waiting to Margaret of Anjou.

Charles Somerset, natural son of Henry Beaufort, Duke of Somerset, and Joan Hill.

Humphrey Stafford, Duke of Buckingham.

Anne, his wife, Duchess of Buckingham.

Andrew Trollope, soldier.

William Vaux, knight in service of Margaret of Anjou.

John de Vere, Earl of Oxford.

Will, servant of Earl of Warwick.

Anthony Woodville, son of Jacquetta Woodville and brother to Elizabeth Woodville.

Elizabeth Woodville (Lady Grey), later Queen of England.

Jacquetta Woodville, Duchess of Bedford. Mother to Elizabeth Woodville.

Prologue

August 1482

A MAN OTHER THAN MY HUSBAND SITS ON ENGLAND'S THRONE TODAY. HE is healthy and still relatively young; he has two fine young sons, an utterly loyal younger brother (another brother, the disloyal one, has long since been disposed of, in the efficient way this man has), a lovely queen, a passel of marriageable daughters. Sometimes as I sit in my chair at Dampierre and watch the sun setting over the Loire, I amuse myself by wondering what would happen if this king suddenly went mad, or simply died young. Would his nobles start to fight among themselves? Would his heir be cast aside? Would those whom he thought most loyal prove disloyal? And above all, what would his queen do? Would she make the same mistakes I did, or would she learn from mine?

For I made plenty. But soon, the Lord and King Louis willing, I shall be laid near my parents' tomb at Angers, having at last followed the men I loved to the grave. Then my maker shall hear my story and theirs as well. When our tales are at last told together as they should be, the Lord—and anyone else who cares to listen—shall judge us all, for good or for ill. There is nothing I can do now, with my life in back of me, other than to pray for mercy and hope that He will be kind.

Part I

Lady of Peace

Margaret
May 1444 to May 1445

IBECAME MY HENRY'S QUEEN LONG BEFORE I SAW HIM: AT TOURS IN 1444, TO be precise. I was fourteen. My marriage was supposed to end a conflict between England and France that had been going on for decades before I was even born.

"You will be our lady of peace," my uncle by marriage, King Charles VII of France, informed me. I had come to Tours with my father, King René of Anjou, whose sister Marie was Charles's queen, and my mother, Isabelle. The English delegation had just inspected me, though "introduction" was the word everyone had used.

"They were satisfied, then?" I asked.

"My dear, how could they not be?"

"I have always said that I had a treasure at Angers," my father said.

Charles halfway raised his eyebrows before he caught himself. I suspected that he was thinking that I was my father's only treasure, for it was true that my father was not, for his position, an especially wealthy man. Though he was known as King of Sicily and Jerusalem, Duke of Bar, Lorraine, and Anjou, and Count of Provence, his title to Jerusalem was flimsy, it had to be admitted, and he had given up his quest for Naples two years before. His lands of Maine were under English occupation. "What dowry shall I have?" I asked. It seemed only right that I as the bride should know.

"Majorca and Minorca," my uncle said, and I winced. If anything was as empty as my father's claim to Sicily and Jerusalem, it was his claim to Majorca and Minorca. "And twenty thousand francs. Well, of course the English shall get a two-year truce; I suppose that counts also."

It was humiliating being sold so cheaply, even with the truce thrown in. My distress must have shown on my face, for Charles said, "You see, my dear, they want this marriage and peace as much as we do, and frankly, they need it more. The sixth Henry isn't the warrior his father was, by all reports. Not a warrior at all."

"But a good man, they say," added my father, putting his arm around me. "Don't worry, my dear."

⁂

I was formally betrothed in the Church of St. Martin at Tours on May 24, 1444, with William de la Pole, then the Earl of Suffolk, standing proxy for Henry. My uncle led me to the choir where the Bishop of Brescia, the papal legate, stood, and Suffolk and I promised to love and cherish each other.

If a heart can break more than once, mine was to break for the first time six years later, when the whoresons—but that is for another time. I like to remember my friend Suffolk as I saw him that day at the altar, his dark eyes alive with amusement as he gave his strong responses following my somewhat shaky ones. "Don't worry, my lady, you'll be an old hand at this when it comes time to marry the king in person," he whispered as the ceremony ended and we processed to the Abbey of St. Julien, where I was to be feasted like a queen.

There was dancing much, much later in the evening. Whether I was a trifle affected from the wine that had been flowing in abundance or simply from it being well past my usual hour of retirement—for my life at Angers was not a boisterous one—I was feeling giddy when Suffolk partnered me at the dance. "If you were a proper husband to me, you wouldn't stare so at one particular lady," I said demurely.

He followed my eye to where his had just been: fixated upon the figure of Agnes Sorel, my uncle's mistress. Suffolk gave an excellent English version of a French shrug. "I beg your pardon, your grace. But it is difficult not to look, you must admit. She is very lovely—though not, of course, as our new English queen."

"Flatterer," I said, and Suffolk did not gainsay me. Agnes Sorel was blond and stately; I was little and darker, though not, I knew, charmless. "She is my uncle's official mistress," I babbled on—quite unnecessarily, I realized later, for Suffolk, who was in his late forties, had been serving in France since he was a young man and probably knew as much about the court here as I did, if not more. "Do you have such things in England?"

Suffolk shook his head gravely. "We are not nearly as advanced, I fear. Our mistresses are entirely unofficial." We paused to take some intricate turns, to general applause, for my grandmother, who had had the rearing of me, had never stinted on dancing masters, and Suffolk was an accomplished partner. "I shall be returning to England shortly. Do you have anything you would like to ask me about the king?"

I considered this question as best I could while dancing. As I turned in harmony with Suffolk, Agnes Sorel once again passed into my line of sight, which suggested a natural topic. "Does *he* have a mistress? I suppose I should know these things in advance."

My partner nearly stumbled, and had to put a hand to his mouth to stifle laughter. "I beg your pardon, your grace."

"I do not see how that is such a foolish question," I said frostily.

"In the case of most men, it would not be—but for anyone who knows our king! He is a very pious man. Indeed, some of the entertainment here tonight would have appalled him. Those rather underclad Moorish dancers we had earlier—There's none such to be seen at his court. Nor will you find any mistresses in your husband's life, in or out of court. You'll have nothing to worry about on that score."

Did that mean I had to worry about anything else? But the dance had ended and it was time to take my place back at the dais beside the Queen of France, so I never got a chance to ask my next question.

Though I was Queen of England in name now, further preparations and negotiations had to be made before I could come to my new country, and my uncle and my father had military affairs to take care of, so I returned home to my father's castle of Angers. There I passed nearly another year before it was at last time to begin my journey to England. Though I kept myself busy learning the language of my new country, I also devoted much time to reminding all at Angers of my new position, for as the youngest of my father's four legitimate children I had hitherto been of limited importance, and previous proposals for my marriage had come to nothing. In enjoying my chance to preen I was, after all, only human, and only fourteen.

At last, in February, my family traveled to Nancy, where my older sister, Yolande (who had long been affianced to Ferry de Vaudemont and thus had missed the opportunity to become Queen of England herself) was to finally marry her betrothed. It was an important occasion for me as well, for I was to travel on to Rouen and thence finally to my husband across the Channel.

It was a grand occasion, at which my uncle King Charles and most of the French nobility were present, and a hugely expensive one, but my uncle found leisure to call me to him during one of the rare moments of inactivity.

"Queenship suits you," he said, nodding at me. "You've grown taller since you were last here."

"Yes, your grace." I forbore from pointing out that I was still at an age where one could be expected to grow.

"It is time we spoke of your duties as queen."

I frowned, hoping that this was not the sort of talk my mother had had with Yolande and me as we traveled to my sister's wedding. "I know my duties," I announced. "I am to be virtuous, to manage my household carefully, to intercede with my husband's subjects, to—"

The king cut me off impatiently. "Yes, yes, all those. But you are a daughter of France, my dear. It is your duty to your country of which I speak."

"I am Queen of England," I reminded him.

"Yes, but you will never cease to be a Frenchwoman. You have the opportunity to do much good with this marriage. Good to our country, and even to England."

"Through peace?"

"Through peace on the terms we want. And what we want is the return of Maine. Suffolk refused to promise it to us when he was here; he said that doing so would exceed his instructions. Well, I can't blame him for that. Such a promise is best given by King Henry himself. You, my dear, are the best person to persuade him to give it."

"Me?"

"Why not? A pretty face and soft words can do wonders." The king gave me a chuck on the chin.

"But won't his people be upset if he simply agrees to give it up?" I discreetly moved just out of chucking range.

My uncle shrugged. "That's his concern."

Were it not impertinent, I would have said that it would presumably be my concern too. "I will do my best, Uncle."

"Good girl. Mind you, the timing must be right; it's not something you need bring up on your wedding night, say. Even Henry will have better things on his mind." I blushed, and my uncle chuckled. "But after a few months of marriage, it will be quite natural to bring it up. I trust your instinct will tell you when. You ladies are instinctive, they all say."

"Yes, Uncle," I said, grateful that I was getting a reprieve of sorts.

By and by, I arrived in Rouen, which of course in those days was still occupied by the English, most notably its lieutenant, Richard, Duke of York, and his wife and young children, who lived at Rouen Castle. The duke and duchess had four children at the time: two daughters, Anne and baby Elizabeth, and two little sons, Edward and Edmund, almost three and almost two respectively. I am not a woman to have premonitions, it appears, for I remember the Edward who was to have such a great effect on my life only as a boisterous little boy who was big for his age and who to his nurse's dismay derived great satisfaction from smacking his thumb, not out of fretfulness but out of the sheer joy of having a thumb so conveniently at hand to smack.

At Rouen, I promptly fell ill. Whether my indisposition was caused by greensickness (for I had just turned fifteen), by the arrival of my monthly course (which for me was an unpredictable event and one that always caused me a great deal of pain), by some ailment picked up from one of the four sneezing York children, or by the sheer exhaustion of having been greeted and feted in every town I passed through in Normandy, I do not know. Still, I had thought myself much improved when I boarded the *Cokke John*, which was to take me to England. Then I discovered that my malady in Rouen was a mild one compared to that caused by the sea.

William de la Pole (now Marquess of Suffolk, thanks to his role in arranging King Henry's marriage to me) and his wife, Alice, had been put in charge of me during the voyage. It had been Suffolk who had taken over my care after I had left the last of my family behind at Paris, and it was Suffolk who held me in his arms in my cabin (when I was not vomiting) and comforted me when I begged him to put me out of my misery then and there. "Let me die!" I moaned over and over again in French, the English I had been learning having abandoned me for the time being. "Just take out your dagger and kill me now."

"Now, now," Suffolk comforted me in his impeccable French, which he spoke with only the slightest English accent. "You'll be in England before you know it, your grace. Think of something pleasant. Think of the hounds the king will be buying you. Think of the beautiful gown you will have for your coronation."

"That is right!" said Alice, who was not feeling very well herself, but was bearing it with far more fortitude than I was. "You will be the most beautiful queen England has ever seen."

I closed my eyes and pictured the pack of bloodhounds my groom had promised me, word having made it across the sea that I was fond of hunting, though one couldn't have guessed it from my prostrate state now. Then I began to miss the dogs I'd left behind in France (for they were my father's, not my own), and my eyes welled with tears just as another bout of nausea began to claim me. "I want to go home to Angers," I whimpered. "I don't want to be queen."

"Well, you are," snapped Alice. I suspected that were it not for her husband's presence, she would have lost her patience with me long ago. "Act like one, for goodness's sake."

Suffolk (usually the most devoted of husbands) glared at his wife, and I myself mustered enough self-command to say, "I will not be addressed in that disrespectful manner."

"That's it," said the marchioness approvingly. "Pluck up some spirit, your grace."

For a short time, I did, even going so far as to walk around the cabin. Then the winds and waves grew rougher, and I sicker, though I no longer had anything in my stomach to bring up. I had no strength left, even to cry or complain. Instead, I simply curled up in a ball on my berth, heedless of the undignified picture I was presenting.

Finally, someone lifted me, and I thought contentedly as I was borne along in a pair of strong arms that death had indeed taken me. Then a man's beard and a cool breeze brushed my cheek, and I blinked to find myself in the open air, being carried by Suffolk. "See, your grace?" he said, smiling down at me. "We've dropped anchor, and that's the English coast. We'll be on dry land before you know it."

Though the day was a miserable one, a band of locals had gathered at Portchester, where we had landed, to give me a proper welcome as their queen. Still in Suffolk's arms—for when he had tested my ability to stand before we disembarked, I had swayed too dangerously—I managed to wave my hand at them and part with a few smiles. But the marchioness was gazing at me oddly, this time without the impatience she'd shown earlier. "Will," she said in a low voice, "I fear that the queen is coming out in a pox."

What if I had died of my illness? It might have saved a great deal of trouble and many lives, and I would have left behind nothing more than a romantic memory as a virgin queen who never lived to see her king or to wear the crown. People might have written mournful ballads about it, and I would have been dressed in my betrothal robes and laid in some beautiful tomb somewhere, my reputation as pure and unblemished as the marble of my effigy. But

I turned out not to have the dreaded smallpox, but a much milder pox, and it was pronounced by my physician, Master Francisco, that all I needed was plenty of rest and quiet. So having been removed to Southampton by barge, a peaceful journey during which I half dozed while enjoying the serenades of seven musicians, I was taken to God's House, an abbey where the principal business was to tend the sick. There I got the tranquility I sorely needed, as did my poor dear Suffolk, now able to attend to other affairs since he no longer had to serve as royal nursemaid.

After a few days had passed, I had recovered sufficiently to sit up in bed. I was listening as one of my younger attendants, Katherine Peniston, read to me, when I heard the now-familiar knock of Suffolk at my door. "Do go on reading," he said. When Katherine had finished, he cocked his head. "I am familiar with much French verse, your grace, but I have not heard that before."

"My father wrote it," I said proudly.

"Aye, I should have guessed. Your father is a man of numerous accomplishments."

"He sent some of his poems with me, for me to remember him by."

Suffolk very kindly did not point out that my father had sent precious little else with me of value. Having spent so much on my sister's wedding, my father had had little left to give me for my journey to England. As I had passed through English-occupied France, where I'd had to give alms and make various offerings in connection with my royal status, I'd found myself borrowing money from Suffolk, and I had finally salvaged my pride by pawning some plate to his wife. My wardrobe was also rather sparse; though I had had grand dresses for my betrothal ceremony and for my sister's marriage, my supply of everyday gowns was more limited. I'd had to wear the same gown twice in a row to banquets in Rouen, and I had seen the Duchess of York (resplendent herself in crimson velvet that practically dripped with pearls) raise her eyebrows when I'd appeared in it yet a third time.

I scowled, remembering the half amused look she'd given her husband. Papa might not have a real crown, but he could write verse and paint, and he had even designed his own tomb. The people of Anjou called him their good king. They probably knew him as well or better than I did, as I had spent much of my childhood in my grandmother's care while my parents struggled for Sicily, but I did miss him and my mother, and the pleasant cadence of French voices around me.

I surreptitiously dabbed at my eye, a gesture which Suffolk caught. "Your

grace, I know you felt it very deeply when you parted from your parents."
I nodded shamefacedly; I'd bawled like a great baby. "My wife and I can be
but poor substitutes, but I hope that we can help you make a home here, and
I can assure you that the king will be a gracious and kind husband to you."

"Thank you," I said, touched. To keep from becoming too maudlin, I said,
"You have a son, do you not, my lord? I was surprised not to see him as part
of your entourage."

Suffolk smiled. "I do indeed have a son, but John was not up for the task
of accompanying us to France. He is not yet three years of age, you see."
I must have looked surprised, for Suffolk was just a few years short of fifty,
an age at which many men were grandfathers. His wife, Alice, had reached
her forties herself. "The Lord did not bless us with a living child until late in
life, and he is likely to be our only one, so he is very precious to us. I have
missed him." He coughed. "He is not *my* only child, though, as I have a
natural daughter, a young lady just a year or so older than your grace, who
was conceived before my marriage. Jane was born in Normandy, but as her
mother is dead, I brought my daughter to England last year after I arranged
your marriage. She is in my wife's household, and I hope soon to find a suitable husband for her."

I nodded in a worldly manner, having several bastard brothers and sisters
myself. My father's pursuits were not entirely artistic in nature. "I shall be glad
to meet her one day."

"She will be honored. But in the meantime, your grace, there is a squire
who has been waiting very patiently outside the door. He bears a letter from
the king."

"I have been so eager to hear from him! Why did you not say so earlier?"

"My mistake, my lady. I will leave you to read it in private."

He withdrew, and a rather awkward-looking young man entered the room
and dropped to his knees. Mumbling something in halting French, he handed
me a letter—written, in consideration of my still inadequate English, in French.

I read it once, then twice, searching in it for clues about the man who would
be my husband. Suffolk had shown me a miniature of him, which depicted a
mild-looking man in his twenties with dark hair, and I had heard fearsome stories
about his warlike father, Henry V, whose name was naturally enough a detested
one in France. I had gathered that my husband was a rather different sort of man,
more inclined to peace than to war, but other than that I had but the vaguest idea
of his character. The letter provided no illumination; it was polite and warm, but

it could have been written by anyone to anyone. "Did your master say when he would be coming?" I asked the still-kneeling squire. So intent had I been on my letter that I had not allowed the poor man off his knees.

The squire could understand French better than he could speak it. "No, your grace," he managed.

"Well, you may go. Here is something for your trouble."

The squire backed away. His exit was followed promptly by the entry of the Marchioness of Suffolk and by Katherine Peniston. Both were wearing ill-concealed looks of amusement. "Pray, what is the matter with you two?"

"My lady, how did you like the squire who was just here?"

"The squire? Should I have noticed something about him? He did his duty, no more or no less."

"My lady, he was your king," sputtered the marchioness.

"That was Henry? *Mon Dieu*, I never let the man off his knees!"

"So he informed my husband," Alice said merrily. "But your grace needn't worry. He was most pleased with what he saw."

I touched my cheeks, which still had faint pox marks on them. "He saw me like this?"

"They are hardly noticeable."

"But why did he not simply introduce himself?"

Alice shrugged. "It was a fancy he had, and I do believe he was a little shy about meeting you formally, without catching a glimpse of you first. He told my lord that he thinks a lady can be observed at her best while reading a letter."

I held the letter in my hand and stared at it as if I were reading it. "I don't see how," I said, putting it down.

"Well, when a man is king, he can have whatever theory he pleases, can't he?"

"So when shall I see him officially?"

"Tomorrow, if you are well enough. He knows you will like to be properly dressed for the occasion."

"Goodness, yes," I said, realizing for the first time that I had received my husband in nothing but a shift. I was glad it was one of my thicker ones; Henry was reputed to detest loose women.

The next day, the Marchioness of Suffolk and the other English ladies who had formed my escort led me—clad appropriately—out to the garden of the House of God, where the Marquess of Suffolk was waiting for me with the squire of the day before, who now that I took the trouble to notice him was a man with a slender but apparently strong build, with dark hair, cut some-what shorter than was fashionable. This time, however, he was clad in robes trimmed with ermine.

I began to curtsey to him, but he would not allow it. "Welcome to England, Margaret," he said in French, taking my hands. "I have waited very long for you."

"And I a very long time for you, my lord."

The king gazed at me, and I looked into the kindest pair of eyes I have ever seen, before or since. "Come," he said, leading me away from the Suffolks and the rest. "You are not strong yet, I know. Let us sit and talk."

We sat on a bench that surrounded a tree, the king holding my hand. "How is your English, Margaret?" he said in that language.

"Not well," I confessed in the same language. I blushed in shame, for Henry's French, while overlaid with a strong English accent, was perfectly comprehensible, as opposed to my awkward English.

"You may speak French with me while we are getting acquainted, then." He smiled. "As you can hear, I speak it rather more fluently than I did the other day."

"I did practice speaking English, my lord, truly. I spoke it with my tutor, and I tried to speak it with my lord of Suffolk and the rest of my escort. But I fell ill in Rouen, and it was easier for all concerned for me to speak in French."

"Yes. The Marquess of Suffolk told me that you had a very rough crossing, and that you had been sick before that."

I nodded. "I could not even ride in the grand procession arranged for me at Rouen. The Marchioness of Suffolk had to take my place, and you had sent such a beautiful chariot for me to ride in!" I sighed, picturing again the splen-did object that had awaited me in Rouen. "Instead, I had to lie in bed at the Duke of York's house, while his children kept finding excuses to come to my chamber to peep at me."

"I cannot blame them, for you are very fair." Cautiously, the king touched my cheek and drew a little closer to me. I closed my eyes and tilted my face upward, expecting a kiss. Instead, Henry drew his hand back. "I hope you are better now."

I blinked, startled at my unkissed state. I was quite virginal, but I knew enough about these matters to suspect that a Frenchman, or indeed most Englishmen, would not have passed up such an excellent opportunity. "Why yes. I am usually quite healthy." I was silent for a moment before I ventured,

"I hope I do not displease you, my lord?" I knew that I possessed the requisites for beauty in my native France—a dainty nose, bowed lips, expressive eyes, a firm, high bosom, a slender figure, pale and unblemished skin, and long, thick hair that was a darker blond than I might have wished, but that was still indisputably blond—but perhaps standards were different here. Or had those who had commended my looks been too flattering?

"Displease me? Far from it." Henry hesitated, then put his hand on my face again. "Marguerite," he said. "In English it is a flower known as a daisy."

"Oh?"

"But your eyes are like violets," Henry said thoughtfully. He placed his other hand on my other cheek. This time, I did not move my face, but let him take the initiative. Slowly, gently, he drew me toward him and kissed me on the lips, very slightly at first, then with more pressure. When he pulled back, he was smiling. "I wish to be married very soon, Marguerite."

⁂

Our wedding was to take place at Titchfield Abbey, to which we moved a few days later. On the day before the ceremony was to take place, Suffolk called on me, the king being occupied with some business. "Your father's wedding gift has arrived, your grace."

"Tapestries? Plate?"

"No, not quite. Come see for yourself, your grace."

I followed the marquess outside, where in an elaborate wheeled cage, a lion—whether old or young or somewhere in lion middle age I had no idea—sat glaring at me, as well might a lion in his circumstances. As I stepped forward, he let out a mighty roar, and I jumped back, almost knocking down Suffolk. "What on earth am I supposed to do with him?"

"Feed him, I would venture to say," Suffolk said wickedly. "He seems hungry." He smiled as I turned to glare at him. "The king does have a menagerie at the Tower, your grace. He can be housed there."

I sighed. Already, I had learned, Suffolk had said a discreet word to the king about my scanty wardrobe, and as a result a dressmaker had been hastily sent to Titchfield to dress me in a manner more fitting for a queen. And now my father had sent a gift that would have to be fed and tended, causing the king even more expense on my account. "My father is not always a practical man," I said.

"I seem to remember hearing that he had a menagerie himself."

"It was one of the first things he did when he came back to Anjou, to start acquiring beasts for it. But there weren't any lions in it when I left."

"Then he must have acquired this one especially for you."

"I would have preferred a songbird. Or some more plate." I cautiously moved forward. My gift roared at me again, but this time I stood my ground. "At least he didn't send me any of his dwarfs." My father was rather fond of them, and any tiny person in Anjou or Provence was sure to find his way to our household sooner or later.

"Yes, they would be rather underfoot," Suffolk said, this time drawing a grin from me. "Come, your grace, don't fret. For some years, we've had a keeper of the lions with no lions to keep. You shall supply him with a purpose in life."

My wedding on April 22, 1445, was not a large one, as so much was to be going toward my coronation in a few weeks. William Ayscough, the Bishop of Salisbury, who was also the king's confessor, officiated. I wore a gold crown set with pearls and precious stones, along with a beautiful but simple blue gown decorated with fleur-de-lis and trimmed with ermine, and the ring Henry slipped on my finger was a large ruby set in gold. All have long since gone into the hands of others.

That evening as I prepared to spend my first night with my husband, the Marchioness of Suffolk, who had been supervising the proceedings, shooed the rest of the ladies out of the room. She began brushing my long, dark blond hair, which had been brushed so thoroughly already that it hardly needed the extra attention. "I always wished the Lord would have brought my lord and me a girl," she said wistfully. "But I am thankful that He blessed us with the son we did have." She cleared her throat. "Tell me, child. Has your mother told you what you need to know about what is to come?"

I nodded. "She told me that Henry would know what to do, and that I should follow his lead."

"That may be the blind leading the blind," Alice said. "At the age of sixteen, the king declared that he would not have sexual intercourse outside of marriage, and as far as anyone knows, he has kept his vow."

"Oh." I grasped Alice's hand. "Then what shall I do?"

"Just be yourself. The king is fond of you already; anyone can see that." She patted my cheek. "Don't fear, your grace. No matter what the king does, he will be gentle about it."

Our bed in the abbey's best guestroom already having been blessed, there was nothing to do now but to let Alice help me into it and tuck me under the covers. A moment or two after Alice left, the king himself, followed by two manservants, came in. I looked away nervously as they stripped Henry of his robe, leaving him clad only in a nightshirt, and put him into bed beside me.

Henry touched my cheek, which still bore a trace or two of my pox. "Are you sure you are well enough for this, Marguerite?"

I noticed with some pleasure that he preferred the French form of my name. "I am very well."

He studied the little part of me that was not hidden beneath the covers. "You're very delicate looking. And small-boned. Perhaps—"

"I am petite, as are my mother and sister. I shall probably never grow much larger."

Henry smiled. "You can tell I'm very nervous, can't you? I've not known a woman before, Marguerite. I chose to wait until this night."

"I am honored that you did." How long could we go on like this? I found myself wishing for the Suffolks, who would surely help us around this impasse. I pictured them holding me while Henry did his business, as I'd once seen a reluctant bitch being held at Angers. A fine litter of bloodhounds had resulted. I smiled, and Henry took me in his arms and tentatively began to caress me.

It has been said that my husband was mad even back then, which is non-sense, and that he was a saint, which I will leave up to the Church to decide. Whichever tale was told, the end result was the claim that he could not or would not perform his most elemental duty as a husband. Those who say that lie. Shy and hesitant Henry might have been at first, but his hands soon grew more assured, and when I made a motion to indicate that my shift was getting in our way, he himself untied it and cast it aside, then lay looking in wonder at my nakedness in the dim light from the cresset lamp that hung overhead. "You're lovely," he said, and lay his body fully against mine.

⌒℘⌒

Indulge me a moment, for I have been paraded through the streets of London twice; once as a queen and once as a vanquished foe, a trophy of someone else's victory. Although it is the latter occasion that wakes me sometimes in the middle of the night, shivering, I find that more and more often, as I sit in my borrowed chariot at Dampierre on the days that I am well enough to go out for a ride, my mind drifts back to those perfect days in May where all London had spread itself out before me in welcome.

On the day before my coronation, I rode from my royal apartments at the Tower to Westminster, where I was to spend the night. I, my horses, and my litter were all in white, in my case, in white damask powdered with gold. Though my marriage had been consummated, custom obliged me to dress as a virgin, with my hair hanging loose beneath the gold crown, festooned with pearls and precious stones, that I had worn at my wedding. The street sellers had been hawking daisies in my honor, and as I admired my surroundings as we passed through the broad street of Cheapside, I smiled to see them in buttonholes and pinned to caps, and even in garlands woven in young girls' hair.

Peace and plenty! It was the theme of all the pageants that greeted me, all of the tournaments that followed my coronation, every sermon that was preached within a mile of London. It was the chant of the people as I made my way through the city streets in my fine litter, and when I exited Westminster Abbey on May 30, 1445, as their crowned queen. Full of optimism and the red and white wine that flowed from the city fountains that day, the people were still chanting long after Henry came to my bed that evening and loved me, noticeably more ardently than he had to date. I myself responded in a manner that I hadn't before, which far from shocking Henry had emboldened him. If I weren't carrying Henry's seed within me before, I thought contentedly, I certainly must be doing so now after all that. "Was it the crown?" I teased, the first time I'd dared to do so.

Henry stroked my hair and kissed me on the lips. "No. Just the fair Marguerite underneath it. You have brought me great happiness, my love."

"And you to me, my darling." I closed my eyes and let myself drift off in Henry's arms as the last chants of "Peace!" died away.

Margaret
July 1445 to December 1445

A S PART OF THE BARGAIN UNDER WHICH I WAS MARRIED TO HENRY, MY uncle Charles, the King of France, had entered into a two-year truce with England. This meant that for any lasting peace, there would have to be further negotiations, and those negotiations came that same July, at Westminster. I stayed at Windsor Castle, for as a woman, I had no place in the negotiations and wanted none. I was content to read the magnificent book, full of romances in my native language, that the Earl of Shrewsbury had prepared for me, to try out my new bloodhounds, and to practice my English with my ladies, who now included a number of Englishwomen as well as some of the women who had accompanied me from France.

One day, having taken a break from the negotiations, which were mainly being conducted by Suffolk, Henry brought a guest with him to Windsor: Bertrand de Beauvau, lord of Précigny. He had long served my father, and my husband had invited him to Windsor as a surprise for me. After we had walked around the castle grounds a bit and he had caught me up on the news of my family, Bertrand asked, "Have you broached the matter with the king yet?"

"No." I began to wish my husband had not thought to please me with this guest.

Bertrand frowned. "My dear child, we spoke of this before you left France. There can be no peace without the ceding of Maine, and as the queen, you are in the best position to influence Henry." He looked sharply at me. "You *are* on good terms with the king?"

"Yes, of course."

"Are you with child, perchance? There would be no better time—"

"I am not with child that I know of."

"Aye? Does the king come to your bed regularly? Don't blush, girl. This is a matter that concerns very many people beside the king and yourself."

"He does."

"How often?"

"That is our own business, sir. Suffice it to say that we are happy together, and I have no doubt that I will bear him a child soon. As for your other concern, he has given me many presents since we have married, more than I have ever had in my entire life." I looked down at my elaborate gown and jewels, all gifts from the king, and at the little dog that trotted beside me, which had come to me from my husband only the week before. "I will only seem greedy if I bring up the matter now. When the time is right, I will."

"This is not a hunting pack or a new gown. This is Maine. It is what your father expects you to obtain from the king, and it is what your uncle Charles expects you to obtain from the king."

"I fully understand that! I am no dunce. I have been told that from the very day the Marquess of Suffolk arranged the betrothal."

"Suffolk," said Bertrand. He stroked his chin. "That's a tack we may want to take. I believe Suffolk's half in love with you, judging from those sheep-eyed looks he was giving you back in France. You must keep your virtue, of course, but perhaps at the same time lead him on; with skill it could be managed. But perhaps you're too young to bring it off. Pity the beauteous Agnes Sorel wasn't more in your company before you came here; she could have—"

"I do not require lessons from my uncle's mistress, sir, and Suffolk has been like my second father. Lead him on, indeed! Every word you say is odious to me."

"Spoken like a good Englishwoman," Bertrand said. "Maybe that's the problem, you are forgetting your own country? Maine is your father's by right."

"I am well aware of that."

"Then I would think you would want to see it back in his hands. Why are you so shy about asking? It would benefit your husband as well as your father; he would have peace, which he seems to want. Which is more than I can say for his uncle, that old fool Humphrey, Duke of Gloucester."

I had met the duke and his grown bastard children, Arteys and the oddly named Antigone, on my way to London. All had been quite pleasant, and the duke's house at Greenwich, which he called Placentia, was stunning. "They say he is a very cultivated man."

"Oh, he is, but a man can quote from the Greek and still be a fool, you know." Bertrand tossed a stick for my dog, his usual good nature restored by his glee in describing Gloucester's folly. "He hasn't quite grasped that he's no longer in high favor with your husband. Your average man would have realized that after his wife was locked up as a witch."

"I heard something about that from the Marquess of Suffolk, but he wasn't at leisure to mention it to me at the time."

"Meaning he didn't wish to be overheard? Oh, it was quite the scandal over here a few years ago." Bertrand sent another stick flying. "The Duchess of Gloucester was tried for forecasting the king's illness and death. Rather a foolish thing to do when your husband is heir to the throne, don't you think? But of course, that's why she did it, and she's lucky to have escaped with her life. A couple of her associates burnt for their part in the scheme, but she was imprisoned. She's still a prisoner, although many have forgotten that she's still alive. Anyway, the witchcraft is just one of the reasons Gloucester's out of favor with King Henry. It didn't help matters that Gloucester ordered the arrest of the king's stepfather, Owen Tudor, for presuming to marry the king's mother. Of course, Suffolk's done nothing to enhance Gloucester's reputation with the king either."

"I am sure if he is in disfavor from such a good a man as my husband, he deserves it."

Bertrand chuckled. "Why, when your uncle Charles was mentioned the other day, King Henry said that he bore him great love, and then he looked straight at poor Gloucester. My, Humphrey was fuming. And then the king looked straight at Suffolk. Smiled and then turned to his chancellor and said straight out that he knew some who had heard his words were not at their ease. No one knew that King Henry had it in him to snub his old uncle so. So you see, dear girl, the ground is fertile as far as Maine goes. You need only sow it."

❦

I pondered the question of Maine in bed that night. Young as I was, I could remember the English rampaging through it; in 1443, they'd scattered their terror through Anjou as well. They'd gone so far as to lodge their captains at the Abbey of St. Nicholas in our town of Angers; though at thirteen I'd been safe inside the walls of the castle there, I could remember being too frightened to draw my bed curtains lest I awake and find my chamber full of Englishmen.

It hadn't occurred to me then that I might soon find myself married to their king.

I remembered the words that my uncle had spoken about my knowing when the time would be right. But would I? I thought now as I lay abed in England. My French ladies could be of no help; all were my age or younger. My English ladies could hardly be impartial, and in any case what did they know of Henry? He was shy around all women but me.

I decided I would consult the man I had come to trust most: Suffolk.

Just a few days later, Suffolk joined us at Windsor. When he arrived, Henry was with his confessor, though what my husband had to confess was and still largely is a vast mystery to me.

"I have a gift for you, your grace." Suffolk handed me a piece of parchment.

"A poem?"

"Of my own composition. I do not pretend to your father's level of accomplishment, or that of my old friend Charles of Orléans, but I thought your grace might enjoy this modest effort."

> Mine heart is set, and all mine whole intent,
> To serve this flower in my most humble wise,
> As faithfully as can be thought or meant,
> Without feigning or sloth in my service…

I looked up. "That flower is me?"

Suffolk smiled. "I will confess that the poem is part of a longer sequence, and that I did not have your grace in mind when it was first composed. But as I know you enjoy verse, I could not resist copying it for you, given that you are a Marguerite."

"And you have even drawn daisies around the border," I said.

"Well, something that looks like daisies. I do not pretend to be an artist."

"It is lovely, the poem—and even the daisies. I shall cherish this forever." I hesitated a little awkwardly. "How do the negotiations go?"

Suffolk half raised an eyebrow at this sudden transition from poetry to politics, but replied, "As one would expect. A few steps forward, then a few steps back. No one wants to commit himself. It appears that King Henry and King Charles will try to meet each other in a few months, however."

"Has the subject of Maine been brought up?"

Suffolk looked at me curiously. "Among others."

"My lord, I am in a dilemma. You must know that my uncle Charles and my father both wish England to cede Maine to France, and that they have asked me to exert myself to that end."

"I have presumed, yes, that they would be unlikely to ignore the usefulness of such a natural envoy as yourself." Suffolk twirled a large ring on his finger. "Please bear in mind, your grace, before you confide in me further, that however much I have enjoyed the company of King René and King Charles, I am an Englishman first and foremost. My loyalty is to King Henry and to my country."

"I understand that," I said, although in truth I sometimes forgot that Suffolk, with his fluent French and his penchant for reading French poetry, was not one of my countrymen. "But we can talk as friends, can we not? For I think of you as my dearest friend in England." I touched his arm. "Truly. I don't speak to flatter you."

"I am honored. Well, then tell me what is on your mind, and I will counsel you as far as I can."

"I do believe Maine should be returned to us. It is but right. But they have asked me to beg it from Henry as if—as if I were a bawd teasing for a trinket. I care for Henry deeply; he has been kind to me and has made me very happy. I don't want to abuse his kindness. I want him to cede Maine because he feels it is right, not because he wishes to please me."

"King Henry is a generous man, your grace, but when he acts, it is because he believes that doing so is right. I can honestly tell you that if he were to make a concession for peace, it would be because he thought it was for the best, and not merely because he was swayed by a beautiful young face."

"Do you think it would be for the best, my lord?"

Suffolk hesitated.

"I promise, my lord, I shall not use what you say against you. I am merely curious."

"Well—Does your grace know that I had four brothers?" I shook my head. "I did. I was the second of the five of us. We were close. All are gone now. My oldest brother, Michael, died in battle at Agincourt. My younger brother Alexander died at Jargeau, fighting against the troops led by the lady you call the Maid of Orléans. He was under my command at the time." Suffolk stared into the distance, and something in his face made me squeeze his hand. "My blundering cost us dearly that day, but that's not here or there just now. I was taken captive that day, and so was my brother John. He was badly injured there, and died in captivity soon afterward. I was freed the following year, but my brother Thomas had to take my place as a hostage. He died in prison before I could get him set free."

"My lord, I am so sorry."

"And my father died just weeks before my brother Michael. He died of dysentery; it was all through the camp at Harfleur. I was with him; it was a horrid death. At least my brothers who died in battle did not suffer long. So you see, your grace, my family has given much to the cause in France."

"I understand, then, that you do not wish your country to cede Maine to those whom you have cause to hate."

"*Our* country now, your grace. Do remember that." I blushed at my mistake. "No, your grace, that is not entirely so. I don't hate France. How could I? I have friends there still, and my daughter was born there. I would consider Maine worth the price for a lasting peace. I would like to see my son reach manhood and thrive, instead of being chopped down in his prime as were my brothers. But there would have to be certain conditions, such as compensation for those English who lose their lands in Maine. And that has been the stalling point in our negotiations. I would not sell us cheap, nor would I advise the king to do so."

"Indeed no," I said.

He shrugged. "Whatever we do, it will be unpopular in some circles, of course."

"Such as with the king's uncle Gloucester?"

Suffolk raised his eyebrows. "Your grace is quick to grasp our affairs."

"I have been told a little bit about the situation," I admitted. "I don't think you like him overmuch, my lord?"

"Does it show? No, I suppose not. We've worked hard to build good relations with France, and he would undo our work if he could. And he can't be disregarded entirely because he is at present the king's heir."

I stifled a sigh. Suffolk had unintentionally hit upon a sore subject, for my monthly course had made its appearance just yesterday, after a period of delay that had caused me to hope and pray that a child had been planted in my womb. But Suffolk could be spared my confidences on that score, I decided. "Is his wife really a witch?" I asked instead.

"She confessed to some of the less serious charges against her. The duchess was lucky. Her physician died in prison, and another associate was hanged, drawn, and quartered. Margery Jourdemayne, from whom she procured potions, was burned." I shuddered. "Gloucester has importuned the king to set the duchess free, I understand, but fortunately he has not softened toward her, as he is sometimes wont to do." I smiled, having heard of Henry's notoriety for pardoning criminals. "I have strongly advised him against it in any case."

"Why?"

"Because your grace's ability to bear a child stands between Humphrey and the throne, and I fear that the duchess might work her malice against you were she free to do so. And I have told the king precisely that." He grinned as I looked up at him, touched by his concern for us. "I would not care to have to spend yet another year negotiating a brand-new marriage for him."

The delegation from France returned home in August, the negotiations having produced, besides a vague feeling of good fellowship, a promise that the two kings would meet each other face-to-face. The next month, a man arrived in England who was to be of some importance to me: Richard, Duke of York. He had been serving my husband as his lieutenant in France, and his term of office was soon to expire. I had stayed with him and his family in Rouen before I came to England for my wedding, but between my indisposition at that time and the tendency of all the people I had met back then to jumble together, he had not made much of an impression on me. Now I had the leisure to observe him: a squat, dark-haired man in his middle thirties. His face was a humorless one but not then an unfriendly one, and his rich gown made it clear that he appreciated the fine things in life.

It is strange indeed—almost comical—to remember that York and I didn't mind each other at all in those days when he first returned to England. "Your grace," he said soon after his arrival back at court, "I would crave your assistance in a matter."

I perked up, proud to be applied to in this manner. "I shall be happy to aid you if I can."

"It is my wish to marry my son Edward to one of King Charles's daughters, the Lady Madelaine. I have written to the king, and have been given some encouragement, but if perhaps your grace might put in a word—"

"I shall be happy to. I rather enjoy thinking of prospective matches for people," I confessed. "They will be a perfect little couple, too. Edward is three, my lord?"

"Yes, my lady."

"And Madelaine is two. She is a pretty little thing, I saw her at Tours. How sweet! I will write to him tonight."

"And my oldest daughter, Anne, is to marry Henry Holland."

"Oh," I said, a little dubiously. I had met Henry Holland, the heir to the dukedom of Exeter. Holland was my own age but already had a reputation for being somewhat combustible. I wondered if he was the best husband for a six-year-old girl.

"He's a high-tempered and proud lad, but time will mellow him, and by the time my Anne's old enough to live with him, he'll have sown his oats, I daresay," the duke said, reading my thoughts.

"She is at Rouen, I suppose?"

"Yes, my wife and children are still there. I hope to return soon and take up my lieutenancy where I left off," he said with a winning smile.

I was silent, not knowing Henry's intentions on this matter, and guessing too that it depended on the negotiations with France. "I am sure the king will make the best use of your talents, wherever they might be employed," I said gamely.

It was not long after that when I began receiving more letters from my uncle on the subject of Maine. Even my father, having sent me a vivid account of a tournament in which he had taken part, interrupted his narrative long enough to wistfully allude that it would be a fine thing to once again hold one in Maine.

I could no longer put the matter off, so I thought at length of how to broach the subject. Ideally, it would be the sort of favor I would ask if I were with child, but to my great disappointment, I showed no signs of that whatsoever. I considered asking Henry after we had made love, but I remembered the crude words Bertrand de Beauvau had said about taking advice from Agnes Sorel, and discarded the idea as being meretricious. Asking Henry after he had attended mass, an event that always left him at peace with the world, seemed nearly sacrilegious.

So at last, one night as we supped privily together as we sometimes did, I simply said, "Henry, I must ask you for something. Not for clothes or jewels or more income," I added hastily. "You have been very generous." (He had been too generous, I realize now, but what lady at fifteen, not a saint, would refuse such gifts?)

"Then what, Marguerite?"

"Something that is very dear to my family, and to our uncle Charles. Something that would help bring about the peace I was sent here for. Maine."

Henry looked at me. I looked down at my lap, hoping I had not blundered.

"I know, of course, that Charles wishes for the return of Maine," he said after a while. "Do you think it would secure peace?"

"I do." Though no one might believe it now, I meant what I said.

Henry smiled and kissed me. "Then I will give it firm consideration, my daisy."

After all the hours I had spent agonizing over the matter, it was just that simple.

In December, Henry wrote the letter that Charles most wanted to see: he agreed to cede Maine out of love and affection for that king, and also "favoring our most dear and well-beloved companion the queen, who has requested us to do this many times." Some weeks later, a letter from my uncle Charles arrived for me that was the written equivalent of another chuck on the chin. I was his little messenger of peace, he said.

I blushed to see myself described so flatteringly by Henry and Charles, and when I went to bed I happily dreamed of my husband and my uncle and my father all meeting in amity and ruling in harmony for the rest of their lives.

If there was a sillier girl abed that night in England, I do not know who she was.

3

William de la Pole, Marquess of Suffolk December 1445 to February 1447

I T WAS STRANGE, I THOUGHT AS I HEADED TOWARD KING HENRY'S INNER chamber in response to his summons to discuss the state of affairs in France, how so much of my life had been determined by a battle that took place thirty years before, a battle that I had never seen. I at least remembered well the day I had first heard of it: it was the autumn of 1415, and I was newly turned nineteen and back in England, just beginning to recover from my illness at Harfleur, when my mother came to my bedside and sat beside me.

"Will," she said quietly, "I have more bad news from France."

Just six weeks before, my father had died of dysentery at Harfleur, leaving my brother as the next Earl of Suffolk. I looked at my mother and saw that she had been crying. "Michael?"

"Yes. He was killed in battle."

Michael, the eldest of us five brothers, was my mother's favorite, naturally enough, I suppose. I had loved him too, and, of course, in my position as the second son, envied him as well. I wondered if my mother wished I had died in his place instead of being sent home to recuperate, but it was a question I did not dare ask. "I'm sorry, Mother." I was too weak to manage anything more eloquent, so I grasped my mother's hand, which seemed to be enough for her. We had been sitting together for a long time with our grief when I thought to ask, "The battle? Did we—?"

My mother smiled sadly. "It was a great victory for England, perhaps the most remarkable since Crécy," she said, smoothing some hair off my forehead with a tenderness that made me decide she hadn't wanted me to die in Michael's place after all. "It was at a place called Agincourt."

Maybe if I had been at Agincourt that St. Crispin's Day of 1415, instead of sick in England, I would have been a different man—certainly if my brother had not died in battle, and I had not inherited his earldom, my life would have been much different. Maybe if I had seen Henry V at his finest at Agincourt, I would have shared the half-contemptuous attitude toward his son that so many held. For I loved Henry; I truly did. I have been accused of working my way into his favor by calculated means, of working to turn him against others—but that is nonsense. Simply said, when I first joined his council after returning from my long sojourn in France, we liked each other. I liked his unworldliness and his gentleness, and his calm certainty that all could live in peace if people would just put their minds to it. What he liked about me I cannot venture to say; perhaps he simply liked me because I liked him. Maybe it was because I forbore, unlike his uncle Gloucester, from constantly invoking the specter of his father.

But even I, fond of Henry as I was, was not prepared for the conversation we had toward the end of 1445 when I came to the king in his chamber at Windsor Castle.

"I have agreed to cede Maine," Henry informed me, flourishing a letter. "In privy correspondence with my uncle of France."

"On what conditions?"

"Well, none." Henry frowned slightly, as if amazed that I should ask such a daft question, then continued cheerfully, "Well, of course, to extend the truce."

"When?"

"It is to be completed by the end of April."

In just over four months, we were to hand over Maine, with virtually nothing in return and without any approval of the king's promise by the lords on the king's council. I must have looked slightly ill, for Henry said, "My lord, do you find this problematic?"

One of my great weaknesses, I have discovered, was my reluctance to disappoint Henry. "I think that it will present some problems, but not insurmountable ones."

Henry smiled. "Peace always presents challenges, I think."

"Indeed."

"It will please Margaret so much," Henry said. He leaned closer. "In confidence, your grace, she is the chief impetus behind this! I might have waited and consulted with my council, but she is so desirous of this peace. How could I say no?"

How indeed? Charles must have known that few men could resist those violet eyes. I had fallen prey to a similar pair myself, and the result was my daughter. In any case, I didn't blame Queen Margaret for trying.

Well, I told myself, perhaps I was being overly pessimistic. Henry and King Charles were still planning to meet; surely, once Charles actually saw Henry in person (for they had never come face to face), we could reach a bargain that was less one-sided than the one Henry had made without consulting a soul except for his girl queen.

Henry coughed politely, and I realized that in my reverie, I had missed what he had been saying. "I beg your pardon, your grace."

"I was saying I think it time we discussed my works at Cambridge. I fear sometimes that they have been feeling neglected there because of my interest in my foundation at Eton."

♋

One thing I can say about our queen—and I came to love her like my own daughter—she had found her way to Henry's heart honestly. Another sixteen-year-old girl with Margaret's tastes (which Henry's treasurer had soon found were by no means inexpensive) might have been bored witless by Henry's talk of his foundations at Cambridge and Eton, but not Margaret. She might like clothes, jewels, and bloodhounds, but she also could sit for hours with Henry and study the plans he was drawing up for his foundations. When Henry traveled to Cambridge in July of 1446, she went with him and stood proudly beside him as the provost of King's College, William Millington, made a lengthy speech of thanks and welcome that would have tried the patience of many a girl of the queen's age.

Henry, of course, listened without the slightest hint of fatigue or inattention; he did not so much as shift his weight. When the provost was finished at last, he thanked him and stepped forward, beaming. "We have long looked forward to this day, my lord. We regret that because of the pestilence, we were unable to lay the first chapel stone here two years earlier, but had to send my lord Suffolk to do it instead. But as our plans for this college have expanded and become more ambitious, we have been given the opportunity to lay this latest stone ourselves. We are sorry to deprive my lord Suffolk of the pleasure!"

The king gestured at me and laughed as two men stepped forward, bearing a giant stone. They carefully placed it in the arms of Henry, who took the burden of two men without visible difficulty. Then as a fanfare played, he stooped and carefully laid it in the place marked out with golden cord. "Soon a great building shall rise from this," he said, getting to his feet gracefully. "It is a grand day for education. Let us give thanks!"

Margaret beamed beside her husband, then bent her head in prayer. Just before I bent my own, I watched Henry's face. Even with his head bowed in reverence, he was still smiling.

Henry and Margaret were happy, and I wanted to keep them that way. Was that such a base wish?

∽

Maine, meanwhile, had not been handed over by the impossible deadline Henry had set—something which, needless to say, had not been forgotten by King Charles. We were, in fact, at an impasse. No Maine, no truce and no meeting, and no peace. There was no choice: we would have to cede Maine. But what of Edmund Beaufort, the Earl of Somerset? He was the governor of Maine, and he also had the most to lose from Henry's promise, for he held the land rights there. He would not give up his holdings with nary a whimper. And there was Humphrey, Duke of Gloucester, to contend with.

Humphrey, Duke of Gloucester, youngest brother of Henry V! It was he I had served under when I returned to France following my non-service at Agincourt, and it was he who had put me on the young king's council when I returned to England after my disastrous encounter with the Maid of Orléans at Jargeau. But he had grown more choleric as the years had passed, and our relations had deteriorated, especially in 1440 when I had been among those urging the release of Charles of Orléans, who had been a prisoner in English hands since Agincourt. Orléans had been in my own charge for a time, and I in turn had been his half brother's charge when I was taken captive, so I had come to like the two brothers, and them me. Gloucester, however, had huffed and puffed and had even stalked out of Westminster Abbey when Charles of Orléans was taking his oath to abide by the terms of his release. His influence with the king had fallen steadily since then, and it hadn't helped matters any that mine was rising at the time.

Somerset, I thought, could be kept sweet easily enough by having his losses made up to him. The Duke of York had been the governor of Normandy and was expecting to be reappointed, but what if Somerset were put there instead, and York sent to Ireland as its governor? York might see Ireland as a comedown, but he was a natural fit for it, being the greatest English landholder there. That was a thought.

But Gloucester would be a different matter. He had little to lose personally from us giving up Maine; for him it would be a matter of national pride and would only confirm his belief that England had been going straight to perdition ever since August 31, 1422, the day Henry V died. Many a time had

I heard him say, "My brother the king would not have done this!" Sometimes I believed that he was in communication with the late king's shade, so insistent was he as to what Henry V's thoughts would have been on any given subject.

No, Gloucester would never be shy of speaking his mind, especially when he heard about something as enormous as ceding Maine. He might be out of favor, but could he rouse the commons to his side? It didn't seem like a chance worth taking.

❧

The New Year passed, and a Parliament had been summoned to meet at Cambridge. I took a deep breath as I approached Henry; what I was about to do was not to my taste, whatever is said now about me. "Your grace, there is a grave matter I need to discuss with you."

Henry frowned. "Is there a problem with our proposed meeting with our uncle Charles?"

"No, but it touches on it. Your grace, I will be honest."

"You always are, I hope, Suffolk," Henry said lightly, fastening his puppy-like eyes on me with vastly disconcerting effect.

"I—I try, your grace. What I am about to tell you may be no more than rumor, but I do not believe it is a rumor I should keep from you. I will start by admitting openly that over the last few months, I have had a spy in the Duke of Gloucester's household."

"Suffolk, that hardly seems honorable."

"I did so, your grace, in order that I might gauge his reaction to the Maine business."

"We really must get on with that, Suffolk. My uncle Charles's patience is wearing thin."

"I fear that your uncle Gloucester is plotting against your grace. Plotting to remove you from the throne and rule in your stead."

I waited for another non sequitur from Henry, but this time I had his full attention. "What proof do you have?"

"Very little. Only that your uncle has been more vociferous and reckless in his complaints lately, and that he has seemed to have more actively courted popularity with his Welsh tenants. And he has been speaking disparagingly against the queen, openly wondering if she is capable of bearing children and describing your marriage as a poor bargain." I did not add that Humphrey called Queen Margaret "the French wench" and myself the "Wool Merchant," an allusion to my great-grandfather's origins. Evidently my family's start in commerce had been preying heavily on Gloucester's mind.

"I see."

"There is another matter that concerns me, your grace. When you travel to France, your uncle would be the natural person to safeguard the realm in your absence. We can agree, I daresay, that given his hostility toward the proposed peace, it would not do for him to travel to France." The king nodded. "I fear that if your grace were to be out of the country, your uncle, whether as regent or simply in a private capacity, might take the opportunity to stir up trouble were he at large. And I also fear that he may disrupt this upcoming Parliament, and perhaps to stir the commons against the peace."

"It almost sounds, Suffolk, as if you are advocating that he be arrested whether or not we have good cause to be suspicious of him."

"It is what I am advocating, for the sake of the peace that means so much to you."

Henry was silent for a time. Finally, he said, "When my uncle was at court, he would always advise me to ask myself, what would my father do? I have asked myself that just now, and I fear that the answer is that my father would take no chances. He would arrest him. Do you think that is the case, Suffolk?"

"I do."

"Then we shall arrest him. Take care of the matter, Suffolk."

If a man is going to do a thing of which he is ashamed, he might as well do it well. I ordered that Parliament be moved to Bury Saint Edmunds, where Gloucester had little influence and I had great influence, and I ordered the leading judges in the country to appear there, to be ready for the trial that would probably be necessary.

Was Gloucester plotting? I honestly don't know to this day. If my spies told me true—and I had a couple of them, not wishing to stake a man's future on a single paid man—he was indeed making plenty of noises in that direction. He dreamed of being reunited with that wife of his, once his mistress and a convicted witch, and they said that after a cup of wine too many on occasion, he would speak of freeing her from her prison. Since Humphrey was next in line to the throne, it was an easy matter to assume that ridding himself of Henry might be next on his agenda. And if he could strike a bargain with his unruly Welsh tenants, God only knew what could transpire.

There was nothing left to do but arrest him and bring him to trial. If he were found guilty by his peers, so be it. Henry's soft heart would ensure that he spent his life in comfortable confinement or in exile rather than face execution. If he were found innocent…well, I hoped he wasn't.

On February 18, 1447, eight days after Parliament opened, Gloucester arrived at Bury Saint Edmunds, trailed by eighty men, including his bastard son. It was a modest entourage for a man of his rank: Henry had instructed him to keep it so. The streets and lodgings, however, were overflowing with Henry's own armed men: we were taking no chances.

It was the coldest day of the year. When the king's treasurer, Sir John Stourton, and his controller, Sir Thomas Stanley, met Gloucester upon his entry into the town and told him to go rest at his lodgings at St. Saviour's Hospital instead of proceeding immediately to the abbey, he was only too glad to agree. It was then that I sent out the delegation I had assembled to arrest Gloucester: the Duke of Buckingham, Somerset, the Earl of Salisbury, Viscount Beaumont, and Lord Sudeley.

An hour or so later, they appeared in my chamber. I stared at their ashen faces. "What happened?"

The men hesitated, as if wondering who should speak, and then Buckingham, the senior among them, said, "Suffolk, something has gone horribly wrong. Gloucester collapsed. We fear he is dying."

For a moment, I thought I might collapse myself. "Tell me of it."

"We asked to see him in private, and then we told him that he was under arrest," Buckingham said. "He laughed at first, and when we didn't laugh back, he asked if the cold had snapped our wits. We told him that we were in possession of our senses and that he was being charged with treason, but that because of his high rank, the cruel weather, and his long journey, he would be allowed to remain in his lodgings, under guard, until the king sent for him. He looked at us as if he were about to laugh again, and then he started shouting. 'Sends for me? I'll not wait to be sent for! The boy can see me now! I'll have it from his own lips, and his alone, what he means by this. Not your lips, not from the Wool Merchant's. Do you understand? Do you understand? I'll not have him treat me so, the ingrate! By God, if his noble father could see this, he would strike him dead!' And that's when he clutched his chest and went down in a heap on the floor. His son got on the floor beside him and held him in his arms. Gloucester was conscious, but nothing he said after that was intelligible. He could manage only a few words here and there. They took him to his bed, and that is where he is now."

"Is he under medical attendance?"

"Yes. His own physician is there. But he holds out little hope."

"Does the king know of this?"

"Not yet. We thought you'd want to be there, it being your—business."

Being your scheme, he meant.

⁂

To my surprise, Henry took the news of his uncle's illness quite calmly. He even ordered that others in Gloucester's household be arrested, as we had intended based on the information I'd received. The plotters included Gloucester's bastard son, Arteys. I at least saw to it that he was arrested out of the sight of his father, who rallied for a couple of days. Gloucester even plucked up enough spirit to demand that the king be brought to him to explain himself. Henry, naturally, refused, but it gave me hope that Gloucester would recover.

It proved futile. On February 23, Henry's sergeant at arms Thomas Calbrose came to me. "My lord, Duke Humphrey is dead. He rallied sufficiently at the very end to receive the sacrament."

I crossed myself. "Thank you. Convey your news to the king." I hesitated. "Did he say anything to you before he died?" Calbrose hesitated. "Well, did he?"

"Yes, my lord. He said that the charges were false and that he had never meant any harm to the king or to his little French bauble, as he put it. 'Twas all talk, he said, and if the king had the sense God gave a sheep he'd realize that. And then he said—"

"Say it."

"He said that all of the sorry buggers who arranged this would pay, my lord. And then his chaplain came in, and I left the room. He didn't last long after that."

"Thank you for bringing this news. Have them lay him out; we will display his body tomorrow in the abbey church so that it can be seen that he died by no foul play. After that he shall be brought to St. Albans; it is my understanding that he had a vault built for him there during his lifetime."

"Yes, my lord." The man bowed and walked out.

Alone, I knelt and tried to pray for Gloucester's soul. But I could not concentrate on my task. I kept hearing the words, *All of the sorry buggers who arranged this would pay.*

4

Margaret
September 1447 to March 1448

I WAS SITTING IN THE GARDEN AT MY BEAUTIFUL MANOR OF GREENWICH— once the great pride of Humphrey, Duke of Gloucester, and now mine—when I saw Suffolk heading toward the landing, his shoulders slumped. "Katherine, run and fetch the marquess for me before he leaves. I must see him."

Katherine Peniston ran as bidden, and I watched, frowning, as she came back with her quarry. The past months had aged my dear Suffolk by years, and he had lost some of the confident bearing I'd first seen at Tours. His brown eyes were downcast as he approached me. "I hope nothing is amiss, your grace?"

"No. I simply wanted to see you before you left. Sit, my lord." I indicated a place on the bench beside me. Suffolk sat, leaving a respectful space between the two of us, which I promptly filled by scooting over so I almost leaned on his shoulder. "I have a surprise for Henry, my lord. No, not that!" I added as Suffolk looked surreptitiously at my belly. "Henry would be the first to know if that were the case. But I hope he will like this." I handed Suffolk a parchment. "Read."

Suffolk obeyed. "You wish to found a college at Cambridge?"

"You read quickly, my lord! Yes, I do. I have read about the ladies I mention there who founded colleges, and it shocks me that no English queen has done so before. Why should I not be the first?"

"It will please him immensely, your grace."

"It was the rector of St. Botolph's who gave me the idea. I only hope the king will not be jealous of my foundation! Queen's College will have to be a little less grand than King's College, I suppose." I laughed, then put a hand on Suffolk's arm. "Walk with me, my lord." When we had proceeded out of hearing range of the others, I said, "You look strained, my lord, and seem listless. I do believe you were going to leave just now without even bidding me good-bye. Has the king been working you too hard?"

"No, my lady. It is Greenwich, I fear. I know it is a pleasure spot for you, but for me it holds ghosts." He sighed. "I cannot come here without thinking of that scene at Tyburn. Soon Gloucester will be the most popular corpse in England."

Two months before, the men who had been arrested at the same time as Gloucester had finally been brought to trial at the King's Bench and had been sentenced to die the traitor's death of hanging, drawing, and quartering at Tyburn in London. Henry had pardoned them, but at the utter last moment. The condemned men had already been half-strangled, and their bodies stripped naked and marked for quartering, when Suffolk galloped up with their pardons. Carried off by their friends, the freed prisoners had been too dazed from the hanging and their sudden reprieve to show any emotion, but the crowd had hissed at Suffolk as he rode off, and someone had shouted "Murderer!" before disappearing into the throng.

"They received a fair trial, and it is all over now," I said firmly. "They have been restored to their lands and positions and are free, and your mind should be free as well. I want you to leave court for a couple of weeks, my lord. Go to Ewelme and rest for a while. I will make your excuses to Henry; I'll tell him that you've been in ill health. As you will be if you keep brooding upon what cannot be changed."

"You sound like my daughter Jane, your grace," said Suffolk, smiling reluctantly. "She is always trying to mother me."

"As someone should. Is Alice not taking care of you properly these days?"

"She is, but I am afraid I try her patience sometimes with my melancholy."

"I will have to have a word with her," I said, so gravely that for a moment Suffolk appeared about to remonstrate. "No, I will stay out of it, but I do wish to see you more cheerful. I do not forget how kind you were in my first days here, when I was lonely. It meant a great deal to me." I touched his arm. "If you cannot leave court—and knowing how diligent you are in Henry's affairs, that is probably the case—at least come back now and listen to my new musicians play. They are superb, and the music is bound to soothe you. And then I wish to consult with you about my college, assuming, of course, that Henry will approve of it. I know you helped a great deal with Eton and King's, and have many good ideas."

Suffolk smiled. "I will obey you, your grace."

∽

During the Christmas festivities of 1447, a new duke appeared at court at Windsor—seventeen-year-old Henry Holland, Duke of Exeter. He was clad in black for his father, who had died just that August. "I believe you are the Duke of York's ward now?" I inquired as we sat down to a game of cards together one evening. I had invited him to play with me, having noticed that out of respect for his father's memory, he was not dancing.

Henry Holland scowled. "Unfortunately."

I looked to see if York was within earshot, which was more than Exeter had done. "Why unfortunately?"

Exeter, taking the hint from my low voice, lowered his as well. "Well, he's married me to his daughter, for one thing."

"I remember his daughter from Rouen. Lady Anne, was it? She was a little girl."

"Aye, there is the problem. She is only eight years of age." He leaned too close to me, and I realized belatedly that he was rather tipsy—a rare sight at Henry's court, for he of course never overindulged, and his courtiers naturally followed suit. "I would have preferred someone of my own age." He smiled again. "And wealthy too."

"You are honest, at least," I said. "But she was a pretty child, as I recall."

"Pretty, but she and I do not suit. She is a little shrew."

I remembered little Anne tossing a fine tantrum during my stay at Rouen and could not gainsay him. "Perhaps she will change when she gets older."

"I very much doubt it. Girls grow up to be like their mothers, and they don't call the Duchess of York 'Proud Cis' for nothing. She's arrogant, as are all of the Nevilles." He reached for a cup of wine, which I neatly intercepted before he could clasp it. Frowning, then shrugging, he continued, "And the Duke of York will be going to Ireland as the king's lieutenant. I suppose I will have to go with him there. Ireland, with the savages and an eight-year-old wife! I don't like it."

"Perhaps Ireland won't be so bad," I said. "After all, your countrymen have been there and must have civilized it a bit."

"That's not what my father-in-law thinks. He's not at all happy about being sent there, though he puts a good face on it in public. He says that Somerset has no business running our possessions in Fr—"

A firm hand suddenly landed on Exeter's shoulder, and the Duke of York glared down at him. "I beg your grace's pardon for my ward's ill behavior. He has monopolized you long enough. Come along, Henry. You have overindulged. It is time you retired."

"But the queen invited me herself! You can't order me about like one of your vassals. Who the hell do you think you are?"

"Your guardian, for one thing."

York began to haul his ward up by force, but I stopped him and placed my hand on his gently. "Do retire, Henry. I shall be retiring soon myself. Tomorrow we shall have another game."

"Yes, your grace." Henry stood shakily but still managed a reasonably proper bow. Ignoring his father-in-law, he let a page escort him from the hall.

York sighed. "I beg your pardon, your grace. My ward is a foolish young man sometimes."

"I expect he must be grieving for his father, my lord."

"Yes, that is this week's excuse. I should follow him to make certain he does not talk his page into taking him elsewhere."

I watched as the Duke of York departed, then smiled as the Marquess of Suffolk approached and motioned toward Henry Holland's vacated seat. "Is this free, your grace?"

"It certainly is. Do you play, my lord?"

"No, your grace must forgive me. I know some games, but I associate card-playing with my captivity, and have avoided it since."

"It is sad to think of you as a captive."

Suffolk shrugged. "It is self-indulgent of me to even mention it, for I was a prisoner for a very short time, compared to the Duke of Orléans and some of your grace's other countrymen. And your grace was not even born at the time." Suffolk pushed Henry Holland's discarded playing cards aside, then picked them up and laughed. "Pity the young duke left when he did. He had an excellent hand, better than any I had in my day."

"See, you should have not said anything, and then you could have started where he left off and won a pretty sum."

"Chivalry is not dead yet, your grace." Suffolk grinned and settled more comfortably in his chair.

"You look more yourself, my lord, than you have in months."

Suffolk glanced around. "Yes, well, Humphrey has been a quieter ghost than I anticipated, for one thing. The rumors of foul play seem to have died down. And for another, Somerset finally has agreed to accept compensation for Maine, and we can at last make the arrangements to cede it. Your uncle Charles has been extraordinarily patient under the circumstances, but that patience is beginning to fray."

"What is his compensation?"

"Ten thousand livres a year from the wine tax in Normandy. And"—Suffolk bent closer—"I shouldn't be surprised if he is made a duke."

I frowned. "If anyone deserves a dukedom, it is you. You have served England much longer, and are much old—"

"'Seasoned' is the word a native English speaker might have chosen, your grace, but I get your meaning. I don't begrudge the man his dukedom if it will settle this business. But enough of this; it is Christmas."

In March 1448—after my impatient uncle Charles brought troops to the very gates of Le Mans—Henry's agents at last surrendered Maine. At the end of the month, Henry formally granted me a license to found Queen's College. "You have indeed been a lady of peace," he told me that night as we lay in his bed together. "I could not be happier. There is just one thing I wish."

"What, my love? I will get with child soon. I know I will."

"I was not thinking of that, my dear. We must trust in God and continue doing our part for that." He smiled; we had just done our part very happily. "No, I was thinking of my old friend, Gilles of Brittany. He was raised in my household, and is now the prisoner of his brother the Duke of Brittany."

"I have heard something about this."

"I would like to see him released. Suffolk knows of my desire, and has a plan for it."

"Oh?" I asked sleepily.

"I shan't bore you with it," Henry kissed me on the cheek. "By the way, I believe it is time we made Suffolk a duke."

William de la Pole, Duke of Suffolk
April 1449 to July 1449

IT HAS BEEN ACHIEVED, YOUR GRACE. FRANÇOIS DE SURIENNE HAS TAKEN Fougères. It took place on the twenty-fourth day of March."

Henry sighed, and I wondered again if he were having second thoughts about my proposal. It seemed a good one at the time: We would start by seizing Fougères, a wealthy town on the border of Brittany, through the agency of Surienne, an Aragonese mercenary in the pay of England. We would then restore Gilles of Brittany to a position of influence and build an alliance between Brittany and England that could be used as a bargaining tool against the French should they be inclined to attempt to win back Normandy now that they had Maine. It was a risky plan, I'd freely admitted to Henry, but ceding Maine had not proven the path to peace. The troops who left Maine had settled on the border between Brittany and Normandy, irritating King Charles, and the English had their own complaints of violence from the French. Brittany was a necessary ally, and the council had agreed. Something had to be done. After much consideration and prayer, Henry had given his consent as well. Much as he wanted peace with his and Margaret's uncle, he did not want to lose Normandy. When he learned that no lesser a person than Charles VII himself had ordered the arrest of Gilles of Brittany—a longtime friend of not only Henry, but of the interests of England—the matter had been settled.

"Well, what is done is done," Henry said aloud. "I shall write to him telling him to keep it diligently and to keep his troops in good order for its safety and defense, and you shall do the same."

"Yes, your grace." I lingered, having the feeling that the king was not done with me.

"I have not told Margaret about this," Henry said after a moment or two. Whenever he spoke the name "Margaret," an undertone of affection entered his voice. It made me feel all the more protective of him, and of her. "Do you think I should tell her that we were behind the seizure? I know she feels it deeply that ceding Maine has not had the results we hoped for. Poor girl, her uncle no longer even writes to her."

"I would keep it to myself."

"Then I shall," Henry said, an unhappy look on his face. "Suffolk, there is something underhanded about this I have never liked."

"I know, your grace. I don't like it much myself. But sometimes such means are necessary. If only Maine had worked out better for us."

"If only," Henry said sadly.

If only, the two saddest words in the English language. If only Margaret's grandmother, Yolande, had never taken Charles VII under her wing years before and helped him to the French throne. If only the Maid of Orléans had never invigorated Charles. If only Henry V had lived to an old age. If only the Duke of Brittany, following the seizure of Fougères, had not declared himself a vassal of France and appealed to Charles to aid him against us. If only Charles, seizing the opportunity to be relieved from a truce that had long ceased to be of advantage to him, had not declared that the seizure of Fougères had broken it. For that was what happened. On July 31, 1449, England and France were again at war, and Henry's dream of peace—the dream I had supported for years—was shattered.

If only I had fallen at Jargeau with my brothers. It would have been better for us all.

6

Margaret
November 1449 to March 1450

R OUEN HAS FALLEN, YOUR GRACE."
I looked into Suffolk's face and saw that it was as gray as the November sky that hung over Greenwich. "Would you believe me if I told you that I was very, very sorry?"

"I would. I do."

"I thank you for that. Few others would believe me. The king, you and your duchess, and my ladies are the only people who do not treat me as a potential spy." I sighed. "I have not heard from anyone in my family since war broke out. I dare not ask anyone else this. Do you know whether my father has joined King Charles's men?"

"Yes. He, your brother, and your brother-in-law were all at the siege. They were all there when Rouen fell. 'Fallen' is the wrong term, actually. Somerset put up only a token fight before he surrendered it. Not only did he surrender it, he also has had to agree to surrender Harfleur, Caudebec, Arques, Tancarville, Lillebonne, and Montivilliers as well. Oh, and Lord Talbot and a few others will have to stay in Rouen as hostages. It's a debacle."

"Sit, my lord. You look ghastly."

Suffolk obeyed. His hand when he picked up the cup of wine my servant offered him was shaking.

"Why did he surrender it so easily?" I asked.

"They say he had no real choice. The citizens there would have cooperated with Charles. They were fearful of being besieged and having the town sacked. They would have offered him no support and might have even put him and his family in danger. Somerset's very fond of his wife and children; there are risks he would take for himself that he wouldn't for them. Anyway, he and his family are off to Caen now."

"There must be some way to prevent further losses."

"We are trying to get troops over. I've lent money to the crown. So have others. Of course, in my case it's the least I can do, having put us into this situation with my mad scheme about Fougères."

I shook my head. "That was rather foolish, my lord."

Suffolk's bleak face lit up with a half-smile. "That's almost refreshing to hear, your grace. Alice tells me not to brood upon it, and the king tells me he knows I meant well. And I suppose it was capable on paper of succeeding. But it did not, and I will have to live with the consequences of my folly forever. As will others, including your grace. These past few weeks can't have been easy for you."

"No one understands that I love Henry and would never rejoice in something that has brought him—and you, my lord—so much misery. They think that all of this delights me, and they could not be more wrong. I am wretched. With this war if I hope for my husband to prevail, my father will suffer, and if I hope for my father and my uncle to prevail, my husband will suffer. There is nothing I have wanted as much as peace."

I sighed so deeply that Suffolk roused himself out of his own misery to say, "We mustn't give up hope yet, your grace. With reinforcements, we might be in a better bargaining position. But I must get back to Parliament. I came here only to tell you the news."

"No one tells me anything these days. I am grateful to you."

Suffolk tried to smile. "That is a sentiment, your grace, in which you are entirely alone."

Between Suffolk and others lending the crown money and Henry—and I—pledging some of our plate and jewels, we managed to come up with enough money to pay the men who had gathered at Portsmouth, waiting to embark under Sir Thomas Kyriell to fight in France. As their pay was far in arrears, their mood was ugly, and it was made uglier on New Year's Day when Harfleur—whose captain had refused to comply with Somerset's orders to surrender it to the French—fell.

Adam Moleyns, Bishop of Chichester, arrived at Portsmouth on January 9, 1450, bearing the men's back pay. Henry saw him off on his mission with relief. "How glad they will be to finally get paid."

Instead, they dragged the bishop out of his lodgings and took out their anger on him. When all was over, the Bishop of Chichester lay face down in the mud in a field near Portsmouth, his skull shattered.

"They are saying that with his dying breath, the bishop denounced me as a traitor who sold Maine and Normandy to the French," Suffolk said in the matter-of-fact tone he announced each new calamity these days. He had come to see Henry and me in Henry's privy chamber at Westminster: Parliament, recessed for one of the most miserable Christmases in memory, was to reopen the next day. "It is in the mouth of every commoner in England, I believe."

I dropped the embroidery I was making a pretense of doing. "How could he say such an outrageous thing? He worked with you!"

"More than that, we were friends. But if he did say it, I don't blame him. He was probably being tormented, poor soul. Most likely he was made to say it. If so, I hope it put him out of his pain. They say he was hardly recognizable by the time they finished with him." Suffolk bent his head. "God assoil him."

"Suffolk, you know we have no doubts about your loyalty," Henry said.

"I know, your grace. Disloyalty is the one thing I cannot task myself with. But the commons have latched onto this like a dog does a tasty bone, and I must answer. Tomorrow, I shall beg you to allow me to clear my name—of treason, at least. Of folly is perhaps another thing."

And so it was, on the next day, January 22, thirteen days after the bishop's murder, William de la Pole knelt before the king. I was not there, of course; some time later, Humphrey Stafford, the Duke of Buckingham, told me what had happened.

"Your grace," Suffolk said, in a quiet voice that nonetheless carried, "it is said throughout the realm that I have been disloyal to you, that I have sold our country to the French. It is said that the dying words of the Bishop of Chichester, whom God absolve, were that I had been a traitor to my country. I beg you, our most high and dread sovereign lord, to allow me to clear my name." Suffolk's voice cracked and he kissed the hem of Henry's gown.

Henry, moved, stared down at Suffolk while the lords shifted uncomfortably in their seats. The commons, meanwhile, perked up. Almost in unison, they moved forward so as not to miss a word.

"My lord, you may arise and address us," Henry said finally.

"Your grace, my father served that king of noble memory, your grandfather, in all of his expeditions, in sea and on land. He died in the service of your father at Harfleur. My eldest brother died thereafter at Agincourt. Two other of my brothers died in your grace's service at Jargeau, where I was captured and paid twenty thousand pounds for my ransom. I have borne arms for thirty-four

winters in the time of the king your father and in your own time, and I have
been a Knight of the Garter for thirty. As a younger man I was abroad in your
service in France for seventeen years without coming home or seeing this land,
and since my return home I have served about your most noble person for
fifteen years, in which time I have found as much grace and goodness as any
liegeman has found in his sovereign lord. And yet men say I would betray all
that I have worked for a Frenchman's promise?"

"Damn right, the sorry whoreson would," muttered one of the commons.

"If I were false or untrue to your high estate, or to this your land whereof
I was born, there would be no earthly punishment great enough for me,"
Suffolk continued, ignoring the outburst. "I beg, your grace, that whatever
rumor might be sown against me, I will be charged of it during this Parliament
and that in your presence, my excuses and defense will be heard."

He knelt again, visibly weeping, and Henry said, "Of course, my lord,
you shall have a hearing. But we do not believe that there is a man in this
Parliament who believes these odious rumors. Still, it is well to get these matters out in the open."

Suffolk, rising at the king's command, bowed and returned to his seat,
and the lords and the commons settled back in theirs, the commons smiling.
"He wants a hearing?" one whispered to the other. "By God, he'll get one.
And more."

⁂

"Your graces, two days before, the commons asked that the Duke of Suffolk
be committed to prison while he awaited a hearing of the charges against him.
The request was denied because there was no specific charge against him, only a
most general one. Now, however, I am appointed by the commons to say that
a serious charge does exist against him, namely, that he has stocked Wallingford
Castle, entrusted by the king into his care, with provisions and that he has fortified it." The Duke of Buckingham started to interrupt, but William Tresham,
speaker of the commons, continued doggedly as he faced the duke and the rest
of the delegation sent to him by the king. "He has stocked it with the intention
of aiding the French when they invade England, as is expected daily."

"That's utter balderdash," said Buckingham.

Tresham, who had been chosen as speaker at several Parliaments but would
have gladly avoided the honor at this particular one, looked uneasy. "But
nonetheless, my lords, it is a specific charge, as was requested to be brought,
and it is a grave one."

"So it is," acknowledged John Mowbray, Duke of Norfolk, with a smile. For years, the Duke of Suffolk had kept him out of any real influence in East Anglia. "I believe, my lords, we have no choice but to advise the king to imprison the Duke of Suffolk."

⁓

"They took Suffolk as a prisoner to the Tower?" I stared at Henry. "Like a criminal?"

"My dear, he was not humiliated. He was taken at dusk, in a closed barge, and let out in my own private water gate. And he will be lodged comfortably. I have appointed three of my most trusted squires to care for him. The duchess may visit him if she wants."

"But you let them imprison him! You gave the order!" I balled my hands up into fists.

"My dear, calm yourself! I had no choice. You know that he himself asked that he be given the chance to answer the charges against him, and when a specific charge were brought, it was of too serious a nature to be ignored."

"But it is a ridiculous one! Suffolk would never aid my uncle against you— or me. He has done nothing like that."

"I know it, my dear." He drew me to him and stroked my hair, even as I held my fists up next to his chest. "I will not let harm come to him; he has been loyal to me and my father for all of his life. Do you think I would forget that, Marguerite? Do you think I am so poor a man that I would abandon a friend to his fate?"

His tone as he spoke the French version of my name was so reproachful that I hung my head and began to weep. "I am sorry," I whispered. "I know you would do none of those things. But after what was done to Bishop Moleyns—"

"I do not even wish to think of it." Henry shuddered.

"But you must. They are vicious people, Henry! They will not be satisfied with keeping Suffolk in the Tower, and that is bad enough. They are capable of any vile act, I think."

"Now, my dear, that was in Portsmouth, and the soldiers were ill-fed and discontent. Do not have so little faith in our commons. They are good men, I'm sure of it. It is just that our reverses in France have set them on edge."

"You have more faith in them than I do."

"We must have faith in them," said Henry, so sincerely that I felt a pang of guilt for my own doubts. "And in the Lord. Remember that, my dear."

⁓

Henry did not trust entirely to faith. In February, when the commons formally impeached Suffolk of treason and misprision, he refused to refer their bill to a judge. On March 9, however, the commons delivered a second round of charges. This time, Henry, under pressure from both the lords and the commons, required Suffolk to make an answer to both sets of accusations. First, however, he moved him to the Jewel Tower at Westminster.

Suffolk was sitting at a small writing desk, quill in hand, the next day when his guards let me, followed by Katherine Peniston and several other ladies, into his chamber. He stood, his face breaking into the first full smile I'd seen from him in months. "Your grace?"

Katherine Peniston and my other ladies discreetly moved into a corner. "I could not visit you before, my lord, because I feared it would only give rise to more gossip about your loyalty when word got out about it. But when they moved you here so close to my own chambers, I had to come see you; I hated to think of you being lonely here. How are you faring?"

"Well enough."

"I am so glad they moved you from the Tower; it is a gloomy place, I have always thought."

"I was kept comfortably there, but I was glad to leave it." Suffolk smiled sheepishly. "I was once told a prophecy that if I could keep clear of the Tower, I would be safe. Why I chose to listen is beyond me; it was more for my own amusement at the time, but the foolishness has stuck with me." He touched a book lying on his desk. "But enough of that. It was kind of your grace to send me poems and so many little delicacies. Each day I had something to look forward to, wondering what would come next. It cheered me immensely."

I blushed. "Alice came to see you too, did she not?"

"Yes, she has come several times, but I prefer her to be at Ewelme with our son. He was not told that I am a prisoner, but children sense when something is amiss, and he has been worried. He needs her with him."

"Jane?" She had married Thomas Stonor early in the previous year. Around Christmastime she had borne Stonor a healthy boy, named William after her father.

"She wanted to come, but I advised her not to under the circumstances; it would do her husband and family no good to associate with me now. But she writes to me, and she informs me that my fine new grandson is growing apace. So, your grace, you see I have much here to occupy myself with, and the commons have provided me with an additional occupation." Suffolk grimaced and pointed toward the sheaf of papers on his desk. "These are the charges against me. I asked for specific charges that I could refute, and God knows, the commons obliged. One thing you can say about the commons, they're not lacking in imagination. See?" He held up a paper and tapped it. "Here's one of my favorites: that I've invited the French into England so that I can depose King Henry and make my son king through his wife, my little ward Margaret Beaufort. Why the French would be willing to help me do that I'm not sure. Oh, and I've delivered Maine to your grace's uncle, solely on my own initiative. I've turned spy for the French, and I've represented myself as being so in favor with your uncle Charles that I can remove the members of his council if I'm so minded. Need I go on?" I shook my head, but Suffolk continued flipping through the papers. "There are other treason charges, but the gist of all of them is that I've allied myself with the French to work against my own country. Then there are the other charges. Generally, I've helped myself to the treasury in all manner of ways. I won't deny having profited from my offices, God knows, but there's not a word here about the service I've given the crown in return."

He threw down the parchment, but not before I had spotted another paper on the desk. I blanched. "My lord. You have made your will?"

"The commons want my head, your grace. That's been made quite clear. The only thing that could change their minds now is if we had a victory in France, and I'm not sure even that would do the job. They might not wish to have their fun spoiled. It's best to have it in readiness if they get their way."

He sighed. I touched his arm. "My lord, I don't understand. All of the business with France—the other lords were privy to your dealings, were they not? Parliament even praised the seizure of Fougères, did it not? And everyone knew of Maine well before it was ceded. No one protested."

"True, and I have reminded them of this in the reply I am writing. But men have short memories when it is convenient for them to do so. I suspect when I give my answer, there will not be a man in Parliament who remembers having been anything but a fervent and outspoken opponent of peace with France. The lords like their heads as much as the next man does, and I've no doubt they will be more than happy to save theirs by sacrificing mine."

My eyes filled with tears. "Henry would surely not let that happen."

"No. He has told me that if pressed, he will send me into exile. Exile, when I have served my country since I was seventeen and when my father and my brothers all died for the English cause! But it is better than the alternative, I suppose." Suffolk crossed to his window and looked out. "Your grace, I am grateful that you are here, for there are two things I want you to promise me in case I am condemned to exile or worse."

"Anything."

"I say this first because I trust you, as you have trusted me. I have known our king since he was a boy, and I dearly love him, but he is not the man his father was. There has always been something in me that wanted to protect him, and perhaps that is part of the reason that I am where I am today. I should have let him make his own mistakes in his own name, to have encouraged him to lead. Perhaps with me gone, he will."

"Suffolk, I don't want you gone! I cannot bear it."

"That is where your grace is wrong. You can bear it, and you will. If I were to choose between you and Henry, I would say that you are the stronger. That is why I want you to promise me that you will stand by him always."

"My lord, that is almost an insult. I have never been anything but a loyal wife to him."

"I know, your grace. But there may come a time when you wish he were a different man, a time when you might be tempted to side with a stronger man simply because his strength attracts you. For your sake and for his, do not give way."

"Very well, my lord," I said irritably. "But if I were not so concerned about you, I would not allow you to be presumptuous."

Suffolk smiled. "I will be more presumptuous yet and tell you that I have come to think of you not as my queen, but as a daughter. It has given me untold pleasure to watch the girl I first saw at age fourteen grow into beauty and grace."

I put my arms around Suffolk, who gently disengaged himself. "That brings me to the other promise I wish you to make, and that is that you will be careful of yourself. You are vulnerable as a Frenchwoman—and, if I may speak plainly, as a woman who has not got with child. You are a natural scapegoat. When I have served my purpose, they will come looking for more, because they will soon find that my being gone has not produced the miracle they expected."

"I will. Oh, I do hope that they will listen to your answer and heed it."

"I do too, for it is not death I fear. It is the disgrace—that I shall die with all of these falsehoods ringing in my ears." He turned to me, his face working. "They are not part of the charges against me, but have you heard what else they are saying? That I abandoned my post and caused my brothers' deaths at Jargeau? That my Jane was conceived when I defiled a nun the night before my capture? Good Lord, I have done wrong in my life, but never have I forced myself upon a woman. Jane's mother was put into a convent by her parents because they could not afford a dowry. She hated it there. We caught each other's eye when my forces were occupying Jargeau. I should have left her alone, God knows, but I was lonely and she was unhappy, and we cheered each other for a short time. When she got with child I arranged for her to live with some friends of mine, where she died while Jane was little. And that my girl shall hear these things of me and her mother!"

He suddenly put his head in his hands and seemed for a moment to be about to sob. Unable to stand by and let him grieve without comfort, I put my arms around him until he gained his composure as rapidly as he had lost it. Almost in his normal voice, he said, "Let the wrong person see you do that, your grace, and you'll only make matters worse."

Remembering how he had rebuffed my affectionate embrace earlier, I stepped back. "Whatever do you mean?"

"You haven't heard?" I shook my head. "Well, I suppose it's natural that you'd be the last to know." Suffolk sighed. "Among the other slanders, I am said to be cuckolding the king." I crinkled my brow, puzzled at an English word I did not know, and he repeated himself in French.

I clapped my hand to my mouth, sickened. "They say something that vile?"

"I am afraid so, my lady. I am sorry I had to pollute the air here with it."

"But that is nonsense. You are so much older!"

"Well, I am not quite in my dotage," Suffolk said with a grim half-smile.

"But you know what I mean! You said just now you thought of me as a daughter, and I think of you as a father. I have been with you longer than I ever was with my father, for he was away so much." My tears began to flow. "None of this would have come upon you if you had not arranged my marriage to Henry and been kind to me. I have brought nothing but grief to you and him."

"Nonsense."

"It is true! They should send me back. I can't bear a child. I have failed to make peace. I am worthless."

"Not true, not true at all. Come, your grace. Cry yourself out here."

"The commons—" I hiccupped as Suffolk took me into his arms.

"Sod them. I'll not let a lady and my queen cry without comforting her."

I put my head against Suffolk's doublet and wept heartily as he gently patted my back. When I had calmed at last, he said quietly, "Henry loves you, your grace, you must know that. His face lights up whenever you come into a room. He has been much happier ever since you came into his life. Never let me hear you say again that you are of no worth."

"But see? I came to cheer you and I only made you sadder."

"No, I have been missing you." He reached for one of the books I had sent him. "Henry's men have been very courteous to me, but they have no liking for verse, so I have not inflicted it upon them. Perhaps one of your ladies can read to us awhile before we part?"

I nodded and beckoned to Katherine Peniston, who despite being the youngest of my ladies had the most expressive reading voice and the best pronunciation. We settled back as she read, and for a short time, I could imagine us in happier circumstances. Suffolk himself visibly grew less tense and even smiled at one or two lines. "Thank you, mademoiselle," he said, as Katherine curtseyed to him, and I reluctantly rose to go. "You gave me much pleasure and comfort. And now I think I can sleep well tonight." He stood and led me to the door, then kissed me on the cheek as I turned, weeping once more, to leave. In a low voice, he said, "You have made my life very sweet, your grace. Whatever happens, remember that. I always shall."

On March 17, Suffolk was brought to a small chamber at Westminster where, in the presence of Henry and the lords of the land, he once again denied the charges against him and declared that he was submitting to Henry's command to be done with as the king wished. Henry, as arranged, ordered him banished from the kingdom for five years, beginning on the first of May.

"Do be careful of yourself," I begged Suffolk later as twilight fell and he prepared to leave Westminster under cover of darkness. The commons, it was reputed, were furious that Henry had banished Suffolk instead of ordering his execution.

"Don't worry, your grace. I'm well armed." Suffolk breathed in the chilly air as he waited for his horse to be brought round. "Despite the circumstances, it is indescribably delicious to be in the open again." He smiled at me. "Don't look so sad, your grace. I am sorry to be going, but I am three-and-fifty and in good health. God willing, I shall live to see both of you five years from now."

"And things may change, and I may be able to bring you back earlier," Henry said. "I will try my best. In the meantime, I am certain the Duke of Burgundy will welcome you within his realm."

"Aye, Burgundy, where all sorts of flotsam and jetsam wash up." In a graver voice he said, "Your grace, I will do all I can to aid England while I am away. Perhaps doing so will help to clear my name as well."

"It was never a clouded one for me," Henry said, shaking his head as Suffolk's horse and the men Henry had collected to escort him home arrived in sight.

"Nor for me," I said, as we embraced Suffolk in turn. "God have you in his keeping, my lord."

"And you too," Suffolk said, mounting his horse so quickly I suspected that his emotions were once again threatening to get the better of him. He raised his hand in farewell, and the procession started moving through the evening mist and out of sight. As I watched it, tears stinging my eyes, Henry put his arm around me.

"Don't fear, my love," he said. "He will come back to England soon."

William de la Pole, Duke of Suffolk
April 30, 1450, to May 2, 1450

*M*Y DEAR AND ONLY WELL-BELOVED SON, I BESEECH OUR LORD IN *Heaven, the Maker of all the World, to bless you, and to send you ever grace to love him, and to dread him, to the which, as far as a father may charge his child, I both charge you, and pray you to set all your spirits and wits to do, and to know his holy laws and commandments, by the which ye shall, with his great mercy, pass all the great tempests and troubles of this wretched world.*

And that also, weetingly, ye do nothing for love nor dread of any earthly creature that should displease him. And there as any frailty maketh you to fall, beseech his mercy soon to call you to him again with repentance, satisfaction, and contrition of your heart, never more in will to offend him.

Secondly, next him above all earthly things, to be true liegeman in heart, in will, in thought, in deed, unto the king our aldermost high and dread sovereign lord, to whom both ye and I be so much bound to; charging you as father can and may, rather to die than to be the contrary, or to know anything that were against the welfare or prosperity of his most royal person, but that as far as your body and life may stretch ye live and die to defend it, and to let his highness have knowledge thereof in all the haste ye can.

Thirdly, in the same wise, I charge you, my dear son, alway as ye be bounden by the commandment of God to do, to love, to worship, your lady and mother; and also that ye obey alway her commandments, and to believe her counsels and advices in all your works, the which dread not but shall be best and truest to you. And if any other body would steer you to the contrary, to flee the counsel in any wise, for ye shall find it naught and evil.

Furthermore, as far as father may and can, I charge you in any wise to flee the company and counsel of proud men, of covetous men, and of flattering men, the more especially and mightily to withstand them, and not to draw nor to meddle

with them, with all your might and power; and to draw to you and to your com-
pany good and virtuous men, and such as be of good conversation, and of truth,
and by them shall ye never be deceived nor repent you of.

Moreover, never follow your own wit in nowise, but in all your works, of such
folks as I write of above, ask your advice and counsel, and doing thus, with the
mercy of God, ye shall do right well, and live in right much worship, and great
heart's rest and ease.

And I will be to you as good lord and father as my heart can think.

And last of all, as heartily and as lovingly as ever father blessed his child in
earth, I give you the blessing of Our Lord and of me, which of his infinite mercy
increase you in all virtue and good living; and that your blood may by his grace
from kindred to kindred multiply in this earth to his service, in such wise as
after the departing from this wretched world here, ye and they may glorify him
eternally amongst his angels in heaven.

Written of mine hand,
The day of my departing fro this land.
Your true and loving father

I sealed John's letter and handed it, along with a letter to my wife and another
one to my daughter, to one of my servants who had followed me to Ipswich,
from where I was to set sail to Calais. "Deliver them with my love."

"I will, my lord."

It was the last letter I might ever write on English soil, I realized with a pang.

⟡

I had spent the last six weeks at my manor of East Thorp with Alice and John,
tidying up my affairs as well as I could and listening for the latest news from
Normandy, which had at first been heartening: Thomas Kyriell, at last in
France with a strong force of men, had taken Valognes. Barely had this good
news arrived when bad news followed right behind it: on April 15, Kyriell
had been caught near Formigny by forces led by the Count of Clermont and
by Pierre de Brézé. Nearly four thousand of our men had been slaughtered,
and Kyriell himself had been captured. At least, I thought grimly as I boarded
the ship that was taking me overseas, I could not personally be blamed for this
latest disaster.

I had two ships and a pinnace to carry me and my small retinue, along with
our horses, overseas. As we headed into the Straits of Dover early on May 1,
I decided to drop anchor and to send the pinnace ahead of the rest to Calais,

where I was to stay before traveling to Burgundy. I had kept the matter from Alice, as we had enough to sadden us during those past six weeks together, but after I left the king and queen at Westminster, I'd been nearly killed by a crowd, furious that I'd escaped a death sentence. Materializing out of nowhere, as foul things often do, the mob had pursued me as far as St. Giles until my men finally beat them off. After this incident, I decided, it would behoove me to determine whether the citizens of Calais were in a similar mood.

As I watched the pinnace sail on and disappear from sight, I fingered the safe conduct Henry had procured for me and tried to preserve the optimism that I had been determinedly cultivating. An exile was not an end, and what was a five-year absence to a man who'd spent over a decade of his young manhood serving in France? Of course, I'd not had Alice or John or Jane to leave behind then, and I was no longer a young man…but there would be letters, and probably visits too in due course. And I would exert myself so hard on Henry's behalf that the commons might be begging for my return, the scoundrels…

Someone upon deck gasped, and I looked up from my reverie and saw a ship bearing down on us. It was twice the size of my own two ships put together. "Pirates?" whispered Henry Spenser. He was one of the king's yeomen.

I looked around and saw that the sailors on my own ship—pressed into my service by order of the king—were watching the larger ship with utter indifference, almost as if they had expected to see it. And then I knew that all was lost.

Presently, the larger ship lowered a boat, and I watched nearly as indifferently as the sailors as the men on it rowed in our direction and hailed us. "Be you the Duke of Suffolk?"

"Yes. Bound for Calais at the king's orders." Surprised that I could speak the words so calmly, I held up my safe conduct. My hand did not shake; I had entered a strange state of resignation.

"Then, my lord, our master wishes to have a word with you."

"Don't go!" hissed Jacques Blondell, who had been in charge of Queen Margaret's horses until she sent him to wait upon me.

I shook my head. "I've no choice." I had a dozen or so armed men with me, not enough to put up a fight even if the sailors with me had shown the slightest inclination to help. All resistance would accomplish would be to get my companions killed. "Lower me down," I said.

My confessor put his hand on my shoulder, and I saw that there were tears in his eyes. "I will accompany you, my lord."

"Me too," my page offered.

Whatever was going to happen, I would not have this boy be a part of it. "No. Stay you here."

A sailor produced a rope ladder in an instant, and I climbed down it, followed by my confessor, and into the waiting boat. My new companions said nothing, and indeed I had no desire to make conversation with them. Instead, I looked for the name of the ship to which we were heading.

Nicholas of the Tower.

Involuntarily, I half rose, remembering the prophecy of doom I'd once heard. The strongest of the sailors pushed me down hard. "You wouldn't be after disappointing my master, would you, my lord? For he sorely wishes to see you."

In a few minutes we were alongside the *Nicholas*. I climbed up another rope ladder, looking down only once at the sea beneath my feet. For a moment I was tempted to fling myself into it, but to jump would be not escape but certain death. When I arrived on board, I saw the master standing before me, surrounded by armed men. He was wearing a fine cloak, of which I suspected he'd robbed someone. He made a mock bow. "The Duke of Suffolk, I presume?"

"Yes. What do you want with me?"

"We'll be asking the questions, my lord, if you please, from now on. But for now, we just want to welcome you." He smiled, showing what struck me as absurdly good teeth for a man of his station. Then he and the crew said in unison, "Welcome, traitor!"

⟞⟝

I thought that my captors would beat me to death, as poor Adam Moleyns had been, but instead they pushed me upon a barrel as the master nodded approvingly. "You didn't dare ask Henry for a trial, did you? Well, you're going to get one now. Judge"—he pointed to himself—"jury, and audience, all here!"

"Does it not matter to you that you are violating the king's safe conduct?" I had been clutching it like some sort of talisman.

"The king's safe conduct," the master mimicked in a fair approximation of my voice, and snatched the paper from me. "The king's next to worthless, and so is this." He ripped it to shreds and tossed its seal over to one of the sailors. "Piss on it, why don't you? We don't know your king, Suffolk. What we do know is the community of the realm, and that's what the crown stands for. We respect the crown. Just not the head it sits on."

"Community of the realm? Those are fine sentiments for a pirate, which is the manner of man you look to me. Who fed them to you? Who put you up to this, whatever your name is? Have the guts to tell me, you whore—"

A single blow to the chest, causing me to crumple and slide off the barrel, was the answer to my question. My confessor bent over me as I lay there gasping, then looked up as I slowly managed to sit upright. "How dare you treat him so?"

"Oh, we can treat him any way we please," purred the master. "His precious king's not going to help him, is he? We can give him a death like a nobleman, following a proper trial, or"—he pulled a dagger from its sheath and waved it in front of my face, then brought it lower—"we can cut his balls off as a preliminary and kill him nice and slow. His decision, really. Yours too. Now, shall we get on with the trial?"

Somehow my captors had obtained a copy of all the charges against me, which one of the sailors, who had evidently had considerable schooling in his youth (I hope none of the lads at the school I have set up at my manor at Ewelme turn out so), read out verbatim in loving detail. The master as judge sat resplendent in yet another stolen robe, costly as the last but more somber in color, as suited the nature of the judicial proceedings. Twelve sailors lined themselves up in an area that had been designated as a jury box; I pass over the squabbling that took place over who got to sit there instead of as a mere audience member. They tried to get me to enter a plea to each charge, but I refused to open my mouth. It cost me a couple of blows until they got bored with that particular farce, but my silence was worth it to me. I just sat on my barrel and listened, trying to remind myself that there was a world beyond this living nightmare into which I'd walked and thanking the Lord that my wife and little son had not accompanied me on my journey.

The verdict being a foregone conclusion, my trial was nothing if not efficient. I was ordered to stand to face my sentence—death, naturally, by sword. I expected it to be carried out straightaway, but to my surprise, the master said, "You've until tomorrow at dawn to repent of your sins. Take the traitor and his confessor below, mates."

I'd not spoken in hours, so my voice cracked when I said, "What will happen to him? And to my men?"

"Released, once you're out of this world and on your way to hell. What use are they to us?"

In the hold, I prayed with my confessor a long time and told him my sins, not that he wasn't familiar enough with them already. When I had finished the formal rites, I said, "I did think I was acting for the best in arresting Gloucester; I did have some evidence. But it wasn't enough. I should have left him alone."

"Yes, my lord. You probably should have."

"And it all ended in disaster anyway. For me and for England." I shook my head. "'All of you sorry buggers who arranged this will pay.' He got the last word, didn't he?"

"My lord, you have done much good. Your almshouses, your generosity to Eton, your grammar school at Ewelme…"

"Yes. But no one will remember those things of me, only the bad, except for my family."

"And the king and the queen, my lord."

"Yes," I said softly. "The king and my little Margaret shall always remember me kindly. That is a comfort to me."

Great as my sins were, they were not so many that they took up the entire evening, so late in the night, my confessor and I laid our heads upon some sacks and tried to doze. He succeeded; I did not. Instead, I lay there, still wondering what man or men had arranged all of this, for I found it hard to believe these men would act as they did for the sheer fun of it, with no hope of profit other than the small amount of money they'd undoubtedly rob my men of before all was done. Gloucester's old supporters? The Duke of Norfolk, who'd been trying for years to reduce my influence in East Anglia? The Duke of York, in revenge for being sent to Ireland, or perhaps in furtherance of a longer-range plan?

It was a mystery that would have to remain tangled, so I wondered instead what sort of man my dear son would grow up into and whether my beautiful Jane would bring me more grandchildren: I was glad I'd taken the time to write both of my children letters before I left England. I was happy that I'd spent my last night with Alice with her clasped tight in my arms, and I was pleased that there were passages in my last letter to her so intimate that she'd never show it to another soul.

And I hoped that the world would not go too hard with Henry and Margaret. If Margaret could bear a child, if we could hold on to something in France…Well, at least I had replaced "if only" with "if."

The door clattered and two sailors hustled me out upon the deck. The sun was breaking over the water; on another day, I would have thought it a glorious sight.

I stood silently as I was stripped of my russet gown and my mailed doublet—more clothing, I presumed, for the master's collection. Then my hands were tied behind my back and I and my confessor were hustled into the same boat on which I'd arrived, accompanied by the most disreputable looking of the sailors, whose name I had somehow managed to catch during the squabble over the jury box. Richard Lenard. My eyes went to the rusty sword he carried, and the master smiled. "Would we lie to you? A nobleman's death. But no need to muck up my ship with your blood." He stepped back and the boat was lowered slowly into the sea as my confessor prayed. I could see my own ship in a distance, my men lining the deck, watching.

"Kneel, Suffolk, and say your prayers if you've any to say."

When I received my confessor's blessing and kneeled, I found that I could not summon more than the simplest prayer, for the long night of confession and absolution had exhausted me spiritually. Instead, my thoughts drifted to a day nearly twenty years before, back at Jargeau. I had fought as long as I could until, weakened from my wounds and surrounded, my brother Alexander lying dead at my feet, I had finally given up, knighting the young man who took me captive so I could surrender to an equal. (It had given me a certain comfort.) With my brother John, badly wounded and delirious, propped against me, I had been conveyed by water to Orléans, where in due course I had been brought before the victorious Maid. Even as I had knelt in submission, mourning my dead and dying brothers and cursing myself for the mistakes I had made, I had sensed that I was in the presence of greatness. "My lady"—how exactly did one address a female in armor?—"I am your prisoner, for you to do with as you will."

"You put up quite a fight, my lord. It was well done." The Maid smiled, very faintly, and said in that gruff voice of hers in the most matter-of-fact tone possible, "But I put up a better."

Let these ruffians play their games with their mock trial and rusty sword; they might have bested me, but I had met defeat from a far more formidable foe: at the hands of the most gallant general France had ever known. And I had put up a good fight; she said so her very self. It was something of comfort to take to my grave with me. I smiled, and I was still smiling when that rat-catcher Lenard raised his sword.

8

Margaret
May 1450 to March 1453

I HAVE BECOME A MASTER AT HEARING BAD NEWS. I STAND FIRMLY ON MY FEET; I ask logical questions—How? Who? What? When?—and no one but I knows that I am shaking inside and want only to find someone's skirts in which to bury my face. But Suffolk's death was the first bad news I had that struck me to the bone, and besides I had just turned twenty and still had the foolish notion that men could act decently and not like savages. So as Henry Spenser, a yeoman of my husband who had accompanied Suffolk on his journey, told me his story, I wept, then finally sank to my knees and hugged them as my ladies clustered around me. It was the chief of them, Emma, Lady Scales, who was managing to ask questions.

"They used a rusty sword to behead him," Spenser said in a flat voice. "It took six strokes—it was the rust that made it difficult, I suppose, and the knave didn't know what he was doing anyhow. They drew near our own ship so we could watch what became of the traitor, they said. The duke's confessor said that the men on the *Nicholas* were laughing, joking that his aim was so bad, calling out encouragement and making bets on how many strokes it would take. There was so much blood, your grace—we could see it from our own vessel, pooling on the floor of the boat as they butchered him."

"For mercy's sake!" I managed. "Tell me that he was not conscious throughout this!"

"I believe the second stroke killed or stunned him, your grace. He made no movement or sound afterward—he had groaned after the first one. The third one I would say most definitely. It went so deep…" Spenser closed his eyes and swayed as I fought back sickness. "I can say no more about it, your grace, I am sorry. Afterward, they rowed to Dover shore and tossed his body there in a heap, like debris from a slaughterhouse. They stuck his head on a pole they had and set it near the body; his confessor had to watch all this. Then they came back for us and stripped us of any valuables we had and brought us to shore alongside him in the same boat they'd used to murder the duke in."

"Does he lie on Dover sands now?" Lady Scales asked.

"No. There was a crowd that collected to jeer at him and us, but a couple of us managed to slip away and borrow a horse to get to the sheriff, and he sent armed men to assist us and linen to wrap the body in. And a wagon to take him away. He lies at St. Martin's in Dover now, and the sheriff has sent to the king for instructions about what to do with the body."

"Does his widow know of this?"

"Yes. She was in London—arranging some of her lord's business, in fact. She is on her way home to Ewelme and is bearing up as well as can be expected."

I commanded myself enough to rise and to say to my chamberlain, "See to it that every assistance she needs is given to her. And make certain the king is informed of this so he can assist her also."

"Yes, your grace."

"And now I wish to be alone. Lady Scales, take me to my chamber."

Lady Scales obeyed and led me to my private chamber. There, I clutched the poem Suffolk had copied for me to my chest and wept for three days straight.

"Your grace cannot keep on like this," said Jacquetta of Luxembourg, Duchess of Bedford, three days later. A Frenchwoman like myself, she had been married at seventeen to John, Duke of Bedford, a younger brother of Henry V. Widowed after scarcely two years of marriage, she had scandalized her family by marrying one Richard Woodville, the son of her husband's chamberlain. The marriage was by all accounts a most happy one, and a fruitful one as well; even in my bleary-eyed state I noted that yet another Woodville was growing in the duchess's belly. "You will die at this rate, weeping and not sleeping and not eating, and what if perchance your grace should be with child?" She patted her belly absently. "It cannot thrive if you mourn so."

"The Duchess of Bedford is right," put in the Duchess of Buckingham, the older of the ladies for whom Lady Scales, fearing for my life, had sent. She sighed, for she had lost four of her seven sons in early childhood. "We know that the Duke of Suffolk was close to your grace's heart, but you can do him no good by starving yourself."

"And the king will be most grieved if you sicken," said Lady Scales. "Please, your grace, for his sake. The Duke of Suffolk would not want to see you ruin your health," she added coaxingly.

I stared listlessly past the gaggle of ladies standing round me to my damsels, who had given way to their seniors. They had been sewing, but now I noticed that they were passing a piece of paper around. "What is that?" I demanded.

Katherine Peniston made a move as if to hide the paper she held. "N-nothing, your grace."

"Of course it is something, or you would not be saying that." I frowned. "I hope you are not receiving letters from William Vaux." William, thirteen like Katherine and one of my pages, had been eying the well-developed Katherine for some time, I had noticed. She had been eying him back as well. "I will not have you conducting yourself in such a manner. Don't you think I have more to concern myself with at present than your love business? Give it here."

Katherine sighed and handed it over. "I wish it were what your grace thinks it is, but it is not. It is a horrid thing. Please pay it no mind."

I took the paper impatiently. As soon as I took it into my hand I found that it was certainly not a personal letter; it bore nail holes and had obviously been ripped from a wall. It read:

> In the month of May when grass grows green,
> Fragrant in her flowers with sweet savor,
> Jack Napes went over the sea, a mariner to be,
> With his clog and his chain to sell more treasure.
> Such a pain pricked him, he asked a confessor.
> Nicholas of the Tower said I am ready, this confessor to be;
> He was held so, that he not passed that hour.
> For Jack Napes' soul *placebo* and *dirge*.
> Who shall execute the fest of solemnity
> Bishops and lords as great reason is,
> Monks, canons, and priests, with all the clergy,
> Pray for him that he may come to bliss,
> And that never such another come after this.

"Jack Napes" was a common name for a tame monkey or ape, and Suffolk's badge was the clog and chain that such an animal would wear. I stared at the ladies. "Jack Napes is Suffolk?"

"Yes, your grace. They are putting copies all around town."

I skimmed the rest, nearly a dozen sickening stanzas. Gleefully, they mockingly described a funeral service held for poor Suffolk, attended by all of those the writer deemed to be enemies of the people. Anyone remotely associated with Suffolk—and with Henry's government—was mentioned there. "This is detestable!" I flung it into the fire and watched it disappear into the flames. "I would like to do that to the man who wrote this."

The Duchess of Bedford, whose own husband was named in the poem, nodded in satisfaction. "Aye, your grace. So would I. But there are plenty of copies of this poem about, sadly."

Unthinkingly, I reached for a wafer that had been left strategically nearby by the ladies and bit into it furiously. "Why are they not being destroyed?" I asked after a moment.

"The writings, or the writers?"

"Both," I said grimly. Just weeks before, while Henry was heading to Parliament in Leicester, a man had run into Henry's path and struck the ground with a flail. This, he had said, was how the great Duke of York would deal with filthy traitors such as Suffolk if he were at Leicester. Henry with his reputation for leniency had shocked many, including me, by ordering that the man be hanged, drawn, and quartered. "The men who are circulating these vile things should be treated as that man at Stony Stratford was."

"I have heard that Lord Saye has threatened to turn all of Kent into a wild forest in revenge for what was done to Suffolk," said the Duchess of Bedford. "But it may be no more than wild talk from the people."

"I hope it is true and that is exactly what he will do," I said. "They deserve it."

Katherine goggled at me. "Well, Katherine? Why look you so? I owe you an apology about this writing, I suppose."

"It is not that. It is only that you sounded so—vengeful just now, your grace. I don't believe you ever have before."

"No one has ever cruelly murdered someone of whom I was so fond before. And smacked his lips over his death as these people do." The girl still looked so worried that I drew her closer to me and stroked her hair. "Come, Katherine. I spoke wildly. There must be good people in Kent who deplore what has been done. But I do intend to write to Henry and ask him to suppress these dreadful writings, and I intend to ask him what is being done to apprehend the duke's murderers and to press him to do some more to hunt them down. My ladies Bedford and Buckingham are quite right. I have been here weeping and starving myself long enough. It is time I took some action."

But others, with very different intentions, were thinking the same thing. Their leader was one Jack Cade.

⤫

Who was he, Jack Cade? To this day, I hardly know. Some said that he was a physician; some said that he was a sorcerer. Others said that he had fought for the French. One story, which I was certainly ready enough to believe, had it that he had fled his master's household after impregnating and murdering a fellow servant there. Some said he was a Kentishman, others claimed that he had spent his life in Ireland and was a distant relation of the Duke of York; indeed, he called himself at one point John Mortimer, the Mortimers being the ancestors of the duke. But whoever he was, by mid-May, he was marching from Kent to London with a horde of armed men, determined to present a list of grievances to the king.

When Henry, who was holding Parliament at Leicester, heard the news, he and a number of his lords hastened to London, where they stayed at St. John's priory in Clerkenwell. I stayed at Greenwich, where I passed the fine June days pacing up and down by the riverside, waiting for the return of the messengers I dispatched two or three times a day to the king for news. At last, on June 18, I learned that Henry himself was riding to meet the rebels at Blackheath, where they had encamped. It was the first time my husband had ever arrayed himself for battle, and I suppose it could be termed a success in a way, because when Henry arrived, the rebels had disappeared the night before. Soon, Henry was back with me at Greenwich.

In no time at all, it seemed, bad news followed us there: two of Henry's kinsmen, the Stafford brothers, had pursued the fleeing rebels into Kent, certain that they could be dealt with easily now that they were out of London. Instead, the Staffords and about forty of their men had been killed near Sevenoaks, and Jack Cade, who by now had become the rebels' official leader, was strutting about in Humphrey Stafford's brigandine, salet, and spurs. Meanwhile, another contingent of Henry's men, itching for action, ran wild through another part of Kent. Instead of intimidating the rebels, they only succeeded in bringing them more adherents.

"Even your grace's men at Blackheath are beginning to murmur in favor of the rebels now," the Duke of Buckingham informed Henry and me at Greenwich. He looked drawn and weary; the Staffords who had died were his cousins. "They have threatened to join them unless you imprison Lord Saye."

Lord Saye had held the hopeless job of royal treasurer since the year before.

I knew better than to ask Buckingham what he had done to incur the anger of the Kentishmen; he had been close to Suffolk, which was enough. "You think they are serious?" Henry asked.

"I fear so. Lord Saye is unpopular in Kent in his own right, your grace must know; he is claimed to have acquired property there through foul means. Whether there is truth to it, who knows? But he is also blamed for our difficulties in France, and having been associated with the Duke of Suffolk…"

I blinked back tears. Henry said resignedly, "I must trust to your judgment. Have young Exeter arrest him." Henry Holland, the sulky young duke I'd played cards with in more innocent times, had returned from Ireland (without his guardian) and had been allowed to take over his late father's duties as Constable of the Tower.

"That will please them," Buckingham said dryly. "One of the complaints of Cade's men is that men of royal blood like Exeter and the Duke of York have been kept from your grace in favor of men affiliated with the Duke of Suffolk."

"God's wounds!" I said unthinkingly. Henry turned grey-faced at the oath, the first I'd ever used in his company. "Must they speak of Suffolk always as if he were the devil incarnate? They have his life. Will they not be satisfied until they destroy every vestige of his memory?"

"They are bitter men, your grace, and frightened ones. Kent has suffered from the war more than most parts of the country, in terms of trade, and it has been raided by the French. Too, they see the soldiers returning from abroad, demoralized. And they believe they lack justice."

They should all be lacking heads, I thought, but Henry looked so miserable I forbore from saying anything. Instead, I excused myself and went back to my garden and my ladies.

⁂

"I am going to Westminster, my dear. And then I am going to Kenilworth."

My jaw dropped. "Withdraw from this area? With Cade's men still in Kent?"

"Yes."

"Wouldn't it be better to stay?"

"It is not for you to tell me my business, Margaret."

It was the first time in our marriage that Henry had spoken coldly to me. "I beg your pardon," I said in a small voice. But I could not stop pushing. "But what of London? What if Cade's men return?"

"London will hardly be ill protected. I will fortify the Tower. But it is best that the court move out of London. I have not made the decision lightly. It has been discussed with my council."

"Shall I go with you?"

"No. You will remain here at Greenwich. It will be useful to have you here, to facilitate contact with London."

I could not but think that my own father and kinsmen, in Henry's circumstances, might have insisted on remaining in London. Evidently my thoughts were quite visible, for Henry went on in the cold voice he had used before, "I do not make this decision lightly, or out of cowardice."

"Of course not." My voice could have held more conviction.

"It is quite possible that with me gone from London, the rabble will melt away. They cannot hope to get to Kenilworth unhindered, and if they stay in Kent, my men can deal with them. What happened with the Staffords was a tragic miscalculation. We know their numbers better now."

I nodded, and Henry suddenly drew me to him and stroked my hair. "Marguerite, please don't think me a coward. I just don't know what to do. Either way I feel that I am damned. I know the Londoners want me to stay, but my council feels that I should go. This is one of the times I sense a ghost whispering to me."

"Your father's?"

"No. I never knew him, after all. No, it is my uncle, Duke Humphrey."

"Does he say to stay or to go?"

"Neither. He says, 'Figure it out for yourself, boy. You should have listened to me when you had the chance.'"

⌘

Henry left that same day for Westminster, which he and the rest of the court left five days later, on June 25. We did not realize it at the time, but the day before, the Duke of Somerset had surrendered Caen to the French. In less than two months England would lose every acre of Normandy.

In the meantime, three days later, Henry Holland paid me a visit at Greenwich. "Your husband was a fool to leave London," he announced as we walked around my flower garden. He sniffed appreciatively. "Very fragrant."

"I trust you remember you are speaking of your king?"

"Yes, and he was a fool to leave London. Cade's men are marching back straightaway, but with a difference. This time, they've all the weapons they seized when they killed the Staffords, and more men than ever."

"How do you know this?"

"The Common Council of London. They sent out spies."

"Is London prepared for them?"

"Well enough. The Tower's been fortified, and there are plenty of men at arms there."

"Shouldn't you be there?"

"I've done all I can for now; it's just a matter of waiting. And I wanted to see how your grace was doing, since your husband—the king, that is—didn't see fit to take you with him."

"He felt I could serve a purpose here."

"His father would have sent you to safety and stayed here himself, instead of vice versa. Most men would, I daresay."

I did not have a ready answer for this. Instead I asked, "How fares Lord Saye?"

"He is in good spirits. King Henry tried to get me to send Saye to him at Westminster, but I refused."

"You refused the king?"

"It would have been foolish to release Saye. It would have only angered the troops, some of whom are men just back from France. They might have revolted, and Lord Saye would have had the worst of it. The Duke of Suffolk might be alive today if he'd been kept in the Tower."

I sighed. Exeter asked, "Do you mourn him?"

"Yes, greatly. He was like a father to me." Remembering the rumors Suffolk had told me of, I added, "And nothing more, whatever you might have heard."

"I never believed that nonsense."

I decided to change the subject. "What do you hear from your father-in-law in Ireland?"

"Very little, which suits me fine," said Exeter with a winning smile. He laughed. "He's probably too busy hearing his wife's complaints to write to me. Lord, your grace, you've never seen discontent until you've heard the Duchess of York wax upon the subject of Irish savagery! France suited her just fine, with the best of everything obtainable at her command. As it is, her stay in Ireland has almost driven the poor duke into solvency." Exeter scratched his chin, which bore a scraggly beard. In a different tone, he said, "Sometimes I wonder if my dear father-in-law isn't behind all of this trouble."

"What makes you say that, with him in Ireland?"

"Well, think of it. Whose name do these people keep mentioning as the man who can put all to rights? York's. Who's next in line for the throne? York. Even if he's over in Ireland, he's not without friends over here who can stir up trouble on his behalf, I'm sure." Exeter shrugged. "Granted, I detest the man, but it's a thought."

"Yes. It is indeed," I said.

∞

Although the Duke of Exeter had promised to return within a day or so to see how I fared, he did not, and I soon found out why from the men I sent sailing down the Thames in search of news: London was under attack. Bit by bit, I pieced together what was happening in London while Greenwich dozed in the July sunshine.

With Henry gone, Cade and his men, just as Exeter had predicted, had hastened back to London—or, more precisely, Southwark, as the gates of London were shut tightly against them. But by the third day of July, the rabble, fighting against the defenders of the city's great bridge, managed to cut the cords that held up the drawbridge, allowing Cade and his men to press through to the gate. Terrified by the threat to set the entire city ablaze, the men guarding the gate handed over the keys, and Cade and his men were inside London. For a time they contented themselves with looting the house of an alderman, but the next day, they turned their attention to trying the men they deemed to be traitors.

The English, I must say, have an odd fondness for making at least a pretense of trying the men they kill. Poor Suffolk had been tried aboard ship; Cade, however, was able to commandeer the Guildhall for his show trials, and commissioners who had been appointed to allow the citizens to air their grievances were forced to hear the indictments the rebels brought. Most of the men indicted were far out of the mob's reach, but under pressure from their unruly troops, the Duke of Exeter and Lord Scales allowed Lord Saye to be brought from the Tower to the Guildhall. While Cade, dressed in the finery he'd taken off the dead body of Humphrey Stafford, paraded through the city, Lord Saye was sentenced to death and beheaded at Cheapside. That afternoon, Cade himself seized Lord Saye's son-in-law, William Crowmer, and had him beheaded at Mile End. For the amusement of the mob, Cade's men had the heads of father and son-in-law, each on a separate spike, kiss each other while the pole-bearers made smacking sounds.

Three other men died that day and the next, for no better reason than they had each displeased the mob in some way. In between and after murders, Cade's men looted. Then they retired to their lodgings in Southwark.

By now, the Londoners, realizing that soon Cade's men might soon display their energies for murdering and pillaging less discriminately, had had enough. Bolstered by the royal troops from the Tower, they gathered on London Bridge, determined to keep Cade's forces from returning. Cade, hearing of this development from his spies, regrouped his men by the bridge, their ranks increased when he freed the prisoners of the Marshalsea in Southwark. An all-out battle resulted, fought not on a field somewhere but upon the bridge. When dawn broke the next morning, poor Matthew Gough, who'd fought in France for over two decades and was admired even by the French for his bravery, lay dead by the drawbridge, killed in the land he had returned to less than six weeks before.

As that same dawn rose, I found the Bishop of Winchester at my chamber door.

"A pardon? You and the archbishops wish for me to lend my name to a pardon of these men? After the horrors they have perpetuated?"

"It is necessary, your grace, to calm the situation. At present there is a truce, and Cade's men are at least shut out of the city, but who knows what will happen? The king had given us authority to act in dire necessity, with him out of the city"—the bishop's face gave nothing away—"and this is the direst necessity. Nearly three hundred men died last night."

I shivered. "But what would a pardon accomplish, other than to sanction murder?"

"It could be used to persuade them to disperse peacefully, without more violence. They have achieved, after all, some of their goals."

"Yes, such as murdering poor Lord Saye and his son-in-law."

"Precisely."

"The pardon could be issued without my name, surely?"

"Yes, but King Henry might not be so willing to issue it, you see, were your name not on it. It is not seen as weakness to give in to the pleadings of a queen for mercy." The bishop's voice grew more urgent. "Please, your grace, consider this request. London is our greatest city. If we do not act, she could well go up in flames. Thousands could perish."

"Very well. Put my name in the pardon if it will help. Use the most florid language you please."

The bishop sighed with relief. "Thank you, your grace. The Londoners will bless your name for this."

(He was wrong, of course; the Londoners have never blessed me for anything, except perhaps on the day when I left England for good.)

After a long morning of negotiations, the pardon, which stated that Henry had granted it in part due to my persistent supplications, was issued in Henry's name that very same day, and the rebels duly began trickling back to their homes. Cade, the fool, joined them, but he did not go his way in peace. Instead, he attacked Queensborough Castle and was declared to be a traitor. With a price on his head, he was captured on July 12. After he died of his wounds a few days later, his body was beheaded and cut into quarters, and soon his head graced the bridge that he had assaulted just days before. Thinking of the vile poem that had circulated about poor Suffolk, I rode down the Thames to see Cade's head and watched in satisfaction from my barge as the birds industriously picked it clean.

Just a couple of weeks after Cade's head had been placed on London Bridge, the Duke of Somerset, newly returned to England after the fall of Caen, knelt before Henry at St. Albans, where he and his council had stopped on the way back to London. "Your grace, I crave your forgiveness. I know that I must take a great share of the blame—perhaps the greatest share—of the disaster in Normandy." It was all but lost now; Cherbourgh, the last fortress there, would fall within a few weeks. "I beg that you allow me to regain your grace's trust by doing service here."

Henry did not even hesitate, but urged the duke up into a standing position. "That is impossible," he said quietly. "It is impossible because you have never lost our trust, my lord."

Somerset bent his head. "Not just in humility," the Duke of Buckingham told me later. "I do believe the man was crying."

A few days after this, Henry and his council returned to London, with the Duke of Somerset in tow. Shortly after this, Somerset came to Greenwich to see me and was ushered to my presence almost immediately after his arrival. He was only in his middle forties, and had looked younger than his years when I last saw him in England, but the last couple of years had taken its toll. He was gaunt and graying. As we exchanged pleasantries, I saw him looking around the chamber. "My lord? Is there something that attracts your attention?"

"I beg your pardon, your grace. It is only that it seems very quiet here. More so than I remember it when I visited in the past."

"It has been that way since Rouen fell," I said bluntly, not altogether unhappy at seeing him wince. "Petitioners shy away from me. Except for my household and my council and my ladies, and Henry when he visits, no one comes here, for as a Frenchwoman, I am suspect."

Somerset smiled sadly. "Trust me, your grace, I can have fellow-feeling with you." He cleared his throat. "Tell me, your grace, since we are free to speak privily, do you blame me for Suffolk's death?"

"I know you did not seek it, my lord. But the blame for the losses in France fell entirely upon him and others in England, when—"

"It was I who caused them," Somerset finished for me. "Your grace, I was much to blame, but do you know how my representatives begged Parliament last year for aid? Do you know how close our plan involving Fougères came to working?" He shook his head. "But I can find no ready excuse for Rouen. The citizens there were only too happy to surrender themselves to King Charles's men, and I and my wife and children were holed up in Rouen Castle with a garrison. We could not have held out long against a siege, I am sure, but we should have resisted anyway. If I knew then what I know now, I would have fought to my death; it would have at least preserved my honor. It was a sorry business. But at least King Henry has given me a chance to redeem myself. I am fortunate."

"And alive."

"And alive," Somerset agreed. "Don't think, your grace, that I fail to appreciate the fact. Or that I do not think myself unworthy of it."

"My lord, why are you here? Now that I think of it, you have never called upon me before except when the king was present, or when your duchess was with you."

Somerset's tired blue eyes shot me an admiring look. "I was thinking you might ask that, but perhaps not so soon. The truth is, your grace, you and I have something in common, something besides being deeply unpopular. We both want to see King Henry strong. Aside from it being a means to better ourselves, I think we each have a deep regard for Henry and want to see him rise out of the mire he's in. Jack Cade's head might deter some from rebelling now, but what in a year, when it's been pecked bare? There's another Cade out there waiting to take his place, if we don't act."

"God forbid. But how can we act?"

"I by bringing the lords together under King Henry—I can do it, for he trusts me, however ill I might have repaid that trust in the past—and you simply by supporting me in front of Henry."

"Against whom, my lord?"

"You're not the least bit slow, your grace. The Duke of York. I firmly believe he will not remain in Ireland for long. He is free to appoint a deputy to carry out his duties there, remember, and if I were him I would find this too good an opportunity to miss. With Suffolk dead and England still nervous after Cade, it's a situation ripe for exploitation, especially since he hasn't been here or in France and can't be blamed for any of what's happened. Though I'm not entirely sure some of the blame can't attach to him. There have been rumors that he has been behind some of the unrest here."

"I have heard such talk. Do you think there is substance to it?"

"I wouldn't discount it. Cade, or whatever he called himself on any given day, dropped his name often enough, and it's hard to imagine there wasn't someone encouraging him to do so."

"My lord, do you think York could have been behind Suffolk's death?" I asked suddenly.

"Him or his followers; it wouldn't surprise me. There wasn't anything spontaneous about that murder. Those men were waiting for the duke, and they no doubt had their orders what to do with him when they found him."

"And none of those seamen who were on Suffolk's ship did anything to resist the *Nicholas of the Tower*'s men. As if it had been prearranged."

"Indeed."

I stretched forth my hand to Somerset. "My lord, we have an alliance."

"I shall be true to it, your grace."

Somerset visibly relaxed, and so did I. "Now that we have formed an alliance, shall I soon have the pleasure of seeing your wife and children?"

My new ally grinned. "As a matter of fact, your grace, they are on the grounds here. Might they join us?" I assented, and Somerset nodded to his servant.

In a few moments, the Duchess of Somerset, Eleanor Beauchamp, and the couple's children stood before me as the duke beamed at them; whatever Somerset might be faulted for, it was not for a lack of affection for his eight offspring. Not all of the five daughters were there; some had married and were living elsewhere. But all three boys were present: Henry, age fourteen, Edmund, age twelve, and little John, age four. There is not much that makes me cry now, but I can still weep to think of the three brothers as they knelt in front of me that day, their faces closely resembling their father's and almost identical to each other except for the gradations of age. I had seen when they entered the room that lively as their young faces were, the expressions of the older two boys were guarded, and the two of them stuck close together as if expecting a challenge, even in my own chamber. I wondered how much of the talk about their father they had heard, and I decided after consideration that they must have heard a great deal of it.

They were forward lads nonetheless, once I bade them rise and engaged them in conversation, and I found that I was enjoying myself for the first time since Suffolk had been sent off on his fatal journey. Because the day was fine, I proposed that we go riding. As the boys trotted on a little ahead of their parents and me, I asked, "Are your older sons to be serving in someone's household now that they are back in England?"

"Henry is to be one of the king's squires, but we have not placed Edmund yet." The duchess gave an almost imperceptible sigh, and I suspected that she was thinking that no noble family might want a Beaufort boy in its household after Somerset's disgrace.

"Then let Edmund serve as one of my pages," I said hastily. "I have room for him"—I hardly needed him, in fact, as my household was rather bloated to begin with—"and he seems a bright lad."

The Somersets smiled their assent, and so Edmund joined my household.

Somerset had been right about the Duke of York, for just a few weeks later, he had landed at Beaumaris in Wales. Evading Henry's men, he had made his way to London and demanded an audience with the king.

"My, he was a study in humility," the Duke of Somerset told me afterward in my chamber at Westminster. I had decided that York's coming would be an ill time to be tucked away at Greenwich. "He'd already sent King Henry a statement protesting his loyalty, and a second statement complaining of his hostile reception at Beaumaris. I'm not sure how else he expected to be greeted, considering that he hadn't sent the king a word of warning that he was coming here. And considering that he's got hundreds of men here with him in London, he surely can't wonder why the king might have his suspicions. But he put on a fine show of having nothing but the best intentions. Said that he always had been and always would be King Henry's true liegeman and servant and that he was grieved beyond measure that the king could think him otherwise."

"What did King Henry say to this?"

"Oh, he was most gracious; he always is. But I've seen him rather more cordial. I believe he has his guard up."

"Henry is getting more wary," I reflected. "Or at least less trusting."

"That perhaps is a good thing, your grace."

"Yes," I said, not without some regret. "It probably is."

For the next year and many months after that, I watched from a queenly distance as Somerset and York struggled for control of the kingdom—limiting my own role to the occasional well-chosen word to Henry in favor of Somerset. York denounced Somerset and even managed to get him imprisoned in the Tower for a time—ostensibly for Somerset's own protection—but Somerset proved a more formidable foe than York anticipated. By March of 1452, York, the arrogant fool, took it upon himself to prepare a petition denouncing Somerset for his losses in France. Henry politely agreed to receive it—and took York into custody when he arrived in the king's presence. As I was at Greenwich at the time, I missed the sight of the proud Duke of York having to swear at St. Paul's Cathedral an oath of allegiance to Henry. York skulked off to his castle at Ludlow, not to be seen again at court for many months.

It was a fine year, 1452. John Talbot, the brave old Earl of Shrewsbury, recovered Bordeaux for the English. Henry's younger half brothers, Edmund and Jasper Tudor, were made the Earl of Richmond and the Earl of Pembroke. There was a liveliness at court that had not been there before, and a hope that what had been lost in France might yet be regained. Even I shared it.

The next year, 1453, began sadly for me: in late February, my mother died. Yet even as I wept for her whom I would never see again and put on blue mourning, I had a secret that brought me hope. For one day in early March, I summoned Richard Tunstall, one of Henry's esquires of the body, to my chamber at Greenwich. He looked back, frowning slightly, at my departing physician. "Your grace is well?"

"Quite. I want you to take a message to the king."

"Yes, your grace."

"Tell him—" I paused as my ladies looked on, smiling. After eight years, I wanted to savor the words I was about to say. "Tell him that my physician has seen me today, and has confirmed what I have suspected for several weeks. I am with child."

Part II

Lady Mother

9

Margaret
January 1453 to December 1454

M<small>Y SON COULD HAVE BEEN CONCEIVED ON SEVERAL OCCASIONS THAT</small> January, I suppose, but I like to think that it happened on January 5, the evening that Edward Tudor and Jasper Tudor were knighted at the Tower. There was a fine feast that night and a disguising, and much wine, and I was dismayed to see during the dancing afterward that fourteen-year-old Edmund Beaufort had overindulged. "Go back to Greenwich immediately," I ordered. "What if the king sees you like this?"

"I'll take him," offered Edmund's older brother Henry, the Earl of Dorset. Hal, as we all called him, was a frequent visitor to my household, as he and Edmund were close and Hal's own duties in the king's household were not particularly onerous. Not quite seventeen, he had inherited more than a generous portion of the Beaufort good looks, and his visits were always received with marked enthusiasm on the part of my youngest ladies. Hal had been enjoying the fruits of the grape himself, but his balance was considerably better than his younger brother's. He gave me a winning smile of apology for his brother's ill behavior. "Come along, Edmund."

"I thought Frenshwomen liked wine," protested Edmund as Hal hauled him in the direction of the royal barge.

"In moderation," I said huffily. "For heaven's sake, Hal, don't let him fall off the barge."

It was much later that evening when Henry and I rode by barge to Greenwich ourselves. As the hour was so late, my bed had already been turned down for me without any of the ceremony that usually accompanied it. As Katherine Peniston dressed me in my nightshift, I heard a rustle from the direction of the bed. I froze. "What on earth is that?"

Then a mouse answered my question by running up my long nightshift. With a single, eloquent shriek, I jumped upon the stool and began beating on the skirt of my garment. Then I saw that the creatures were all over the place—gamboling in the bedclothes, scurrying along the bed curtains, frisking among the drapes. "Take them away! Call my pages! Call the rat-catcher! *Do* something!"

"Leave the room, your grace," Katherine said reasonably. Was it my imagination, or was she trying very hard not to laugh?

"I will not leave my bedchamber to those creatures. And who knows where else they are lurking?" A mouse scooted across the floor and into my slipper. "More pages! Now!"

A handful of pages rushed in, predictably headed by William Vaux, who never missed an opportunity to be in Katherine's presence. "You know, my lady," Katherine observed as the boys slowly began rounding up the rodents, "I believe that they have been put inside your chamber deliberately."

Nearby, William, holding a mouse by the tail in each hand, snorted. Still on my stool, I turned to stare at him. "Do you know something about this, boy?"

"Your grace…"

"Answer me!"

"Well…I think Edmund Beaufort might know something more about it."

"Call the king and the Beaufort brothers here immediately."

In no time at all, my husband and the Beaufort brothers appeared, Edmund leaning on Hal. Henry blinked at me as I stared down at him from the vantage point of my stool. "Marguerite?"

"There are mice in this room."

"Sisteen of them," offered Edmund Beaufort proudly. "Would have been seventeen. Cat," he added gloomily.

"Henry, what are you going to do about this?"

"My dear?"

"That—creature—has infested my chamber with mice! And he knows I hate them! It is one of the first things my pages are told when they enter my household."

"It is partly my fault," admitted Hal. He had been gazing, I suddenly realized, in the direction of my nightshift, which was not one of my thicker ones. With a scowl, I crossed my arms over my bosom. "Edmund just wanted to play a prank, and I—er—helped a little."

"Helped *a little*? You got all of the mith."

"Well, that's gratitude for you," snapped Hal. He pushed Edmund to his knees, a task that required very little effort given his brother's present difficulty in remaining upright, and followed suit himself. "Your grace, please forgive us. We had too much wine, and knowing of your—susceptibilities—we could not resist temptation."

"Do forgive them, my dear," said Henry. Was he hiding laughter as well? "It was nothing but a silly prank."

"But I can't sleep in this chamber! It may still be infested!"

"There are two I can't account for," reported William Vaux.

"You see? I cannot sleep here!"

"Then you shall sleep in my chamber tonight," Henry said. He lifted me from my stool, his hand brushing my breast as he did. "Come, my dear. Forgive Hal and Edmund, and let us go to bed. It is very late."

"Oh, very well," I said grudgingly. "But it had better be free of mice in the morning."

"See to it," Henry ordered Hal. Then he led me to his chamber, where he dismissed his attendants before we even were completely inside the room. He stepped close to me and laid his hand on my cheek. "You looked very beautiful in your nightshift back there, Marguerite."

"There are two mice unaccounted for! What if one is hiding in its folds?"

Henry reached for the fastenings of my nightshift and began to untie them. "Then I will check," he assured me. "Very carefully."

And so there you have it. I had prayed, fasted, bargained with God—done everything in my power to be granted a child. All it took in the end was, it turned out, the earthly intervention of the Beaufort brothers.

⤳

Henry was at Reading, where Parliament was being held, when I sent him word of my pregnancy. I received a loving note from him, short and joyous, and early in April, when Parliament had adjourned for Easter, I received Henry himself. He kissed me, then tenderly touched my belly. "There's nothing much to feel yet," I said apologetically. "I am just a little plumper there, that is all."

"God be thanked," whispered Henry, taking me into his arms. We stood there embracing for a long, long time, both of us weeping for joy.

Though I probably owed my pregnancy to the Beaufort boys' mischief, I could not leave out God entirely. Already I had given a rich New Year's gift to the shrine of Our Lady of Walsingham, in what had become my increasingly desperate hope that it would help influence God to send me a child. Now that my prayers had been answered, it was time to go to Walsingham in person. I traveled there leisurely in mid-April, in the company of Henry's half brother Jasper. "So what do you think of your new ward?" I asked as we plodded along. Jasper and Edmund had been made the guardians of ten-year-old Margaret Beaufort, the daughter of the Duke of Somerset's late brother, John. Poor Suffolk had married little Margaret to his son at around the time of his imprisonment, but the unconsummated marriage had been dissolved just last month. I involuntarily sighed, thinking of this posthumous blow to my late friend's ambitions. "She seems to be an intelligent child."

Jasper laughed. "She was certainly pleased to be the center of attention at court!" So that the child could meet her prospective guardians, Henry had summoned her to court in February, generously presenting her with new gowns. "Edmund will marry her, I suppose."

"And you? Shall you take a wife? A man with a title needs a wife."

"I am content with my single state as of now. But you do like matchmaking, don't you, your grace?"

"I like to see people married, especially now that I am in such a happy state." I smiled and blushed. "I have waited so long for this, Jasper. I don't even care whether I bear a boy or a girl; I just pray that I can carry my babe to term and that the little one is healthy. I do not think I could bear it if—"

Jasper patted my hand as I started to give way to my emotions. "Your grace must not think of that. You are young and healthy and"—he bit his lip—"if the very worst were to happen, you are young enough to conceive again. But we must hope that this is the first of many children to come."

A mile from Walsingham at the Chapel of St. Catherine of Alexandria, I removed my shoes and walked barefoot the rest of the way to the shrine, as was the custom for its pilgrims. The well-trod path was smooth and easy to walk; had it been covered in sharp stones, I would not have cared even if they had torn at my tender feet. When I at last knelt before the holy shrine, I spent a good hour there, first in saying the assigned prayers, then in adding the fervent prayers that I had composed on my own. They all amounted to the same plea. *I have failed to bring Henry peace. Let me succeed in bringing him a child. A healthy babe who will rule this country in peace and prosperity. Grant me that one petition, and I will ask for nothing more.*

≈

As I made my way back to London, I was accosted by a servant wearing a livery that I did not find entirely agreeable: that of the Duke of York. Cecily, Duchess of York, was staying at her husband's manor at Hitchin in Hertfordshire. Would

I be gracious enough to accept her hospitality? Given that Cecily had waited even longer than I to bear her first child—ten years—and now had a brood of healthy ones, I thought that this might be a good sign. I readily consented.

Tall, blond, and slender, Cecily was so unlike her shortish, dark, and squarish husband that I wondered if the couple's elders had not mated this pair of opposites as some sort of experiment. Cecily had been a great beauty in her youth, I had been told by the Duchess of Suffolk and others, and she still carried herself as if she were used to being admired. "I hope your health is good, my lady?" I said after we exchanged a few formalities. I knew that she had given birth to a son, Richard, the previous October.

"My son is thriving, but I myself have been slow to recover."

"Was it a difficult birth?"

Cecily nodded. "Slightly, but I believe that the primary cause of my indisposition has been my anxiety about my husband, your grace. He is a loyal subject. It distresses him so to be thought otherwise."

"His actions last year were disturbing to Henry, of course," I said blandly, noticing that Cecily was eyeing my belly. "He has tired of being told that he should imprison the councillors who have been loyal to him."

"My lord only wants the best for the kingdom, your grace."

And for himself, I thought. "Henry is a man who readily forgives, but he has become more cautious," I said. "I am certain, however, that when he feels quite assured that the Duke of York can work with him, and not against his councillors, he will welcome him at court."

Cecily sighed, and I found myself feeling sorry for her. It could not be easy living with a disgruntled duke. "I shall certainly encourage good relations between your lord and the king," I said. "I know that is what Henry most desires. And"—I could not resist a little thrust, given that the Duke of York was the heir to the throne—"I have hopes that the king will have more cause than ever to be in charity with all of the world. You see, I went to Walsingham to give thanks for my pregnancy."

To her credit, Cecily smiled and curtseyed. "I am thankful beyond words that the Lord has at last blessed your grace with a child. But you cannot be far along?"

"I expect to be brought to childbed in October."

Cecily said with some hesitation. "Without being presumptuous, your grace, I know indeed the pain this must have caused you. For nearly ten years of marriage, I never got with child, though I was of the age to conceive when

I married. I had despaired; I had tried everything I knew." She shook her head. "I should not say this, but I even consulted a wise woman and obtained a love potion. I was that desperate."

"I would have obtained one myself if I had not feared someone finding out," I confessed. "It has been horrid. The rumors! People have said that Henry's confessor told him he should not lie with me, that Henry had taken a vow of chastity, that he spurned me after Maine was ceded, that I had been told not to lie with him until King Charles regained France, all sorts of nonsense!"

"Queen or no, someone will always talk scandal about a woman who fails to conceive a child immediately. It is the way of the world."

"No doubt if I had conceived straight away there would have been talk that I had anticipated my wedding day," I fumed before I brightened. What did that hurtful gossip matter now? "But now that I have conceived, I hope that I shall follow your example and have many more babes."

"It can be frightening the first time one is with child. Do ask me anything you wish to ask about child bearing. Has your grace began to look for a midwife?"

We engaged in similar conversation throughout the evening until the next morning, when I left to resume my journey. It was a pity, I was to think later. I had truly liked the Duchess of York. In a kinder world, we might have become friends.

⁂

Like any woman great with child, my greatest fear in those early months of pregnancy was that I would miscarry. But day by day my belly grew larger, and at the expected time my baby began to kick within my womb—a sensation that I could not feel too often. Henry was as transfixed as I and would spend up to an hour lying beside me, feeling my child move.

"I am sorry this business up north must take me away from you," he said in mid-July. There, the Nevilles and the Percies were feuding, for reasons that were obscure to me then and that I recollect only vaguely now. "But it is the sort of problem that must be contained before more families are swept up in it. The best way of doing so is for me to ride to the North myself.'

"Of course." Whether it was our recent success in Gascony, or impending fatherhood, or the forlorn state of the Duke of York, or the amicability of the most recent Parliament, I did not know, but I had never in our marriage heard Henry speak so determinedly and confidently. It was almost a pity, I thought with a hidden smile, that my pregnancy prevented Henry from demonstrating this heightened manliness in my bed. "I will be fine. I have never felt better, in truth. Why, I believe that being with child agrees with me."

"I do not think you have ever looked better, my dear."

"Oh, I look enormous," I said cheerfully. Each day as my ladies undressed me I examined my disappearing waistline with satisfaction, thoroughly delighted at my increasingly bovine state. I held up my hands. "Even my fingers are getting fat, I think."

"Then I am glad I did not order a ring for your gift."

"Gift?"

Henry nodded to a page, who handed him a large casket, which my husband presented to me. "Open it, my dear. It is a very small token of my gratitude to you."

Inside the casket was a girdle, set with magnificent precious stones. "Henry!"

"I ordered it the day after Richard Tunstall brought me the news." He looked on as I tried on the girdle just below my disappearing waistline. "Of course, in your ninth month you may find it difficult to wear. But for now..."

I threw my arms around Henry. "It is not just my beautiful girdle that makes me so happy," I whispered as we hugged each other tight. "It is that I have finally made you so happy."

ॐ

Women expecting their first babies often become so wrapped up in the state of their own bodies, they ignore the world around them. I was no different. With Henry on his progress, I passed the next few weeks sewing garments for my child, scarcely concerning myself with what was happening outside of my chamber. The Nevilles and the Percies could have exterminated themselves for all I cared. I was hardly more attentive to the affairs of my household. Where once I had badgered my council with my attention to minutia, I now nodded placidly as my men brought their reports and their accounts to be examined. Had my men been dishonest, God only knows what they could have got past me in those days. Even the campaign we were still waging in Gascony failed to capture my attention.

Only in one affair did I take any interest: that of my damsel Katherine Peniston and her suitor, William Vaux. Now sixteen, they had spent years making sheep's eyes at each other and exchanging tokens, and one day as I strolled in my garden at Greenwich, I heard a rustle—too loud to be caused by any small creature—in a secluded area. Investigating, I found Katherine sitting on William's lap, kissing him with no unpracticed air. His lips were active but his hands were behaving themselves, though not for long, I foresaw. "Katherine! William! Stop that and come here immediately."

Katherine let out a little cry of dismay and rose from her perch, William helping her up sheepishly. "Your grace—"

"This cannot go on like this, the two of you. You will be getting with child yourself if this keeps up."

"We have not done anything more than kiss like this," Katherine said hastily, and William's rather wistful look confirmed it.

"Well, I believe you. But it is too much. Indeed, I have suspected your little affair for some time, and have written to your father, William. I have just heard from him today, as a matter of fact. He agrees with me that this situation cannot continue as it is." I made my voice as stern as I could. "It has come down to this: As Katherine's family has little to give, I have offered William's father a sum toward Katherine's dowry, and he has accepted it. The two of you will be married before the year is out. Here is his letter to confirm it."

Katherine squealed and fell into my arms. "No," I said, gently pulling away. "It is your future husband you ought to be hugging so. Goodness knows you were doing it adeptly enough a few minutes ago."

"How can we thank you?" asked William, coming up for air after Katherine complied.

"Just be happy," I said. I smiled. "And behave yourselves until you are married. I would not like to explain an eight months' child to the king."

This was in early August. A few days after this successful venture into matchmaking, Edmund Beaufort came to me, a frown upon his young face. "Your grace, my father is here."

The Duke of Somerset had accompanied Henry on his progress. To have him back, without Henry, was exceedingly strange. "Why? Is something the matter?"

"I think so, but he would not tell me anything. He wishes to see you privately."

Was one of the other Beaufort children sick, perhaps, or worse? Perhaps this was the news he had refused to give to his son. "Send him in, straightaway."

Somerset came in, looking as gray-faced as in the days when he had newly returned to England from France. "My lord, what is it?"

"Pray, your grace, sit here."

"What means this?" I said, looking up as Somerset practically pushed me onto a stool. "Is it Henry? Is he ill? Is he dead?"

"Ill, but not dying. Pray, my lady, be calm. Promise me you will be calm."

"Somerset, stop speaking to me as if I were a child."

"I am sorry; I simply do not know how to tell you this. Let me start by asking you a question. Have you heard of what happened in Gascony?"

I shook my head. "Gascony? Why do you talk of Gascony? What of my husband?"

"It is all connected. In Gascony we had another reversal, two weeks before. At Castillion. Four thousand of our men perished, and it is in the hands of the French."

Two weeks before, I had been playing at bowls at my garden in Greenwich, surrounded by my giggling ladies. "The Earl of Shrewsbury?"

"He was killed. So was his son Lord Lisle."

I thought of that beautiful book the earl had given me when I first came to England. It was a collection of pieces on an entire array of subjects, written in French so that I could read it back in those days when my English was still inadequate, and I still treasured it and enjoyed leafing through its familiar pages. Now the old earl, kind to me in person as he had been fearsome to his enemies on the battlefield, lay dead, along with England's hopes in Gascony. Tears began to slide down my face. "Go on," I managed.

"The news arrived when King Henry reached Clarendon. The king took the news badly, as you might expect—we all did. He wept and asked why God was punishing him, and England, so. Afterward he closeted himself with his confessor and it seemed to do him good. He went to bed, not in good spirits, but in a better frame of mind than he had been at first, at least. He was eager to meet in the morning to discuss what could be done to retrieve the situation. Nothing unusual happened during the night; he slept soundly, as he always does. Then in the morning his men came in to wake him and found him lying in bed, awake but without the power of speech."

"A stroke."

"No, your grace. It is something different. One can speak to him, but he does not comprehend. He opens his eyes, but he seems to see nothing. Yet he can be led from room to room, and he can chew his food, though he requires help in eating and shows no interest in what is offered to him. He does not speak, and he makes no response when prodded."

"Somerset, what are you telling me? That Henry is—"

"Mad." Somerset, gripping my hand, finished my sentence. "He has lost his reason."

I turned aside and wept while Somerset awkwardly patted my hand. "You are sure?" I asked stupidly when I could at last speak. "It could be nothing else?"

"No, your grace. His physicians have examined him. We will call others in, of course, but there can be no real doubt about the matter."

"But he seemed to be so much more—more manly lately. More confident, more sure of himself. How can it be?"

"No one can say, your grace. But you might remember his grandfather—"

"Charles the Mad," I whispered. "Lord help us." I groaned, remembering what I had been told of Charles VI, for he had died long before my own birth. "He thought at times he was made of glass, they say, and once killed some of his own men in a fit of delusion."

Somerset nodded. "He was not constantly insane, though. He had periods where he was well."

"So Henry could turn violent like his grandfather." But I could not imagine Henry violent, even when insane. "Or he might alternate between periods of madness or sanity. Or—he might not recover at all."

"That may well be."

My child kicked me, and I cradled my belly. Next month, I had been scheduled to go to my confinement at Westminster, where I would pass the weeks in company with my ladies while waiting for my child to be born. I had expected it to be a dull but serene time. Instead, I would spend it fretting about Henry, for even if he recovered, how long would it last? Would he ever be fully himself again? And how would his illness affect my child's future? Oh, could not the Lord have allowed me to spend the most happy time of a woman's life in peace, as He did other mothers-to-be? Tears began to form in my eyes again, this time at the sheer unfairness of it all. Then I remembered Suffolk's words to me that night at Westminster. *If I were to choose between you and Henry, I would say that you are the stronger. That is why I want you to promise me that you will stand by him always.*

I took a deep breath and straightened my back. "Well. What do we do now?"

For the time being, we—I and everyone around Henry, that is—said nothing about his condition. "Let York hear about this, and he'll exploit it to the fullest," Somerset said. "Even if he recovers soon, York will be on the lookout for any slightest indication of a relapse." He snorted. "And I wouldn't put it past him to try to cause one."

"But surely people will notice when he just keeps staying at Clarendon and when no one but a few people have access to him."

"We'll deal with that when the time comes," Somerset said. "In the meantime, the people will be occupied with anticipating a royal birth. Your grace must go into confinement as if all is normal."

I did not protest anymore; the idea of pretending that all was normal and that this was a confinement like any other did not lack appeal. Perhaps I hoped that pretending might make it so. Thus, on September 10, I put on my best smiles as Somerset and Buckingham, accompanied by the scarlet-clad mayor and aldermen of London, arrived at Greenwich to accompany me by barge to Westminster, where I would be conducted to my chamber with great pomp. As the barge moved gracefully down the Thames, I daydreamed that the birth of my child would bring Henry back to himself.

While Somerset continued to issue warnings to me about the need to conceal Henry's madness from York, Buckingham quietly answered my questions about my husband. "He's no better, your grace. One day he raised his hand and made a noise as if he were trying to speak, and we all waited—but nothing. Since then there's been no sign that he's cognizant of his surroundings."

"Perhaps the knowledge that he has a child will rouse him?"

"I am praying that it does."

"I am thinking that I should have gone to see him before I went into my confinement." I looked on my other side and found that Somerset was occupied with speaking to the mayor. "Somerset advised me against it."

Buckingham shifted on his seat on the barge beside me. I knew that he had been in favor of telling York of Henry's madness. "In this case, I must agree with him. Seeing the king so might upset your grace and cause you to deliver your child prematurely."

"Am I such a fragile creature?" I said irritably.

"It is upsetting for those of us on his council to see him in his present condition," Buckingham said mildly. "It would be far worse, I would think, for his queen to see him so. Best wait, your grace."

"I shall. But will you—will you give him daily messages of love from me, in hopes that it might rouse him?" Much as I had come to rely on Somerset, it was Buckingham to whom I felt more comfortable making this request.

Buckingham smiled. "Of course, your grace."

On October 12, at Westminster, I went into labor. I am small-boned, and my ordeal was long and hard, so much so that there were doubts, I heard later, as to whether I would survive it. Newlywed Katherine Vaux, who had left her newfound marital bliss to attend me in my confinement, became teary-eyed each time I let out a yelp of agony, which was quite often, and in the short intervals when I could think, I hoped I was not frightening the poor girl from having children of her own. But it was she whose hand I was nearly wringing in two when I at last pushed my child into the world on October 13, after nearly a day of effort, and it was she who clapped her hands and hugged me when the midwife held up the baby. "My lady! It is a boy!"

"Boy," I whispered, almost too weak to appreciate the significance of the words.

A few minutes later, the midwife placed my son in my arms, and I stared at him. He was large and red and wrinkled, and it is safe to say that I have never seen a more beautiful creature in my life. "*I* managed to bear *him*?" I asked dazedly.

The Duchess of Buckingham, who had accomplished a similar feat ten times over, patted me on my naked shoulder. "You did, your grace. You have given England a great gift."

Katherine Vaux, shaking out her hand—I had left bruises on it with my squeezing, I saw later—said, "My lady, shall he be named Henry?"

"No. Today is the feast of the translation of Edward the Confessor, King Henry's favorite saint." I clutched my son close to me, and my tears—half from happiness, half from grief that my husband would not come to me to see his child—began to fall. "We shall name him Edward."

I have long since lost count of all of the men who were later said to be the father of my dear boy. The Duke of Somerset and his two oldest sons, the Tudor brothers, a traveling player, various and sundry nobodies—all have been counted among my lovers by the tale-bearers. At the time, though, it had yet to suit anyone's convenience to question my virtue, so news of Edward's birth was greeted joyously, with ringing bells and a singing of the Te Deum. Only my son's father remained oblivious to his existence.

Christening gifts poured in from the nobles, and as my baby thrived, I happily contemplated the possibility of at last being forgiven for being a Frenchwoman and for having so signally failed to bring the hoped-for peace. Even the news that Henry's advisors had overruled Somerset's wishes and summoned York to an upcoming meeting of his great council failed to dampen my optimistic mood as I dandled little Edward and contemplated which foreign princess would have the great good fortune to be his bride.

Then, one morning in late November, not long after I had gone through the churching ceremony that marked the end of my confinement, Hal Beaufort was shown into my chamber. He did not even wait for me to greet him before he said, "That whoreson York has arrested my father. He is a prisoner in the Tower!"

"What on earth for?"

"France, what else? The loss of Normandy and Gascony, when Father did his best to save Gascony! York will never let that business lie; what did he ever do to help the situation? Nothing! Sat on his estates in Ireland while Normandy was lost, then came back here and arrested Father instead of standing behind King Henry as he should have. Not a word about how my father sent one of our best soldiers, the Earl of Shrewsbury, to fight in Gascony. Not a word! And—"

"Hal! Calm yourself if you can. I know it is distressing for you, but you must tell me what happened and not go off into a rage. Give me the details."

Hal took a breath. "Actually, it's Norfolk who accused Father of treason, but Norfolk is York's creature. I'm sure of it. He hasn't the brains to organize this business himself—or the balls." The colloquialism did not escape me, and I gave Hal a frosty look. Undeterred, he continued, "York probably wrote the speech he gave in council for him. It's typical of him to let someone else do his unpleasant work for him. Norfolk can come off as the belligerent one, while York stands there nodding calmly, the soul of sweet reason."

"But what did he say, Hal?"

"That a man who gave up towns without siege and who fled from battle should be beheaded." Hal's voice faltered at the last word. At seventeen, he suddenly looked very young. "I was there with Father in France! Norfolk and York don't know what it was like there. The people of Rouen were leagued with the French; a siege would have been hopeless. My father might have made a misjudgment but he's no coward."

"Of course not," I said. I patted Hal on his shoulder. "I will summon York here and see what his intentions are," I said after some thought.

"Norfolk couldn't have made them clearer. They want to kill my father. Just like they wanted to kill the Duke of Suffolk," he added.

I found myself unable to gainsay him.

That very afternoon, I summoned the Duke of York to my presence, and he arrived promptly the next day. He thanked me for my kindness to his wife, who had written a letter to me shortly before my lying-in, begging me to intercede with the king to bring her husband back into favor. I had not told her of the state of Henry's health, but had gone so far as to suggest to Buckingham that it would be a good thing, perhaps, if York were allowed to return to court on conditions of good behavior. "You paid me back ill by arresting Somerset," I said bluntly. "He has his faults, I acknowledge, and has made mistakes, but he has been nothing but loyal to Henry since his return to England. Is it not time to let bygones be bygones? Yes, we have failed in France. Yes, some of it was probably Somerset's fault. Much of it, we can even say. But what good does it do to fight about it now?"

"With due respect, your grace, this is a matter of honor, of knightly honor. It is a concept a woman cannot understand as well as a man."

"I am no knight, but I understand that with my husband ill, you lords should be working together instead of fighting one another. I understand that our son will be ruling England someday, and I wish to see him presiding over a secure one."

"Somerset's trial and punishment will be beneficial to the realm and to the prince, your grace."

"How?"

"It will rid the king of a councillor who has done him nothing but harm and who has served his self-interest."

The unctuous tone was beginning to grate on me. "And you have no self-interest yourself, my lord?"

"No man is free of self-interest, but my interest is far more with seeing England restored to her former strength and glory, which will serve us all. And in any case, Somerset's fate is not in my own hands, but in that of the lords of the land. I was not even the one who impeached him. That was the Duke of Norfolk, though I certainly concurred with his sentiments."

"The king is much attached to the Duke of Somerset. He will be vexed and grieved if Somerset comes to any harm."

"If he recovers."

"Do you wish for the king's recovery, my lord?"

"Why, of course," York said, his response just a beat too slow.

When I dismissed the Duke of York, I went to the place at Westminster in which I was happiest—the nursery.

The nurses promptly brought me Edward, whose light blue eyes gazed back at me with the vague interest of a very young baby as I took him in my arms. "Did you miss me? Are you being a good boy?" His nurses assured me that he was the most good-natured of babies, though of course I would not have believed them if they had said otherwise. I turned to the wet nurse. "Is he still suckling well?"

"Beautifully, your grace. The prince has an excellent appetite."

I smiled and sat as Edward drowsed in my arms. Content as I was to hold my boy, I could not push the encounter I just had from my mind. Since York came back from Ireland, his single goal had been to get rid of Somerset, and with Henry incapacitated, he might just achieve his goal—against a man who was my husband's chosen advisor. To strike at Somerset was in its way to strike at Henry.

Though both the Duke of Exeter and the Duke of Somerset believed that York had been behind Suffolk's death and the Jack Cade revolt, no one had ever proven his involvement—but then again, no one had proven his lack of involvement either. I stroked my son's hair and frowned into space. I could not help but believe that for all of York's grand words about acting for the good of the realm, he was also acting for the good of himself. How far might his ambition take him? My little son stood between York and the crown; could York ignore this fact? If the worst happened to Somerset and Henry never recovered his wits, what might happen to my Edward in a kingdom controlled by York?

I turned my gaze back to Edward. "Whom can we trust, little one?" I asked softly.

And then the answer came. *Myself.*

✍

The Duke of Buckingham stared at me for a good minute, then sputtered, "Your grace. Are you mad?"

"No," I said. "One mad spouse in a marriage is enough, I believe."

Buckingham flinched at my sardonic tone. I had caught myself making grim little jokes like this more and more often; if I did not, I might well cry to think of the Henry I had married and the Henry who sat insensible at Windsor. "But a queen—to have the governance of the country! A woman!"

"Most queens are women, surely? Come now, Buckingham. I am not attempting to be another Queen Matilda." I knew little about her, but I had observed that the mention of her name had a tendency to make Englishmen blanch, and Buckingham predictably shuddered. "I am only asking to be made regent until Henry recovers or until our son is old enough to rule. Then I will go back to stitching altar cloths, I promise you. And I will not be without good counsel. You and others shall make sure of that."

"England is not ready for a woman wielding that sort of power."

"Nor was England ready for a mad king, but we have one, don't we? And in any case, women have been regents in France, and yes, I am aware that this is not France." Buckingham smiled slightly, just enough to encourage me to press ahead. "My lord, it does make sense. I pray that no harm comes to Somerset, for I am fond of him, and even more so of his children. But if he does survive, then he will doubtless take his revenge upon York, and then York will be taking his revenge upon him, and on and on while the kingdom suffers. If I were regent there would be one less thing for them to quarrel over."

"Don't be so sure, madam. We men will always find something to quarrel over."

"Do at least consider this, Buckingham. I shall have to prepare my bill to put before Parliament. You will have time to ponder it."

Buckingham made a sound that might have been a grunt, then recovered his natural politeness. "I will think upon it, but I can promise nothing else."

"That is enough for now. And now, my lord, I think it is time to show the king his son. Perhaps that might help heal him."

"I can agree with your grace on that."

I sighed. "I dread it, you know, even as I know it might be our last hope. To see Henry being fed and walked about, completely helpless..." My eyes filled with tears. "In truth, I have put off mentioning it because I fear the sight so much."

"He is kept well. But it is a grievous sight, I must admit, at least for those who have not seen him so before. I am compelled to say that I am used to his altered state now, but it took time." I must have looked as forlorn as I suddenly felt, for Buckingham added, "My lady, I shall be with you."

"Shall the Duke of York be there?"

"Not if you do not wish him to be."

"Good. I don't."

Soon before Christmas, on an unusually mild day, I and my son rode by barge from Greenwich to Windsor. There we were conducted to the chamber where Henry's attendants brought him every day to sit in his chair of state in the hope that this routine might push him back into a state of normalcy.

We had agreed that seeing both Edward and me at the same time might shock Henry and do him more harm than good, so I handed Buckingham my son as we stood outside the half-open door. "Don't drop him."

"I've held my own sons many a time, your grace, and they've thrived," said Buckingham good-naturedly. "See?" He nodded at his eldest son, a man in his early twenties who had accompanied us. "The Earl of Stafford is living proof of it."

I smiled nervously as Buckingham went through the door. From my position, outside of Henry's line of sight, I could not see Buckingham, but I heard him say in a hearty voice, "See, your grace, your queen has given you a fine prince! We crave your blessing."

There was no sound except for my own deep sigh. The Duchess of Buckingham took my hand as my lip began to tremble in spite of my efforts to keep my face calm. "It may take time, your grace."

Buckingham kept on speaking in a bright tone, telling Henry about my son's christening and about his godparents, who were the Archbishop of Canterbury, poor Somerset, and the Duchess of Buckingham. After once again begging for the king's blessing, he said in a lower voice, "Your grace, your queen has come to Windsor as well."

I was inside the chamber before Buckingham had even finished his sentence.

I dropped to my knees in front of Henry. For the first time in months, I looked upon my husband. Henry was paler than usual, having not spent time riding each day as had been his wont, but he was properly shaven and his hair had been trimmed just as he liked it, a trifle too short for fashion. His robes were immaculate. I had feared that having to be fed his meals would have caused him to lose too much weight, but although he was visibly thinner, he was not starkly so. It was his eyes that were most changed. The gentle eyes that had looked at me so lovingly when we met at Southampton were blank, like those of a corpse, and they stared toward the floor, never varying their downward gaze except to blink occasionally and give me false hope.

Buckingham gave me a moment to absorb the shock of my husband's appearance, then carefully put Edward in my arms. His familiar, dear weight made me recover myself. "Henry," I said in the same forced, bright tone Buckingham had used, "I bring you the great gift we have received from God, our son. He is healthy, thanked be the Lord, and he needs only your blessing."

Henry's eyes flickered, and suddenly he turned his eyes straight upon our son. Buckingham and the attendants nearby gasped. Then Henry dropped his eyes again. His expression had never changed.

"Henry, please. Your blessing on our fair son." I rose and handed Edward to Buckingham, who looked near tears. I took Henry's limp hand in mine, then kissed his cold cheek. "My love," I whispered. "Do you not remember me, Marguerite, your queen? I love you so dearly. Please come back to me. I miss you so much, and our son needs a father. Our country needs a king."

Henry remained motionless in his great chair, oblivious to my kisses and caresses. Even Edward's growing fussiness, culminating in an outright wail, did nothing to rouse him. "I will come again and see you with our son," I said finally, stepping back, trying to keep from my voice the hopelessness I felt. "God keep you, my husband."

Outside Henry's chamber, I broke down and wept on the duchess's shoulder. "Still, there was that one movement he made," the Duke of Buckingham said tentatively when I had recovered. "It is little enough, but it is more than anything we have seen before. Perhaps in a month or two—"

"I do not think I can bear it," I said, wiping my eyes. "Get me out of this place. Now."

∽

I wept my fill about Henry, and then I set to work with my councillors, drawing up my petition to be named regent. Meanwhile, Somerset languished in prison while the rest of the lords gathered together weapons and followers, seemingly preparing for war instead of for the Parliament that was supposed to meet in February. Even the elderly Archbishop of Canterbury, John Kemp, thought it prudent to arm all of his servants. No one knew what to expect from anyone, and everyone was coming prepared for anything.

"At least I am not coming with a group of armed men like all the rest," I told Katherine Vaux as she brushed out my hair the night before I was to ride to Parliament. "That surely will count for something in my favor."

"Do you think they will grant your petition?"

"I can only hope, but I am pessimistic," I said, sighing as my long hair swirled around my face. Henry had loved the sight and would sometimes brush it for me. "York has been given the commission to hold Parliament in lieu of Henry, and before Parliament even began, he brought a lawsuit against the Speaker of the Commons and had him thrown into the Fleet after judgment was entered against him. York wants Thorpe out of the way, of course, because he is an associate of Somerset's. And Norfolk, York's creature, is attempting to get Archbishop Kemp dismissed as chancellor."

"It doesn't look good."

I nodded. "But by appearing and presenting my petition, I may at least influence Parliament to create Edward as Prince of Wales and Earl of Chester.

That would be some security for my boy." I gazed in the mirror as Katherine finished braiding my hair for the night. "At least I must try my best for him."

⁓

I arrived at Parliament the next day and duly presented my bill before the assembly, whose members looked faintly ill or scandalized as I did so, as if I had chosen to don a bishop's miter and take to the pulpit. There was nothing to be done now but to wait in my chambers at Westminster as Parliament debated. Its members seemed to be in no hurry.

Then one day as I reading through a book that poor Suffolk had given me, Katherine Vaux came inside, a paper clutched in her hand. "My husband gave me this," she faltered. "He felt your grace should know about it. It is—horrid."

I snatched the paper and read it. It was a diatribe, rambling and barely legible in parts, but its gist was only too clear. Not only was I trying to seize power to which I, a woman and a Frenchwoman to boot, had no right, I was trying to foist my bastard son off upon the country as Henry's heir. My bastard son by the Duke of Somerset. "Where did this come from?"

"On the door at St. Paul's, your grace. There are others of the same nature nailed there, William said. This is the worst."

"By God, the man who wrote this should be hanged, drawn, and quartered. I wish I could do it myself." I rose, shaking with rage. "Is Parliament still in session for today?"

"No."

"Good." I called my parting words over my shoulder as I hastened through the chamber door. "I have some business to discuss with the Duke of York."

⁓

York was sitting at a table in his own chamber, looking over some papers, when I barged in. "Your grace? I must say the common courtesy of announcing yourself is requisite, even from a queen."

"Never mind the common courtesies. Read this." I thrust the paper in York's face, all but stuffing it into his mouth. "How dare you say the prince is Somerset's bastard?"

"Your grace?"

"Don't play the innocent! It is written here, for every common churl in London to see."

"I have heard the rumor before this," York said calmly. He took the paper and scanned it. "Yes, this is what I have heard. But I did not spread it."

"You lie!" Without realizing it, I had begun speaking in my native French.

"Who would have better cause to spread such a rumor? You hate Somerset and wish to destroy him, and you are in line for the throne should my son be put aside as a bastard."

"I have no ambitions for the throne, I assure your grace. Now calm yourself. I did not put up this paper or direct its posting, and I do not know who did."

"You said you have heard the gossip before this. Have you done anything to counteract it?"

"That is hardly my place. Nor am I in a position to offer proof to the contrary."

"Well, I am. I will swear an oath before every bishop in England—before the Pope himself if necessary—that I have known no man but King Henry. And my ladies and the men of Henry's household can swear as to when and where Henry came to my bed, and how long he stayed there."

York shrugged. "But what good will they do? Your grace's ladies cannot swear as to whether the king was capable of the act once he arrived in your bed."

I slammed York across the face, putting my full weight behind my blow so that I teetered forward. York grabbed my wrist, and for a moment I thought he might throw me to the ground. Instead, he released me and stepped back. His cheek was bloody from where my ring had caught him, but he was smiling. "Do you realize what you have done? You have just proven, conclusively, that you are utterly unfit, with your ungovernable temper and your hasty ways, to serve as regent. Ill-advised as your proposal was, I have thought at times that one woman in a hundred might be capable of handling the task, but you certainly are not that woman."

"No woman with an ounce of spirit would listen to such vulgarity and not react as I did."

"Oh? Well, I do not pretend to be able to speak for your sex. In any case, even before your attack upon me, I could not possibly support the idea of your grace's regency." York sneered as he said the words *your grace*. "Aside from your unsuitability, I've no doubt that you would restore Somerset to a position of authority, and soon we would likely not only lose Calais through his incompetence and treachery, but perhaps find the French at our very shores. I'm not at all sure that as a Frenchwoman you would not find that entirely acceptable. You have, after all, been screeching at me in French for half of this conversation."

"My son—Henry's son—will be King of England. I would protect that throne for him against any man in France, including my own dear father, if it came to that."

"Very touching, but I would not like to see your grace's protestations put to the test. Now, may I reason with you? I will repeat what I have said previously, that I did not start the rumors about the prince's parentage and have no idea who did. No doubt when the prince is older he will bear a more decisive resemblance to the king than he does at present. That should silence the gossips once and for all, more readily than any oaths you and your ladies might take. In the meantime, if your grace drops this ridiculous bid for the regency, I will do my part to see that the rumors are stopped."

"I don't believe you."

"Then I shall not waste your grace's time or my own by protesting further." He took the paper and read it more closely as I turned to take my leave. "But really, your grace, if these were written at my dictation, don't you think I would express myself better than this? This writer can barely express a coherent thought."

Whether it was the rumors about my son's parentage, or the disadvantages of my sex, or a general fear among the lords of winding up in prison with Somerset I shall never know, but my bill to serve as regent was firmly rejected. My one consolation was that my son was indeed created Prince of Wales and Earl of Chester, thanks largely, I suspect to the exertions of the Archbishop of Canterbury and of the Duke of Buckingham.

Then, on March 22, the near-octogenarian archbishop, who had tottered more than walked into Parliament over the past few days, took to his bed after one exhausting day and was dead within a couple of hours, worn out, it was said, by his age and the strain of the last few years. When the news was brought to Henry—as it had to be, as England was now without a chancellor—he was even more unresponsive than he had been when I showed him our child. With no hope of my husband recovering, there was no avoiding a protectorate now, and York became that protector.

I would not say it then, but I suppose he was not a bad one—unless you were Somerset, who remained in prison, untried and kept in closer captivity, or the Duke of Exeter, who thanks to his feuding up north soon was a prisoner himself. My son's rights had been shielded when York was made protector—my Edward would have the right to hold that office himself when he came of age—and my household was not reduced, as I had feared. The placards about Edward's birth were no longer seen in London. I began to reconcile myself to the possibility of a lengthy protectorate and to concentrate on the upbringing of my son.

Then, just after Christmas, Henry was moved to Greenwich, where I brought him some of the wafers that had been baked for the festivities and of which he was particularly fond. As expected, he paid no attention to the basket in my hand; it could have been full of asps as far as he was concerned. I had kissed him good-bye and was halfway through the door when I heard my name, uttered in an otherworldly, guttural voice. "Marguerite."

I turned, open-mouthed. The voice came again, louder this time. "Marguerite?"

Henry sat on his chair, blinking. As everyone in the chamber froze, he reached down awkwardly and stiffly. He slowly grasped the basket, then lifted and opened it. Gradually, his lips curved into the slightest of smiles. "You brought these for me?"

The tears began to pour down my face, and I walked up to my husband and knelt by his side. "Yes. God be thanked, I brought them for you."

10

Margaret
December 1454 to May 1455

ENRY'S PHYSICIANS ADVISED CAUTION AFTER HE RETURNED TO HIS SENSES, lest he relapse into madness. He had no knowledge of anything that had happened since August of the previous year, it soon became apparent, and it was important that his perhaps still fragile mind not be overburdened. Accordingly, I told him nothing of our son or of Somerset's arrest. In any case, his long sickness had left him exhausted, and he slept much of the time during the first few days after his recovery. Each time he closed his eyes, I and his attendants held our breath, terrified that he might awake insensible as he had when he first took ill. But each day, he took more and more interest in his surroundings, and when he asked about the state of his foundations at King's College and Eton and insisted that the accounts there be brought for his review, we began to feel safe again.

So soon after the New Year began, I took my fourteen-month-old son's hand in mine and entered the hall at Greenwich. Henry stared as Edward toddled into the room alongside me. "Can it—?"

"My dear lord, on St. Edward's day, the Lord blessed you with a son. We named him Edward."

Tears formed in Henry's eyes, and for a moment he was speechless. "God be thanked," he whispered finally, and held up his hands in a gesture of thanksgiving. "Come here, my child." Henry indicated his lap. Fortunately, Edward was a gregarious boy, and he was happy enough to sit with the stranger on the great chair.

Henry laughed as Edward played with the collar of interlocking S's that my husband wore around his neck. "Who are his godparents?"

"Archbishop Kemp, the Duke of Somerset, and the Duchess of Buckingham," I said reluctantly, for the first was dead and the second was in prison.

"They were good choices, my dear." Henry nodded at the Duchess of Buckingham, who had accompanied me and stood at a distance. "But where are the godfathers?"

"The archbishop was called to God, my lord. He died in March after a short illness."

"Aye. One of the wisest men in this land is dead, then." Henry sighed. "I suppose the news was brought to me?" I nodded. "I remember nothing of it," Henry said. "Nothing of the last—what was it, a year and a half? I could not even remember for certain that you were with child when I fell ill."

"It is over now, my love. You are well, and getting better every day."

"Aye," Henry said as Edward, bored with the collar and with sitting relatively still for the last few minutes, began to squirm. "And this fine fellow is helping. Thank you, my dear."

⁓

That very evening, one of Henry's pages told me that the king wished to spend the night with me.

After being so long apart, and with Henry having been so ill, it was almost as if we were two virgins coming together again, but soon we became familiar with each other and began to caress each other with more abandon. "The physicians advised me against this," he whispered as we lay together afterward.

"I am glad you disobeyed them."

"I am sorry I lasted such a short time."

"Next time," I said lazily, stroking his chest, thinking of all those lonely nights I had lay solitary in my great bed, thinking that at age twenty-four I would never lie with my husband again. "We have the rest of our lives now." I hesitated, wondering if I should ask my next question, but unable to resist. "Do you really remember nothing of the last year and a half?"

"Nothing. And not all that much of the days just before that. I remember getting the news of the Earl of Shrewsbury's death and our defeat in France"—I touched Henry's cheek gently as his voice faltered—"and I remember looking forward to our child being born. But it is all hazy. I suppose I shall never remember those days."

"They were rather dull," I said mischievously, to break the somberness of Henry's mood, and he laughed and pinched my cheek before turning solemn again.

"Marguerite, there are things they are not telling me. Aren't there?"

"Yes."

"I know York has been made protector. No one has mentioned the Duke of Somerset to me, save except when you told me he was our Edward's god-father." He hesitated. "Did York—kill him?"

"No, no," I said, grateful that the news I was about to impart was not as grim as that. "But he has imprisoned him—he has been a prisoner in the Tower for well over a year."

"On what grounds?"

"The old business of France. York refuses to allow him bail, and he refuses to bring him to trial. He has not even brought formal charges against him. That is against Magna Carta, is it not?"

"Indeed it is."

"He is not allowed to see his family, and I am not at all sure he is being treated as a duke should be. I have not been able to visit him or to send him any comforts whatsoever. And—" I wisely stopped myself from telling Henry of the rumors about Edward being Somerset's son. Instead, I continued, "The Duke of Exeter is also a prisoner; he is at Pontefract. I suppose there is some justification for York's actions with regard to him; he has allied himself with the Percies in their feud against the Nevilles, and has been wild and ungovern-able. They also say he was angry at not being made protector himself, as he has a claim to the office through his birth. But even there, York has behaved unjustly. Exeter came up to London to attend a meeting of the council, but went into sanctuary at Westminster when he feared arrest, and York broke sanctuary and imprisoned him."

"They shall both be released."

"And I have a confession to make, Henry. I sought to become regent after Edward was born. It was for his sake," I added quickly, sensing that Henry's silence was a shocked one. "I feared York's own ambitions, and I feared for our son and for Somerset and our other friends."

"A woman as regent? My dear, I do not think we English are ready for that."

"So I found. My proposal died in Parliament. Few supported it. But I would have done my best for you if it had been accepted."

"I've no doubt you would have," Henry said, clasping me close once again as we settled to sleep. "Good night, my love."

❧

A couple of weeks after this conversation, the Duke of York came to Greenwich, where he looked somewhat surprised to see me in Henry's chamber, and somewhat more surprised when I made no sign of leaving. Having evidently resigned himself to my presence, he said stiffly, "Your grace, I thank God for your recovery, and am glad to find you well."

"We thank you, my lord, and we thank you for your services that you have rendered during our illness. As you can see, however, we no longer have need of them."

"Yes, your grace. I have come to resign my office as protector."

"We accept your resignation." Henry's voice bore little trace of its usual warmth.

I smiled. "Would you like to see the Prince of Wales before you leave, my lord? He is growing apace, and I believe he has Henry's nose and my chin, but some of my ladies insist that he has my chin and Henry's nose, while others are plumping for both Henry's nose and chin. I should like an impartial opinion."

Even today, it gives me a little bit of satisfaction to think of the look of sheer disgust on the Duke of York's face.

At the end of January, the Duke of Buckingham, the Earl of Wiltshire, and Lord Ros entered the king's chamber at Greenwich, followed by a gaunt, pale, and heavily bearded man I at first did not recognize. Then I gasped. "Somerset!"

"Yes, it's I," said Somerset as Henry and I, having forestalled his attempts to kneel, embraced him in turn. He smiled when we had released him. "I gather I am not the most prepossessing sight."

"I knew you were coming, and even then I did not recognize you," I admitted. "Good God, did not York give you any comforts whatsoever?"

"He promised to cut back on the crown's expenses, and I gave him great opportunity for that," Somerset said dryly. "But it is not all due to him; I had an ague, and under the circumstances I found it hard to shake off." He took the seat Henry offered him with a gratefulness that hurt to see. "I am glad beyond words, your grace, that you have recovered, and I do not say so only because it has meant my own freedom. But I thank you for that too. Does the Duke of York know?"

"No. He is not protector any longer and need not be consulted, though the matter will have to come before the council. It will meet soon to discuss the terms of your release. But I wanted you out of the Tower and into more comfortable quarters, more than ever now that I see you have been ill. Your wife and children will be much concerned, I fear."

"I am hoping, your grace, that I will be allowed to travel to see them, even without being put to bail."

"There is no need." Henry nodded to two of his household knights. "Take the duke to the chamber we have made ready for him. You will find your wife and children there waiting for you, Somerset."

Somerset's face worked, and I think he would have knelt to Henry and kissed the hem of his gown had not my husband shaken him off and pushed him in the direction of the door. "A good new year to you, Somerset," he said softly.

❧

"Your grace, I genuinely like the Duke of Somerset—though I must say that mine is not the prevailing opinion. My eldest son, as you know, is married to his daughter Margaret. I am glad that you dismissed the charges against him. But put Somerset in York's place as captain of Calais? It is most ill-advised." Buckingham ran his hand through his hair, as if to imply that Henry's policy was responsible for its rapid graying.

"Perhaps, my lord, you wish Calais for yourself?" I asked before Henry could speak.

Buckingham turned his irritated gaze on me, and I knew he was searching for some way to tell me my presence was not wanted. But since Henry had recovered, he liked to have me with him when he spoke in private with his lords, and I would not refuse him this desire—not, of course, that I ever thought about trying to thwart it. "Your grace, that is unjust. I am concerned about what this decision will mean for the king, not plumping for Calais."

"My lord, as you know, the Duke of York resigned the office," Henry said.

"Freely? It matters not. York might not be the best person for it, but give it to someone else—not to me, but not to Somerset either."

"Somerset still has men in Calais who have served us well."

"Yet all the charges against him originated in his conduct as to France. Nothing can be gained, and everything can be lost, by giving him such an office; it will infuriate York, and to no good purpose. Keep Somerset employed in England; send him on a diplomatic mission; send him on pilgrimage to Jerusalem. But for God's sake, don't give him Calais!"

"Are you done, my lord?" Henry asked in the same cold voice he had used when York resigned the protectorate.

Buckingham sighed. "Yes," he said wearily. "I am done. Whatever happens, your grace cannot say that you were not warned."

❧

Richard Neville, the Earl of Salisbury, had resigned as chancellor in protest at Somerset's restoration to power, which took place in March. (He had been appointed by York after the death of Kemp.) The Duke of York and the Earl of Salisbury soon withdrew to their estates. Good riddance, I thought. When the Duke of Exeter was released from captivity in early April, it seemed that all would at last be back to normal.

Soon after Exeter returned to court, Henry called a great council to meet at Westminster. There it was decided to hold another council at Leicester in May, to discuss the safety of the king and to implement a settlement between Somerset and York, who prior to York's huffy exit from the court had entered into bonds to keep the peace until June. An arbitration panel of lords had been appointed to settle the remaining disputes between the two dukes, and its decision was to be announced at Leicester. The council also planned to discuss the governance of the realm in the event Henry fell ill again, for he was well aware of his grandfather's malady and of its recurring nature. Those were the council's only purposes, and innocent and worthy ones they were.

Unfortunately, York and the Neville family did not see it that way.

11

Henry Beaufort, Earl of Dorset
May 1455

MUCH AS I LIKED KING HENRY, BEING A YOUNG MAN AT HIS COURT HAD never been easy. He took pride in resisting the temptations of the flesh (of course, it helped that he himself had the most beautiful woman in England to supply his fleshly needs for him) and could never understand why the rest of us in the household were not so restrained. Even his scholars at Eton, mere boys that they were, had been known to roll their eyes behind the king's back when told by Henry about the moral cesspool that the court could be.

So as often as I could, I sneaked off to Eastcheap to find the sort of company I at nineteen quite naturally craved. Not a whore, mind you, but Joan Hill, a confectioner's widow who was a few years older than myself. Shortly before the king lost his wits, the delicious smell that had wafted through Joan's shop had attracted me off the street, whereupon I discovered that Joan (plump, but not too plump) looked nearly as delicious as the wafers she cooked. For some time after that I had busied myself with trying to get her into bed, satisfying my sweet tooth almost daily in the process, but it took my father's imprisonment for me to at last succeed in my task. There is nothing, it seems, as successful as having a father in the Tower to win feminine sympathy.

And yet when my father was released, Joan remained my mistress. I would have to marry sooner or later, I knew—now that Father was out of prison, it was just a matter of time before he found me a suitable bride, who certainly couldn't be Joan Hill—but that seemed a long ways off. All in all, then, it was a pleasing state of affairs that day in May 1455. I was to head to the king's great council in Leicester (my first), where the Duke of York would finally be given to understand once and for all that the kingdom was not his to run any longer. Perhaps my father might send me to Calais as his deputy, who knew? Maybe I could even take Joan with me. "Do you perchance happen to speak French?" I asked her as she curled closer to me to ward off the slight chill of the morning.

"That's an odd question to ask a lady first thing in the morning."

"Well, do you?"

"Not a bit, love. Though I do make some French pastries."

"That'll do. Everyone in Calais will be speaking English anyway."

Joan was about to question me further, as well she might, when a knock sounded. "My lord?"

I frowned, recognizing the voice of one of my servants. What did he want with me so early in the day? "Come in. What is it?"

"Your lord father. He wishes you to come to Westminster immediately. There is disturbing news about the Duke of York."

"There's always disturbing news about the Duke of York," I said to Joan, who shook her head sympathetically, and I hoped regretfully, as my servant helped me into my clothes and she concealed her splendid figure beneath a sheet. It was at daybreak when she was most avid for me, though I was eager for her at any time. "The whoreson."

"Why all of you cousins just can't get along together is beyond me," said Joan.

I noted with approval that the little genealogical lesson I'd given Joan the other night, in which I had laboriously explained the common descent that most of the nobility in England had from the prolific Edward III, had not been wasted. "It's precisely because we're all cousins that we can't get along. We all can picture ourselves on the throne through some descent or the other, if we sit back and think about it hard. Edward III would have done well to take a vow of chastity after the fourth or fifth child or so."

Joan blew a kiss to me as I made my reluctant exit. "Well, cousin or not, I'll say this for the Duke of York: he certainly knows how to spoil a morning."

"At your service," I said airily when I arrived at Westminster. "The Duke of York is causing trouble?"

"He's raising troops," said Father in a tone that suggested further airiness on my part would be unwelcome. "So are the Earl of Salisbury and the Earl of Warwick."

"Ah, yes, the Triumvirate." Richard Neville, the Earl of Warwick, was Salisbury's oldest son and the nephew of the Duchess of York. Lately, the Nevilles had been sticking close to the Duke of York. Warwick, then six-and-twenty, happened to be my uncle by marriage—his wife was my mother's half sister—but our families had never been close. Aside from the fact that nearly everyone disliked my father, my mother and her sisters, not to mention their husbands, had been quarreling over their father's inheritance even before the man was cold. "But why are they raising troops?"

"Why do you think? To force the king to bend to their will. So we need to raise forces of our own to bring to Leicester." He stared disapprovingly at me. "We need you to help us, instead of gadding about London, drinking and gaming and God knows what else. Why, you're still in yesterday's clothes."

"I wasn't drinking and gaming," I said. This was true: Joan and I had spent a very decorous evening at her house before retiring to bed and behaving rather less decorously.

Father did not overlook my reminiscent smile. "I suppose that means you've a trollop, then, but you'll have to give her up for the next little bit. We've got business to take care of before we go to Leicester."

It wasn't like my father to be this brusque and stern with me; if anything, he'd been overindulgent toward his offspring, especially me, in the years since he had surrendered Rouen. I had so much pocket money, I was one of the few young men I knew who had no debts. "They want you, don't they?" I said suddenly. "York and his cronies want the king to hand you over to them."

"Quite possibly," conceded my father. "Now get busy."

Getting busy meant writing to my father's retainers, demanding that they send men to St. Albans, where they were to join us on our journey to Leicester. As a clerk put the finishing touches to a letter I'd dictated, I sat with my chin in my hand, remembering a day six years before.

I was thirteen on November 4, 1449, the day my family left Rouen, which my father had agreed a few days before to surrender. Under the terms, we could take our possessions with us, and all of my coffers had long since been hauled down to the carts by our servants, who carried out their task as silently as if they were disbanding our household after a funeral. So when my half brother Thomas, Lord Ros, came looking for me, he found me in a bare room huddled in a window seat. "Hal, it's time to go."

"I don't want to go! They can't make me."

"Can't make you? King Charles himself will be here in a few days. Do you think he's going to adopt you as his heir?" Tom, two-and-twenty, sat beside me. "It's time, Hal. Your staying here isn't going to change a thing."

"Why hasn't Father come to get me? Is he afraid to face even me?" I turned my face, which was embarrassingly tear-stained, toward my brother. "He wasn't man enough to stand up to the French. Why should I think he's man enough to stand up to me?"

"Hal, don't speak like that of your father."

"Why not? I can speak any way I please about him. He's not your father."

"He's been good to me since Mother married him, and I respect him."

"How can you do that after what happened? He caved in to them, Tom! He caved in! He's a damned coward, and you know it!"

Tom dealt me a stinging blow across the cheek. As I blinked at him, he said calmly, "Your father's no coward. I don't like what happened here any more than you do, especially since I'm to be a hostage."

"Yes, and that's so unfair—"

"Shut your mouth. Things aren't always as simple as they seem when you're thirteen, Hal. The duke's been under immense strain; he's had others to think of besides himself. How long could he have withstood a siege here? Just because we've given up Rouen doesn't mean it's the end of Normandy for us."

"You know it is."

"Not necessarily." Tom's eyes did not match his words. Quietly, he said, "Hal, it will take a lot of courage for your father to face down the anger that's going to greet him when this gets back to England."

I nodded. "Yes, it is. And that's why Father's not going straight to England. He's going to Caen first."

"How did you know that?"

"Eavesdropping. How else? I heard him talking to Mother." I was silent for a few moments. "He was crying about it, Tom."

Tom put his arm around my shoulders. "Hal, you know what happened to his older brother when he had a reversal like this."

I nodded; what had happened to John Beaufort, the first Duke of Somerset, after a blundering military campaign in France was the shame of the family. "He made away with himself. You don't think that Father—"

"No. He's too strong, and he'd never give his enemies the satisfaction. And that's why you should be supporting him instead of sulking in your chamber." He looked around. "Besides, where the hell are you going to sleep tonight, with your bed gone? Come with me, Hal."

I let Tom lead me from my chamber to Rouen Castle's great hall, where my parents and my brothers and sisters stood, plainly having been waiting on me.

They said nothing, however, and my father merely nodded at Tom in thanks as he took his place among the men who were to stand hostage for the terms of the agreement my father had made. "Ready, son?" he said softly.

"Yes." I managed to look my father in the eye, though I really didn't want to.

Father patted me on my shoulder. "Someday I'll make this up to you," he said, so low only he and I could hear.

Instead, eight months later, he had surrendered Caen, though at least that time he'd resisted as long as he could.

"My lord? My lord? Are you ready to dictate another letter?"

"Yes," I said. "Sorry. I was daydreaming."

On May 21, we left Westminster, anticipating the arrival of our reinforcements at St. Albans. We needed them: without them, we were ready only for a council, not for a battle. Whether we were going to be faced with one was something we didn't know: the king demanded that York and the Nevilles disband their armies, but whether they would obey the order was something about which we were all pessimistic.

Where York's men were, I don't know, but one thing was clear: they had pen and ink with them. Before we even got within spitting distance of St. Albans, the Triumvirate (my own term; sadly, I couldn't get anyone else to adopt the usage) had sent us two letters. They laid it on thick. After calling for the excommunication of the enemies about the king—that is, of course, my father—and terming themselves King Henry's true and humble liegemen, they protested, in injured tones, against the mistrust of them and hoped that they would be cleared of it. How they expected to be trusted, while at the same time they were raising troops, was a matter about which they were less clear.

Having encamped at Watford for the night, we pressed on toward St. Albans, only to hear just minutes after we had begun moving that York's men were already just outside the city, with over a thousand more men than we had. And many of those with us were not fighting men, but clerks.

"We should stay here," Father said to the king. "Stay here, and fight when they arrive. The reinforcements—"

"We should negotiate," the Duke of Buckingham said flatly. "They're traveling quickly; what if the reinforcements don't reach us in time? It's a battle we could lose. And—" He hesitated. I knew he was thinking that some of our number might throw in their lot with York were battle to be joined, but he could hardly say it aloud. Instead, he repeated. "Negotiate, your grace. York may have a genuine misapprehension of your intentions. Perhaps he fears arrest, like the Duke of Gloucester so many years ago. If so, he can be reassured that your grace's only intent is to see to the greater security of the realm."

"York can't be trusted," Father said. "Negotiation with him is a waste of time."

The king hesitated. Finally, he said softly, "Peace is always to be desired over war, my lords. Buckingham, I appoint you Constable of England."

My father, who held that office, began to sputter. The king cut him off. "The constable is the best person to conduct the negotiations, and you, Somerset, being the person York wishes me to give up, are hardly suited to enter into them yourself. Come. Let us move on."

Father opened his mouth, closed it again, and shook his head. Buckingham's son, the Earl of Stafford, who was married to my sister Meg, saw the expression on my face. Too softly to be overheard by our fathers or by the king, he said, "Hal, don't worry. If anyone can make York see reason, my father can."

I did not like the sound of that qualifier.

If—speaking of which word—this had been a normal journey, the king would have lodged himself at St. Albans Abbey and no doubt been treated to a discourse by Abbot Whethamstede on the myriad virtues of Humphrey, Duke of Gloucester, the abbey's greatest patron. But this was no normal journey; York's men were already encamped in Key Field. So instead, Henry set up his headquarters near St. Peter's Street, in the home of a citizen who could not have looked less excited by the prospect of a royal guest. Lord Clifford and his men went out to bar the roads that led across Tonman Ditch into the town, while Buckingham and York negotiated through heralds—a three-hour process that was hopeless from the start, for all the high-flown words came down to one point: York wanted my father turned over to him, supposedly for trial, and the king refused to give him over.

"This could go on all day," I told Stafford. Standing with most of the other nobles near the king, we were only half clad in our suits of armor; with the negotiations dragging on as they were, it had hardly seemed worthwhile to arm ourselves head to toe. I glanced at our fathers, who were conferring together. Then I pointed to a tavern. "Why not get an ale? They don't need us. We'll be back before they've even miss—"

"To arms!" One of Lord Clifford's men ran up, coming from the direction of our barriers at Shropshire Lane. "To arms! York has begun attacking!"

Gabriel, the bell in St. Albans Clock Tower, began to ring frantically as our pages, who had been dicing nearby, raced to help us into our remaining armor. The townspeople, who had been leaning from their upper windows as if watching a particularly dull pageant they kept hoping would get better, screamed warnings to each other and slammed their shutters tight. Men ran out of taverns, dropping in the street the ales they'd been drinking.

York's men were attacking the barriers at Shropshire Lane; Salisbury's, we learned just a minute or two after the first man had arrived, at Sopwell Lane. King Henry looked to his left, then to his right, stymied—at age thirty-three he'd never fought in a battle. As his servants frantically tried to get him into his armor, the king's face changed, and he lifted his arm, as if he had suddenly recalled that he was Henry V's son. "Unfurl our banner! I shall destroy them, every mother's son, and they shall be hanged, drawn and quartered that may be taken afterward!"

Then an arrow hit the king in the neck.

Men were swarming into the marketplace, pushing their way in between buildings, knocking down market stalls, forcing their way through houses and into the street, their way assured by the arrows that were whining through the sky. Buckingham caught one in his unprotected face; so did my brother-in-law the Earl of Stafford. The Earl of Northumberland was down.

And I was fighting for my life, side by side with my father.

At St. Albans that day of May 22, 1455, armed scarcely better than a common soldier, taken completely off guard, and outnumbered, my father fought as I have never seen a man fight before, or since. As the few archers we had with us desperately tried to fend off Warwick's men, he and I took down as many men as we could, our desperation lending us strength. But it was a hopeless task. Our men were falling, others were running, and when it became clear that all was lost, Father threw himself against the door of the Castle Inn, hard by the marketplace. It gave and we tumbled inside as the innkeepers—an elderly couple who hadn't had the strength to drag furniture to barricade their doors—ran shrieking up the stairs.

For what seemed an eternity, we remained side by side by the door, doubled over and gasping. There was no doubt a back way out of the inn, but if York's men had any sense, which I decided on reflection they probably did, they would have blocked it by now. And my father wasn't looking for an exit anyway. He got his breath, then straightened and laid his arm across my shoulders. "Son," he said. "About Rouen and Caen. I disgraced myself with that, and I disgraced your name as well."

"Oh, it wasn't that—"

"Don't tell me it wasn't! I saw your face the day when we left Rouen. You thought I wasn't looking. There was nothing in it but contempt."

"I was thirteen. Stupid."

"No. You were a bright lad who knew a stain on a man's honor when you saw one. I told you then I'd make it up to you. I never have. I will today."

"Father! You don't have to make up anything to me."

"Yes, I do. And I have to make up something to myself as well." He embraced me for a long time. "Be a good son to your mother, Henry. Give her and the rest my love. And God keep you." Then he released me, smiling. "Here they are. Good timing."

Warwick's voice came from the street. "Somerset! We know you and your whelp are in there. We have possession of the king. All's lost, you cur. Surrender!"

"Father! Please!"

My father shoved me aside and rushed through the door, sword raised high despite the blood dripping from his arm, and I and the men who remained to us followed. There were ten of us at the most; a hundred or more of them, circling us. My father took out four men, at least, before Warwick himself swung his battle ax and my father fell. As Father struggled to rise, his blood seeping around him, Warwick smiled. "Finish him off, men. Orders from the Duke of York."

Three men, two with daggers, one with a mace, surrounded my father and raised their weapons as he lay helpless. This was no death in fair battle; this was an assassination.

I rushed with my sword toward the men closest to me, but it was too late. As two other men dragged me back, I heard my father mutter a fragment of a prayer, heard his skull crack, then crack again. As I struggled and cursed, my captors knocked me to the ground with their clubs, and a blinding pain shot through my head and through my arms as I landed next to my father and into a pool of his blood.

Someone was raising his dagger over me, I saw through the blood pouring down my face, but I could not move my arms to resist or even hold my eyes open to watch my killer. Then a panicky voice, close by but sounding miles and miles off, said, "For God's sake, leave off!"

"You don't want a brace of Beauforts? You shock me."

"My quarrel wasn't with the younger one. I'll not have unnecessary blood on my hands. It invites trouble."

"I should think leaving the whelp alive would invite even more trouble, but they're your orders to give and mine to follow. In any case, I suppose it wouldn't accomplish much anyway, as there are two more at home where he came from. Somerset was capable in one respect, anyway." Warwick chuckled. "Fine armor he brought here too, what there is of it; it was a stroke of luck that the fools hadn't fully protected themselves, wasn't it? I trust my men can have it, or would yours prefer it?"

"Yours," said York.

"Where's Clifford?"

"Dead. It wasn't necessary to see to his death. He was killed fighting at the barricades. Northumberland is slain too."

Another pair of feet halted near me. A youthful voice asked with interest, "Father, is he dead too?"

This had to be Edward, Earl of March, York's thirteen-year-old son, who no doubt had been brought here to wait upon his father and to get a taste of battle from a safe distance. In reply, York bent and prodded me. "He's alive. Post a guard here so no one harms him further."

"You're not going to kill him?" asked the Earl of March. The brat sounded vaguely disappointed.

"We've been through that," snapped York. "No. Go see to the horses as I ordered you to."

Warwick gave me a casual kick. "He probably won't survive anyway, though. Look at the blood he's lost, or is that all Papa's?"

"For God's sake, let's go to the king and get this behind us. It can't end well."

Warwick snorted. "You should have thought of that earlier."

After they walked away, I remained lying there, my own blood blending with my father's as I drifted in and out of consciousness. Then I saw a familiar face staring into mine. "Tom?"

"Yes, it's me," my half brother said.

I made an effort to stay conscious. "They killed Father. They murdered him."

"I know. Hal, don't try to move. I've got some monks coming to take you to the abbey, and I'll get a surgeon for you once we're there. York only just gave the word that the monks could bury the dead. They'll be coming for your father soon."

I looked at the figure next to mine. Someone had thrown a cloak over it. I struggled to rise but could not move off my back. "I want to see him before they take him away. Move that thing off his body."

"No," Tom said. "I'll not let you see your father like that." He took a flask from his side and raised my head slightly. "Have a little wine."

I managed a sip. "Won't they take you prisoner if they find you with me?"

"Probably." Tom shrugged and helped me take another sip of wine.

In a few minutes, two monks arrived, carrying a bier. As they loaded Father's body onto it, not removing the cloak, Tom wrapped his arms around me. I tried to say something, but instead tears just ran down my face.

By and by, two more monks came and gently lifted me onto another bier as Tom superintended. Even so, the pain of my removal must have made me lose consciousness for a moment, for when I next stirred, I heard one of the monks asking the other in a whisper, "Do you think he'll live?"

"No. Just look at him."

But he was wrong, I told myself as they carried me away, Tom holding fast to my hand. I would not die; I would live to kill the men who had murdered my father. Vengeance would keep me alive.

12

Margaret
May 1455 to February 1456

Y OUR GRACE, YOU WERE NOT SENT FOR."

"I am well aware of that," I said, trying to force my way around the Duke of York into Henry's chambers at the Bishop of London's palace the day after Somerset had been murdered at St. Albans. "When did you plan to send for me? Michaelmas?"

Very late the previous evening, one of Henry's knights, who had somehow escaped the strict surveillance of York following the slaughter, had come to Greenwich and told me what had transpired after Somerset's death. York, Salisbury, and Warwick had gone to the abbey at St. Albans, where a shocked and wounded Henry, along with a badly wounded Buckingham, had taken shelter. The three whoresons had first demanded, and received, Buckingham's surrender, having threatened to take him by force, and Henry, terrified of despoiling the abbey with bloodshed, had agreed. Then the victors had knelt before Henry, begged his forgiveness for endangering him, and assured him of their loyalty. The next day, they had escorted Henry back to London, York on his right, Salisbury on his left, and Warwick bearing the sword of state. With Henry still in tow, they had even held a grand procession through the streets of London, ostensibly to show their loyalty to Henry but in reality to flaunt their newfound power. The mummery had ended only a half hour or so before.

"The king needs to rest," York said.

"Of course he does, after you dragged him from St. Albans, wounded and grieving." Taking advantage of an opening around York's squat body when the duke switched position suddenly, I pushed my way past him into the inner chamber where Henry, his neck bandaged, sat in a chair, Warwick standing beside him. For a horrid moment, I thought from his dazed look that my husband had relapsed into madness, but then he stood and let me take him into my arms.

"Marguerite. You have heard the news, I suppose."

"Yes, that these brave men have murdered Somerset and the rest."

"We have relieved the king of the burden of those who worked against his interests," corrected York, as if reciting the words by rote. "With the canker removed, the whole kingdom will heal and thrive."

"The canker you speak of was a father and a husband. A good one. As were the others who died."

"Then he should have been a better subject," York said coolly.

"And the king!" I looked at Henry's bandage. "If that arrow had gone only slightly to the left or right, he might have been killed. Did you people have no care for your anointed king? Or was his life as cheap to you as the others'?"

"My lady," said Henry, "have done. I have extended my forgiveness to them."

"Henry, you would forgive the devil himself!" I tried to compose myself, though. "Well, what of the others? Buckingham and his son survived with wounds, I heard, but what of the Earl of Dorset?"

"He's badly hurt," York said, not a trace of concern in his voice. "He was taken away this morning in a cart."

"Taken where? Home?" York shook his head. "Then do so, or better yet send him here, where he can be cared for by our own surgeons."

"I am afraid that cannot be, your grace," Warwick put in. "He is in my custody."

"*Your* custody? After—" I bit my lip.

"The young man is getting medical attention," York said in a polite, bored tone. "Your grace need not concern yourself with that. Though his injuries were grave, he's young and fit and will probably mend quickly."

"Is he even conscious?"

Warwick snorted. "Quite so, at least he was this morning. Indeed, once he was cognizant that he was in my custody, he said some most disagreeable things. I have sent him to be tended by my lady; she is, after all, his aunt. I just hope he does not try her temper."

"Can you blame him? For God's sake, let him be tended by his own people. Or by someone from here."

Henry roused himself to say, "The queen is right. The Earl of Dorset has been like a son to us. You must allow our surgeon to attend him. And a chaplain as well. You cannot deny him spiritual comfort in light of what he has suffered. If you are our loyal subject as you claim, you will comply with our wishes in this small matter."

"Very well," Warwick said.

"Now, let the king rest."

"Your grace, there are some matters we had wished to discuss with the king—"

"Your damned discussion can wait! You yourself said earlier that he needs to rest. No doubt he does, after his ride here and that farce in the streets."

Warwick looked at York, who grimaced an apparent assent. After they took a suitably cringing leave of Henry, I sat beside him, holding his hand tightly. When some moments had passed, he said, "I don't want to talk about it. It was too horrible. But I must talk about it, or I shall go mad again. What they did to Somerset..."

"Surely to God they did not make you witness it?"

"No. But they carried his body into the abbey to lay him to rest there, and I was lodged there overnight. When I heard he was brought there, I went to pay my respects and pulled down the sheet they'd wrapped him in before they could stop me. He'd been so loyal to me, and he was my kinsman—I couldn't just let him go without a look. I shouldn't have. They'd beaten his skull in—you could see his brains, for pity's sake!—and there were knife wounds all over his body. All inflicted when he was past fighting back, one of his men who saw it told me. I was almost sick at the sight of him."

"He must have been beyond all pain when they did most of those things to him, Henry. His soul had long since fled his body."

"I pray that was how it was."

"You know that was how it was."

"Dear Marguerite," Henry whispered. He sat staring straight ahead for a few minutes. "The Earl of Dorset must have seen all that was done to his father; he fell beside him. I sat with him an hour or two that night at the abbey infirmary. The monks tended him well and he was better when we left the abbey, Warwick wasn't lying, but for a time that night he was delirious and didn't know me or Lord Ros, who was also taken prisoner. He just lay there talking out of his head, mostly begging his father not to leave the Castle—he was killed by the Castle Inn. But once in a while he called out for a Joan. Do you think in his disturbance of mind he could have meant the Maid of Orléans? Or maybe one of his relations?"

In spite of myself, I smiled. "Hardly, Henry. Joan is his mistress, and has been since about the time our son was born. Hal was not discreet in proclaiming his conquest to all and sundry, I am afraid."

"His mistress? But I thought he would avoid the ways of the flesh. He once promised me he would."

How could I help but love my unworldly Henry? I kissed him tenderly. "I am sure he tried his very best."

Henry sighed. "Hal was such a lighthearted lad. After St. Albans, I fear he will never be the same again."

None of us would, I thought.

My husband gazed at his hands. Finally, he said, "You know, my dear, that after it was all done, York and the others came to the abbey and begged my forgiveness. They said that they were acting for the good of the realm, not against me. I did forgive them; it is what the Lord teaches. But I also know I had no real choice. Somerset, Percy, and Clifford dead, Buckingham and his son wounded, Dorset wounded, my men scattered—I could not have resisted them. And now I can only hope their intentions are good, for they are the men I must work with now."

"For now," I echoed, giving the last word an emphasis that Henry, who did indeed look and sound exhausted, missed.

Shortly before Christmas, a visitor was announced at Greenwich. "The Earl of Dorset, your grace."

My eyes filled with tears as Hal Beaufort entered the room, and I forestalled his attempt to bow with a hearty embrace and a kiss. As we moved apart, I saw for the first time that his right cheek bore a large scar. I touched it gently. "Oh, Hal."

"It's not so bad. Mother said it makes me look like a pirate, but Joan said it made me look mysterious."

I frowned in mock outrage. "You visited your mistress before you visited your queen?"

"Well, there are certain inducements with her that your grace lacks," Hal said, grinning.

Silently, I thanked the Lord that St. Albans had not robbed Hal of his sense of humor. "But how did you get free?"

"Much as I would like to say that I overpowered Warwick and made my escape, the ignoble truth is that he simply let me go. He really couldn't come up with a good excuse to keep me in ward indefinitely, after all, and I suspect it was beginning to become an embarrassment for York, with all of his lofty talk about reconciliation. So he made a pious speech about the season of the birth of the Lord being a time to show mercy, and here I am. He was actually quite pleasant toward the end. It was rather unnerving; he even suggested that we joust sometime. Joust, as if I would trust him to fight fairly! I don't think he realizes how much I heard and saw at St. Albans." Hal's brown eyes clouded over, then grew hard, before he continued, "But I am sorry. I spoke of the topic that must not be named in polite company."

"Ah, you have heard that?" The York-controlled government had strictly forbidden anyone from discussing the events of St. Albans. "I daresay you may have a dispensation here."

"I'm not sure I want one," Hal said quietly.

"Well, how does Joan fare?"

Hal visibly brightened at my hasty change of subject. "I was afraid she would take another lover in my absence, but no. I got quite the welcome. Oh, and she told me that an unnamed friend of mine sent her a sum of money for her support while I was imprisoned, in case she was in need. My mother is a kindhearted lady, but her charity doesn't extend to my harlot, as she calls her. I suspect it came from another source." I blushed tellingly. "Thank you, your grace."

"I think we had better not mention this to the king. He would not approve in the least. How fares your mother?"

"Edmund said that she was a wreck at first, terrified that York might harm her or us; she dragged the family to my aunt's at Maxey Castle. She's better now." Hal grimaced. "There's even talk that she might remarry. One of my aunt's servants, Walter Rokesley, of all people. It seems a little sudden to me to talk of remarriage, but he's been kind to her, and she's been lonely without my father. She loved him very much."

"As he loved all of you, Hal."

Hal cleared his throat. "Tell me, your grace. Is what I heard true? Is the king ill again? I heard that York had been named protector once again."

"He does not suffer from the same malady as he did before, God be thanked, but he has not been entirely himself either. He sleeps far too much—he goes to bed much earlier than a man his age usually does. He becomes agitated very quickly, and he seems to get confused more easily than before. I noticed it just slightly after—after St. Albans—but it has been gradually going worse. One can't give him too many details in a single conversation or he gets overwhelmed; it can almost be seen on his face. And he thinks much about his own death, too much for a man of only four-and-thirty. He has even been talking of where he shall be buried. And—" I bit my lip.

"Your grace, what is it?"

What I had been about to blurt out was that Henry no longer had sexual relations with me. We needed another child; what if our little Edward succumbed to one of the illnesses that could take the healthiest of children? And yet Henry these days did no more than lie beside me, gently rebuffing my tentative attempts at lovemaking. But this was hardly a topic I could discuss with a man, and particularly not with a handsome young man like Hal. "Nothing. I was merely running on."

Hal did not meet my eyes again, and I wondered if he had guessed my thoughts. Then he said briskly, "Who knows, perhaps in a few months his situation will improve. So that is why York took over as protector? The king's state of mind?"

I nodded gratefully. "Mind you, I don't think he would have needed much of an excuse, but with Henry so abstracted recently, and York so alert for the slightest sign of incapacity, it was easy for him to get Parliament to agree. He even convinced the king that it was in his own best interests to take a rest from his duties for a time." I hesitated. "Hal, I don't want to cause you pain, but I suppose you have heard what York's Parliament said about St. Albans."

"Yes. That it was all the fault of my father. Not a word about York's men attacking while negotiations were still going on. Not a word about his being butchered by those cowards when he was helpless, lying on his back, not even able to raise his hand."

"I want Henry out of York's control. How could he not have realized that he was putting my husband's life in danger when those arrows were shot?" The words, so long repressed, were tumbling out of my mouth so quickly that my English was inadequate for them, and I switched to French. "If Henry had died, there would have been a protectorate for our son, and who would then rule in all but name? York! And what security would our boy have, being controlled by the man who stood next in line to the throne? I do not trust him, Hal. I don't believe those sugared words he speaks about loyalty to Henry and to the realm. There is one person the Duke of York is loyal to above all others, and that is the Duke of York."

"I don't merely mistrust him. I want him dead, even though he kept Warwick's thugs from killing me. He gave the order that my father be assassinated." Hal stared around the chamber, and I suddenly remembered, with a pang, the day his father had brought him and his brothers there after their return from France. "But for now, I'll settle for removing him as protector."

"Alas, he can be removed as protector only if Parliament assents," I said. "He took care to have that provision inserted, so the king couldn't change his mind and have him removed on his own volition. But there is some hope there, actually. The resumptions." Claiming that the royal household was living beyond its means, the commons had been demanding for some time that Henry take back the grants he had made over the years. I stood to lose by the resumptions, and so did those lords who could not obtain exemptions from them. York, in his favorite guise as man of the people, had stood behind the commons, who had somehow failed to notice that York had his own ambitions to acquire some of the resumed property. "The lords cannot be happy with them. If we could just take advantage of their unease…It is a pity you aren't in Parliament, Hal."

"And won't be until I'm one-and-twenty; I don't see York and his cronies summoning me before that. But I'm not without friends there; I can make my views heard. And as for you, all you have to do is smile sweetly at the lords, in that certain way you have like *this*"—Hal managed a most peculiar looking smile that I hoped did not resemble any expression of my own—"and they'll do anything you please."

"Hal!"

"It's true. Try it."

❧

I did *not* smile sweetly at the lords, as that impertinent young man had suggested, but I settled down with my council that day, and the next, and the next, and composed a letter to the lords whom I thought would be sympathetic, expressing my deep reservations about the wisdom of the resumptions and begging that they would ensure that the rights of my son and my own rights were protected. More cautiously, I begged them to consider whether York, so close to the throne, was the best man to serve as protector, if a protector was needed at all. This second thread of my argument was what occupied my councillors for so many days, as its meaning had to be implied rather than said. Were I to openly say that York should be removed, my words would simply be disregarded as those of a meddling woman, and might end up only fixing him more firmly in power. "But it is time someone meddled," I said to Katherine Vaux soon before Parliament was to open. "If poor Henry cannot, it must be me. Why, William? What in the world?"

William Vaux had rushed into the chamber. "Your grace! Kate! Do come outside. It is the most wondrous sight."

We followed William outside to the lawn at Greenwich, where most of the household had gathered. And then I saw it, the brightest star I had ever seen, gleaming in the blackness of the night like the Star of Bethlehem must have glowed. "I have never seen such in my life. What could it mean?" Katherine asked.

"An omen, surely," one of my older ladies said.

I smiled. "A good omen, surely. Nothing so beautiful could be a bad omen."

And I was right. When Parliament met shortly thereafter, the lords talked of the marvelous star—and of the high-handed resumptions proposed by the commons and the Duke of York, which even threatened poor Henry's beloved foundations at King's College and Eton. So disgusted were the lords that a delegation of them went to Henry, who walked into Parliament on February 25, clad magnificently, and ordered York to resign as protector. Save for York and Warwick, the lords assented.

And that same afternoon, the Duke of York himself paid me a visit. "So, my lady. You may congratulate yourself on a job well done."

"Whatever do you mean, my lord?"

"You will not attempt to deny that you sought my removal as protector. I saw the letter you wrote."

"I had not been planning to deny it, but you must have noticed that I was not among the lords in Parliament. As I am not in the habit of wearing male dress, I would not have blended in. The lords acted as they would; I merely informed them of my opinion. They were free to disregard it; it appears that either they did not, or they happened to hold the same opinion as I did."

"Tell me, your grace. What do you think will happen to the realm now that I am not protector? Do you truly think the king is fit to govern?"

I shrugged. "He has his council, does he not? And you remain on it. My lord, face the truth. Pleased as I am to see you gone, it was not my doing. It was yours." I paused. "I do understand your frustration, my lord."

"Oh?"

"Yes. As I am a woman, you cannot arrest me, or do battle with me, or have your men beat my brains out as I lie helpless in the street, as you did the Duke of Somerset. It must be extremely irritating to you." I gazed at the interesting shade of red York was turning. "My lord, before you leave, there is one thing I would like to request of you."

"Oh?"

"That tiresome fellow, John Helton, who posted those bills claiming that the Prince of Wales was a changeling. I do not know if he was one of your creatures, or Warwick's, but if he was yours, I hope you shall refrain from inciting any more of them to such deeds. Henry ordered him to be drawn, hanged, and quartered, and he hates commanding such things. Please spare him the further necessity of it."

13

Margaret
October 1456 to May 1458

THE DUKE OF BUCKINGHAM HAULED HAL BEAUFORT INTO MY CHAMBER AT Kenilworth Castle and shoved him upon the floor, where he rested unsteadily upon his knees, his hands tied. "Good lord, what has happened?" I sniffed. "Is he drunk?"

"He's drunk, and he's an utter fool," snapped Buckingham. "He and his men decided it would be *amusing* to attack the Duke of York and his men at Coventry."

"I heard just now that there had been a disturbance there. Was that the trouble?"

"Aye, all owing to this fellow. And there was trouble indeed. In the fracas two of the city watchmen were killed."

"Hal!"

Hal hiccupped and mumbled, "Forgive me, your grace."

"The city officials would have arrested the young fool, and some of the townspeople might have done worse to him, but I prevented it," Buckingham continued. "No, don't thank me, your grace. 'Tis only because his sister Meg is married to my son, and she frets herself to death over her favorite brother, and then Humphrey frets himself to death over her. I did it for their sake. If it weren't for that I'd have told them to keep him."

"But you should have seen the Duke of York," Hal interjected, attempting to stand until Buckingham, who was not a particularly imposing-looking man but who could rise to an occasion, stopped him with a mere glare. "He was riding at the head of all of his men, looking so damned smug. We were coming out of the tavern and saw him, and we just couldn't stand it. Or at least I couldn't stand it," Hal added sullenly. He looked up at me. "I'm sorry about the watchmen, your grace. We only wanted to fight with York, and they got in the middle of it."

"And what else did you expect them to do? Tomorrow you will make reparations to their families. It is the least you can do."

"It is the *only* thing he can do, unless he can raise the dead," snapped Buckingham. "For God's sake, your grace, keep him here until the council finishes meeting. He's only likely to cause more troub—"

"Hal, what is this?" Henry, who had entered the room noiselessly, bent beside Hal and touched him gently. "They tell me your men were in a great affray."

"I beg your forgiveness, your grace." Hal's eyes were filling with tears; either he was genuinely contrite by now or he was the lachrymose breed of drunk. "I saw him and I thought of Father; I *miss* him, your grace. And it drives me mad to see the Duke of York living, and not having suffered at all, and—" He took a breath. "I didn't mean for anyone else to die, your grace."

"I know, I know." Henry patted Hal on the shoulder. "But you must forgive the Duke of York, haven't we discussed that? Come. Let me take you to your chamber so you can rest. Tomorrow we can speak of these things more in depth."

He raised an unprotesting Hal to his feet, untied his hands, and led him from the room, murmuring soothing words to him as I stared at my feet.

The court had for all purposes moved itself to Coventry and its environs earlier that year. That had been chiefly my doing; my estates mostly lay in the surrounding area, and I had realized that here, instead of in volatile London, I could find support against any mischief York might care to do to the king and to me—and to our son. It was also a chance for the people to meet their Prince of Wales. Taking him around was of course a task I delighted in anyway, for Edward at three was sturdy and bright and well worth showing off. Henry, strained from a summer of unrest in London that arose from long-simmering tensions between the locals and the Italian merchants who resided there, had joined me in September.

It was to Coventry, then, that Henry had summoned his council, and it was at Coventry, again mostly due to my efforts, that the Bourchier brothers, who had ties to York, had been removed from their positions as treasurer and chancellor and replaced with men I could trust. Yet the Bourchiers were Buckingham's half brothers, to whom he was close, and I knew their removals had vexed him. He wasn't a man I wanted to vex. I liked him, and I indeed wanted him to like me. I had never forgotten his kindness to me at the time of Henry's madness.

I would have to find some way to get back on good terms with Buckingham. "Thank you, my lord, for intervening on Hal's behalf."

"He must learn to govern himself, your grace. Antics like this do nothing to help him or those who favor him."

I flushed at this reference to myself, for it was true that Hal had been much about me since the court had moved to Coventry. I found his company pleasant, especially with Henry so tense and fretful, and I had believed—up until now—that my company had a softening effect on Hal, who otherwise was greatly inclined to dwell on the prospect of avenging his father's murder. "I will use what influence I can, and Lord Ros may be able to reason with him. Of course, the king may work a good influence upon him. You saw him listening to him just now."

"Listening; yes, well, that's one thing. Whether young Beaufort actually acts upon what he hears is another matter. If he won't heed your grace's advice, I doubt he'll heed anyone's."

I decided that a subject change was in order. "You spoke of your son and daughter-in-law, my lord. How does your grandson fare?"

"Harry does well," Buckingham said, visibly softening, though with obvious reluctance, at his mention of his year-old grandson, born the September after St. Albans. "At present he looks more like a Beaufort than a Stafford; poor Somerset, God assoil him, would have been pleased by that, no doubt. He would have doted on the boy, as do I." He sighed. "I know young Hal genuinely mourns the man, and I understand he wants retribution. I saw his father's body, and trust me, even a saint, not to mention our hot-blooded Hal, would have difficulty not lusting for revenge after such a sight. But he needn't drag all of Coventry into his grief and grievance either. I had best go back there and see that order has been restored."

"I don't know what we would do without you, my lord." I was sincere, and I hoped Buckingham realized it.

Evidently he did, for he smiled faintly. "Me neither, your grace."

*

"I have paid for the watchmen's burials, offered prayers for their souls, and provided compensation for their families," a hung-over Hal informed me the next afternoon.

"Hal, that's commendable, but you cannot involve innocent people in your quarrels like this. Not only have men doing their duties died because of this, your actions put the whole court in a bad light."

"I know, your grace."

"You must do better in the future."

"Yes, your grace." Hal bowed his head. "I have also thanked Buckingham;

he went with me this morning on my rounds, and I sorely needed his presence as a mediator or I might have found myself in a spot of trouble. Now that I have made what amends I could in Coventry, the king has given me leave to depart from here. My servants are packing. I'll be gone within an hour."

"That is best, I think."

Hal raised his head and fixed his dark brown eyes on me. All of a sudden, I felt as if I had kicked a puppy. "Do you hate me that much, your grace, after what happened?"

"Hate you? Goodness, no. Come sit with me a while before you leave."

Hal obediently sat on the stool I indicated, and my ladies flocked into a corner to give us privacy, though I had not requested that they do so. I took his hand, which like the rest of Hal was lean and strong. "I only want you to keep the peace. It is something the king wants so much."

"I know. I try, I truly do, but it's harder than you might think. When I'm not thinking of my father running out of that inn, then getting slaughtered by those whoresons, I'm dreaming of it. It makes me wake up screaming sometimes. Only Joan and my pages and now you know that." He managed a smile. "I hope your grace is conscious of the honor."

I squeezed Hal's hand, which I had neglected to release. "I am glad you can confide in me."

"And then I see York swanning around Coventry as if he's the Messiah come back to earth, and my blood boils, especially when he looked at me the way he did last night, as if we Beauforts were dirt beneath his feet. He seems to have forgotten that his duchess's mother was one of us." Hal snorted. "What does that make his own children? An eighth Beaufort? My head aches too much to cipher it."

I sighed. "The king seems to be on good terms with York. He believes that he has the good of the realm at heart."

"And you, your grace? Do you believe that?"

"Not for a moment."

We smiled at each other, and then Hal brought my hand to his lips and kissed it. "I should be off, your grace. I think Kenilworth will be more than glad to see the back of me, and Mother will be glad to see me home."

"You are staying with her, then?"

"Yes, for a few days, but naturally, it is Joan I shall be staying with most of the time. But that's not what I told the king. That will be our own secret, won't it, your grace?"

"Yes," I said a little coldly, not caring to analyze the odd pang I felt in my heart or the even odder sensation I had felt when Hal's lips brushed my hand. But that night when I lay in my bed, unvisited by Henry, I found myself imagining, as I had begun to do on these lonely nights, myself in the ardent grasp of a man. A man, I realized with a start, who looked a great deal like Hal.

I blushed with shame and turned over on my side.

There was sad news a few weeks later: Edmund Tudor, the Earl of Richmond, Henry's younger half brother, was dead, leaving behind a very young widow, Margaret Beaufort, who was great with child despite having just turned thirteen. Her father, long deceased, had been the older brother of the late Duke of Somerset. There were doubts as to whether the poor girl, who was really too young and small to safely bear a child, would survive her forthcoming ordeal, but she gave birth to a healthy son, named after the king, in late January, and lived through the experience herself. In a matter of months, the Duke of Buckingham and Edmund's brother, Jasper—with my blessing—were negotiating a new marriage for the young widow, with Buckingham's second son, Henry. This, I was pleased to see, improved my relations with Buckingham.

Meanwhile, in March 1457, Hal Beaufort returned to Coventry to take formal possession of his father's dukedom and his lands, and to explain his latest escapade, this one over Christmas. "I was riding in London from Joan's place, and who did I see riding toward me but John Neville?" John was a younger brother of Warwick. His feuding with the younger Percy sons, which had started years before for reasons no one outside of the families involved had quite figured out, had caused Henry much irritation before St. Albans. "So he started giving me hard looks, and naturally I started giving him hard looks, and before we knew it, we were trading insults."

"Fancy that."

"I would say on the whole that I did better with mine," Hal said reflectively. "Anyway, we decided to have it out once and for all, but neither one of us was properly armed, so we rode off to gather our men to fight in Cheapside."

I groaned. "How many lives were lost this time?"

"Oh, none. The mayor sent the watch out and kept us from fighting."

"You promised me at Coventry you would not do this sort of thing again."

"This was different. It wouldn't have been an attack, but an honest fight. No need for outsiders to be involved."

"An honest fight between dozens of men on either side? Hal, you are not even of age yet! Try not to get yourself killed before you turn one-and-twenty. Joan would miss you, for one. And your mother and the rest of your family."

"And you, your grace?"

"And me." I dropped my eyes. "And the king would miss you as well," I added firmly.

In August, the quiet we had enjoyed in England was broken abruptly when Pierre de Brézé, the seneschal of Normandy, attacked the town of Sandwich. I knew Brézé from my father's court—in those innocent days when I was preparing for my marriage, he and Suffolk had arranged an archery contest during the festivities at Tours—and he was to be one of the best friends I ever had later. But to say, as some did even then, that I had encouraged the attack was nonsensical.

"No sensible person would believe that," Henry said mildly one evening at Coventry after I had held forth on this topic for a time.

"Well, these are not always such sensible people," I muttered.

Henry's long stay in the Midlands had improved his mental state greatly—so greatly, in fact, that he had resumed marital relations with me, though without resulting in the second pregnancy for which I so longed. "This incident makes me realize how important it is that England be as one again," he said, stroking my hair one night after we had loved each other. "I must return to London, and I must exert myself to bring the lords together." They had not been causing trouble lately, but their quietude in itself was somehow ominous and had more of a sullen quality than a peaceful one.

"If there is a man who can do it, I am sure it is you. You have the patience."

Henry tapped me on the nose. "I hear the emphasis you put on *if*, my dear skeptic. But I am determined to do so."

And somehow he did, although the situation could have hardly looked less promising when a great council convened in January 1458. Every lord arrived with a small army at his back: the old Earl of Salisbury with five hundred men; the Duke of York with four hundred, the Percies and Lord Clifford with fifteen hundred. How in the world Somerset and Exeter managed to raise eight hundred men between them baffled me, for neither was very rich for a duke. Warwick, who had been appointed Captain of Calais and who had been residing there, arrived with six hundred followers, each wearing a red jacket bearing his symbol of the ragged staff.

The poor mayor of London! He could scarcely wait to see the backs of all of the lords. Somerset, Exeter, the Percies, and Clifford had to be lodged out-side the city for fear that their men would attack those of York, Salisbury, and Warwick, who lodged inside the city. The mayor had to set a watch of five thousand men around the area just to keep the groups from fighting, and I am constrained to say that given the chance, Somerset would have gladly done so.

Henry, having begged the lords to work for peace, left the appointed arbitrators to do their work without royal interference and retired with me to Berkhamsted. When in mid-March, matters seemed to be a standstill, we traveled back to London, Henry to pray for peace at the forefront of a great procession, me to pray in the privacy of my chapel at Westminster that God grant Henry's wish. "It is the least you could do," I told the Lord after having exhausted my formal prayers. "Grant this good man what he wishes for the most."

The Lord did. York and his allies were to endow a chantry at St. Albans for the souls of those who had died there; they were to pay compensation to the families of Somerset, Clifford, and Northumberland. To demonstrate the newfound harmony between the lords and Henry and myself, we all—Henry, me, the lords spiritual and temporal, the arbitrators—were all to process to St. Paul's on March 25. Our public showing of mutual goodwill and of the formal resolution of our differences would be known, in accordance with tradition, as Loveday.

Poor Henry's day of love has since been mocked. But who could prophesy the future? For Henry's sake, I for one was willing enough to make a new beginning when I took my assigned place beside the Duke of York and put my hand in his. Before us, Somerset joined hands with Salisbury, the father of the man who had killed his father, and Exeter sulkily gripped the hand of Warwick, who had been made keeper of the seas despite Exeter's hereditary position as admiral. Henry, wearing his crown, walked happily behind the two pairs of men, while York and I brought up the rear. "You must walk a little slower, my lord," I hissed graciously to York. "I cannot keep up with you."

York flashed a smile to the onlookers and amended his pace to mine.

⸎

To cap the Loveday celebrations, Henry ordered that over Whitsuntide, jousts be held at the Tower and at Greenwich—an unusual thing for his court, as Henry had never had much interest in jousting, either as a spectator or as a par-ticipant. Somerset, however, turned out to be an avid jouster, as was one of his friends, eighteen-year-old Anthony Woodville, the eldest son of the scandalous match the Duchess of Bedford had made with the late duke's chamberlain.

"A fine family you have," I said to the Duchess of Bedford as she and her husband took their places alongside the dowager Duchess of Somerset, the Duke and Duchess of Buckingham, and the Duke and Duchess of York in the stand erected at the Tower. The seats around us overflowed with Beaufort, Stafford, and York offspring, but the Woodvilles put them to shame in sheer numerosity. I indicated Elizabeth, the eldest and the prettiest of the Woodville girls sitting below me, who wore a sky-blue gown that matched her eyes and complimented her golden hair and fair complexion. "Lady Grey in particular is quite the beauty."

"So the Duke of Somerset has noticed." Hal was resplendent in shining Italian armor and a surcoat bearing the Beaufort symbol of a portcullis. ("Not a humble *gate*," he had informed me once when I used that simpler English term for it. "A *portcullis*.") He handed his lance up toward Lady Grey for her to deck with a favor, amid a general sighing from the ladies, the majority of whom were in some degree pining for handsome Hal. Only his sisters were indifferent, reserving their own longing looks for Elizabeth's handsome brother Anthony.

Elizabeth dimpled as she fastened a ribbon onto Hal's lance. "I do hope he realizes that she is married," I said, wondering if a young woman married to a mere knight could withstand Hal's ducal charm if he cared to exert it.

"Oh, I've no worries on that score." Out of sheer habit, the Duchess of Bedford patted her belly, though she for once was not carrying a child. "My Elizabeth may have the looks of a seductress, but she is remarkably prim, and very attached to her John. Not even a king could tempt her to stray." She smiled mischievously at her own handsome husband, who thanks to his marriage and his faithful service to Henry had become Lord Rivers and a Knight of the Garter. "They say children of unconventional matches are always the most conventional themselves."

"You have raised her well, madam," Henry put in. "It is good to see young ladies who are not only beautiful but virtuous." He smiled at me. "Like the queen."

I squeezed Henry's hand and shifted my position so I could better see around York's son Edward, the sixteen-year-old Earl of March, who himself was admiring the profile of Lady Grey. Finding a vantage point that did not include the young earl was a difficult task: the boy was six feet tall and showed every sign of growing taller. He bore not the slightest resemblance to the Duke of York; his good looks must have come from further back along the generations.

Sensing my difficulty in seeing the jousting, Edward moved over and flashed me a charming smile. "I am surprised you do not joust, my lord," I said after thanking him. "I should think that with—"

"My size, your grace?" The Earl of March's teeth shone in the sun as I nodded. "I do suppose I'd be a natural, but the truth is I just never had any interest in participating in a joust. Watching is good enough for me."

"You mean to say, you just never had any interest in practicing," the Duke of York said. Throughout the jousting, and especially when Hal had ridden out, he had worn a look of grim endurance. "Lazy."

"Quite true," conceded the Earl of March. "But you'll find me active enough when it suits my purposes, Father, never fear."

York harrumphed, and the Earl of March returned to his former occupation of eyeing Lady Grey, who was utterly oblivious to this male attention.

Henry pressed my hand and smiled. Like the Earl of March he was ignoring the jousting below, which had reached an exciting point: Anthony Woodville was running against one of my own household knights, Katherine's husband William Vaux. "This is what I have longed for all these years, my dear. A splendid May day in England, with my lords enjoying themselves and their ladies and not making war upon each other. Who would have thought three years before we would be at this happy pass?"

I nodded. Just after Loveday, Henry and I had gone to St. Albans, a gesture to show that all of the old wounds were healed. Quite calmly and without rancor, Henry had pointed out the spot where he had been injured and the spot where Somerset had been bludgeoned to death in front of Hal, but I had not been able to look at either without trembling with anger—though for Henry's sake, I pretended I was merely suffering from feminine vapors. "You are right. It is something to marvel at and to give thanks for."

Henry smiled and turned his eyes back to the jousting, evidently deeming it polite to take a kingly interest in it. With the exception of the still-sour Duke of York, the lords among us fell to discussing the merits of the jousters—Anthony Woodville, it was generally agreed, was the most accomplished despite his youth—while the ladies discussed their handsomeness, modestly refraining from praising their own sons or husbands. Only I remained abstracted, thinking that trouble was looming but not sure how or from what quarter.

It all just seemed too good to be true, I thought. And as it turned out, I was perfectly right.

14

Margaret
September 1459 to November 1460

EDWARD TUGGED AT MY ARM, STARTLING ME AS I PACED IN THE GUEST chamber at Eccleshall Castle. I had not known he was in the room with me. "Are we winning, Mother?"

"I don't know."

"We *have* to win."

Henry's Loveday peace had proven sadly short-lived. Commissioned by the king to investigate piracy in the Channel, the Earl of Warwick had instead taken to piracy himself, attacking Spanish, Hanseatic, and Genoese fleets. It made him popular among his men in Calais, who shared in the profits, and among certain elements of the people, who thoroughly enjoyed a pirate earl, but it did not please the Spanish, the Hanse, or the Genoese—all of whom were either our friends or at least not our enemies. Ordered to Westminster in October 1458 to answer the complaints against him, Warwick had not seen fit to arrive until November. While the earl was at Westminster, one of the king's men had trod upon the sensitive foot of one of Warwick's men. A miniature riot had ensued, with the men from the kitchens even grabbing cooking spits as weapons, and Warwick had had to be hustled to his barge by some of the king's men. Making haste to Calais—unpunished for his piracy—he had embroidered the toe-trodding incident so it had developed into an assassination attempt. Soon he and his father, and naturally York as well, were plotting again. Summoned to a council at Coventry in June 1459, they failed to appear and were indicted for their absence, for it was not lassitude or indifference that kept them away: they were, in fact, preparing for rebellion yet again.

But this time there would be no St. Albans; we were ready for them. I myself had traveled through my Cheshire estates, Edward in tow, showing my son to the men there as a prince worth fighting for. I had stood by proudly as Edward had handed his badge, depicting a white swan, to each man we encountered. "We will be pleased if you wear this and serve us well," he piped to each one.

"He looks just like his grandfather the fifth Henry," said one of the oldest men there, who had served that king in his wars, and I beamed. There was nothing that could please me more than to have my son associated with the memory of that mighty warrior.

We had need of those memories and the men's loyalty. By September, Warwick was sailing from Calais, the Earl of Salisbury marching from Middleham, the Duke of York gathering men at Ludlow. All were heading toward the midlands to place their grievances before the king—or so they claimed; I did not doubt for a minute that they planned another St. Albans. While Henry raised men at Nottingham and then moved into Staffordshire, I, in Edward's name, sent out summonses at Cheshire. From there, we had moved to Eccleshall Castle with the intent of joining Henry.

Instead, Salisbury's men moved into a position where we could intercept them, and my Cheshiremen, eager for a fight, had decided to make it one. "We outnumber them," James Tuchet, Lord Audley, a man in his sixties who had fought in France long before I was born, told me. "Why not prevent the lot from ever reaching the king?"

"You don't think you should wait for Lord Stanley?" Although he was Salisbury's son-in-law, he had promised to join us.

Audley bristled. "We can do fine without him. And what good will a man fighting against his wife's father be? He'll be thinking about the feelings of his sweetheart when he should be striking home. No, your grace, we're better off without him. We shall go—if we have your blessing."

"You know these matters better than I. You have it."

Three hours had passed since Audley's men had set out, resplendent with their white swan badges that Edward and I had also pinned to our clothes. Not a word. Three more hours passed, and I put a loudly protesting Edward into bed. "I will wake you when I hear news," I promised.

It was past dark when a young squire finally stumbled into the great hall, his arm bleeding through a makeshift bandage. "What has happened?" I asked as the others crowded around.

"Not—nothing good, your grace."

"I gathered that." I glared at the bystanders. "Why do you stand still? Fetch him a surgeon, get him some ale and some dressings for his wound. Sit." The squire obeyed, and I began to carefully remove his bandage. "Don't squirm.

I learned to tend a wound quite well when I was a girl. Now tell me as best you can."

The squire took a sip of ale with Katherine Vaux's help. "We met Salisbury's men over by Blore Heath. Salisbury was clever, your grace. He tricked us into thinking that he was retreating by withdrawing some of his men—and we fell for the ruse. Audley led a cavalry charge downhill and over a stream—and right into a hail of arrows. Many of us went down there and then. But we regrouped and came back again—and this time Lord Audley was killed." The squire stared wonderingly at the wound I had exposed.

"I'm listening." I patted his shoulder and began dabbing at his wound with a cloth. "Go on."

"It's just a scratch," the squire said manfully. He took a long drink of ale. "Lord Dudley took over then, and had us fight dismounted. We got over the stream—we had to walk over the dead in it—and began to fight them hand to hand. We must have been fighting for a couple of hours. Dudley did his best, but he was finally captured. After that some of the men lost heart and began to desert, and some began to turn their coats." The squire looked at me with regretful eyes. "That finished us, your grace. I'm sorry we lost it for you."

"I know you did your best." I looked at the hall, which was beginning to fill with the wounded, and blinked back my tears at the thought of all of my brave Cheshiremen who would never come back with their fellows. "Next time will be different," I promised him.

Two thousand men fell at Blore Heath, Salisbury having suffered nearly as much of a loss as we. My men soon had the satisfaction of capturing two of his younger sons, Thomas and John Neville, and shut them up to bide their time at Chester Castle. It did not occur to us to execute either of them; I wish that it had.

In the meantime, I and Edward and our men traveled south to meet Henry's, now augmented by forces from Somerset and many others. "I feel like a camp follower," I said as we embraced each other. "And I must look as grimy as one too."

"You are a sight for my eyes nonetheless," Henry said fondly, holding me more tightly and for a longer period than he normally would with onlookers present, then embracing Edward. "How are you, my son?"

"Our men lost at Blore Heath," Edward informed him gloomily.

"So I have heard, but right will prevail," said Henry, smiling down at him.

"Where are York and the rest?" I asked.

"Ah, we were just speaking of them." He indicated a letter in his hand. "York, Salisbury, and Neville have sent us a letter, through the prior of Worcester."

"Oh, Henry! Not another one of York's exercises in self-justification and humility. Let me guess. He and the rest are your loyal subjects, who wish only to relieve you of your evil councillors, who are robbing you blind. All will be well if you only allow yourself to be guided by the noble and excellent Duke of York."

"Why, that sums it up perfectly," said Henry, and I saw Somerset and some of the other lords smile. "And I intend to offer York and Warwick a pardon, though not Salisbury, as he fought against my own son's men."

"A pardon?"

"They must submit to me, Marguerite, and lay down their arms. It is only right to offer them one, in any case." He smiled, and for a moment his smile was as near to a cynical one as I had ever seen my husband manage. "Whether they take it is another matter. But at least it cannot be said that it was not offered."

They did, of course, shun Henry's generous pardon. Pursued by our army, they went into Tewkesbury and would have continued going south had not we forced them into Wales. I say "we," but I was back at Worcester with my household men, prepared for anything from total victory to utter defeat.

Yet I was not prepared for the news that Somerset brought me late on the evening of October 13, 1459. "We have experienced a difficulty, your grace."

"For God's sake, Hal, don't speak in riddles! What is it?"

"Namely, the lack of an enemy. The noble Duke of York and his kinsmen ran off when we were by Ludlow."

"*Ran off?*"

Somerset nodded. "Oh, York and his cronies started out well, putting up fortifications, setting out guns and traps—all very impressive. But there were some problems, namely, that a lot of the men from Calais hadn't realized that they would be fighting against the king. I must give myself credit here, for I sent a messenger to old Andrew Trollope, reminding him of his years of faithful service to my father at Calais and asking him if he could reconcile his conscience to fighting against the king and his old master's sons. When darkness fell I got my answer: Trollope and dozens of his men from the Calais garrison, deserting York for the king."

"Oh, Hal!" I hugged him.

"It gets better. When York and the rest got wind of their men's discontent, they began dragging out men to swear that the king was dead, so he couldn't give out the pardons he had promised. They even trotted out a priest to pray for his soul! The men didn't find this particularly convincing, and soon we got a whole new batch of deserters, sneaking away throughout the night. And then York and his kin gave up. Everyone was lined up, ready for battle in the morning, and York and the others said that they were going to go refresh themselves. They're still apparently refreshing themselves, for they never came back. When dawn broke, their men realized there was no one left to lead them. Not York, not Salisbury, not Warwick, not York's sons the Earl of March and the Earl of Rutland. All flown, save for the Duchess of York and the younger York children."

"He left his duchess there to take her chances? The knave!"

"Yes, but she was unharmed. Buckingham had her and the children escorted out of the town. They'll stay with his wife, I suppose." The Duchess of Buckingham was an older sister of the Duchess of York.

I sensed there was something Somerset was not telling me. "I hope there were no—outrages."

"Against the duchess? No, except for her goods. Against the townspeople, well—some of the men did get out of control. Some were sore at being deprived of a fight, and some, I suppose, were angry about Blore Heath. They pillaged Ludlow Castle and the town, with all that entails."

"There was rape, in other words."

"Yes. But not much. Don't look at me that way, your grace. I don't condone that in my men. The king and the rest of us did get things under control fairly quickly, but it's a large army. Their discovery of the ale and wine stored at Ludlow Castle didn't improve matters."

I sighed. But I could not put aside my joy at York's ignominious departure. "Where have they gone?"

"Who knows? My guess is that some will go to Ireland, others to Calais. And I shall be going to Calais myself, did you know? With Trollope; he has all sorts of useful ideas." He snickered. "Trollope. Father once told me not to consort with trollops, you know."

"You will have to explain that to me, I'm afraid."

"By and by. We'll get the task of driving Warwick out from Calais if he flees there. It will be a pleasure." He paused. "I rather wish I could take Joan there with me, but it wouldn't do, not until I get myself well settled in. She can't rough it; she's with child."

"Hal! Yours?"

"Who else?"

I felt a twinge of envy that I decided would not bear very close analysis. "You will be an excellent father, I am sure. I trust Joan is in good health?"

Hal smiled. "It's kind of you to say that. Yes, she's doing well, and is busy making baby things. It's a slow process, I fear. Joan isn't much of a needle-woman." He paused. "She has other abilities, of course."

"Which I don't want to hear about."

"I was referring, your grace, merely to the excellence of her cooking. Every time I visit her for an extended period I come out heavier."

"I deserved that," I admitted.

As it happened, York and his second son, the Earl of Rutland, fled to Ireland, where York was still governor in name; Warwick, Salisbury, and York's oldest son, the Earl of March, were in Calais. We knew we had not seen the last of them, though it was certainly our hope that we had.

In November, Parliament met at Coventry. Foremost on its agenda was the attainder of York and his confederates. Their wives' jointures were spared, Henry not being the sort of man who would make a woman suffer for the sins of her husband.

The chief sinner's wife, the Duchess of York, arrived at Coventry in December, accompanied by her three youngest children. Cecily looked as soignée as ever, and I thought rather uncharitably that she was bearing up fairly well under her husband's exile. "I hope you are comfortable with your sister the Duchess of Buckingham, my lady?"

"I have no complaints, your grace, though our relations do become a bit strained at times."

Fancy that, I thought, remembering the scar from St. Albans that the Duke of Buckingham bore. "I daresay. I understand there is something you wished to speak to me about? As one woman to another, I will help you in any way I can if it is within my power. But I do not believe I have met your children, my lady."

"These are Margaret, George, and Richard." The duchess indicated a tall girl of about thirteen, a tall boy of about ten, and a shortish boy of around seven. Only the youngest boy favored the Duke of York in appearance, though he lacked the distinguishing scowl the duke usually bore in my presence. "They are missing their father," she added, and the children put on suitably woebegone looks.

"I am sorry to hear that, but it is quite beyond my power to influence the king in his favor. His council is quite adamant against the duke too, I fear."

"But Mother says that your grace controls the council," put in George. Margaret gave a half-suppressed groan, and Richard, who seemed an unusually sharp lad, cocked his head up at his older brother with interest to see what became of his faux pas.

"I merely said that I believed that the king much respected your grace's opinion," Cecily said with admirable quickness. "As all men should respect their wives' opinions."

"No, you said to our aunt when you had that fight the other day—"

"Perhaps your grace would give my daughter permission to take my sons out?"

"Of course," I said, and Margaret hustled the offending George away, trailed by Richard. "Odd what children get into their heads, isn't it?"

"Odd indeed," agreed the duchess. For the first time she looked ill at ease, probably wondering if the sharp-eared George would make a reappearance. "I will come to the point, if I may. With my husband being attainted, I have been left with no means of support, and a jointure has not been provided for me. I would ask that your grace help me in my petition to the king that I be granted an adequate income to support myself and my three children here. Without it we are nothing but a burden upon my sister and the Duke of Buckingham."

"What sum do you need?"

"A thousand marks would be adequate."

And York had called me extravagant? But I supposed that for the duchess this was a rather modest income. "I shall recommend it to the king."

"I thank you," said Cecily. She looked genuinely grateful, even humble. Probably she had thought that George's indiscretion had doomed her request, but I could feel for a sister woman, then and now, and took no pleasure in seeing her and her children, even loud-mouthed George, suffer for York's presumptuousness. Who knows? Perhaps when everything changed, she put in a word of kindness for me.

All in all, though, I rather doubt it.

It is one of the sadder ironies of my existence that when the day came that I needed the Earl of Warwick's services as a fighter, he failed miserably. When he was fighting against me in 1460, he seemed invincible.

Hal, having managed to establish himself at Guînes, could make no headway against his garrison at Calais, and his situation became even more desperate when the fleet we had assembled at Sandwich was seized by Warwick's men, who captured poor Lord Rivers and the Duchess of Bedford as well and hauled them to Calais as prisoners. Doggedly assaulting Calais nearly every day, Hal succeeded in April in engaging Warwick's forces in combat at Newenham Bridge—and had to retreat. Short of men and funds, by the summer he was barely holding on to Guînes. Exeter, in charge of the seas at last, lost the chance to intercept Warwick, traveling between Ireland and Calais, because he could not be certain that his own unpaid men would be loyal. Even my old family friend Pierre de Brézé, whom I secretly begged for aid in seizing Warwick, was unable to capture his ship.

When not making the lives of my friends miserable, Warwick was plotting with York. In June 1460, the news we had been anticipating finally came: Warwick, Salisbury, and March had arrived back in England, minus the Duke of York. "He is making the others do his filthy work for him," I said when I heard the news. "As ever."

"May I tell your grace how tired of all of this I am?" Buckingham asked as we strolled outside together. He had been attending a council meeting with Henry at Coventry, where I was staying also. As Henry had been exceptionally nervous over the last few days, I had taken the opportunity of catching Buckingham alone to press him for details.

"Yes, you may."

"I can tell you this also: when we confront him, there will be no negotiation at this point, and he will not escape." Buckingham tightened his fist. "I have come to the conclusion that all of York and Warwick's high-flown language about their loyalty and their plaints about their grievances come to one point: York wants the crown."

"Well, I have been thinking that for years," I snapped. "If only someone had listened to me."

Buckingham's careworn face brightened into a faint smile. "We men underestimate your sex, I sometimes think," he admitted.

"Do you think he wants to depose the king?"

"I don't know if he has the ba—er, the nerve for that. No, your grace, I fear that he wants to be named as the king's rightful heir, in place of the Prince of Wales, who they are saying is a—Well, your grace must have heard the rumors."

I nodded. This year there had been a fresh spate of gossip about the parentage of my son. The rumors were even spreading abroad. "Soon I shall have a truly international reputation as a great whore. I do not believe there is a man at Henry's court I have not been said to have lain with, with the exception of Henry himself, of course." I blinked back my tears. "I can bear those rumors for myself, but they hurt Henry so deeply."

"No one here believes them."

"But everyone else does."

Buckingham did not deny it. After a silence for a while, I said, "So Henry is moving to Northampton?"

"Yes, and summoning troops to meet him there. We will be ready for Warwick and the rest if they attack, which I have no doubt they will. Nonetheless, I will warn your grace now: if it should go ill for us, you would be well advised to flee with your son."

"Where?"

"The Earl of Pembroke's estates in Wales."

I nodded. "I will remember that." Impulsively, I put out my hand. "My lord, I have not always valued you as I ought to have. Forgive me for that. I know now that you have been one of Henry's truest friends."

"He is lucky in his queen. I have not always fully realized that myself."

We smiled at each other. No doubt, I thought later, someone would soon be adding poor Buckingham to my list of lovers.

Henry set out for Northampton the next day, looking pale and distracted. "My dear, take care of yourself," he said, kissing me tenderly and quite at length. "You know our token. Do not come to me unless it is given to you."

I nodded. Following Blore Heath, Henry and I, concerned that we might be separated, had devised a code known only to the two of us. I and our son would not come to him unless the messenger asked for Daisy. "I love you, Henry," I said, hugging him close to me. "I will pray for you constantly."

"And I love you, my dear. There is no need to tell you that I will pray for you too." Henry bent and smiled at six-year-old Edward. "God bless you, my boy."

"I wish I could come with you," Edward said. "When do I get to see a battle?"

Henry's face turned gloomy again.

"Not for a good long time yet," I said firmly. "You have much to learn. And when these traitors are subdued, there will be no need for it anyway."

This time, it was Edward's turn to look gloomy as I gave Henry one last kiss good-bye.

Midway through July, I was sewing in my chamber when Katherine Vaux came in, her face ashen. "William is back."

There was no need to guess what had happened when William, limping, followed his wife through the door. Everything on his face bode ill. I forced myself to stand up straighter. "We lost."

"Yes." William swayed on his feet, and I quickly motioned him to a stool as Katherine sat beside him and put her arm around him. "Badly. The king is in the hands of Warwick and his men. My lord of Buckingham, the Earl of Shrewsbury, Lord Egremont, and Lord Beaumont are all dead. They died fighting in front of the king's tent."

I crammed my fist into my mouth and bit my knuckle.

"Grey of Ruthin ought to be dead, but he is not. He deserted to Warwick. It was planned ahead of time; it had to have been. Warwick's men did nothing against Grey's. We began to suspect something when Warwick's men refused to fight his men, even though they were in the vanguard. And then Grey's men actually began to help Warwick's men over the trenches! It was lost after that, for we had been outnumbered from the start, and when Grey's men turned on us, it was over in minutes. Buckingham and the other lords surrounded the king's tent, trying to protect him, and were all cut down." William crossed himself. His voice broke. "We had guns, but it started raining just as Warwick and his lot attacked, so they were useless. Nothing went right."

"William, tell me about Henry," I said.

William composed himself. "I am sorry, my lady. When I think of Grey's treachery, and poor Buckingham dying after having been loyal to us for so long…Well, the Earl of March, Warwick, and the rest knelt to the king and told him that they were his loyal subjects. I didn't see the sight myself; I was one of the lucky ones who escaped. Many didn't; they drowned in the river. I'd have been dead if I hadn't got away. Warwick gave the order to spare the common soldiers but to slay the lords, knights, and squires." He caressed Katherine's cheek. "I came very close to making you a widow, my love."

They clung together. I let them do so for a couple of minutes. Then I said, "We have to get out of here. Buckingham said that we should, and I shall take his advice, God rest his soul, for this last time."

Three hours later, six of us, including my son and the Vauxes, were riding away from Eccleshall. Gone were the tall hennins Katherine and I fancied; we were dressed in the simplest clothes we owned, as were the men and Edward.

No one spotting our party at a distance would have taken us for a queen and her entourage. Only the very good quality of our horses and saddles might make for suspicion, and I could only pray that the men in my party could deal with that sort of situation as it arose.

We made good time, stopping only once to rest the horses and—in my case and Katherine's—to rearrange the jewels that were tucked into our bosoms for safekeeping. By dusk, we were just outside of Malpas. "I know of no one here who would put us up," I said regretfully as our horses took a long drink and we stretched. "But there are plenty of inns, and Lord knows we have plenty of money with us." In addition to what Katherine and I were toting around in our bosoms and in our saddlebags, the men had sizable amounts of gold on them as well.

"Don't be so sure of that."

I turned to stare at John Cleger, Edward's groom. He had been particularly eager to be of help to us on our flight. "Whatever do you mean?"

"I mean"—he pulled out a dagger and yanked my son against him—"if you value your boy's life, you'll hand me those jewels inside your breast. Lady Vaux's too."

"Are you mad?"

"No. I'm poor, and I expect that if I stay in your service I'll be poorer yet now that the king's a captive. So instead, I intend to be richer, starting now. Hand them over, your grace. The rest of you, don't even think of moving against me, or I'll cut the boy's throat. And that would put a crimp in your plans, wouldn't it?"

Katherine Vaux let out a string of curses in French, so quickly and fluently that even I did not understand entirely what she was saying. Cleger simply laughed. "For God's sake, stop that noise! I'll be glad to be done with you lot of Frenchwomen as well."

"Hand your jewels over, Katherine," I said. "William, put away that dagger. You too," I said to my groom and to fourteen-year-old John Coombe, one of my pages. "We're better off without the whoreson."

Katherine, trembling with rage, reached inside her bosom and began pulling out jewels as I did the same. Katherine, who was rather well endowed, was still retrieving jewels when I was finished. Even Cleger seemed surprised at the quantity. "Take them, you knave!"

Still holding Edward, Cleger stuffed the jewels in the saddlebags of the horse he had been riding. Then he shoved my boy aside and mounted. Tipping his hat in a mock salute, he galloped off.

My three remaining men turned in unison toward their own horses. "What are you doing?"

"Your grace, we can catch the whoreson! And kill him as the faithless knave deserves."

"No! It would waste time, and killing him might call attention to us. We must move on."

Edward, who had seemed more puzzled than scared throughout the proceedings, tugged at my hand as the men reluctantly obeyed. "Mama? Can we go find an inn?"

"Indeed we shall," I promised, stroking his hair. Then I snorted. "*Malpas.* The very name sounds troublesome. I should have known. Katherine!"

Katherine had sunk to her knees and was retching. As William and I both bent to help her, she whispered, "It is all right," then smiled and with our assistance rose shakily to her feet, patting her belly. "I suppose this is not the best time to announce this, but I am with child."

William turned as white as Katherine as I gave way to gales of nervous laughter.

"And look!" Katherine put her hand daintily inside her bosom, then flourished a large ruby in the air. "There's still some treasure left where that came from."

With me riding behind John, Edward riding behind my groom, and the Vauxes riding together—William holding on to Katherine like a fragile object—we finally made our way to Harlech Castle. I knew its constable, David ap Eynon, to be loyal to the Earl of Pembroke, and he did not fail me. Safe inside its mighty walls, erected by the equally mighty Edward I, I could plan what to do next.

Cleger, the rat, must have made his vile way to Warwick and his men, for a couple of weeks after I arrived at Harlech, messengers began to arrive from that scoundrel, all promising me and my son the best of treatment if I would come to London. Desperate as I was for news of Henry and the lords who were my friends, I sent the messengers away unheard and unanswered, for none bore Henry's special token.

Then, in September, Henry Holland, the Duke of Exeter, appeared at Harlech Castle. He was thirty now, as was I; it was strange to look at him and think back on the time when we each had been fifteen. "I have come to be of what help I can, your grace," he said, with none of his old sullenness. "God knows that I have been a hindrance in the past, but I hope I can do you good service."

"I know you can. But first, what has gone on?"

"I suppose you heard the Tower had been under siege?" I nodded. "It surrendered shortly after Northampton. Lord Scales, who was in charge of the garrison, had no real choice. They were running short on food, and the Tower was full of ladies—my wife included—who had decided to take shelter there. They didn't leave much for the garrison, and the ladies were a nervous lot as well, which made things even worse. So Scales surrendered, and was allowed to leave—but then his barge was attacked by a mob. The Londoners were upset with him because he had been bombarding the city from the Tower. They killed him, stripped him naked, and dumped his body at a church in Southwark."

"Christ," I whispered.

"Warwick then executed some of my own men who had been in the Tower. Hanged, drawn, and quartered."

That was the horrible death reserved for traitors. "But they were fighting for the king!"

"That's nothing to Warwick. He's power-mad. Somerset in Guînes had to surrender to him also. The king—that is, Warwick—issued an order for him to give it up, and he had no hope of holding out longer if he had refused. He and Warwick came to terms and kissed."

"Oh, poor Hal! That must have been agonizing for him."

Exeter, perhaps not as sympathetic toward Hal's sensibilities as I, raised an eyebrow but went on. "Somerset went into France. King Charles is sheltering him; he was impressed with his actions at Guînes. I have been in communication with him; he is ready to sail to his castle at Corfe when the time is right. And I believe the time will soon be right. The Duke of York is expected back from Ireland any day. He may be here in England already, in fact."

I shivered, then asked the question that I had been most wanting, and most dreading, to ask. "And Henry?"

"I have not seen him, of course—his household has been swept almost clean of all his own men, so access to him is controlled by Warwick's creatures. The king went to pilgrimage to Canterbury in August; he even hunts. But the few of our friends who have seen him say he is like a man in a daze. They believe that the deaths of Buckingham and the others, and his worry about you and the Prince of Wales, have shattered him."

I put my head in my hands and began to weep as Exeter gingerly held me. "I will do anything in my power to help you," he said quietly after I had calmed. "Just give me the word."

"Good," I said. "Then you must help me raise an army. We need Henry out of these men's hands."

⁂

As Exeter and I began our task, York finally returned to England and began to move slowly toward London, his arrogance and presumption growing with every step he took. He'd sent for his duchess to join him, and Cecily was borne into her husband's presence seated in a splendid chariot, covered in blue velvet.

If Cecily was traveling in fine state, her husband had decided it was time to travel in royal state. At Abingdon, he sent for trumpeters to accompany him on his progress toward London, and the banners he unfurled bore the royal arms. He even ordered that the sword of state be carried before him. When he reached Westminster, he forced Henry out of his own chambers and into mine.

And then, on that same day, October 10, 1460, York walked into Parliament and put his filthy hand on the throne.

York's gesture did not received the rapturous assent that he had expected. Instead, the lords had looked on in shocked silence until the Archbishop of Canterbury pricked up the courage to ask York if he wished to see the king. York had made a belligerent reply to the effect that it was York the king should be seeking to see and had stalked out of the chamber and into the rooms he'd commandeered from Henry. York was still polluting Henry's chambers while the lords discussed this new state of affairs.

Warwick and his men had not come to England alone. With them they brought a papal legate, Francesco Coppini, the Bishop of Terni, with whom they had thoroughly ingratiated themselves. At Northampton, he had been supposedly negotiating between the two sides, but poor Buckingham, recognizing that Coppini was no more than Warwick's tool, had ignored his overtures. It was even rumored that he had excommunicated everyone who had supported Henry at Northampton, and I for one did not doubt the rumor. Naturally, the good bishop had followed his new friends to Westminster, and it was from one of his subordinates, the friar Lorenzo de Florencia, that I had heard of York's attempt to claim the throne.

The reply I had made to this piece of news really will not bear repeating.

November was about a week old when Lorenzo de Florencia appeared at Harlech again. "Your grace," he said, speaking in French, "we have reached a settlement."

"Oh?"

"The king—"

"King Henry, I trust? Or is York calling himself King Richard now?"

"King Henry," said Florencia, with a look that suggested that he was beginning to wish he was back in his city of origin.

"Well, that is something. Tell me about it, then."

"The king shall keep his crown, and reign the rest of his natural life."

"And then?"

"And then upon his death, the crown shall pass to the Duke of York, and then subsequently to York's heirs."

"So you are telling me that our son is disinherited."

"I am telling your grace that King Henry has accepted that the Duke of York has a superior claim to the throne than King Henry himself, and that in order to preserve peace, he has agreed to this compromise. You see, your grace, York's lawyers have made a persuasive case. King Henry's grandfather, the fourth Henry, had an inferior claim to the throne. When he took the throne from the second Richard—"

"Damn the lawyers, and damn the second Richard, and damn the Duke of York and his heirs! The fourth Henry was accepted as king, and his house has held the throne for sixty years!" I leaned into Florencia and shook my finger in his face. "Where were these lawyers when the fifth Henry was conquering France? Where were they when the Duke of York was accepting favors from the king he now claims has no valid title to the throne? I am no naïve fool. I know my husband has been ill, and I know that he will be never be the king his late father was. But I know he is an anointed king and that he has expected his son to reign after him. If he agreed to this—this travesty—it was under duress. Has his life been threatened? Has my own life been threatened?" I stood back. "That is it, isn't? York's men have told Henry that if he does not agree to this farce, I and our son will be killed. That is the one thing that would make him agree to disinherit Edward."

"Your grace, there has been nothing of the sort! You talk too wildly, too passionately. Your husband did not agree to this out of fear, but out of his love for peace and his affection toward his dear cousin, the Duke of York."

"Oh? Tell me what else he agreed to."

"The Duke of York and his eldest two sons are to have ten thousand marks a year in land, apportioned among them—"

"Nothing for the two youngest sons? Well, no doubt their snouts will be at the trough when they are a little older. Pray tell, from where is this land to come?"

Florencia ran his tongue over his teeth. "Well, your grace, it must naturally come from your son's lands, as he is no longer the heir to the throne. But he might be allowed to succeed to the duchy of Lancaster."

"So my son will not be king, but at best the Duke of Lancaster?"

"Yes. A perfectly respectable title, held by no less than the great John of Gaunt, after all." Florencia paused in case I wanted to say something, but I simply stared at him. "Your grace, the Bishop of Terni—and I am certain, the king and the Duke of York also—would be greatly pleased if you and your son would accompany me to Westminster, and show yourselves to be in harmony with this agreement. I have given you all of its salient points. I fully realize that the settlement is not entirely palatable to your grace, but your grace must understand that the lords and the king found this agreement to be necessary to the peace of the realm—"

"The peace of the realm be damned. You tell the Duke of York that." Once more, I leaned into the unfortunate friar. "I will not let my son be disinherited by a terrified man, a greedy duke, and a pack of cowards. Who sat in this puppet Parliament, anyway? Not the noble Duke of Buckingham, murdered by your Duke of York's followers as your good bishop stood by and yawned. Not the Duke of Somerset, one of the bravest men I know. Not the Duke of Exeter. And my husband to rule the rest of his natural life! How long a natural life do you think he will be allowed to have, with York and two grown sons waiting for him to die?"

"Upon my word! I assure your grace the Duke of York would never let any harm come to King Henry!"

"No, not if he can get Warwick to do his filthy work for him, like he did at St. Albans and at Northampton. But I have no intent of prolonging this conversation. You can take this message back to your Duke of York and that creature in a bishop's miter you serve: I am not friendless or helpless, and I will not see my son deprived of his birthright without a fight."

"So you will not accompany me to Westminster?"

"I would as soon journey to hell."

"You do not even have a message for your husband?"

"You tell my husband that I love him dearly and that I pray for him daily. You tell the Duke of York I will see him soon." I spat out the next word. "Dead."

Part III

Lady of War

15

Margaret
December 1460 to March 1461

I LIKE TRAVELING BY WATER," EDWARD PRONOUNCED AS HE LEANED OVER THE side of the ship while two of my servants kept a firm grasp on him. "Seasickness is for women."

"It certainly is," I agreed, willing my food to stay down. It had been fifteen years since I had been to sea, and it had not improved in my absence. "But there is really no need to boast about it."

Edward—always a loving boy, God bless him!—obediently put on a humble expression, and I laughed and tousled his hair. "At least we have one sailor in the family."

My son and I were taking ship to Scotland, where I planned to meet with that nation's queen mother, Mary of Gueldres. Her husband, James II, had died just months before while besieging Roxborough, leaving his eight-year-old son, James III, king. Unlike me, Mary had been named regent during her son's minority; also unlike me, she had three more healthy sons and two daughters. I was making my trip on the advice of Somerset, now in England, He and Exeter and others were raising an army to oppose the Duke of York. Any help we could get from the Scots, Hal had told me, would be much desirable. And while I was there, could I pick up a recipe for their biscuits for Joan, as they were said to be delicious?

I smiled, as I could not help doing when I thought of Somerset, and for a moment even my thoughts of seasickness disappeared.

Mary of Gueldres was several years younger than me and, I am sorry to say, far more pleasing in her person, even when she was dressed in widow's weeds. A worry line had begun to etch its way between my eyes, and I had begun fasting once a week in a desperate attempt to get some heavenly help on my side. As a result, I had become too thin, whereas Mary's six pregnancies had left her pleasingly plump and with an ineffable glow of self-satisfaction that was not much dimmed by her recent bereavement. This was irritating, as was the perpetual chilliness of Lincluden Abbey, where I was staying in early January 1461. Since coming to Scotland I had developed a permanent sniffle. "You'll get used to it, my dear!" Mary said, snuggling herself more deeply in her fur-lined cloak that reminded me painfully of the fine clothes I'd left behind me in my flight. "It was hard for me coming here from Burgundy, trust me. Now, do you really have hopes of defeating the Duke of York?"

"I have some of the finest men in England bringing troops to the North. All I ask from Scotland now is that hostilities at the border cease so that my men in the North can feel free to leave their lands and fight for me. When the Duke of York is defeated, then perhaps we can make a permanent peace."

"But what can you offer in the meantime?"

It was irritating as well to realize that for all she reminded me of a pampered lap dog, Mary of Gueldres was not the slightest bit stupid. "I am offering to make one of your daughters my son's bride."

Mary batted her eyelashes, a gesture wasted on me but perhaps one that had worked with the men who had made her regent. It was a trick, I thought sourly, that I should have tried myself on the lords after poor Henry went mad. "That hardly seems enough, my dear, given that his position is so uncertain at present."

"Well, then, what were you thinking?"

"Berwick would be nice," Mary said sweetly.

I winced. "It has been in English hands since 1333."

"Oh, yes. Which is why we miss it so much." Mary studied her nails. They were beautifully shaped; mine, which I bit from time to time out of tension, were scraggly.

"I do not think the English will countenance its being ceded." I had a certain gift for understatement.

Mary shrugged. "Yet it might be necessary for your husband to recover his throne. It depends, I suppose, on how badly you want it."

I was in the midst of formulating a reply, other than the slap on Queen Mary's smug face I longed to deal out, when a knock came and a servant obeyed Mary's answer to come in. "Your grace, a man is here for Queen Margaret from the Duke of Somerset. He says that it is most urgent."

"Then by all means allow him to come in." Mary rose and shook out her skirts. "I will leave you to discuss your business in private."

Somerset's man did not so much as bend to me as to drop before me, so exhausted did he appear, but he was smiling when he held out an object. "Your grace, my lord asks that you and the Prince of Wales travel to York, where he shall be waiting for you. And he has sent you this with his compliments, your grace."

I stared at the cloth he slowly unfolded. It was blue and murrey and bore a familiar emblem: a falcon within a fetterlock. It was also stained with blood. "This means—"

"Yes, your grace. The Duke of York has been slain. He met his death on the next to last day of December, just outside of Wakefield."

At York, Somerset and Exeter and a number of other lords were waiting for Edward and me at Micklegate Bar. I was about to accept assistance off my horse when Somerset stopped my page. "Wait, your grace, you'll have a better view from your horse. Look at the top of the gate."

I craned my neck upward obediently. Perched upon Micklegate were three human heads. "Here on the left, madam, you see the Earl of Salisbury," Hal said cheerfully, pointing with a flourish. "And here on the right, madam, you see the Earl of Rutland. And here in the center, madam, you see the noble Duke of York. Wearing the crown he so deeply desired, you see. We felt that it was only proper to give one to him, albeit made of paper."

My lips curved into a smile, and if you think that wrong of me, remember that these were the men who had schemed to deprive my son of his crown and who would have surely shortened my husband's life so that York and his descendants could sit upon the throne sooner rather than later. "How can I thank you?"

"It is Somerset your grace must thank," said Exeter with some reluctance. "He was chiefly responsible for winning the fight."

"No," said Somerset. "It is Andrew Trollope your grace must thank." He grasped the shoulder of the man twice his age who stood next to him. "York got wind of our movements toward the North and marched here himself, leaving Warwick in London and sending the Earl of March to Wales. He didn't bring that many men with him, and thanks to Trollope here, we deprived him of quite a few of them near Worksop. But they were his advance guard, so York was able to press on to his castle at Sandal, where he holed up and celebrated Christmas. And as we had all arrived here, we decided to make it his last one." Somerset took his sword and drew a sketch in the snow that blanketed the ground. "See? Here's Sandal Castle—notice the little turrets, if you please—and here we are, all round."

"How on earth did you lure him out?"

"Well, to a large extent, it was pure luck. They were getting hungry in Sandal Castle, and they really hadn't bargained on having so many of us in the area. They sent out a foraging party, and Trollope suggested that we seize our opportunity and attack it. York got wind of this—I do believe he spotted our forces and thought that some of us were men coming to relieve him—and rode out. And by the time he realized how outnumbered he was, it was too late. He put up a fight before we dispatched him, I'll grant him that. None of us can personally can take credit for his death, I'm sorry to say. It was a group of Devonshire men who took him out."

"Good work," I said grimly. I nodded upward in the direction of Rutland's seventeen-year-old head. "Did Rutland die beside him?"

"That was my work," Lord Clifford put in. "He fought well, I'll say, but when his father fell, the rout began, and I caught him on Wakefield Bridge, trying to flee. He's young, I know, but we had the same orders that Warwick gave at Northampton, my lady. Go for the lords. He'd have killed me if our positions were reversed, I know it."

"As York's son, he could hardly expect otherwise," I said, trying not to think of the small boy who'd peeped at me at Rouen when I'd stopped there on my way to England. "You did right. And Salisbury?"

"Him we captured and sent to Pontefract. We would have held him for ransom, as he would have been a profitable hostage for us, but unfortunately for him he's not popular in the area. The people mobbed him and beheaded him. And so there you have them: the Unholy Trinity. Though I'd sacrifice that epigram to have Warwick's head perched up alongside the others. The Foul Four would have been pleasantly alliterative."

I dismounted and embraced each of the men in turn. "You have served me well, and I heartily thank you." I turned to Trollope. "You should be knighted, but I would rather have it done in my husband's presence."

Trollope bowed. "Then I will be most honored to wait."

"And I do have a good bit of news—though it pales beside this." I tilted my head in the direction of York's and smiled. "Queen Mary and her council have agreed to a truce while we head south, and to further negotiations once we recover the king. Before the news arrived, she thought we were well and truly desperate—that she could get me to cede Berwick. The audacity!" I laughed.

"You have never seen a woman's face change so much as when I told her York was dead. Why, what is it, my dear?"

Edward had been staring up in fascination at the heads. "Mother, won't they blow down?"

"If they do, we will put them right back up," I promised him. For the first time, I noticed the sharp wind that was rustling York's paper crown. "Come, gentlemen, let us go inside and speak of what we are to do next."

"Can't you sleep, your grace?"

I started as Somerset, a cloak thrown over his shoulders, joined me at the bottom of Clifford's Tower at York Castle. "No."

"Neither can I. Were you about to climb up? Then it's good I'm here to help you."

He led me up the winding stairs until we finally stood at the top of the tower, where we stared down at the city of York below us. "I didn't mention it before, your grace, but I have had some disturbing news. My brother Edmund is a prisoner. I left him behind to hold Carisbrooke, and he was captured last month."

"Oh, Hal."

"It's one of the reasons I agreed to hold Salisbury for ransom, and it's one reason why I would rather have not had the Earl of Rutland killed. But Rutland was fighting, as Clifford said, and would have slain Clifford if he'd been able to, I daresay." He crossed himself, a gesture I'd seldom seen him make except during mass. "I can only hope Warwick and the Earl of March don't take revenge on Edmund."

"If Henry has any say, you know he will prevent it."

"Aye, if he has any." Hal's shoulders sagged. "But the good news is, I am a father. Joan gave birth to a healthy boy. Charles. She named him for the Count of Charolais and for your uncle Charles, who were gracious to me when I was abroad."

"And you haven't had a chance to see him."

"Joan assures me that he is the image of myself. Not that I had any doubts about the matter, but it is good to know. But I do hope I get to see the lad. I would hate to end up like Exeter, who's seen his daughter only a couple of times."

"You and the rest of the men have sacrificed a great deal, Hal. Don't think I forget it for an instant."

"You've sacrificed too, your grace." He touched my shoulder cautiously. "You're too thin, and your clothes are shabby. I don't like to see you this way."

We were standing far too close together. "Oh, it is just that I have no one but a laundress taking care of my things," I said, moving back a little.

Hal took the hint and moved back himself. "So what keeps you up at this hour?"

"Henry. I am afraid of what they might have done to him, what they still might be doing. He is so vulnerable, and there is hardly anyone there he can trust. What if they have turned him against us?"

"Don't worry. Henry might be weak but as long as he has some degree of sanity, I don't think he could ever be turned against you."

"And that is what frightens me. What if he has lost his sanity again? Or is in danger of losing it? I think sometimes I would almost rather see the crown on the head of York's son than to see Henry in that state again. And then I start to doubt myself."

"You mustn't. How could his resigning the crown that his father and his grandfather wore possibly help his state of mind? It would wrack him with guilt, more likely, and might well topple him over the edge. Don't worry. Being reunited with you is bound to improve his state of mind, whatever that is."

"Thank you, Hal. That does make me feel better." Without consciously intending it, we had stepped close to each other again. "I am getting very cold. I should go inside."

"Yes." Hal moved even closer to me.

"You have done so much for Henry and me over these past weeks. I do not know if I properly expressed my gratitude for what you did at Wakefield."

"I wish I had been the one to have slain York for you."

"It hardly matters as long as he is dead."

"It matters very much to me." Hal moved so close to me that I could feel his breath come and go.

My heart began to pound. "I had best go now. Edward will be wondering where I am," I said lamely.

"He's sound asleep." Hal brushed my cheek with his fingers, then tipped my chin upward. "I want to serve you, my lady," he said softly. "In every possible way."

Was he about to kiss me? I stepped sharply back. "I must leave now."

Somerset half suppressed a sigh. He took my arm almost roughly to guide me toward the steps, then stopped and took the cloak off his back and gently draped it over me. "Wear this. You're shivering, your grace."

The lords and I met the next morning. Hal and I sat far apart and acted so jumpy whenever we came within two feet of each other that the others must surely have thought that we were guilty of the sin we had managed not to commit—if that was indeed what we had been on the verge of doing. Was I misreading Hal's actions, perhaps? The casual flirtations that were part of some other courts had never been a part of Henry's, and my youth and rank had sheltered me from such attentions when I was at my father's court. Had Somerset's behavior been no more than the innocent gallantry of a young man toward his queen?

I had more pressing matters to occupy my mind, however, than my encounter with Hal: our course of action following our victory. My men and I decided to waste no time in marching southward to London. This time, I did not stay behind. Instead, Edward and I rode at the front of our army, flanked by the Duke of Somerset on one side and the Duke of Exeter on the other. All of the leaders, including me, wore the badge of my son the Prince of Wales: a bend of crimson and black with ostrich feathers. There were twenty thousand men with me—and with Henry in spirit, even though he was in the hands of his enemies, being marched north by them even as we were marching south.

A swarm of locusts, a band of savages, a pack of demons—those were the names that the Yorkists have used to describe the brave men who made up my army. They are said to have snatched nuns from their prayers in order to rape them and pregnant women from their childbed in order to rob them, to have slaughtered monks and priests who tried to protect their abbeys and churches and chapels. What lies the House of York tells! Of course the men helped themselves to food and drink; they had to in order to eat as they moved south in the freezing winter. But to think that I would countenance the dishonor of my sister women, or that I would dare to affront the Lord when I needed his help most, is to paint me not only as heartless but as quite stupid. If I was that, it was in showing too much mercy when—But I anticipate myself.

I slept in abbeys when I could during our march; when I could not, I slept in a tent, accompanied only by the Countess of Devon, who was my bastard cousin Marie—pregnant Katherine had stayed behind in Scotland—and a couple of servants. It hardly mattered where I lay at night: after hours in the saddle, with my face being buffeted by the winds for hours on end, I slept like the dead when I at last took to my cot.

"Your grace? Forgive us for intruding, but you must hear this."

I blinked foggily and gathered my blankets closer around me as the Duke of Somerset and the Duke of Exeter, scarcely less presentable than I, barged into my tent just after dawn one February morning. "What is it?"

"Bad news, your grace," said Exeter. "The Earl of March encountered the Earl of Pembroke and the Earl of Wiltshire in Wales, at a place called Mortimer's Cross, and was victorious."

"That boy?" The Earl of March, York's heir, was not yet nineteen.

Somerset nodded grimly. "Either he's damn lucky or damn skilled. I'd like to think it was the former, but it might be the latter. Anyway, Pembroke and Wiltshire escaped, but old Owen Tudor was executed at Hereford on March's orders."

I gasped. Owen Tudor had been Queen Katherine of Valois's second husband; he was Henry's stepfather, of whom Henry was fond. To execute him instead of simply imprisoning him could be nothing more than an act of spite directed at Henry himself. "The whoreson!"

"That's the politest thing I can think to say about him," said Somerset.

"Poor Tudor thought until the last moment that he would be spared, being so closely connected to the king," Exeter added. "When they ripped off his collar to bare his neck for the ax, they said that he looked shocked. But he plucked up his spirit and said that the head that was to lie on the stock had once lain on Queen Catherine's lap, and then he said his prayers as calmly as if he were in his own chapel. It was a gallant death."

"And a gallant life," I said. "How many miles did we cover yesterday?"

"Thirty or so."

"Let us do better today, in brave Owen Tudor's memory. Come, gentlemen. Leave so I can dress."

With the shameful act of Owen Tudor's execution spurring us on, we continued to push southward. Warwick, we heard, had stationed himself—irony of ironies—at St. Albans, while the Earl of March appeared to still be in Wales. Why he tarried there, I have no idea; perhaps Warwick in his arrogance assumed that the young earl would not be needed.

At Dunstable, we handily overcame a few hundred men who had been posted there by Warwick. Most, fortunately for their own sakes, simply ran off, terrified by our sheer numbers. Our only casualty was a fine gilt-painted swan badge that Trollope wore; during the pursuit it fell off, never to be seen again.

We rested for a couple of hours at Dunstable, then pushed on to St. Albans via the old Roman road of Watling Street, the moon lighting our way through the darkness. It was our hope to arrive by the city late at night and to take Warwick's men by surprise at dawn. Tired as I was, I was in no danger of falling asleep: the wind biting into my cheeks and making my eyes tear kept me wide awake.

Somerset, riding beside me and clearly preoccupied with his own thoughts, roused himself to look at me as I drew my cloak closer around me in a vain attempt to warm myself. "We can get you into the litter beside the Prince of Wales, your grace," he said in the excessively formal way we had spoken to each other since our encounter at York. "You'd be a little warmer that way."

"I am fine," I said, willing my teeth not to chatter.

"You look utterly frozen. I wish you had taken our advice and stayed at Dunstable."

"But I did not want to take your advice," I said frostily—aptly enough under the circumstances. "I told you, I want Henry to know that Edward and I are there waiting for him, and to know that we are fighting for him."

"I would think you have proven that quite adequately." Somerset glanced at Trollope, who was in conversation with Lord Clifford, and at Exeter, who was talking to his bastard brothers. Satisfied that he would not be overheard, he said, "Your grace, is it my folly the other night that is driving you to forsake a comfortable, safe place to stay in order to prove your devotion to your husband? For if it is, please allow me to have you escorted back to Dunstable. You are guiltless and have nothing to atone for by putting yourself at risk."

So I had not misinterpreted Hal's behavior. I laughed nervously. "Men, always thinking their breeches are the center of the universe! No, it is not that foolishness. I simply want to be there with my husband, as I could not be at Northampton. And if the worst happens, I want to know about it on the spot, and not be left waiting in agony a dozen miles off."

"We'll do our best to make sure it doesn't come to that," Hal said a little touchily. "But since you *are* accompanying us, really against all reason in my opinion, let me stress again that you must obey our orders. We can't have you and the prince falling into the hands of Warwick."

"I will not wander into the town to look at the shops or out into the field picking posies, if that is what you are worried about."

"No. More about you picking up a sword and following us into battle. You're tough, madam."

"I think I can count on you without my aid for this particular battle," I said gently, having guessed the primary reason for Hal's preoccupation.

Somerset nodded. "Yes. I'd like to fell Warwick where he felled Father. But I'd settle for simply having him dead. And then I can stand in front of Father's tomb at last and tell him that he has been avenged."

He lapsed into silence again and we rode on into the night, the men around me ever alert for signs of an attack by Warwick's men. There was no sign of them whatsoever, though our scouts had assured us that they were camped in the town and had devoted the last several days to preparing their defenses. They even had handguns, brought by some of the mercenaries Warwick had recruited in Burgundy.

And they had Henry. What if they had somehow enticed him into putting on armor and riding at their head? My men could happily fight Warwick to the death, but would they attack their anointed king? And what must Henry be thinking, to be arrayed against an army that wore the badge of his seven-year-old son?

The sighting of the dawn breaking over the River Ver, which ordinarily would have been simply a lovely sight, brought me out of my reverie. Over the bridge lay St. Albans, and it was in those city streets that the future of England might be decided. My men conferred with a forerunner for a few minutes, and then Somerset turned to me. "Your grace, you and the Prince of Wales shall stay at St. Michael's. Remain there until you are sent for."

His voice brooked no argument, and I made none. "God keep you and lead you to victory," I said as a group of heavily armed men led me and Edward away. Not having a sword, I raised my fist. "For our king! For the Prince of Wales!"

"For our king! For our Prince of Wales!" The men's cries echoed as we went our separate directions, and my eyes filled with tears as I thought of the possibility of not seeing some of them again.

The church's priest had been informed of our coming and opened the door to us with the air of one who expected to be massacred for his pains—like everyone else in the South, I was soon to find, he had been convinced by Warwick's fear-mongering that my army intended nothing less than the destruction of the entire region and its people. Finding that my own pillaging did not extend further than asking him for some bread and ale with which Edward and I could break our fast, he brought us the food and then went out to reconnoiter with the neighbors and, no doubt, recount his narrow escape from certain death at my hands.

There was nothing to do but to wait, my apprehension not much eased by the painting of the Last Judgment that hung inside the church. I saw with my own eyes that our vanguard had to fall back to the area surrounding the church—the Yorkists, I learned later, had gained word of our presence just in time to bring their archers into the streets—but my men soon rallied and found another gap in Warwick's defenses to penetrate. After that I could hear only the distant sounds of battle in the center of town, near the abbey, and as the hours wore on I could not hear even that. I paced up and down outside the church, watching for our returning men, and when I grew tired from pacing, I prayed.

And then, at last, I saw several horsemen galloping toward St. Michael's. Could it be...? "Henry!" I shouted, almost throwing myself into the horses' path.

Henry dismounted and wrapped his arms around me as I flung myself against him. "I feel as if I were dreaming," he said wonderingly. "I thought they had taken you away from me forever, my love."

"No, no, they could never do that," I said in between my sobs.

We pulled apart at last and gazed at each other. Only in the other's eyes could either of us have been a pleasant sight. Henry looked gaunt and ten years older than when I had seen him before Northampton, and I, wearing the simplest of headdresses and dressed in a gown that was none too fresh, looked scarcely less grimy than my foot soldiers. "Is the fighting over?"

"Almost." Henry nodded at the men, who wore Somerset's portcullis badge. "They brought me here. I don't want to talk about it."

"Then we shan't," I said soothingly.

Henry turned his attention to Edward, who had been playing football with some of our men. One day, I knew, Edward would awake to the fact that his father was not quite the same as other men, but that day had not come yet. "I missed you, my son," Henry said as they embraced. "Have you been a good boy?"

"Oh, yes!" Edward pulled back and began chattering. "We got robbed!" he announced cheerfully. "And we went to Scotland, and then we fought a battle at Wakefield, and we won! And we chopped the Duke of York's head off, and the Earl of Salisbury's, and the Earl of Rutland's..."

As Edward regaled his father with our adventures, I took the opportunity to turn to Somerset's men. "We've all but run them off, your grace—just mopping up now, really. The Duke of Somerset told us to seize King Henry and bring him here when the time looked right, and so we did. We captured two of the men who were holding him against us, Lord Bonville and Thomas Kyriell."

I frowned at their names. These men had once been in Henry's household, and had fought for him and been favored by him, but Warwick had lured them to his side the previous year with the Order of the Garter. "They should lose their heads for their disloyalty. Is Warwick taken?"

"No, but his younger brother John, Lord Montagu, has been seized. We've only lost one man of quality," Somerset's man added, anticipating my next question. "Sir John Grey fell, fighting most valiantly."

"Sir John Grey of Groby? The one who's married to the Duchess of Bedford's oldest daughter?"

"I am afraid so, my lady."

I sighed, thinking of the pretty girl who had watched the Loveday jousts, now a widow with two young sons. Then Somerset himself rode up, followed by a multitude of men. Dismounting, he knelt beside Henry. "Your grace, the victory has gone to us."

"God be thanked," Henry said. He raised Hal and embraced him, then beckoned the rest of the lords and knights toward him. "You have restored my son to his rightful place as my heir and protected my most gracious lady, and for that I am grateful. I should like to knight my son and to then have him knight the most deserving."

"Your grace, I must first ask you what is to be done with our prisoners. I would ask that the life of Lord Montagu be spared and he be imprisoned, as my own younger brother is in Warwick's custody. For the same reason I would ask that Lord Berners, as the brother of the Archbishop of Canterbury, be spared and imprisoned."

"So be it, my lord."

"But Lord Bonville and Thomas Kyriell, who themselves had your grace in custody after having once been your loyal men—"

"If they kept you prisoner, Father, they should die," said Edward cheerfully.

Henry's pain and indecision were almost palpable. These men had served him since he was a child; yet they had played him false. To spare him more agony, I stepped forward. "The Prince of Wales speaks wisely, my lord. The men are traitors and should pay with their heads."

My husband closed his eyes. After a moment or two, he said in a barely audible voice. "See to it, then."

John Morton, a churchman and lawyer who had been my son's chancellor for several years, stepped forward with a prayer book in his hand. "Your grace, I am ready to assist in knighting the Prince of Wales."

Henry's face unclouded, and he bowed his head both reverently and grate-fully as Morton began reading the ceremonial prayers.

That night, Henry and I, who were lodging at St. Albans Abbey, gave thanks for our victory and paid our respects at the tombs of the men who had fallen there six years before. Hal, Lord Clifford, and the Percy brothers spent a great deal of time kneeling in front of their fathers' respective tombs, and no one disturbed them. I heard too that Hal had gone to the spot near the Castle Inn where his father had died, and that he had spent well over an hour there in silence, with his head bowed. I never asked him about it, but I noticed when I saw him the next morning that something seemed to have lifted off of him at last.

In the meantime, I lay side by side with Henry for the first time in eight months. We did not even try to make love to each other—I knew that there had been too much damage done to my husband for that to take place—but we held each other close and tenderly. "Forgive me, Marguerite, for disinheriting our boy. I never wanted to, and it grieved me beyond measure. I felt I had no choice. York and Warwick told me there would be years of war, and you and my son might be put to death."

"I knew it. I knew that you had been coerced."

"They tried to poison my mind against you. They reminded me that you had been friendly with Somerset—the father, that is—when Edward was con-ceived and said that he could be his or anyone's son. Did I want to foist off someone's bastard as my heir?" Henry's voice broke. "My boy, the pride of my life, referred to as someone's bastard! They told me that after Northampton you had surrounded yourself with handsome gallants and would happily marry young Somerset if you could but be rid of me."

I closed my eyes.

"I did not believe them; I would scream at them to stop telling me such awful things. They wouldn't serve my food on time so I was hungry and faint. I should have stood up to them better; I know that now. Time after time I have smote myself, knowing how I had betrayed you and our boy. When I saw you today, thin and—dirty, I must say—and so tired-looking and thought of all that you must have been through…And you were robbed, Edward said. My little Marguerite."

"All is well now," I said, holding him tightly against me. "Don't dwell on such things."

"I knew too that once I had agreed that York was to be my heir, my own life was hardly worth the purchase. How hard would it be for them to slip some poison into my food, or to have me shot by a stray arrow when I was hunting? No grown man who is the heir to the throne wishes to wait his turn forever. I went to Westminster to look at the spot I had assigned for my burial, wondering if I would soon be lying there. I almost hoped I would be. I could have left the world without much regret—except for realizing that you were still in it, fighting for me and my son." He shook his head. "I should be fighting for you, my dear. You deserve so much better. I wish at times like these I was like my father."

"You are what you are, and I love you for it," I said, closing my eyes. "I am very tired, Henry, after marching all the night before. Let us rest now."

Henry cradled my head in the crook of his arm and stroked my hair as I fell asleep.

∽

Though our men had helped themselves quite liberally to the provisions St. Albans had to offer, we needed more supplies. Accordingly, we sent messengers to London, both to request supplies and to determine how we would be received.

Two days later, we had an answer in the form of a delegation of aldermen, accompanied by the Duchess of Buckingham, Lady Scales, and the Duchess of Bedford. The first two wore mourning for their husbands, killed just months before, and the Duchess of Bedford was puffy-eyed from the news of the death of her daughter's husband, John Grey, here at St. Albans. "We come bearing the city's fervent hope that your grace will show her and her citizens mercy," Jacquetta said as if reciting a speech.

"My lady, talk to me as a friend, not in that formal manner. What have they been saying of me? I mean no harm to the Londoners; I have never meant them any harm. I told them so after York claimed the crown, when his creatures were putting it about that I planned to storm the city and pillage it."

"I know," Jacquetta said unhappily. "But they do not believe your grace."

"The Londoners are terrified of your grace's army," the Duchess of Buckingham said. "Warwick has convinced them that you mean their destruction."

"If they only knew that what I want more than anything is my chamber at Greenwich, and a warm soaking bath," I said. "And the ultimate atrocity of obtaining a couple of extra gowns and a warmer cloak." I made a gesture of irritation with my hand. "If I meant to destroy the city, why are we talking here instead of marching upon it when it is undefended? But issue my reassurances. Tell them we have no intent to pillage the city or to despoil its people. We will even send part of the army back to Dunstable, as a token of our good faith." I paused, looking at Lady Scales. "But that does not mean we will not punish evildoers, such as those men who murdered your husband, my lady." I turned to Jacquetta. "I am very sorry that Sir John died here. He was a fine young man."

Jacquetta sighed. "I have not seen poor Bessie, but I know the news will break her heart; she was very fond of John, and he of her. And it is so sad to think of her little boys growing up without a father."

"With her lovely face and graceful ways, she will not go without offers," I said. Once Warwick was out of the way and we were back to normal, I reflected, perhaps I could find a suitable husband for the girl myself.

The ladies and the aldermen having left to bear my assurances to the jumpy Londoners, I sent Sir Edmund Hampden, Edward's chamberlain, and two other men to Barnet to negotiate for our entry into the city, at the head of a force of four hundred men. No sooner had they left, however, than the carts of provisions sent to us were seized and looted by the London rabble. And worse was to come. When some of our men were admitted to the city by the aldermen, they were attacked by the same rabble.

Then we heard that the Earl of Warwick, joined finally by the Earl of March, had combined their forces and were marching on London.

"We must enter the city ourselves," said Somerset. "This negotiating is for naught; they don't want us in, and protesting our good intentions will make no difference. We need to force our way in, and do it before the Earl of March—who is quite likely to assert his father's claim to the throne—does so himself. He's no laggard; Mortimer's Cross proved that. Your grace, we have to make a decision."

Exeter and others nodded. Henry, at whom Somerset's words had been directed, remained silent for a minute or two before he said, "I know not what to do. It grieves me that the Londoners should think we mean them harm."

This, it was clear, would be all of Henry's contribution to the discussion. Somerset turned to me. "Madam, you must agree. London can be ours if we move quickly. We could begin moving there in a couple of hours, with a force of picked men."

"No. I believe that we should return to the North."

Hal stared at me. "Are you mad, your grace?"

"The Londoners have never supported us in the past. What makes you think that they would this time? They have always unaccountably admired Warwick; they will support him and the Earl of March. In the North, the men are our friends. Let March and Warwick come to us there, if they dare, and we can finish them off."

"We have an army here! Why not finish them off here too?"

"I do not think we can, for one thing. Our men are underfed; Warwick's and March's are relatively fresh. And what might happen if they trapped us in London? If they gain possession of the king and the Prince of Wales and me, all will be lost. They will find some means of ridding themselves of Henry."

"I never thought I would say this of you, your grace, but you are too timid. We should have entered London days before; let us do so now. March's army need not ever enter London's gates. We can destroy them before that. Send one force into London and another one to intercept March. For God's sake, we had a great victory here, and another at Wakefield! Let us follow up strength with strength."

"Too many of our men have deserted, and many of those we have now are growing impatient for want of victuals. We will have difficulty fighting March on one front, much less two. And there is yet another consideration. I promised the Londoners that they should not be despoiled."

"Who plans to despoil them? If they allow us in, they should come to no harm."

"You have forgotten what happened when the Tower was under siege. The bombardments we sent out angered the Londoners so much, they murdered poor Lord Scales. That should be a sign of what is to come if they suffer yet again."

Somerset was making ready to launch yet another counterargument when Henry, who had been watching us volley our arguments at each other, like a spectator at a tennis game, spoke. "My lady is right, Somerset. We shall not enter London. I will not risk having my queen and my son fall into the Londoners' hands."

"If that is your chief objection, your grace, why not send them north to safety?"

"No," said Henry. "I shall not be parted from them again."

"But—"

"The matter is closed." Henry stood, grasping my shoulder for support like an old man as he rose. "I shall lie down for a while."

Hal watched as Henry exited the chamber at the abbey where we had been conferring.

"It is folly, madam," he said when Henry's footsteps could no longer be heard in the distance. "Mark me; you will rue this." Then he turned and stalked out of the room.

⁓

As we began to move out of St. Albans, the Londoners flung open the gates of the city to Edward, Earl of March. On March 4, he was proclaimed as King Edward IV.

He did not waste time, this oversized brat, this pretender. Within days, he was taking an army north to seal his claim in blood.

We, back at York when the news reached us, did not stint in preparing for them. "God keep you and lead you to victory," Henry called, over and over again, as our troops—well over twenty thousand men—filed out of York Castle in late March, twenty-four-year-old Somerset at their head. A gentle snow was falling, dusting the men's armor and the heads that still sat on Micklegate Bar.

By Palm Sunday, March 29, the snow had turned into a near blizzard. Henry and I went to mass at York Minster and spent the rest of the day apart, him praying, me pacing. I had given up on hearing any news and was preparing for bed that evening when I heard the sounds of hooves, slamming doors, and screams. Scarcely decent, I flung off the lady who was braiding my hair and rushed into the great hall.

Somerset, Exeter, and Lord Ros, Somerset's older half brother, stood in the center of the hall, gasping for breath. Around them, men were pressing into the hall, some walking, some being carried by others. Some were dripping blood onto the rushes. All were covered with snow. "Somerset! For God's sake, what has happened?"

Somerset did not look up. It was Exeter who said, "All is lost, my lady. We must get out of here immediately. You and the king and the prince will be taken prisoner if you do not."

"Lost!"

"Tom!" The Countess of Devon rushed to a man who had been brought in on a makeshift bier. His face was barely recognizable as the young Earl of Devon's.

"He's dying," Somerset said, his voice toneless. He wiped melting snow off his face and continued. "Northumberland's dead. So is Trollope. There must be thousands of men dead—on the fields, drowned in the river. They're every-where." He chuckled. "All covered with snow by now, I suppose. It's pretty, snow, don't you think? It covers a multitude of sins. Beautifies everything." He stared at the snow he had been rolling into a ball. "Shall we finish this glorious day with a snowball fight, men?" He tossed the ball into a tapestry, laughing, then suddenly sank to his knees, sobbing.

"Good Lord! Has he gone mad?"

"No," said Lord Ros. "He's utterly exhausted, and it was sheer hell out there." He gestured to two of Somerset's men. "Sit him down over there and make him rest until we're ready to go. Try to get some warm drink into him. Exeter's right; we can't waste any time. We're dead if York's men catch us, and they were close upon us."

"The Earl of Devon?" I looked at Marie, who sat beside him on the floor, speaking to him soothingly in French while he groaned in pain.

"He won't last more than an hour or so if he tries to travel; it was all we could do to get him here. He had best stay."

"But if York..."

"Come," interrupted Exeter. "There's no time for this. Where is the king? Is he actually sleeping through this? Wake him and the prince; they cannot stay abed!"

"Stay?" Henry suddenly appeared in the great hall, blinking.

"Take the king to his chamber! Dress him! Madam, you must get dressed yourself. We've a long ride ahead of us."

"Marguerite? What is it?"

"We must flee," I said, putting my hand on his shoulder. "We have lost a battle and many men, and that is all I know."

"Oh." Henry closed his eyes. "Let us pray for the dead, then."

"Not if you want to add yourself to them! Hurry!" Exeter virtually shoved Henry into the arms of his page. "Get him ready for travel immediately. You too, your grace!"

I obeyed Exeter and joined my ladies in my chamber, where they were already packing. "Pack light!" hollered Exeter, looking in before racing off again. "Just take what you need for warmth."

Marie stumbled in, half blind from crying. "He is making me leave," she said, tears choking her voice. "He says that if they find me here, they might capture me because I am a Frenchwoman. Marguerite, he is dying! I do not want to leave."

"You must, if he wills it, and he is probably right. Honor his last wishes. Go back and sit by him until it is time to go. We will get your things together."

In a half hour we were all back in the great hall. Henry stood in the middle, looking scarcely less confused than Edward, who had been roused from a sound sleep and still was only half awake. Marie gave the Earl of Devon one last kiss, then another. "Go," he whispered. Filled with those men who were too badly injured to flee with the rest of us, the great hall now looked like a hospital.

Somerset, sitting on a bench with his face in his hands, rose on command like a man sleepwalking and joined the sad parade out of the great hall. More out of instinct than out of conscious courtesy, he took my arm to help guide me in the darkness. "We should have entered London when we could," I whispered, more to myself than to anyone else. "Christ, but I was a fool."

Hal turned and looked straight at me. "Yes," he said hoarsely, "we should have. And you were."

I hung my head and wept.

16

Margaret
March 1461 to July 1461

PALM SUNDAY FIELD, THEY CALLED IT WHEN THEY COULD BEAR TO TALK OF it—that terrible battle near Towton on March 29, 1461, that cost us—and England—so dear. For hours upon hours Lancaster and York had hacked at each other in a blinding snow, blowing in the faces of our own men and keeping our archers from properly shooting their arrows.

Until almost the very end, though, it could have gone our way: we had more men, and none braver. No one had been more active in the battle than Somerset, even after Trollope had fallen near his feet. But then the Duke of Norfolk, whose illness had prevented him and his troops from reaching Edward's side earlier, suddenly arrived at the head of hundreds of men, fresh for battle. Our men, exhausted from fighting for hours with a wind buffeting them, had not been able to withstand them.

The rout had been almost worse than the battle proper. As our men fled the field, some had plunged to their deaths into the River Wharfe; others had been slaughtered on its banks by the pursuing Yorkists. Men said that the river ran red with blood and that the snow turned crimson, that the bodies in the river were piled so high that they formed a footbridge over which the lucky could escape. When all was over, more than twenty thousand men lay dead. Edward executed forty prisoners immediately afterward, and when he arrived at York on March 30, he executed four more, including Marie's husband, the Earl of Devon, who was barely able to walk to the scaffold.

I never saw any of the slaughter, of course. Yet I still dream of it regularly, and each year on March 29, I do not even attempt to sleep at night. I stay on my knees, praying for the men who died that day and for the widows and orphans they left behind.

It was to Newcastle that we fled after Towton. Fearing that the Earl of March—I am sorry, it still pains me to call him king—would send men after us, which he soon did, we tarried only a day or so before we moved on to Berwick. There we awaited a safe conduct to Scotland, which seemed our best hope for a refuge. Very soon a reply came, and by mid-April we were established in Linlithgow Palace, licking our wounds.

We were a ragtag group. In addition to Henry, Edward, Somerset, Exeter, William Vaux, and me, we had a few knights and clerks, Hal's brother Lord Ros, and the Earl of Devon's brother John—a great comfort to poor Marie, who would otherwise have been quite forlorn. Katherine Vaux had been waiting for us in Scotland, having added a newborn daughter, Jane, to our entourage.

Mary of Gueldres had sent instructions that we be entertained like visiting royalty instead of the almost penniless refugees we were. For the first couple of days at Linlithgow all of the members of our battered party, even the men, were content just to eat the good food we were provided and to sleep in the comfortable beds we were offered, secure in the knowledge that no Yorkist troops would come to drag us out of them. Henry, a heavy sleeper at the best of times, lay in his chamber like the dead, and I spent an untold time in a steaming bath, not coming out until my skin was shriveled.

"Your grace, Queen Mary is expected to arrive tomorrow," Somerset said the third day of our stay there. I was standing by Loch Linlithgow, idly throwing bread to the ducks that had gathered around me expectantly.

"Oh?" I said stiffly.

"I imagine she is going to ask for Berwick."

"Well, this comfort does not come without a price." I glanced at the skirts of my new gown, made of material given to me by my Scottish hosts. "I suppose we will have no choice but to give it to her. If doing so makes me a fool, so be it."

Hal took my hand, which I let lie limply within his. "Your grace, I have told you that I was half dead with exhaustion and grief that night, and did not know what I was saying. Many a man—many a wiser man than I—would have done the same thing you did and not enter London. Try to forgive me for my unkind words that night."

"I have. It is myself I cannot forgive. If I could do it all over again…"

Somerset put his arm around me and held me close to him as we stared mournfully across the loch. After a while he said, "I never told you how Trollope died at Palm Sunday Field. He caught an arrow in the neck and was lying there helpless in that damnable snow, choking on his own blood. So I kept the promise we had made to each other when we fought our first battle together: that we would not allow the other to die in agony. I kissed and blessed him, and then I cut his throat, neatly and cleanly as I could. I do believe there was thankfulness in his eyes in the moment before he died."

"Hal…"

"It was like cutting the throat of my own father." Hal crossed himself with his free hand. "Give Berwick to Queen Mary, if that is what it takes for the Scots to provide us with men. Just don't stand here full of self-blame and give up on our cause. We owe it to those who died on that miserable field, to Trollope and all of the rest."

"Who said anything about giving up?" I snapped, pulling out of Somerset's embrace and lobbing a piece of bread into a startled duck. "This very morning I dispatched a messenger to Pierre de Brézé, asking him to seize Jersey for us. It would certainly be of help."

Hal grinned. "It certainly would. I apologize, madam. I've underestimated you. But what does the king think of it?"

"The king," I said softly, "does what I wish now. He has put everything into my hands—and of those who advise me. Some might tell you that sort of power is gratifying; I am here to tell you that it is terrifying."

∽

Mary of Gueldres did indeed arrive the next day, bearing a gift of a hundred crowns and so smug a countenance, she might have already established her household at Berwick. I made a pretense of attempting to negotiate, to save my pride, but our hosts were in a vastly superior bargaining position, and they knew it. Had they chosen to do so, they could have taken us prisoner and turned us over to Edward of York, and that realization pervaded the negotiations like an unwanted dinner guest.

To my irritation, Mary's big blondness made a distinct impression upon Somerset, and his own good looks did not escape her attention either. Even Henry noticed the attraction between the two. "I do hope that woman is not taking advantage of our poor Hal," he said as Mary and Hal went off on one of their never-ending confabulations, all in the name of negotiation. "He is still very vulnerable after Towton."

"Oh, I think he can handle himself," I said dryly, rather wishing for a moment that Henry was a different sort of man so I could add, "and that she will handle him." Nor could I mention my hope that Hal's manly charms might lead to better terms, for Mary had not only hinted that Berwick might not be enough, she had also mentioned that King Edward, as she insisted on calling him, was making civil overtures toward Scotland.

"Perhaps Exeter should talk with her instead."

"Exeter means well, but he lacks the temperament of a negotiator." And, I added privately to myself, Mary did not find him the least bit attractive, at least beside Somerset.

"Well, you know best." Henry, who was lying beside me, patted my hand. Even though we often slept together, we'd not made love since our reunion, and I was beginning to suspect that we probably never would again. I tried not to imagine what Hal and Mary of Gueldres might be up to, and tried even harder not to recall the feeling of Hal's arm around me the other day.

Instead, I changed the subject. "We must think of something to do with Edward," I said, referring not to the usurper but our son. "All of these travels of ours are making him quite wild."

On April 25, we ceded the Scots Berwick, which to their delight we were able to turn over immediately, and Carlisle, which had to be taken. Soon afterward, our makeshift court moved to Edinburgh, at the Convent of the Dominican Friars. We did not have long to stroll the picturesque streets of Edinburgh, though, for we did not intend for the Earl of March to wear his crown in peace. In June, young Edward and I personally accompanied the Duke of Exeter to besiege Carlisle, while Henry himself took a group of men to Ryton and Brancepeth in June. Meanwhile, in May Pierre de Brézé had sent a fleet under the command of his cousin to capture Jersey.

John Neville, Warwick's younger brother, raised our siege of Carlisle, giving me cause to regret having not executed him when I had the chance, while forces raised by the Bishop of Durham—who had once been my chancellor but like so many others had made their peace with March after Towton—repelled us at Brancepeth. Brézé's fleet, however, took Jersey, and we still held a few castles in Wales, where Henry's brother Jasper was still stirring up trouble on our behalf.

"We need more forces than we have available now," I fretted after we had all gathered back in Edinburgh in varying degrees of disrepair. "I know Bishop Kennedy here in Scotland is our friend, but Queen Mary wavers"—I gave Somerset a significant look—"and I have heard that March is still trying for a truce."

"And they have finally held his coronation," Henry observed. "They say it was a magnificent ceremony."

"I don't want to hear a single detail," I warned. "I think it is time we took another tack. When I came to this country, my uncle Charles urged me to do everything in my power to get my lord to cede Maine, and I did. No one in England has had a kind word to say of me ever since. So it is time, I think, that he did me a great service in return. We need men and we need money. He can supply us both."

"So you plan to write to him?"

I shook my head. "He was very much impressed with my lord of Somerset when he was attempting to recover Calais. I would like him to go and ask my uncle in person. And to see what help the Count of Charolais can be to us."

Hal nodded. "I'm willing." He grinned. "Edinburgh is a bit gray for my taste."

"And you, my lord?" I prompted my husband. "Do you approve of this mission?"

Henry nodded, just as I thought he would.

The evening before his departure, Hal caught me as I was strolling—or, to put it more accurately, pacing—around the convent grounds. "May I speak to you?"

"There is no need to be formal, Hal."

"But you have been formal with me lately, *n'est-ce pas*?" I shrugged, and Somerset turned my face to his. "Is it the Queen Mother? You look disapproving whenever I speak to her in a friendly manner."

I turned my head. "She is a widow, and you a single man. You can speak to each other as you please."

"Yes, and that is all we do. Queen Mary and I are not lovers."

"Really?" I said, ashamed of the girlish note that crept into my voice.

Hal, of course, caught my tone. "Really. We amuse each other, and I must say that I did offer to warm her bed, it being chilly in Scotland. But she is as annoyingly practical as she is amusing. She quite enjoys being the king's regent, and she could hardly retain the position if she were to turn up pregnant with my child. So she very graciously refused."

"But you spend so much time together—"

Hal shrugged. "What can I say? It is the Beaufort charm. She prefers me to her Scottish councillors, 'tis all."

"Well, that is a relief to know. I would not like to see your bed sport harm our cause." I started to turn away, but Hal caught me by the arm.

"Just our cause?" he asked softly. "I believe that you are a bit jealous of the Queen Mother, Margaret."

"No! I—"

Hal drew me toward him and kissed me. For a moment, I gave myself up to the pleasure of having his lips against mine. Then Hal's hands began to wander, and I pulled back. "It cannot be, Hal."

"Margaret, I am fond of the king. I would do nothing to hurt him. But—"

"Then we will do nothing to hurt him."

"Need he know? We need not risk getting you with child. There are other ways of giving—and getting—pleasure."

I wondered fleetingly if Hal had tried this argument on Queen Mary. "I am aware of that, and they are just as wrong for a married woman and a queen to indulge in."

"A married woman and a queen whose husband no longer touches her. I'm right, am I not?"

"That is none of your con—Yes, you are right."

"Then why not give yourself a little pleasure? I promise, we will be discreet."

"If I thought only to give myself a little pleasure, I would have fallen into your bed long before this." Absently, I put my finger against my lips, warm from Hal's kiss. "But don't you understand? Surely you must have heard the rumors about your father and me, that he was my son's father."

"Yes."

"He most certainly was not, if you have ever wondered. What do you think would happen if word got out that I was lying with you? For word would get out, you can count on it. Half of the men in Mary's court want to align with the House of York, don't you realize that? They would be more than delighted to pass along the rumor that I was moving from one Beaufort to the next, and that if one wasn't the father of Edward, the other surely must be. Everything we have fought for—everything our men have died for—could be for naught, if enough could be convinced that my son were a bastard."

"Yes, you must always think of your cause."

"Hal, it is our cause, not just mine! Don't be like this."

"I will see you tomorrow at my departure. Good-bye, madam."

Hal turned away, leaving me to lean against the abbey wall and weep with frustration.

*

That night, Henry joined me in bed. This time when he gave me his customary good-night peck on the lips, I pulled him close to me and kissed him hard, trying my best to replicate Hal's expertise in this area. "Love me," I whispered, and Henry did tentatively explore under my shift, almost as if we were both virgins again, as I caressed him and made encouraging noises.

He tried; I give him that. So did I. I employed all of the arts I knew of, which were not numerous given Henry's very conservative nature in bed. But probably even an experienced courtesan would have met with defeat. After a while, Henry sighed and gently stopped my browsing hands. "I am sorry, my dear."

"Perhaps some other time," I said, trying to keep the misery out of my voice. Two-and-thirty, and I was a married woman living the life of a nun while being derided by my enemies as a strumpet. If the Duke of York had made it into Paradise, perhaps he was having a good laugh at my expense. I kissed Henry and rolled over before my tears began to fall. "There is always another night."

The next day, we gathered at the harbor, where a brisk wind promised to send Hal and his party to France quickly. As his companions said their own farewells, Hal made a great show of double-checking to see that all of the letters he had been given were accounted for, then bantered with young Edward about the probability of getting seasick. Then he embraced Henry, and at last turned to me. Would he give me a warm good-bye, or a formal one? He could hardly leave without saying anything. "I wish you a safe voyage," I said tremulously.

His voice was quiet, but not cold. "Is there anyone to whom you wish to send a message? Such as your father?"

"Yes." I looked into Hal's eyes. "Tell him that I love him very dearly."

"I will, your grace." Hal kissed my hand and smiled. "I look forward to seeing all of you shortly, and with good news."

But the next news we heard was ill: my uncle Charles was dead. By the time Hal left his ship, a new king, Charles's surly son Louis, sat on the throne of France.

Margaret
May 1462 to December 1462

"MY DEAR, HOW LONG THE TIME HAS BEEN!" MY FATHER STEPPED BACK TO gaze at me. "And this is my fine grandson." Father bent to address Edward confidentially. "*Parlez-vous français?*"

"*Oui*," said Edward, and proceeded in fluent French to tell his grandfather the story of our journey from Brittany, where we had landed a couple of weeks before.

Louis XI, France's new king, had been proving himself to be most unpredictable. Just days after becoming king, he had ordered the arrest of Pierre de Brézé, against whom he bore an old grudge. Louis and my uncle King Charles had long been on ill terms, and when Louis learned that Hal had arrived in France to see the late king, he had promptly ordered his arrest and held him in close confinement for several months. I had been terrified when I heard this news, convinced that Louis would send Hal to King Edward—as I suppose I should start calling him for clarity's sake—in chains and that he would promptly be executed. Instead, in one of those abrupt volte-faces that was to typify my cousin Louis, he had suddenly decided it was time to discomfit King Edward and had ordered Somerset's release. Unable to cross back to Scotland for fear of being intercepted by Edward's agents, Hal had traveled to Flanders under the protection of his old friend Charles, the Count of Charolais, who had helped persuade Louis to spare his life in the first place. Supported by Charles, he was living in Bruges. From there, with the help of the count, he had plotted with John de Vere, the Earl of Oxford, and his son Aubrey to land at Essex, but poor Oxford's side of the plot was discovered, and the earl and Aubrey had been beheaded on Tower Hill in February 1462 along with several others. Add to that the fact that the Earl of Pembroke and the Duke of Exeter had been defeated in Wales the autumn before by Edward's men, and that Edward was making more overtures to the Scots, and it looked bleak for us that spring of 1462.

So I had decided to try my luck with Louis myself. First, however, I visited my father, whom I had not seen in seventeen years. As my father chatted with Edward, I gazed around Angers Castle, overlooking the River Maine. I had schooled myself upon coming to England not to feel homesick, and thanks to Suffolk, I had largely succeeded, but now that I was back in France at last, I felt an overwhelming urge to stay the rest of my life in this comfortable castle with my boy, safe from all that threatened me. I choked back a sob, and Father at once looked up at me. "My dear, what is it?"

"It has—it has been so hard lately, Father." *And I have been so lonely*, I had to fight myself from adding. Henry still did no more than lie beside me.

Father put his arm around me. "Come, Marguerite. You have had a long journey. I have had your old chamber made ready for you. You must rest." He smiled at Edward. "And you, my boy, shall see my lions!"

In the chamber where I had spent much of my maidenhood, everything was largely as I had left it—my old tapestries, taken out of their chests and rehung, my old bed, my old coverlet and furnishings. I climbed into my bed and lay there, sipping the wine I'd been given, while Marie and my other ladies unpacked my belongings. Jeanne de Laval, my father's second wife, who was three years younger than myself, superintended. I had known her when we were children and remembered her as being very good natured, but now she looked scandalized at the speed with which Marie and the others were accomplishing their duties. "My dear, this is all you brought with you?" I nodded. "Is this all you carry in England?"

"We are not all quite barbarians there, but I have been reduced to traveling light," I said. "My husband and I are very poor now, and live on others' charity."

"Well, I daresay your dear father will replenish your wardrobe, poor darling." She shook her head at the gown that Marie was unfolding, which was downright threadbare in spots. "After all, so many people are curious to see you, and you won't want to appear in front of them looking less than your best."

"Curious to see me?"

"Why, of course! You are thought to be quite the heroine here, fighting for your husband and your son."

I snorted. "The people of England think quite differently of me, I can assure you that."

"Oh, well, they are fools, are they not? And it helps matters here as well that the gallant Duke of Somerset is so plainly enamored of you."

I almost dropped the cup I was holding. "Enamored of me?"

"Indeed, he is quite the knight-errant, and you the lady of his heart. It is all quite chivalrous. Of course, it helps that he is said to be so very handsome. We have never seen him here at Angers, of course, but those who have seen him say he is like a young King David. Is he?"

"He is good-looking," I allowed.

"Oh, you seem rather underwhelmed."

I shrugged. "I have known him since he was fourteen, which is a rather unimpressive age for most men in terms of looks. I suppose I am simply so used to seeing him now that I cannot see what other women see."

"Dear me," said Jeanne, shaking her head as she drew the bed curtains so that I could settle in for a nap. "You have become quite the cold Englishwoman, I fear. I quite agree with your father; you need to tarry a while in Angers."

"I saw the lions!" Edward told me as we walked around the castle grounds a few hours later. "And look—there are ostriches! With feathers just like on my badge!" A pair of those birds sauntered by us. "And there are these strange dark people all about."

"Moors."

"And dwarfs! How come Father never kept Moors or dwarfs?"

"Your father is more concerned with spiritual pursuits."

"And do you know there is a tennis court here? When I become king I shall have one at Windsor. Maybe Westminster too." Edward considered. "And I think I'll have some Moors there too."

"No dwarfs?"

Edward scrunched his face up to ponder the matter. "Well, maybe," he said finally. "And Grandfather said there will be a farce tonight in our honor. Have I ever seen a farce? Grandfather says it is a comic play."

"No." Having two kings in one tiny island was farce enough for my taste.

"Father's court—when he had one—is not very amusing," Edward commented.

"When it is yours, you can make it so." I ran my hand through Edward's hair. "I know it is hard to be wandering from place to place with so little money and so little amusement, but someday we will have your father's throne back, and it will have been all worthwhile."

"Oh, I understand." Edward pulled at my hand. "Look, Mother! A monkey!"

While I enjoyed a semblance of my youth again (and indeed the face in the mirror that my father bought me looked less careworn with each passing day), King Louis tarried in the south of France, sending envoys to greet me but making it clear that I would have to bide my time before I met with him personally. In the meantime, there arrived some welcome additions to my party: Pierre de Brézé, whom Louis had freed from prison, and Jasper Tudor, Earl of Pembroke.

And Doctor John Morton, my son's former chancellor, also appeared one day at Angers—much to my shock, for he had been captured after Towton and sent to the Tower. "You were released?" I asked after I had greeted him joyously.

"No," said Doctor Morton cheerfully. "I escaped.'

"*Escaped?*" Men like Roger Mortimer, Queen Isabella's virile lover from the century before, could manage the feat of breaking out of the Tower, I supposed, but this plump little man? "How?"

"No great feat of strength, I fear. I simply picked the most amicable of my guards and reasoned with him. Was it not wrong, I asked, to take an anointed king from the throne that he and his father and his grandfather had held for sixty years, in favor of the grandson of a man who had been executed as a traitor? Even if King Henry was"—Morton coughed delicately—"not entirely himself at times, did he not have a fine young man, whose soundness I could attest to, to succeed to his throne, and who would be capable of acting as his regent in just a few years? Mind you, this seed took many weeks to plant, but it at last bore fruit, and when it did, my guard procured old clothes for me and allowed me to slip out in the dead of night, where he had friends waiting to convey me abroad. And so—here I am! As is my kind guard who helped me escape. So you see, madam, I have not only brought you myself, but a convert as well."

"Lancaster should have more such as you," I said, smiling broadly. Not in months had I felt so optimistic. Let so-called King Edward treat with the Scots! We had other means of unseating him.

Lord Ros, Hal's older half brother, also joined us. By this time I was able to ask about Hal without betraying anything more than the natural solicitude of a queen for a loyal supporter. "He's doing what he can for us in Bruges, your grace, stirring up trouble for Edward from there." Ros laughed. "And I suspect he's not so unhappy to be there, as rumor has it that the ladies of Burgundy find him quite agreeable." He touched his face, a good-humored one but not a particularly good-looking one. "Oh, to be blessed with that angelic Beaufort visage."

I managed a smile.

Finally, in June, I was summoned to Chinon to meet Louis. I remembered him from my sister's wedding celebrations at Nancy in 1445 as a long-nosed youth of twenty-one, who'd been feuding with his father, King Charles, and had made a great point of parading his unhappiness with being at court. Now I saw that although his nose had not improved with time, he had certainly become more urbane. "Dear lady and cousin," he said, kissing my hand. "We are delighted to have you in France. I do wish my queen were here to greet you."

I smiled sweetly, knowing full well from my men that Louis had been issuing orders that I not be allowed to see his queen, lest I put her in the position of begging Louis a favor for me, and him in the position of having to grant her petition. "I am sorry to have missed her." I hesitated, then decided to get past these niceties and to the heart of the matter. "But you must know I am not here to visit. I am here because my king and I need your help."

Louis's impenetrable face betrayed a slight hint of approval at my straightforwardness. "So I hear. What are you prepared to offer?"

"A hundred years' truce."

"Truces are made to be broken. You might as well say twenty years, or two years, or two months, my dear lady. It's all the same."

"Safe conducts for our subjects in each other's dominions."

Louis yawned, not at all discreetly, behind his hand.

"Calais."

Louis put down his hand, and my own men repressed gasps. Though I had told them beforehand that this was an offer I was willing to make, and Henry had empowered me to make it, they might well have thought I would lose my nerve. For Calais had been in the hands of the English since 1346, when it was won by the great Edward III, and Englishmen, even those who had never seen the coast of England, much less Calais, cherished it as they did their own acres of land. I could not have possibly made a concession more likely to earn me the hatred of the English people.

"My dear lady, you certainly do not pander to the people by courting popularity with them."

"My popularity does not matter a whit to me now. I lost any love the people might have had when Normandy fell, and nothing will gain it back, save perhaps for me drowning myself in the Thames."

"What of your husband's popularity?"

"They will blame all on me, and his reputation will go unscathed. And when my son is old enough, he will gain the people's love, with or without Calais. He has the makings of another Edward III or Henry V. I feel it in my very bones."

"Mothers," said Louis.

"And in any case, our bargain about Calais need not be made public for now."

"True."

"I do not, of course, expect that we would give up Calais without compensation. That will have to be determined."

"Oh, yes." Louis smiled. "I trust, by the way, that your husband has empowered you to make this very intriguing offer?"

"Yes. I have his full authority."

"Such an interesting marriage you have. But the English are quite a unique people."

"Well? Can we talk further?"

"Oh, yes." Louis had the look of a man already remodeling Calais to his satisfaction. "We certainly can."

The next day, on June 23 at Chinon, Louis and I signed our secret agreement, in return for a loan of twenty thousand francs. Once we won Calais back from Edward's men, it would be delivered to Louis within a year, at which time Henry would receive forty thousand crowns. A few days later, we went to Tours, where we signed a public agreement, under which Louis agreed to proclaim that he favored our cause. Better yet, once the ink was dry, Louis permitted Pierre de Brézé to raise an army that he and I would bring to Scotland.

Twenty thousand francs to the better, thanks to Calais, I traveled to Rouen in July, Edward having remained at Angers with his grandfather. As part of what seemed to be our friendship, Louis had ordered the citizens there to give me a grand welcome as I rode in, richly dressed (thanks to my father) and riding a fine horse. "They're even wearing marguerites," I said to the Archbishop of Narbonne, who was escorting me. My eyes filled with tears as I stared at the crowds thronging the streets. "That is what the people wore at my coronation procession in London."

"Your courage and devotion to your husband are admired here, your grace."

"And this is where my dear Suffolk and his wife stayed in Rouen when I visited here before I went to England," I said, pointing to a handsome house and wiping my eye at the thought of my murdered friend. "And the Duke and the Duchess of York met me here. I stayed with them and their children..." My voice trailed off as I thought of young Rutland, killed fighting against me. I shook my head. "Seventeen years. So much has chang—Why, could it be?"

Riding up to greet us was a group of local officials. But there was one handsome English face among them that made my knees turn weak and caused me to jerk at my reins.

"Why, it's Hal!" said Lord Ros as I occupied myself with soothing my startled horse, which really did not require a good deal of comfort. "I was hoping he might meet us."

"I am glad to see him here," I said feebly.

After the welcoming festivities were at last over, Somerset asked to see me at my chambers at the Golden Lion to talk of recent developments, and for a good half hour that is precisely what we did as my ladies busied themselves inside an outer chamber. Louis had written to the Duke of Burgundy, asking him to allow his son, Somerset's friend the Count of Charolais, to take charge of the army he planned to use to attack Calais, and to allow the army to pass through Burgundy's territories. "I am not sure of the Duke of Burgundy," I fretted. "But we can only hope." I paused and looked at Somerset, who had been letting me do most of the talking. "But I have never asked why you came here. I did not expect you."

"For one, to see my brother. For another, to assist you in what way I can, though I doubt Louis will tolerate my presence here for long; we didn't exactly become the best of friends. For yet another, to warn you against him. Louis is a slippery fish; I spent enough time in his prison and in his company to realize that. Don't put too much faith in him. He might speak fair words to you and espouse our cause today, but if he sees an advantage to allying with Edward tomorrow, don't think for a minute he won't take it."

Our cause, he had said. "I will keep that in mind."

"I just don't want you to be disappointed." He hesitated. "There is another reason I am here: to apologize to you, for my conduct in Scotland has been gnawing at me. I asked for what I had no right to, and I should not have been angry when you refused."

"It is all behind us now." I made a dismissive gesture with my hands. Then

I met Hal's gaze, and as I did I knew that all was lost. There was a longing in Hal's eyes that was matched only by my own.

"I lied," he said quietly. "I came here to try again for you."

There was a banquet that night—an interminable one. I drank my wine sparingly, as always, but there was a haze about everything I said and did, and I could make only the most rudimentary conversation—a failing, fortunately, that everyone attributed to fatigue from my journey. All I could think about was Hal, sitting at the dais some distance off, and the meeting we had arranged for that night, in my own chamber. I did not fear betrayal by Marie and my other ladies, whose sleeping quarters lay in an adjacent, connecting, chamber: the troubles of the past few years had weeded out those who were not absolutely loyal to me.

Alone in my chamber at last, I gulped a cup of wine and waited for the expected knock. It came just as I was pouring myself a second cup, which Somerset took from me after he entered the room. "I want you sober, sweetheart," he said, taking me into his arms.

I leaned into him. "It is so wicked of me, but I have tried so hard not to, and Henry just can't, and I have been so lonely, and—"

Hal put a finger to my lips. "Easy. I'll take care of you, my sweet. I promise you, no harm will come to anyone from this."

"I wasn't sure whether to leave all of my clothes on or just wear my nightshift," I babbled on.

"Clothes on," Hal said. "It is very pleasurable taking them off." He expertly removed my hennin and the coif beneath it, then watched as my loosened hair fell to my waist. He ran his hands through it, then began to unfasten my clothing, kissing my breasts as he bared them. At last I stood nude before him, torn between shame at what I was about to do and hope that Hal would find me pleasing to his eyes.

Hal gazed at me. "Since I was a boy, I've always wanted to say what I am about to say now: 'Your grace looks very lovely stark naked.'" When I failed to smile, he said, "You're more beautiful than I ever imagined. And I have done my fair share of imagining, my dear."

"Hal, we shouldn't—"

"Come, sweetheart. Help me undress."

I fumbled nervously with Hal's fastenings until Hal, chuckling at my incompetence as a valet, stripped himself bare without a shred of self-consciousness.

At twenty-six he was perfectly formed, but he bore the scars of each battle in which he'd fought, especially on the arm that had been broken at St. Albans. I reached out in sympathy to touch it, and he shook his head. "Don't think of any of that," he whispered. Leading me to the bed, he lay beside me and caressed me until I at last relaxed against him. Then he slowly, tenderly brought me to a state of ecstasy before he entered me in response to my frantic urgings.

I am quite unequal to saying more about that first time with Hal. When it was over, I sobbed, half from guilt and half from the release of my long-pent-up passion, and he soothed me to sleep on his shoulder, where I dozed for several hours before awakening and finding him smiling at me. "You look so content when you are asleep, Margaret. Like a carefree girl. I almost hated to see you begin to stir."

"I have never been so content before. That is why." I put my arms around Hal, delighting in the feel of his bare flesh against mine; Henry had always come to bed in his shirt the past few years and had made it clear that he preferred me to keep on my shift. With Somerset's encouragement and guidance, I began to explore his body and soon felt his arousal. "You like this, I think, my lord," I teased, daring for the first time to play the coquette in bed.

"Christ, you learn quickly," Hal murmured and pulled me astride him.

"I love Henry," I said much later that night as I snuggled against Hal. "You must understand that, Hal. I never would want to hurt him. If I thought he might find out about this—"

"I know, sweet. I'm fond of him myself. But I have longed for you since I first saw you when I came to England from Caen."

"You were but fourteen."

"I was precocious."

"Joan Hill?"

"She is very dear to me, and she is the mother of my child. But she's not you." He sighed. "When the king could make you happy, I could control myself, and when you refused me back in Scotland, I tried my best not to think of you any longer. But I could not keep out of Rouen when I heard that you were traveling here, and when I saw you here, looking so ripe and lovely after your stay at Angers…"

"You will have to marry someday, Hal, when we get England back, and I would not have you be unfaithful to your duchess."

"We'll worry about that when the time comes." Hal yawned and held me closer to him, and in a few minutes I saw that he had fallen asleep. This time, it was my turn to study him as he slept. I could give him the attention that propriety forbade in public and admire his features—his dark hair with the reddish tints that served as a reminder that he himself was of Plantagenet blood; the high, sharp cheekbones; the eyelashes that were just long enough to be attractive without being feminine, the faded scar on his face that reminded me of the loss for which I knew he still grieved. I kissed him, and in his sleep or half-sleep he smiled.

I had sinned grievously, I knew even as I admired my lover. Worse, I had become the adulteress all my enemies said I was. Yet as I lay next to Hal, all I wanted to do was to sin again with him.

Hal had vowed to withdraw himself just in time, but in our passion neither of us had been willing for him to do so. Though it would have been the cruelest of ironies for I, who had had so much difficulty in conceiving my legitimate son, to become pregnant with Somerset's bastard, I was not particularly worried about this possibility. Even when I was in the prime of my child-bearing years, I had gone for three or four months without bleeding, and in the last couple of years, I had hardly bled at all. My physicians and the midwives I had consulted had given up on giving me potions for child-bearing even before Northampton. No, I was most likely barren, and with God's grace I would stay that way where Hal was concerned. And if I did conceive, Hal and I would find a way around that difficulty, I told myself in my love-fogged state. I could be hidden in my father's castle, perhaps, and my child passed off as one of his own bastards…"Don't worry, I'll take care of you," Hal had whispered, and I knew I could trust him utterly.

For the next two weeks, Hal remained at Rouen, where we planned our English campaign during the day and spent our nights loving each other until we were exhausted. I had a little room at the Golden Lion where I held my makeshift little court and discussed our plans, and I delighted in sitting across from Hal at our cramped conference table there, knowing that none of the men there but Ros, who had a knack for conveying Hal to my chamber with no one seeing his progress there, were aware that Hal and I were lovers. I was like a giddy girl, thrilling when our sleeves brushed or when we caught each other's eye. On two occasions we even had some time outside together, strolling through the town that Hal knew better than I because of his father's residence here, and on both occasions we managed to slip away from the sight of our attendants for a moment or two and steal a lingering kiss.

God forgive me, but I cannot to this day think of that time in my life without a smile.

With Louis expected to arrive in town in August, Hal had deemed it expedient to leave for Bruges, from which he planned to hazard the sea and join Henry in Scotland, where I and my army would arrive soon. In early August, therefore, we spent our last night together, on a pleasure barge that Hal had borrowed from a rich townsman he'd been friendly with when he had lived in Rouen as a boy. "See, madam?" he said when he led me onto the barge. "A picnic!"

Spread out on a dainty cloth was a meal of bacon, cheese, nuts, apples, mushrooms, and onions, along with a jug of wine. I wrinkled my brow, knowing I recognized this menu from somewhere. "Why, this is from my father's poem!" He had written it in honor of my stepmother.

"'Regnault and Jehanneton,'" Somerset agreed. "I remember you reading it to me. Except that whereas the good shepherd and shepherdess have milk, we shall have wine. And plenty of it, my dear, for I want our last night to be a merry one."

"But there is a little dog, Briquet, as well. You left him out."

"He would be rather in the way," Hal said.

Lounging outside our barge's private cabin, we enjoyed our meal, and especially the wine, as the barge lumbered down the Seine. It was a beautiful summer night, and only after we had held hands and watched the sun set did Hal lead me inside the cabin. "I feel more like Cleopatra than Jehanneton," I said, reclining tipsily on my elbow on the cushions that had been so amply provided for us.

"A blond Cleopatra? I don't know, my dear. But you are as beautiful as she. Or Helen. Or Petrarch's Laura."

"You are very well read, Hal." I stifled a slight hiccup.

"We Beauforts all are."

I took a languid sip of wine from the cup we were sharing. Never in my life I had been this deliciously light-headed. "But do you know what? If I were not Queen of England, I would not wish to be Cleopatra, or Jehanneton, or Helen, or Laura, or any of those ladies. Do you know who I would be?"

"Who, my sweet?"

"The Duchess of Somerset." I clapped a guilty hand to my mouth.

Somerset only laughed. "You would make a lovely duchess, my dear."

"We would live on the Isle of Wight."

"And have eight children by now."

"Eight? I'd lose my figure!"

"Well, five then."

"You just want me to look like Mary of Gueldres," I snickered. "Large." I made as if to set down my wine cup, which slid out of my hand and rolled lazily across the barge. "How did that happen? And why you are laughing?"

"Because, my dear, until tonight I had never encountered the phenomenon of a Frenchwoman with a poor head for wine. It's an impressive one. But then, much about you is impressive."

He brought me onto his lap and kissed me, cupping my face between his hands as if to stop my head from spinning. "I love you, Hal," I said dizzily.

"I love you too, my sweet. It is going to be damned hard to walk away tomorrow." He settled me on my back among the cushions and began to untie my garters. "I don't even want to think about it."

Hal brought me back to my chamber at the Golden Lion before dawn, our entrance aided as usual by his obliging brother and my obliging ladies. Though reasonably sober by then, we were too exhausted to be eloquent in our good-byes; instead, we simply clung to each other until he finally gently disengaged himself from my embrace and slipped out the door. Late in the morning, he returned to bid me and my party a formal farewell, kissing my hand so decorously that no one could have guessed that hours before his lips had been upon other parts of my body entirely. "I will see you soon," he promised. "And we will restore England to her rightful king."

He might have added, "and you to your husband," I thought guiltily later. For now, however, I went back to my chamber and sat in the window seat, watching the boats glide down the Seine and thinking of my lover.

I could not moon around pining for Somerset for long, however, for King Louis and Pierre de Brézé arrived in Rouen just a few days after Hal left it. With them they brought a train of troubles. The Duke of Brittany had refused to allow Louis to bring his troops through Calais, making a siege of that city impossible, and King Edward, having learned of Louis's proclamations on behalf of our cause, made a great point of assembling a fleet at Sandwich—just in case, it was given out, it became necessary to attack France.

That made Louis nervous, but there was another way we could get into Calais and win the garrison over to our cause: bribery. I moved to Boulogne, where I promised to pay the long-overdue wages of Edward's men if they would come over to our side. But Edward, damn him, was no fool, and he miraculously found the money to pay the garrison. To rattle Louis even more, Edward sent a party under the Earl of Kent to raid the coast and began to make friendly overtures toward Castile. Suddenly Louis's aid to me stopped, just as Somerset had predicted it would.

"We can do it anyway," Pierre de Brézé said as I sat despondently at Boulogne.

"But we only have eight hundred men!"

"We'll pick up some in Scotland. And more will come when you land in England. The northerners have always been with Henry."

I pondered. What choice did we have? Louis in his present skittishness would not tolerate me staying in Boulogne forever, the Scots were no doubt getting tired of Henry, and we could accomplish nothing by slinking back to Angers. "But can we pay their wages? I have enough to hire the ships, but—"

"I will pay the men," said Brézé. He patted my hand as he saw my astonished face. "Your family has long been dear to me, and besides it is not in my nature to see a lady so brave founder for want of friends."

"God bless you," I breathed.

So in late October, our forty-two ships and eight hundred men at last sailed for the coast of Northumberland—first stopping at Edinburgh to take my husband and Somerset on board and to leave my Edward in the household of Bishop Kennedy, who had always supported our cause.

It was a smooth voyage, and by now I had traveled enough not to be seasick, so I had full leisure to pace upon the deck, wondering about how I would meet Henry—and Hal. Surely my guilt would show upon my face when I saw my husband for the first time in well over a year? And Hal... I was not so base or so stupid, I told myself, to lie with him underneath my husband's very nose, but my stay in Rouen had taught me that I could not entirely trust myself in these matters.

Beside me, Edward peered into the distance, as he had been doing every few minutes, leaning so far over that I instinctively grabbed him. "I see land, Mama! Land! Soon we will be in Edinburgh harbor!"

I managed to say calmly, "Indeed we will."

The wind brought us quickly and safely into harbor, where, our ships having been sighted, Henry and Hal and a few others were waiting. Henry was the first to come aboard the ship. "Marguerite. Edward," he said simply, and took us both into his arms. Edward, all boy, broke free quickly enough, leaving Henry to hold me close to him. "I have missed you greatly, my dear."

"And I have missed you," I said truthfully. "But I think I have done good work for you."

"When do you ever not?" He stepped back and clapped Hal, who had been hanging back at a respectful distance, on the shoulder. "I was just telling Hal here that no man has ever had a better wife than I."

My eyes stung, and I was grateful that the sea breeze could account for any tears that might escape them. Hal stepped forward and kissed my hand, "Welcome back, madam." He bowed to Edward and smiled. "And your grace? Did you have a good journey?"

"I never got seasick. Not coming to France or coming back," Edward boasted. He frowned as Bishop Kennedy came aboard. "Must I go with him? Can't I stay and go with the rest of you to fight?"

"Not this time." I ruffled his hair.

"But what if we win and I don't get another chance?"

I smiled, and for the first time my eyes met Somerset's. "Win? I think that would be absolutely lovely," I said. "But don't you fear. No matter what, there will always be another battle."

⁂

We disembarked in Northumberland near Bamburgh, where the great castle stared down at us as we unloaded our ships and unfurled Henry's standard. I had hoped that some adherents of Henry's would have been there to greet us, but only a few loyalists joined us. We were not long disheartened, though, for Bamburgh was in the hands of William Tunstall, whose brother Richard was with us. After a lengthy brotherly discussion, William opened the castle gates. That very evening, we dined in Bamburgh's great hall.

"So what is next, your grace?" asked Pierre of Henry that evening as we sat in the cleanest solar that we'd found. Keeping the rooms fresh had not been anyone's priority here in some time.

"Margaret believes we should move on to besiege Alnwick. William Tunstall says that it is short of supplies."

"I like that he has been so cooperative," I said. "Thank goodness we had Richard with us; it is good to see brothers so loyal to each other."

Lord Ros, who had smuggled Hal to my chamber at Rouen so many times, looked at the table. I winced, not having considered my remark before I spoke it.

Hal said in a businesslike manner, "Whom shall we send?"

"I believe that you and Lord Ros should stay here at Bamburgh," I said, avoiding Hal's eyes. "The rest of us will move on to Alnwick."

"Ralph Percy holds Dunstanburgh," Ros said quickly, as if expecting an outburst from his brother. "I believe he might be persuaded to hand it over to us."

"Then to Alnwick we shall go tomorrow," Henry said. He stood. "I believe I will retire for the night. You may leave, my lords."

The men obeyed. I remained in the solar, which was adjacent to Henry's bedchamber. "It is the first time we have been alone in many a day, Henry."

"Yes." He touched my face, gently. "I have missed you very much. Has a chamber been made ready for you?"

"Yes, but I would much prefer to share yours."

"It is not as comfortable as you would like, I fear. There was some difficulty with the fire."

"Then come to mine, Henry."

"Very well." Henry kissed me lightly on the cheek. "I will see you soon."

My ladies dressed me in my warmest nightshift and I settled into bed, waiting for my husband. When an hour or so passed with no sign of Henry, I put a cloak over my shoulders and a pair of slippers on my feet. Grabbing a lantern, I made my way cautiously to the ramparts and stood there, watching the sea below.

Behind me, I heard footsteps. "Ah. I hoped I might find you here."

"You knew you would."

"I wasn't sure, actually." He took my hand. "You've hardly spoken to me since you picked us up in Edinburgh. I was beginning to think you'd forgotten all about Rouen."

"There have hardly been opportunities. And there is Henry right here in Bamburgh with us. We cannot carry on like we did in France. It is wrong."

"I fail to see the role geography plays in morality," Hal said. "It is no more or less a sin for crossing the Channel."

"You know what I mean."

He cupped my chin. "Tell me, sweet. Did Henry come to your chamber tonight?"

"Hal—"

"I gather not, then. How long has it been since he saw you? A year and a half? Good Lord, Margaret, after a separation of that length from you, a normal man would have taken you back at Edinburgh in the ship's cabin!"

"He is a good man, Hal," I said hopelessly.

"The best in the world." Hal slipped his hands under my cloak and smiled as my nipples hardened in response to his inquiring touch. "A saint, practically." His hands drifted lower and I groaned in response to his expert manipulations. "You're ready. I could take you right here," he whispered, backing me against the wall. "Would you like that, darling?"

"It's too cold," I said as all of the fine resolutions I had made aboard ship evaporated under the force of Hal's kisses and fondling. "Please. If we're going to sin, let's be warm at least."

Hal grinned. "Ever practical Margaret." He let the skirt of my nightshift fall back into place and took me by the arm. "I have been so presumptuous as to have a chamber made ready for us. Very private. And with a blazing fire," he added coaxingly. "Like Twelfth Night come early, in my humble opinion. Well? Shall we repair to Chez Somerset, madam, or stand freezing on these ramparts?"

"A chamber made ready? You knew I wouldn't say no to you."

He smiled and fingered my nightshift. "Especially since you already came dressed for the occasion."

The chamber Hal had found was high up in a turret and indeed had a blazing fire, but even then the room was so chilly that I was happy enough to leave my nightshift on as Hal and I lay together on a narrow cot. He himself remained in his fine linen shirt, which I ripped as I clutched him to me during my climax. "I love you," he gasped as he took his turn at peaking.

"And I love you."

"Even if you do ruin a perfectly good shirt," Hal said, rolling off me and kissing me. "And you mean it, my dear?"

"You know I do. I told you so in Rouen."

"Yes. But you were a wee bit touched by the grape, lass, as the Scots say. I wanted to hear it from you sober."

I sighed and raised up on my elbow to look into Hal's beautiful brown eyes. "But you know this is all hopeless, Hal. How can it last? Why should it last? It is wrong of us. I am wracked with guilt when I leave you. I will be wracked with guilt when I return to my chamber tonight."

"Is that why you are leaving me here when you go off to Alnwick? To avoid me?"

"I did not want you and Pierre to quarrel over who was to direct the siege. They are French troops, after all, and he is paying their wages; it is more his right than yours. But yes, partly it is because I knew if you and I were there together, I would soon find my way into your tent. Already I have shown how weak my resolution is." I sat up and hugged my knees. "I should leave now; I have been away from my chamber for too long."

"But this fire has a couple more hours in it, I'd say." Hal sat up and stroked my cheek. "Please? I've missed you."

"And I you. But we cannot take these sort of blatant risks." I rose. "Hal, do think of what I said while I am gone. We must end this, before something dreadful happens."

"Oh, I shall." Hal reached for my cloak and draped it around my shoulders, then kissed me tenderly. "I shall think of it, and I shall think of how you looked just this moment with the fire lighting up everything that's beneath your pretty French nightshift, and it shall likely be a hopeless task, my love. But I will make the effort."

⟡

Katherine was waiting for me when I returned to my chamber. "The king is here. He is in your bed waiting for you."

With a trembling hand, I parted the curtains of my bed. Henry, who had been dozing, stirred at my approach.

"Henry? I thought you were not coming."

"I was praying, my love, for our success. It took a long time."

"I see." Never in my life have I hated anyone as much as I hated myself at that instant.

"Your ladies said that you had a headache and went to the ramparts to get some fresh air."

I breathed a sigh of thanks for the loyalty of my women. "Yes. I think it was the voyage. The moonlight was pretty on the water; I stood there watching it for a while. Then Somerset was kind enough to come upon me and escort me back."

"He's a fine young man. We must get him married when things are settled."

Was there a hint of knowledge there? No, I decided. I kissed Henry on the cheek. "I can sleep now; my headache is gone. Good night, my love."

Henry did not reply. Instead, he drew me closer and began caressing me until, perhaps as much as to his shock as mine, he became aroused. With a cry of triumph and with a force that made me gasp, he entered me nearly as vigorously as Somerset had just an hour or so before.

⟡

We left early the next morning for Alnwick, Somerset and his brother staying behind with a small garrison. As we discussed our plans and said our farewells,

Hal, seeing that Ros, perhaps deliberately, had engaged Henry in conversation, turned to me. "You've lain with *him*," he said in an undertone. "I can see it in his face."

"*He* is my husband. Do be reasonable."

Hal resumed his normal tone of speaking as Henry turned away from Ros. "May I?"

He was offering to assist me to my horse, but Henry was already there, helping me into my saddle. Hal forced a smile. "God be with you, your graces."

⁓

Ralph Percy, as predicted, handed over Dunstanburgh—like Hal, he had seen his father die at St. Albans and had never had much love for Edward. Alnwick, which had been short of supplies, fell after a short siege, and we left it in the hands of Pierre's son and a largely French garrison. But though we could now claim three castles, we would have to keep them garrisoned, and hardly anyone inside England had rallied to our cause. Could they be content with Edward and forgetful of our own rightful claims? I refused to entertain the possibility.

Then, after we returned to Bamburgh, we heard that Warwick was coming to relieve the castles and that Edward himself was speeding north.

"We can't win a battle with them," said Brézé, putting what we were all thinking into words. He shook his head at Hal, who was building a castle out of a couple of sets of playing cards as we spoke. "Not with the few men we have."

"If we can't raise men here, we'll have to get them from Scotland," I said.

"If they'll come." Hal cautiously tested a card. "They haven't been that dependable, in my opinion."

"Oh, lay the card on, Hal," I said. "Bishop Kennedy is still our friend."

"About our only friend, though. The queen is certainly not on our side now. Did you know that Warwick has proposed that she and Edward marry, and that she has given it consideration?" Hal smiled at me, not particularly pleasantly. "Now, there's a couple for you!" He snorted. "Big as they both are, they can wrestle when they get bored with hunting."

"But Bishop Kennedy is a powerful friend to us," said Henry softly. He cleared his throat. "And I believe the Earl of Angus will support us too, with a little encouragement. I believe that the queen and I should return to Scotland and ask them for their support. Brézé, you shall come with us."

"Then it is settled," I said.

Somerset flicked his wrist and sent his castle tumbling down.

✑

"As you are to leave tomorrow, I came to wish you a good-bye in private."

"Who let you into my chamber?"

"Your obliging ladies. Don't worry. I saw the king go off to Dunstanburgh with Brézé just now. He certainly is vigorous lately."

"I believe he has hope he lacked before."

"And he is lying again with you regularly. Isn't he?"

He was, in fact, almost as often as he had in the earliest days of our marriage. "That is none of your business, Hal. What is wrong with you?"

"I've been looking for you on the ramparts. Every night. You haven't come."

"I told you, it is dangerous."

"And Henry is keeping you so satisfied that you don't need my services. Is that all I have been to you? A plaything?"

"Hal, you're talking wildly. I lay with you in France and that night here because I love you, and love made me reckless." I took my hands in his. "But you must be sensible. This has been an idyll, which we will look back upon fondly in our old age, but it cannot last. It is wrong whether or not Henry comes to my bed."

His voice softened. "Then you want that night in that turret room to be our last? That narrow cot in that cold, drafty room? I think it only fair to both of us that we have a last time together that is more pleasurable. Such as here, in your comfortable bed with the sun warming us—well, as much sun as you get up north." Somerset kissed me playfully. "Please? After all, we're bound to be besieged here soon. Isn't a bit cruel to leave a man here with nothing but his fellow men to look at, with no pleasant memories to think upon?"

I am not made of stone. "But it must be our last time. Hal, promise."

"I promise." Hal began to undo the fastenings of my gown.

Twenty years later, I can still perfectly recall it all: the sun glinting on our hair as it mingled on our pillows; my cries of pleasure blending so harmoniously with the squawks of the seagulls that I started giggling until Hal brought me to such a height that I could think of nothing except for the sensations claiming me; the incoherent endearments we whispered to each other; Hal's gasps of pleasure after I'd slowly teased him to climax; the long, delicious sleep in each other's arms afterward. It was sin, Lord knows, but it was sweet, and when the sunlight plays on the walls of my chamber a certain way and I think of all in my life who have come and gone, I remember it still.

❦

"I don't like the looks of that cloud," Pierre de Brézé said the next morning as our ships sailed toward Berwick.

I came out of my reverie long enough to gaze upward. *I shall never forget yesterday afternoon, my love, no matter what happens in the future*, Hal had whispered just before Henry and I were rowed off to our ship. As best as I could without betraying myself, I had kept him in my sight until I could no longer make out his form. "It does look rather nasty," I said lackadaisically.

Brézé gave me an irritated look. "That's an understatement." When I had nothing more to say for myself, he added, "I think we should head back to shore. I'll speak to our captain."

He had been gone for no more than a minute when the tempest came upon us, stirred up as if by some angry god of antiquity. The wind howled, the rain pelted us, and the waves tossed around our caravel as easily as a child might toss around a toy ship. Soon we could not even see the rest of our fleet.

Ordered into the cabin by the captain, my ladies and I could do nothing more but huddle there and pray as the ship's rocking sent us skidding from one side of the tiny space to another. Then I screamed as the sea tossed our ship upward and threw her down again amid a great spray of sea and a sound of shattering wood.

We stumbled out of the cabin just as the cry went up to abandon ship. Through the rain and blowing sand, I could just make out the rocks that we had been wrecked upon. "What will we do?" Marie wailed. "We'll die!"

"No," I said. "We'll launch the boat, and we will get into it and be safe." I looked at Pierre de Brézé. "Won't we?"

Pierre nodded, then looked at our flowing gowns critically. "We're going to have to lower you ladies down into it, and those skirts of yours will be a nuisance. My advice is cut them to your knees. May I?"

I nodded and offered my skirts up to Pierre, who hacked at them with the dagger he wore at his side until I stood exposed from my knees down, save for my stockings. Marie looked on mournfully as he repeated the process with her. "My trunk! It will soon be at the bottom of the sea. Won't it?"

"Along with all of our treasure," I said. "But we can't worry about that now."

With a great deal of cursing and shouting, the sailors had succeeded in launching the boat, which looked pitifully tiny next to even our sleek caravel, especially with the waves swirling around it. Two men promptly clambered down the rope ladder into it. "I shall go next," said Henry. He shook his head as a sailor offered to tie a rope around his waist. "You don't need to tie me. I place my life in the Lord's hands."

"Henry—"

My husband kissed me. "You shall go after me, and I shall be there to make sure you arrive there safely. Tie her very carefully."

"Henry!" I clutched at him as he set his heels upon the ladder. "If we die, there is something you must know. I have sin—"

Brézé pulled me back. "There's no time for that! Let him go."

Because the ship was built low for cruising, the distance to the boat was not more than twenty feet or so, but to me it looked three or four times that as Henry descended. He landed in the boat safely and called up, "Now, Marguerite, you come. Trust to the Lord as I did, and all will be well."

Brézé looked at my feet. "Best do it barefoot, your grace. You'll slip right off otherwise."

After kicking off my sodden slippers, then shedding my stockings, I put my bare foot on the first rung of the rope ladder. From the ship, it had looked deceptively stable; now that I was on it myself, I found that it swung back and forth. Praying, or to put it more accurately, mumbling God's name like an incantation as I went on, I found the next step and began to descend slowly, each step downward feeling like a free fall into an abyss. Then at last Henry's arms came around me. "You're safe, my brave girl," he whispered, lowering me into the rocking boat and wrapping his cloak around my freezing legs as he sat me down.

Late that evening, we finally made it in our little boat to Berwick, where the garrison stared at us women in our mutilated gowns as we straggled into the great hall. My ladies and I sank in front of the fire, but Henry went with the constable himself to make certain that I could be accommodated comfortably. Pierre de Brézé, unwilling to prop himself before the fire while the king was being so active himself, would have followed, but I stopped him. "Please stay for a moment, my lord." Reluctantly, I moved away from the huddled ladies before the fire. "When I thought we were in danger of death, I almost made a confession to the king."

"Yes. I believe I know what it is. Does it involve the Duke of Somerset?"

I nodded shamefacedly. "How did you guess?"

Brézé snorted. "No great perceptiveness on my part, trust me. Somerset's not a model of subtlety, despite what he might think. He undresses you in his mind whenever he looks at you; any man over sixteen can watch him and see him doing it. And you're not exactly circumspect yourself. If your husband weren't Henry, I daresay he would have guessed by now. I did back in Rouen. Lovers are insane, most of them, in what they think goes unseen, and you're no better than the rest of the lot as far as that goes."

"You stopped me from telling him."

"Yes. Aside from the timing being poor, some things are better kept to oneself. I'm not sure even King Henry would be able to refrain from putting the duke to death. What would that accomplish?" He coughed as I hung my head. "I'm old enough to be your father and he's not here to tell you this, so consider this advice in the spirit of *in loco parentis*. Put this affair to an end. I know it's difficult for you, Somerset being a charming young blade and King Henry being—unique, as we shall say, but it will get around sooner or later, and you will lose your reputation for virtue."

"I don't believe I ever had one among the English in the first place," I said. "But I have anticipated you. I have broken it off." But would I be proof against Somerset the next time I saw him, if he pressed himself upon me? "At least, I have tried."

"You must do more than try, my child. You must be firm."

"I know. But I love him so much."

"The king, or Somerset?"

"Both," I said. I stared toward the fire. "Thank you for your advice, my lord."

Four hundred of the men who had set out with us from France were wrecked upon Holy Island during the storm that had claimed my own ship. Some were killed by Edward's men, some were taken prisoner; most simply escaped and found their way back abroad. I had nothing to pay them with anyway; my treasure was at the bottom of the sea.

By Christmas, Henry and I were back in our borrowed quarters at Edinburgh, as if we'd never left. Warwick had been besieging Bamburgh, Dunstanburgh, and Alnwick since late November, and I knew that all three castles were inadequately provisioned and could not long hold out against a winter siege. But help was on the way from the Scots, given only after Henry promised the Earl of Angus an English dukedom and I hinted to Bishop Kennedy that the Archbishopric of Canterbury might be within his reach. If the castles could hold out just a little longer, we would be able to raise the siege with an army headed by the Earl of Angus and Pierre de Brézé, who were heading south as quickly as they could.

Christmas had come and gone when, coming back from my son's chamber, I entered my own and saw my ladies standing together in a knot. "Oh, Christ," Marie whispered. "This will kill the queen."

My hearing has always been sharp. "What will kill the queen?" I halted as my ladies turned pale faces to me. "What on earth is it?"

"We have lost Dunstanburgh and Bamburgh."

I winced. "Our men?" They stared back at me. "Well, what of our men?" A chill ran through me. "Speak. Are they captured? Dead?" My voice pitched upward. "My lord of Somerset. Is he captured, or dead? Tell me, for mercy's sake!"

"He ought to be both," Katherine Vaux said finally. "But he is neither."

"For God's sake, what do you mean?"

"The Duke of Somerset has joined Edward's men. He is besieging Alnwick—alongside Warwick's forces. He has turned against us."

For a moment I stood frozen there, absorbing the unthinkable. Hal, whom I had trusted, loved, given what should have been given only to my husband, had betrayed us.

With all my strength, I drove my fist into the wall beside me.

"God damn him to hell!" I screamed as my ladies dragged me backward, my hand bleeding over all of us as I struggled to free myself from their grasp. "God damn the filthy whoreson to hell!"

18

Margaret
December 1462 to July 1463

Aᴛᴛᴇʀ Sᴏᴍᴇʀsᴇᴛ ʙᴇᴛʀᴀʏᴇᴅ ᴜs, I ᴛᴏʀᴍᴇɴᴛᴇᴅ ᴍʏsᴇʟғ ᴀs I ʟᴀʏ ᴀʙᴇᴅ ᴀᴛ night, picturing him and King Edward chortling together at my folly in bedding Hal. Perhaps they were laughing at me for loving a man six years younger than myself; perhaps Hal was amusing Edward and his new Yorkist friends with tales about my merits or lack thereof as a sexual partner. What basis, after all, did I have for comparison? By-and-by, he might even point out the chambers where we had made love at Bamburgh, as sort of curiosity pieces.

It did no good, in my more rational moments, to reason with myself that I had never known Hal to be unchivalrous in that manner and that surely he could be trusted to keep the secret of our liaison to himself. I had thought that he would be true to Lancaster, too, and what had happened? My only consolation was in thinking of what would be done to that handsome body of his if he ever fell into our hands. Hanging, drawing, and quartering would be his lot, I promised myself—and castration as well. In my worst moments, I pictured myself performing this latter task personally.

The tidings of Somerset's treachery had come from an unimpeachable source: Hal's brother Thomas Ros, who came to me soon after I heard the news from my ladies. "We offered to surrender Bamburgh on Christmas Eve," he said, glancing at my bandaged hand and wisely deciding not to comment. "We didn't know then that troops were on the way to raise the siege. We were almost without provisions, and we had started eating our own horses by then."

I briefly indulged myself in a pleasant mental picture of Somerset dining on one of his beloved palfreys. "Go on."

"Our condition was that the castles remain in the hands of Percy, provided that he swore allegiance to Edward, and that we be spared our lives. They offered the Earl of Pembroke and I safe conducts here, and they brought Hal and the rest to see Edward at Durham. Edward had been sick with measles."

"Measles," I said. "The boy king."

"I don't know what Edward said to Hal at Durham. I do know that when we were at Bamburgh, Hal was beginning to lose heart—and it wasn't just the horsemeat. He's not seen our mother in years; he has a son he's never seen; he's never married; he's poor; he's worried about our brother Edmund in prison."

"But you haven't seen your mother or your wife or most of your children in years either, and you are worried about Edmund too, surely? And you stayed faithful to us. He has no good excuse for his treachery."

"I don't seek to excuse him, but he's my younger brother and I've always been fond of him. I can't judge him harshly. Perhaps in his case I would have done the same. When he went off to see Edward, I feared that he might be heading into a trap, that he might be killed. When I found that he had joined Edward, I wanted to beat him black and blue, but I was also glad to hear that he was still alive."

"I was not. I hope he rots in hell." I glared at Ros, "You helped him meet me back in Rouen. Why?"

"Because I love him," Ros said quietly. "Your grace must know that I was never pleased by the arrangement, but he would have met you anyway with or without my help. I hoped that with my help the two of you would not be discovered and that the affair would run its course, as it did when your grace very sensibly ended it. I regret having played the role I did."

"You should."

Ros hesitated. "Your grace, there is something I must ask. Could you be—?"

"Carrying his brat? No. And it is lucky that I am not, for if I were, I would use any means I could think of to get rid of it. Including sorcery, if that were my only hope." Ros shivered, and I stared stonily into his eyes. "I spoke too harshly just now; it is hardly your fault that I played the whore with your brother. I am grateful for the good service you have given to me over the years. But I warn you, if you ever communicate with that false traitor, brother or no brother, you shall pay the price."

"Yes, your grace." Ros backed out of the room.

⁂

"This is precisely how I want to spend a beautiful day in July," Queen Mary said as we rode toward Norham Castle. "Besieging a castle with a fellow mother. And our sons! Quite a family party."

"They seem to be enjoying themselves," I said, glancing at the boys.

Soon after Somerset's perfidy, Pierre de Brézé and the Earl of Angus had ridden out to relieve Alnwick Castle, still under siege, and had freed our garrison. But the earl—ailing, as I later realized, as he died from an illness that March—had been overcautious and had avoided battle, and so in the end Alnwick had fallen into Warwick's hands. Yet our fortunes, at their nadir then, had improved. In March, Ralph Percy, left by Edward in charge of Bamburgh and Dunstanburgh, had sent a messenger in secret to let us know that he would give them up to us, and Sir Ralph Grey had followed suit with Alnwick in May. With these favorable augurs, and with our ally Bishop Kennedy in the ascendency in Scotland for the moment, we had decided to lay siege to Norham Castle.

This was not to say that all of our party was enthusiastic. King James, who was just a year or so older than my own son, appeared to be liking his taste of warfare well enough, as were my Edward and the triumphant Bishop Kennedy, but Mary of Gueldres had not given up her hopes for a peace with York. Rudely, I wondered whether she harbored thoughts of marrying King Edward.

"None of your schemes has worked! Not one."

"Well, if this one does, we shall be out of your hair and at Westminster where we belong." I made a conscious effort to keep my temper. "And I feel confident that this one will work."

"Why, my dear? Why this one?"

Because something has to go right for us, sooner or later. "We have men and great ordinance. And I believe our recent success has given us heart."

"I should hardly call having three dreary castles handed over to you by traitors success," mused Queen Mary. "But I can see where it might be a decided improvement from your point of view. Now you will forgive me, dear, but there is someone I really must speak to." She prodded her horse ahead of mine and trotted briskly away.

I glared at the rear of her departing horse, wondering what Somerset had ever seen in her.

For eighteen days we laid siege to Norham. Each night Henry and Edward and I, as well as King James and Bishop Kennedy, rode among our men, calling out words of encouragement. (Mary of Gueldres, who I learned later to my considerable guilt was genuinely not feeling well, and who indeed died late that year, stayed in her tent.) "Do you think we'll ever get England back?" asked Edward while we were riding back to our tents after one of these excursions.

"We pray so," Henry said. He smiled at me. "And if your mother has any say in it, our prayers will be answered."

"I don't like living like this, always having to move from place to place. I liked Grandfather's court."

I sighed as I looked down at my stained dress. Sometimes, though I tried not to, I could not help but think of my wardrobe at Greenwich, stuffed with fine dresses and jewels. How pampered had I been in those days, and how little appreciative of it. "It will not be forever, Edward. Now, hush. Having Queen Mary complaining is bad enough without you joining in."

"Yes, Mother."

Henry gazed at Edward for some time after that. Later that evening, as we were preparing for bed in the tent we shared, he said, "My dear, I have been thinking about what Edward said. Win or lose, when this siege is over, I want you to return to France."

"You don't want me here?" The guilt I felt daily over Somerset descended upon me. "Have I offended you?"

"Don't want you here? I shall miss you every hour." Henry put his arms around my waist. "But this is no life for you and for our son, living in tents and in castles where we can be turned out at someone's whim. I want you to live in comfort. And my reasons are selfish, too, for I worry constantly that you will fall into the hands of Edward's men. I will be much easier in my mind, knowing that you are safe abroad."

"But—"

"It is decided, my love. I have written to your father to ask him to give you and Edward the use of one of his castles. Do not think you will not be of any use to me there. You will be able to meet with King Louis and our other relations."

I hesitated. "But you? Would you join me there?"

"No, for now I think it best to stay here. It would not do to have others fight for me while I stay abroad."

I did not trust myself to go abroad without Henry again, not after what had happened in Rouen. But I heeded Pierre de Brézé's advice. "Very well. I will do as you wish."

⁊

Just before dawn the next day, a messenger arrived: Warwick and his men, traveling north to raise the siege, lay within a short marching distance from Norham. All would be decided in a couple of hours. We were ready for a fight.

Instead, we ran. At the first sight of Warwick's banners, the Scots—deaf to Pierre de Brézé's orders, curses, and finally pleas—fled, bearing young King James and Mary of Gueldres in their midst. "God curse the sorry cowards!" Pierre screamed as he sat astride his horse, flanked by the few French troops we had remaining. "We can't possibly fight with them gone. We'll be annihilated."

"Is there nothing we can do?" I said, tears stinging my eyes.

"Nothing. Whoresons!" Brézé let go a volley of expletives in French, then stopped in mid-curse. "Warwick's men! Good God, they mean to capture you and the king! Fly!"

We galloped away, the press of men and horses beside us causing Henry's and Brézé's horses to become separated from Edward's and mine. My nine-year-old son, though he promised to be a fine horseman, lacked the experience of the rest of us, and the vagabond life we had been living had not allowed him to practice riding regularly. Panicking and completely out of his control, his horse ran off the path we were traveling to Berwick. Screaming advice to my son, which he either could not hear or was too terrified to heed, I followed. "Edward!"

Edward lay face down in some mud, his riderless horse vanishing into the woods. I scrambled off my horse and knelt beside him. "My God. My God. Speak to me."

My son sat up. "I'm fine," he muttered.

I helped him to stand. Nothing had been broken, but a knot was beginning to appear on his forehead. "You must get on my horse. It has a sidesaddle, of course, but we can man—"

"No. We have a sidesaddle now." A rider wearing the ragged staff insignia of Warwick swung easily from his horse, and grabbed me by my cloak as five or six other men trotted up behind him. "And look what else we have, boys. The little French bitch who started all of this. Ain't I right?" He raised his sword and smiled at me. "I can cut your pretty little head off with this, like you did the good Duke of York's. Did you know that?"

"Leave my mother alone!"

"Well, if it isn't the little bastard himself," said our captor genially. "Whose son are you, anyway? Suffolk's?"

"Too late, you fool. Suffolk died years before this one was hatched."

"True. Must be a Beaufort, then. But who knows? Could be anyone's, really." He pushed me to my knees. "Ever had a fighting man, Meg? Maybe I'll have my pleasure with you before I kill you. Would you like that?"

Edward ran to my side and drew his dagger. "Don't you dare hurt her!"

My captor chuckled. "The bastard has spirit, I'll give him that." He considered. "Now, if there is an off chance that he's Henry's, he needs to be got rid of. If he isn't Henry's, he's a nuisance no one will miss. What of it, men? Shall we kill the boy as well?"

"For our Savior's sake, spare us!" I stared up at the men. "You can have my jewels, my horse, my cloak—everything. You can have my body if that is what you want. You are Warwick's men, don't you think he will give you a generous reward if you bring us to him alive? Don't you think my father would pay dearly to ransom us? You'll get nothing if you bring Warwick our corpses; even he won't want his hands stained with a woman's blood and a boy's. He might even punish you." I held up my hands in supplication. "At least spare my boy!"

"The wench has a point," observed the youngest of the men, who had been watching me plead with less amusement than the rest. He gave me a look that I could not read, then walked over to my horse and opened a saddlebag. "Christ, there's half the crown jewels in here!"

"You'll not be taking them all for yourself," his leader warned. He turned as the men around him all swarmed round the booty. "What, you think you'll cheat me out of my just share? Will! Guard the bitch and her whelp, damnit!"

Will, the young man who had spoken earlier, left the treasure with a sullen look and yanked me to my feet. Then he whispered into my ear, "See the dappled horse there? When I signal, grab your boy and run for it. Hesitate and all three of us will be dead."

I nodded. For an agonizing few more moments, the men squabbled over my goods, their voices rising as they fought over who should get what. Then one punched the other. "Now!" hissed Will.

We scrambled on the horse, I in front of Will and Edward hanging onto his back, and galloped into the woods, our departure lost in the melee. "I'll not see a lady raped or killed, and I suspect they would have done both to you," Will said when I gasped out my thanks. "But I warn you, your grace, these woods are full of brigands. We might have exchanged bad for worse."

"For now, I'll be pleased to take my chances," I said, clutching the pommel and thanking the Lord that I had always been a confident rider. Every small tree looked to me like another menacing figure coming to rob or ravish me, and I had no idea whether we were riding toward Berwick, but I at least did not fear falling off this horse. I turned. "Edward! Are you holding on tight?"

"Yes, Mother," said my son, with sufficient irritation for me to smile.

Then a horseman galloped toward us, clearly bent on blocking our path. "Let us pass!" demanded Will as he reluctantly halted our horse.

The horseman said nothing, and indeed, he looked so menacing that he needed no words to aid him. He was easily one and a half times Will's size, and his stare as he sized up my escort was a fearsome one to behold. "What have you got for me, boy?" Will made no response. "Answer me, boy, or I'll kill you here and now, before the lady." He moved closer to me and fingered my gown. "That gown's of quality; you'll not have me believe you've no valuables." He eyed Edward, who was attempting without much success not to look scared. "That boy's well dressed; if you'll not pay me to recover him, I reckon some of his people will. Give him here!"

"Let him go!" I dropped to the ground and stood before the brigand. "Do you know who I am? I am your queen, Margaret, wife to your rightful king, Henry the Sixth, and that is your prince!"

The robber stared.

"It is true. Go a little ways from whence we came, to Norham Castle, and you will find it has been under siege, with me present."

"She speaks true," said Will.

"I have no jewels; I was robbed of them back near Norham. I have only the clothes on my back. If that will satisfy you, I will give them to you, though as you can see they are much worn. But why settle for that, when I can give you something far more valuable?"

"Say what?"

"A new life! Aren't you secretly ashamed of this life, robbing innocents and the unwary, lurking, knowing that you will end up on the gallows? But if you help my son and me and my friend here, and bring us safely to the king, you will have done a good deed that will atone for the evil you have done. My husband will reward you, be certain of it, and more important, God will reward you as well. It is never too late to change."

The robber hesitated. "You are really the queen? You sound more like a female preacher."

I smiled. "I am the queen. When you take me to safety, my friends will tell you I speak the truth. Now, come. What will it be? The clothes we are wearing, which will feed you for a short time before you are hanged, or your immortal soul?"

The robber swung off his horse and knelt awkwardly at my feet. "My lady, I am yours to command."

"Rise, then, and show us to Berwick, where my husband awaits me."

"It's not far," said the thief. He looked at Edward, still sitting behind Will. "I can take the boy up behind me, my lady, if it would be more comfortable for you and him."

I hesitated, then nodded. The robber swung Edward onto his horse, and we trotted away after Will had settled me behind him. Will hissed behind his shoulder, "Your grace, why did you tell him who you were? He might have taken you back to Warwick's men for a reward! And why did you give him your son? Wasn't that taking a risk?"

"I don't know." I looked at Edward, who was chattering now quite amicably with the robber. "Maybe it was because it was what my husband would do."

It was mid-afternoon when our oddly assorted little group finally came to Berwick, where I found that a search was being mounted for Edward and me. As soon as I passed through the gate, a messenger dashed off to find Henry, who had me locked in his arms before I could even reach the bailey. "Thank the Lord you are safe," he whispered into my hair. "And you, my boy!" He embraced my son, then stared at Will with his ragged staff badge and my would-be robber as they kneeled before him. "And these are—"

"This is young Will, who saved me back at Norham," I said. "And this is—" I frowned, remembering I had never learned the name of the man to whom I had entrusted our son.

"They call me Black Jack, your grace."

"Black Jack," said Henry, the name sounding so ridiculous on his lips that I could not help but smile in my exhaustion.

"Black Jack could have robbed me in the forest, but instead helped us here to safety. He has treated me with all of the respect due to a queen, and I trust he will do the same to you as his king."

My companion nodded.

"Rise, then, both of you," Henry said. "Young Will, you can return to your people, or stay here in my service. I hope you will choose the latter, but I know you may have family waiting for you."

"I do, your grace. I am sorry."

"Then take some refreshment before you leave, and rest your horse. And you, Black Jack? Would you like to stay?"

"I've no one waiting for me, your grace. If I can serve you and your brave lady, I'd be honored."

"Then so it shall be."

Before my adventures, I had half hoped that Henry would change his mind about sending me to France, but after getting an uncensored account of the episode from Edward, Will, and Black Jack, Henry could not get me out of England fast enough. He did not even wait for my father's reply to his message. "Had those men murdered you, or ravished you"—Henry shuddered— "I might well have gone mad again. I almost did when I heard from some of those Scots that Warwick's men had been seen near you. No, you and Edward must go to France. Why, what is wrong, my dear?"

"I deserve to have been ravished and murdered." I dropped down to my knees. "I have been advised not to tell you this, but I cannot bear it any longer. You must know the truth if you are to send me to France again. I have wronged you in the worst way a woman can wrong a husband."

Henry stared down at me as I huddled by his feet. "With another man?"

"Yes. With Henry Beaufort." I swallowed. "He has been a traitor to you by deserting you and will have to answer to God for that, but I am to blame for our adultery. I am the woman and the married one; I should have known better. I did know better. If you will only forgive me, I will do any penance I am asked to do. I will fast. I will walk barefoot through the streets with a taper. I will end my days in a nunnery. I will—"

"Margaret, stand."

Shaking, I obeyed. Calmly, Henry asked, "Edward. He is my son?"

"Yes. I will swear to it. I did you no wrong until I went to Rouen. *Ruin*. It is aptly named, is it not?" I stared at the floor. "I will never wrong you in that way again; I will swear an oath to that too."

Henry took me into his arms. "I forgive you, Marguerite. There is no need for solemn oaths."

"You are too generous," I whispered.

"You have had much to bear these last few years." Henry stroked my hair as I began to sob into his neck.

"But can you ever trust me again?"

"I can and I will." He smiled sadly. "Even when you were in Rouen, you did your best for me. How many queens have been asked to do so much? How many have suffered robbery and shipwreck and exile for their king's sake? I do not condone your behavior with Somerset, but under the circumstances I cannot let it outweigh all of the devotion you have shown to me and our son."

"*Our* son. Believe me."

"I do." Henry was silent for a time while I rested in his embrace. "I would even forgive Hal if he asked it," he said. "Perhaps someday he will."

I shook my head. "They say that Edward has made him very welcome at his court. The traitor will be too comfortable there."

"You must have loved him, and I was fond of him myself. The man cannot be all bad; indeed, I know he is not. Do not give up on him, Marguerite."

Only my dear Henry could speak more kindly about my former lover than I could myself. "I will try. After all, you have not given up on me."

I spent the night clasped in my husband's arms. The next day, I once again made my farewells to Henry at Edinburgh. Traveling with me and Edward were the Duke of Exeter, Doctor Morton, Marie, William and Katherine Vaux, and a couple of dozen others, each of us in varying degrees a tatterdemalion. Would we ever see England's shores again? Yet as uncertain as our future was, it was Henry I worried about most, left to no one but the uncertain protection of the Scots. "I wish you were going with us," I said as I embraced him.

"I must stay here and be ready for whatever happens," said Henry, hugging me closer to him. "Who knows? Perhaps when we see each other again, it will be in London."

I smiled and turned to Lord Ros as Henry bade good-bye to our son. "Do take care of him."

"I will. I and Black Jack," he added, for Black Jack had taken a distinct liking to Lord Ros and could generally be found rendering him some service or another. "Don't you fear, your grace. We will keep the cause of Lancaster alive here."

"As I will abroad." I turned to Henry one more time. "I love you," I said simply.

"And I love you. Remember, my darling. In London!"

"In London!" I said, smiling and waving as Pierre de Brézé led me toward our waiting ship.

19

Henry Beaufort, Duke of Somerset
December 1462 to December 1463

KING EDWARD, AS I HAD BEEN REMINDED NONE TOO GENTLY TO CALL HIM, was a tall man, who looked even taller when one was kneeling before him in supplication. Six feet four, I estimated. "Up," he said cheerfully, extending a hand himself to assist me, for my hands were bound lest, I'd been told, I had some harebrained notion about assassinating the rightful king. "So! You have agreed to become our liegeman. A sensible decision. What made you do it? I must say, you're the last one I'd have ever expected to come over to our side."

"I thought I might as well give in to the inevitable," I said. In fact, I could pinpoint the exact moment when I had decided not merely to surrender to Edward, but to pledge my loyalty to him: the morning of Christmas Eve, when I had sat down to yet another plate of horse. I was six-and-twenty and unmarried, with a bastard child I had never seen. I was poor; I hadn't seen my mother in years; my brother Edmund was languishing as a Yorkist prisoner. I loved a woman I never could have openly, and she herself had begged me to break off our relations. I was fighting for a cause that had been lost long ago at Palm Sunday Field. That Christmastide as I stared around me at the cheerlessness of Bamburgh Castle, it had suddenly seemed so simple, so seductive to throw in my lot with the side that was winning.

Seductive it had been; simple it had not. I hadn't dared to tell even Tom, my own brother, my intention. Even as Edward's men led me into the king's presence, I had had second thoughts. I could tell him I had changed my mind, and then I would go to my prison or to my death with a clear conscience.

But my courage, and my conscience, had failed me.

Edward snorted when he heard my reply. "That's what they all say when they come over to me. *I decided to give in to the inevitable.* Or *One can't fight against fate*. Always the same answer. And they all have the same expression on their face, like they've taken a gulp of bad wine."

"Oh?" I said gloomily. "I had hoped that I was more unique."

My new king smiled. "Someone told me that you had a certain charm, Beaufort. I was beginning to doubt it." He settled back in his chair and looked at me with interest. "Why, I believe we might even become friends."

I tried not to think of Margaret in those early Yorkist days of mine, which of course meant that I thought of her nearly constantly. When I had been brought to Alnwick to assist Warwick (a role that was as nearly as unpleasant to think about as my betrayal of Margaret, but I was wisely kept far from his presence), I passed the dreary hours of the siege in dialogue with myself: *She dismissed you, after all, and she was right. Continuing as things were could only lead to disaster. Her place is with her husband, not with you. It's all for the best.*

But you didn't have to abandon her cause when you left her bed.

With all of my conversations with myself ending like this, I couldn't have been more unpleasant, and more tedious, company for myself. Needless to say, then, I quickly sought out more congenial companionship as soon as the king's household, me in tow, arrived in London. "Your grace, I would like to ask leave to visit my son in London. I've never seen him."

Edward threw me an exasperated look. "Beaufort, when will you realize that you're not my prisoner? You can see the boy any time you want. How old is he?"

"Three. He was born when I was abroad."

"And you've never had a chance to see the lad? Well, I suppose not, if he's been here. Who's the mother?"

I hesitated, and Edward laughed. "Good Lord, man, I'm not poaching on your territory." He smiled in that endearingly boyish way of his. "In fact, I've a bastard son of my own, just newly hatched. Arthur, the boy's name is, by an Elizabeth Lucy. I rather like the name, don't you?"

"Do you still see the mother?" I asked, since Edward evidently liked this topic and it had occurred to me that I had been rather standoffish.

"Oh, once in a while," the king said airily. "There are other women now."

Sometimes I marveled at the fact that the same island had managed to produce two kings so diametrically opposite as Henry and Edward.

That very afternoon, I set off for Eastcheap, where I found that unlike everything else, Joan's shop had changed very little in the past few years—if anything, it looked better than when I had seen first seen it. It smelled as tempting as it had when I had first come across it at age seventeen, and I wondered if Joan was as tempting too.

Well, I would find out soon enough. I pushed open the door and there Joan stood, setting out wafers. "Smells good in here," I said.

"Thank you, sir. My cooking is good, you'll find. Won't you try something?" Joan gave me her full attention and clapped a floury hand to her chest. "Hal?"

"The same."

"My God," Joan said, and locked me into a flour-filled embrace. "It's safe for you to be in London?"

"Yes." Well, there was no point in delaying the truth. "I serve the House of York now."

Joan's face changed. "I had heard that, but I never believed it. You? A Yorkist?"

"Me."

"I can't believe it even when I hear it from you."

"Well, it's true. Is that all you can do, stare at me as if I had horns?"

"I—I just never expected it."

"Maybe you lack imagination." I slammed the purse I was carrying—full of coins courtesy of Edward, who had given me a generous allowance—on the counter. "I'll take myself off now, if that's the welcome I'm going to get. Here's some money for Charles. You can wash it before you use it in case it's too filthy for you."

"Hal, no!" Joan caught at me. "Don't get your back up so quickly. I am sorry. I am glad to see you back. But it's confusing. Don't you realize that? I've been raising Charles as a Lancastrian through and through. He knows that his father's been fighting for the king and the queen and understands that's why you haven't seen him before. And now you're with the House of York—it's not something I ever expected. Not after what happened to your father—and you—at St. Albans. I remember how you were when I first saw you afterward, how I just wanted to take you in my arms and comfort you as if you were my boy instead of my lover. And now you're fighting for these men?"

"Times have changed. King Edward"—I'd had to train myself to add the word *king*, and as a result I always gave it an odd emphasis—"is a better man than his father."

"Yes, so they say. But he's still got Warwick, hasn't he?"

This was a question best ignored. "It's best for everyone. For Mother, for my brothers—King Edward's going to set Edmund free soon, I hope—and even for you and Charles. I can provide for him now, marry him well."

"But is it the best for you? Love, I don't want you coming to hate yourself."

"Why not? Everyone else does—except for King Edward. His men treat me like a leper, and you can just imagine what Henry's men think of me now. I'd hoped for something different from you."

"I don't hate you, Hal. I am very, very glad to see you. And Charles will be glad to see you also. Will you come see him? Please?"

"Joan, I've not been around children his age much. How do I act?"

Joan patted my cheek. "You'll do fine. Let me just get Joe to mind the shop—just as he's been minding us, I warrant." A boy bobbed into view, and I wondered how long he had been eavesdropping. "Oh, I should warn you that my mother's back there; she helps me with Charles. She believes I've made it up about you being the father, by the way."

"Who does she think is the father? The Holy Ghost?"

"More like the innkeeper a few houses down. Come on, Hal."

In the living area behind Joan's shop, an older lady sat sewing as a small boy played with cherry stones. "Charles. This is your father. Mother, this is the Duke of Somerset."

I gazed down at a perfect replica of myself at three years of age. I'd never doubted Joan for an instant when she had told me that I was the father of her coming child, but I had not expected that my son would resemble me so completely. Neither, evidently, had Mrs. Hill, who stared in turn at me, Joan, and Charles before muttering, "Well, I'll be damned."

"I told you he'd come back when he could, Ma."

"And here I am," I said. "My pleasure, madam." I hesitated, then crouched beside Charles, who looked at me as one could expect a child to look at a total stranger who has just been announced as his father. "Can I play?"

"Do you know 'ow?"

Look like me this boy might, but his voice was pure London. "I'll have you know that no one in my family was better than I at bowling stones in my youth," I said. "Just watch the master in awe and learn, boy."

"He talks funny," Charles observed, but obediently watched as I aimed one stone toward the other and set them to colliding with a satisfying click. Soon we were making quite a match of it, though naturally I let Charles win.

Mrs. Hill took the first opportunity to rush home, presumably to tell her neighbors that her daughter had indeed been mistress to a duke. I spent the rest of the afternoon with Joan and Charles, Joan leaving the shop in what I hoped were the competent hands of Joe. We played at stones for a while, and then we walked out into the open fields to play at ball. Joan cooked us supper when we returned (her cooking was even better than I remembered), after which we put our tired son to bed, I carrying him up the stairs. "You've worn him out, and I didn't think that was possible," Joan said as I laid him in his tiny bed and kissed him good-night on the forehead. "He likes you."

"And I like him. You've done a good job with him, Joan." I supposed at some point, though, that his education would have to be taken in hand: the letter aitch and Charles, for instance, could certainly stand to become better acquainted. "I'm very proud that he's my son," I added lamely, revolving in my mind whether I should stay longer. It had been over three years since we had been together; perhaps Joan had found another man—though, base creature that I was, I had looked around and hadn't seen any signs of one.

Then Joan answered my unspoken question. "I expect that you've had other women, Hal, after all this time, and I can't blame you. But I've never had another man since you left, and I won't have another. It wouldn't be right to have Charles thinking he could have been fathered by any gentleman I happened to fancy."

I stroked her cheek. "I've missed you."

"I've missed you too, Hal. Even if you have gone Yorkist on us."

"A Yorkist takes off his drawers the same way as a Lancastrian," I told her, leading her into her bedchamber opposite Charles's tiny chamber. "I'll prove it."

Making love to Joan was a world away from making love to Margaret. Physically, the women themselves could not have been less alike—Margaret was petite and fine-boned, whereas Joan was tall and ample—and with Joan there was none of the guilt and fear of being caught that had always lent a certain desperate edge to my couplings with Margaret. Instead, our lovemaking was easy, comfortable, and uncomplicated, and when it was over I felt more at peace with the world than I had in many a day. Only one thing concerned me. "You don't think Charles heard, do you?"

Joan shook her head. "He sleeps like the dead," she said contentedly. Draping her arm around me in preparation for sleep, she kissed me. "Welcome back to London, Hal."

I spent every night I could at Joan's, for as I had told her, people at Edward's court kept their distance from me, especially when Ralph Percy, who had turned his coat at the same time I had turned mine, went back to Henry and Margaret's side. I wasn't that much bothered by the coldness of Warwick and his brothers—they were not people I could envision myself holding a friendly conversation with under any circumstances—but even the urbane and jovial Lord Hastings, Edward's closest friend, was coolly polite toward me, and others were downright hostile. It made me feel like I imagined a lonely schoolboy must feel.

Only the king treated me with warmth: dining by my side, joking with me, and even doing me the honor of allowing me to share the royal bed—an honor I could have really done without, for not only was half the court jealous of me and the other half convinced that I had plans to assassinate Edward, it turned out that the king snored. Each time my nagging conscience settled down adequately enough for me to fall asleep at night, he would start up, and I would lie tossing and turning until he finally shifted position.

"We'll have to find you a wife one of these days, Somerset," Edward mused one evening in April as we settled side by side. I'd been restored to my title and lands by Parliament in March, and I had to admit that it was a pleasure to hear my ducal title on the king's lips once more.

"Yes, one of these days," I agreed, trying to put from my memory the image of Margaret sitting on my lap in that barge at Rouen. *I would be the Duchess of Somerset*, she'd whispered artlessly, so sweetly. "I suppose your grace will be finding a wife soon?" At least then, I thought, I could sleep in my own bed or Joan's more often.

"Oh, one of these days," the king said offhandedly. "I'm still young, and Warwick keeps proposing these perfect frights. So far they've all been too old, or too homely, or too dull. I know the field is limited for a king, but surely he can do better than that. Sometimes I think I'd like to pick for myself, just to see the look on Warwick's face. But enough of that. You joust, don't you?"

"It's been a while," I said evasively, thinking it impolitic to mention that the last tournament I'd been in was after poor Henry's ill-fated Loveday.

"Well, you'll be jousting again. I'm holding a tournament in your honor in May. I won't be in it myself—I'm not particularly accomplished, and I'm in no hurry to see my brother George land in my throne—but we should be able to attract some fine jousters. Lord Scales, for instance."

This was Anthony Woodville, who along with his father had switched his allegiance to York after Palm Sunday Field. *See?* I reminded myself. *Other men had changed their loyalties*. Surely they didn't feel as miserable as I did some nights when I walked through the king's elegantly decorated chambers and pictured poor Henry living in borrowed lodgings in Scotland. "I'm honored. But don't you think it might irritate people?"

"Oh, sod them. You can even bring Joan Hill," he added coaxingly. "She can't sit with my sisters, mind you, but we'll find her a nice place with the merchant's wives to sit. You're too melancholy; some jousting will do you good."

I blinked, taken aback as usual at his perception. For all Edward seemed to have genuinely loved his father, the men couldn't have been more different; if York had possessed a shred of sensitivity, I'd never noticed it. "I thought I hid it well."

"Not at all. You're still fond of old Henry, aren't you?"

"Yes," I admitted, hoping that Edward didn't ask me if I was fond of Margaret. "When my father came back with us from Rouen back in 1450, Henry was kind to us," I said, staring up at the bed canopy as the memory came back. "Father was in disgrace at the time, and Henry treated us as if we'd come back full of glory. I was fourteen and feeling ashamed, and being treated that way meant a great deal to me at the time. It could have been so much different."

Not, my ever-alert if not always effective conscience promptly reminded me, that Henry's kind treatment of me had stopped me from lying with his queen or deserting him. I sighed.

"Well," said Edward briskly, "he's a kind man, no doubt, but his claim to the throne is inferior to mine, and he was a damn bad king when he wore the crown. But when we catch him, we'll treat him kindly, if that makes you feel better." He yawned and rolled over. "Good night, Somerset."

"Good night, your grace."

In five minutes, the snoring had begun. I lay on my back and waited it out, still staring at the canopy and thinking what a convenient thing it would be if the ceiling caved in upon me.

⁕

"What in the world are you wearing?" Anthony Woodville asked me as our pages dressed us for the tournament. There had been some murmurs of anger when the other jousters had seen me there, but Edward had made a great show of coaxing me to take my turn in the lists.

"What does it look like?" I preened. "A straw hat." It was large and floppy brimmed, like a peasant might wear while working in the fields.

"You'll get killed without a proper helm if you're unhorsed."

"But I won't get unhorsed. I've been practicing, I'll have you know. My son and his mother are here, and I mustn't disgrace them."

"Your opponents will be aiming at that damned hat of yours."

I grinned at Anthony. "Better than at my balls."

Anthony looked mildly distressed; I'd forgotten that he had a distinctly straitlaced side. Still, I'd been pleased when he arrived in London for the tournament and actually proved willing to converse with me, so I changed the subject. "Tell me, Anthony. When you came over to the king after Palm Sunday Field, how long did it take anyone to say a civil word to you?"

"Not that long, but there were a lot of us who made our peace then, you know. We didn't stick out the way you do. But Warwick's still chilly to my father." Lord Rivers had been admitted to Edward's council the year before. "But that's because my father's not of noble stock, and the same can't be said of you. They'll come round after you've been here a few more months." He fingered the brim of my hat and shook his head. "If they don't put you away as a madman first."

As I rode out, I saw that Edward's sisters were sitting in the stands, along with the king's mother, the Duchess of York, who fixed me with a glare. I wondered what on earth Edward had promised her to get her to this tournament, which after all was unofficially in my honor. I couldn't imagine her holding out for less than a manor. Elizabeth, the Duchess of Suffolk—married to the son of William de la Pole, Margaret's murdered friend—merely scowled, while Anne, the Duchess of Exeter, whose estranged husband still served the House of Lancaster, made a point of studying her fingernails. The Lady Margaret, at seventeen the king's only unmarried sister, was a pretty, gawky girl who even seated towered over the other ladies: she must have been nearly as tall as most men. As she was not glowering at me like her mother, but staring at my straw hat and giggling, I decided to offer my lance to her. "The Knight of the Straw Hat wishes a favor of the Lady Margaret," I called.

Margaret sneaked a look toward her mother, who gave a clipped nod and heaved a martyred sigh. She tied a ribbon around the lance and I swept my hat off my head in thanks. "My, he's handsome," I heard her say as I rode off.

"He's a turncoat and a murderer," the good Duchess of York corrected her. "I hope someone breaks that handsome head of his."

But no one did; I had been practicing. Anthony Woodville carried off the top honor, but I was right behind him. The next day, Mrs. Hill and Charles vied with each other as to who could tell the most people in Eastcheap about my prowess as a jouster, and Joan insisted upon me wearing my straw hat in bed with her the following night. "It'll fall off," I protested.

Joan set it firmly upon my head. "Not if you're on your back," she explained, and proceeded to prove her point.

⁓

But an even more pleasant event happened during the early part of that Yorkist summer of mine: Edward ordered my brother Edmund to be set free from the Tower. I was waiting for him when the guards took him out. After a year in the place, my father, who'd been lodged in some comfort, had looked bad enough; Edmund after two years of confinement looked even worse, his face listless as he stepped out to freedom. Then he caught sight of me and his expression brightened so much it hurt to watch. "Hal!"

We embraced each other for a long time; I could feel the bones in his back. "Come along," I said finally as I released him, both of us close to tears. "There's a barge waiting for us."

"What about my things?"

"I've arranged with the constable to have them sent."

"But he might forget."

"Edmund, no one's going to forget, I promise."

He reluctantly let me lead him along before coming to a halt. "Where are you taking me?"

"To my house." I'd rented one in London for when I wasn't staying at Westminster or with Joan in Eastcheap, though I hardly ever used it.

"I don't want to be around Edward."

"I'm not taking you around Edward. Don't worry. Now come. I've a surprise at my house."

"Hal, if it's a woman, don't even think of it. I'm not up for carousing."

"Not even a drink at your favorite tavern?"

"I don't have a favorite tavern in London."

"Then we'll go straight to my house. And I promise, no woman."

Edmund nodded and walked silently beside me, staring at the cobblestones beneath our feet, as I studied him covertly, trying to see if anything of my old prankster brother remained. When we approached the landing, he at last flickered to life. "That's yours?"

He was indicating the handsome barge awaiting us. "No. The king has let me use it." I watched as my men helped him in. "You won't get seasick on me, will you, having been so long on dry land?"

For the first time, Edmund managed a grin. "I'll aim for the side if I do." He pointed to a turret as we glided away from the Tower. "That's where I was held. But I couldn't see more than a bit of the river from my window."

"They must have kept you close," I said gently.

"Yes. It was your being in favor with the king that got me out, I suppose?"

I nodded. "It helped, you might say. The hope that you'd be set free was one of the reasons I deserted Lancaster."

"I hated it there. Sometimes I thought I'd never see the outside of the Tower. Thank you."

He relapsed into silence, though this time he was at least looking with some interest at the structures lining the Thames. Presently, we arrived at my house near Westminster. Compared to some of the grander residences surrounding it, it was a small place (I wasn't a particularly wealthy duke even at the best of times), but it was a pleasant one, which I hoped would make my jumpy brother a little more relaxed. As we walked up from the river landing and headed toward the entrance, I said, "Edmund, I lied to you. There is a woman here."

"Hal, I told you—"

My mother stepped forward and took my brother in her arms. "My dear boy," she whispered, and burst into tears.

*

Mother and her husband, Sir Walter Rokesley, had arrived in London the day before, along with my youngest brother, John, and several of my sisters. Settling on the lawn that sloped down to the Thames, we spent the day eating and talking. I couldn't remember the last time all of us had been together. "I just wish my Tom were here with the rest of you," my mother said after a while. "Hal, do you think he'll ever make his peace with York?"

"I don't know," I said, trying to shut out the memory of that day we'd separated at Bamburgh, Tom to rejoin Henry and Margaret, I to betray my allegiance. "If he hasn't by now, I rather doubt that he ever will."

My mother fingered the necklace that my father had given to her years ago. "I still mourn your father," she said softly. "And I hate to see Warwick so powerful. But some days I just wish that Henry and Margaret would just give in, so I could have my boys all here with me in England."

*

But Henry and Margaret weren't giving up; soon word came that they were planning to invade England with a Scottish army. Warwick went up north to deal with the problem himself. By early July Edward had decided to bring his own force up—with me in his entourage. What if Henry and Margaret accompanied their army to battle? Leading forces against either or both of them was the situation I'd most dreaded since I joined Edward's forces. But if I did not go, my loyalties would be forever suspect.

"Do you really think you'll be able to fight against them?" Joan asked me the afternoon before I was supposed to depart from London. The two of us were riding on my horse, and Edmund and Charles were riding on my brother's horse. To put it more accurately, Edmund, Charles, and I were riding and Joan was clutching me for dear life. Only my insistence that Charles be taught to ride had induced her to get upon a horse, though this was the gentlest I owned.

"Christ, I hope not." I'd never told Joan, or anyone else in my family outside of Tom, about my relationship with Margaret, but I supposed that my family ties with Henry were enough to account for my earnest tone of voice. "I don't even want to think of it."

"Hal—oh! Can't you slow this thing down?"

"This *thing* is a magnificent beast, and she is not even trotting. She's barely walking. But if you insist." I patted Grisel, who turned her head and gave me a quizzical look. "Easy, girl."

"I was saying," Joan resumed when we had settled into such a stately pace that my horse could have grazed if she had chosen to, "maybe if you don't want to think about fighting against them, you shouldn't be going with the king."

"It's not that simple. What if I were to abandon Edward? Edmund would be clapped back into prison. Our son would be a traitor's bastard. My mother would have to go back to borrowing money from her sisters. That's how she'd got along these past few years, you know, up until this year when the king restored her annuity. And I've come to like Edward." I looked at Edmund and Charles, trotting into the distance. "You know, I could catch up on my correspondence here while we're riding. If only I'd brought pen and parchment."

"You're changing the subject."

"I know. It's a beautiful day and I don't want to think of disagreeable things." I turned and kissed her. "I love you. You've made these last few months very happy for me, and it's really more than I've deserved."

"I love you." Joan sighed. "But if you do stay true to the king, you'll soon be getting yourself a wife."

"Let's face that when the time comes." I nudged Grisel to a stop and dismounted, roped Grisel to a tree, and lifted Joan to the ground, then pointed to a secluded area nearby. "What do you say we take a break from riding?"

"What if Charles and Edmund come back?"

"Edmund will give us time. Brothers have a sense about these things."

Joan smiled and let me take her on the warm soft grass, the birds chirping merrily in accompaniment to our soft whispers and groans. Afterward, I lay there stroking her hair, reluctant to let reality intrude in on our golden summer day. But something did have to be said, and with the sharp-eared Charles gone, now was the best time to say it. "Joan, there could be a battle up north. I need you to promise me two things. First, that if you or Charles ever needs money or help of any other kind, you'll come to Edmund or one of my other brothers or sisters, or even my mother. She might fuss about it, but it will all be for show; she'd never let you or my child be in want. Second, that if you ever feel that Charles is in danger, for whatever reason, you'll send him abroad. You have those names of my friends in Bruges I gave you, and the men in London who can help you contact them."

"I promise," Joan said. She held me tightly against her, then rose on her elbow and adjusted her clothes as we heard the sound of an approaching horse. "Aren't they going awfully fast?"

"Compared to your average snail, yes," I said, making myself presentable and emerging into the open just as Edmund and Charles appeared.

"Look, Papa! Uncle Edmund let me take the reins."

"And a good job he's done with them," Edmund said, grinning at us knowingly.

"Did you get lost?" Charles asked.

"Your mother needed a rest from riding, that's all," I said solemnly, tousling my son's head. "But come! It may be a while before I get to see you again. Would you like to ride with me a while?"

"Yes!"

"Then you shall," I promised, and settled first Joan, and then my son, in their places. I grinned as our little family made its way in the direction of London, Charles holding the reins. "Easy there, lad. We don't want to scare your mother."

⁂

The next morning, Edward and his men, myself among them, departed for the North. In my own good-sized entourage came Edmund and John. Edward had eyed them a little askance, perhaps thinking that three Beauforts were two more than he had bargained for, but he'd said nothing.

By nightfall, we were in Northampton, where we stayed as guests in the castle there. After supper, where I sat at the high table with the king, I and my brothers decided to take advantage of the merriment and dancing afterward to slip over to the Grey Friars and pay our respects at the tomb of the first Duke of Buckingham, who'd fallen in battle here. His eldest son, dead himself through the plague, had been married to our sister Meg, and I knew she would appreciate the gesture.

My youngest brother, however, at seventeen had other thoughts in his mind as we pushed our way through the castle's crowded great hall. "Are there any good—er—houses here?"

"Didn't you have a chance to visit Southwark when you were in London?"

"With Mother around so much?" John asked plaintively. "And that's like saying a man shouldn't eat on Thursday because he ate on Tuesday, anyway."

"Let's visit the duke's tomb first, shall we?" I said sternly. "And don't expect me to join in; I have to attend the king to bed to—What the hell are you about?"

Two men, not in the king's livery but evidently some of the townspeople who had been invited to dine here tonight, had seized me and were wrestling me against the wall. "Filthy Lancastrian dog!"

Edmund and John tried to drag my attackers off me, only to be knocked away by two more men, who were quickly joined by others. John fell to the ground, while Edmund was able to reach for his dagger. All he could do, though, was defend himself; there were too many of them on me now, punching, kicking, yanking on my jewels and clothes as I fought back as best I could. As my own men ran over, followed by more townspeople and turning what had been an isolated attack on me into a full-fledged brawl, the largest of my attackers shoved me to my knees and held up a dagger. "What say we kill him, mates, as he did the good Duke of York?"

"Kill the traitor! Kill the traitor!"

"Halt!" Edward stormed through the crowd and knocked the dagger out of my would-be assassin's hand. He pulled me to my feet, then spun the man to face him as everyone fell still and silent. "What means this?"

"We only tried to rid you of a traitor, your grace. One who means to do you harm."

"The Duke of Somerset has been attending me for months now. He has slept in my bed, gone hunting with me when three out of six of the men present were his own. Do you not think that he would have done me harm long before this if that were his intention? Well? Don't you?"

"We—we didn't think, your grace."

"Well, that's damned obvious." Edward laid a hand on my shoulder, which made me wince with pain as I stood gasping for breath against the wall. "Now, gentlemen, we are heading north to subdue the Frenchwoman and her foreign armies. While I appreciate your concern for my welfare, it would be much better directed toward our enemies than toward loyal men like the duke here who have repented of their past allegiance. Now, don't you agree?"

A rather sullen affirmative murmur ensued. Edward grinned. "I don't like to see loyalty, even misguided loyalty, go unrewarded. Hastings, arrange for a tun of wine to be brought into the marketplace for these good men and their fellows to share. Now, come! Let our hearts be light. Musicians!"

The king's minstrels struck up a tune as Edward turned to me. "Go to your chambers. I'll speak to you later."

Half supported by Edmund and John and trailed by my men, I limped out of the great hall.

<p>

"I was nearly killed down there, and you're sending *me* away? Your grace! I was minding my own business, talking to my brothers, not provoking anyone, when I was attacked."

"I know. But it's a delicate situation. With Margaret staging this invasion of hers, and your having been so closely allied with her, men are suspicious."

"No one tried to attack me in London. No one may try to attack me in the next town." I glared at my servant as he scrubbed too hard at some dried blood on my cheek. "Easy there."

"It's a chance I can't take, either for your own safety or the realm's—or mine. There are men who have never reconciled themselves to my reign, men who never will. One more incident like this could bring them to the fore. And I'm sending you to Chirk, one of your own castles. Hardly exile."

"I've never seen the place."

"Time you did, then."

I stared down at the latest bruise beginning to announce itself on my arm. God only knew what I would look like the next morning. "So I rusticate, and the townspeople get free wine. How come it seems that I'm getting the worse of the bargain?"

Edward shrugged. "It placated them, what I can say? And your stay in Chirk will only be for a few months. Maybe less, depending on developments. And I shall send a contingent of your own men to guard Newcastle for me, to show my trust in you." He started to clap me on my shoulder, then thought better of it this time. "We'll be staying here for a few days. You can wait for a day or so before departing as long as you stay out of public view here; you'll be miserable if you try to ride in your condition."

"I'll not stay where I'm not wanted." I pressed a cold cloth against my blackening eye. "I'll be off at first light tomorrow."

Located on the Welsh march, not far from Chester, Chirk was a large, well-kept castle—after all, my great-uncle, Cardinal Beaufort, had thought well enough of the place and the lordship that came with it to purchase it from the crown a couple of decades before. There was good hunting there, and since my lands had been in the hands of others for so long, there was plenty for me to do in getting my affairs back in order. But I could not escape the feeling that I was a sort of prisoner, especially when the king did not send for me after news arrived that Henry and Margaret's invasion had failed. On the couple of occasions when I wrote to remind Edward that I was still alive, I was told politely but firmly that I had best stay on my estates.

Then in late September, I had a visitor—not an envoy from the king, but my older brother. "Tom!" I said, staring at him as he came into my chamber. He was thin, his clothes threadbare and his hair unkempt beneath his faded cap. I moved to embrace him, but he stepped back. "You've left Henry?"

"Do you think I'd ever do that?"

"Well, you're here," I said reasonably. "It's a possibility."

"I'm dead if Edward's men catch me. And the queen would probably kill me as well. But I stole here to see you." He stared at me in my rich clothes—there really wasn't much to do at Chirk except to dress well and hunt. "And now that I'm seeing you, I'm not sure whether I like what I see. You're living quite well as a Yorkist, aren't you? Is it worth the price of your soul? No wonder you stole off from me at Bamburgh, not telling anyone that you planned to go over to Edward."

"It's not that simple." I looked at Tom, who'd taught me how to ride, patiently stood by while I learned to shoot at butts, knelt by my side after St. Albans. If he had ever resented the fact that our mother's grand second marriage had made me a duke and him a mere lord, he'd never shown it. "I couldn't tell you; I was afraid you'd talk me out of it. I wasn't even entirely sure myself until the words came out of my mouth. And I didn't know how generous Edward would be."

"I see you didn't call him the king. A slip? Or does it stick in your mouth?"

"Tom, leave off, for Christ's sake."

"Oh, hell. Maybe I should just go back from where I came."

"Go back? Are you mad? Not until I get some food in you and some decent clothes on your back. Please, Tom. Stop looking at me as if I have leprosy. That's the way everyone in Edward's court looks at me. I don't need it from you too. Would you just sit down and talk to me like my brother, and not like an enemy?"

Tom finally nodded. "I still want to shake you."

"Have some wine first." I waved to a servant. "Bring us some wine and something to eat. I won't be going hunting today. Sit, Tom."

My brother obediently sat in the chair I indicated. He looked even shabbier sitting than he did standing. "Does everyone in Henry's court look as bad as you?"

"No, not quite. Henry's at Edinburgh in Bishop Kennedy's care, and is comfortable enough under the circumstances. I've been at Bamburgh, stirring up what trouble I can. Conditions are pretty harsh there." He stared at me. "I can trust that you won't tell Edward that?"

"Tom, if you can say that, you must not know me at all. Why don't you just leave?"

"I'm sorry. You're right. I do know you better." A servant poured wine for us and set down some bread. "Thank you."

I watched as Tom tried not to show how hungry he was. "You're not eating horsemeat there again, I hope?"

"No, things aren't that bad. Yet."

I hesitated before I dared to ask my next question. "How is she?"

"She?"

"For God's sake, Tom, don't be like this. Margaret. And no, I don't mean Margaret our sister, or our cousin Margaret. I mean that Margaret."

"I figured as much," Tom said. "She's in France with her father."

"Then she's safe and comfortable, at least."

Tom's eyes flashed all of a sudden. "I suppose your precious king gloated about Norham to you, about how the filthy Scots abandoned us?"

"I heard about Norham, yes. Not from the king personally. I've not seen or spoken to him since July."

"Well, did you know the queen almost got killed by brigands after that fiasco at Norham, when she was escaping? That's how safe and comfortable she was."

"For God's sake, leave off!" I leaned forward, fighting off sickness, for I'd not heard this story. But I did need to know more. "Did the brigands—"

"Rape her? No, it appears that she came close to it, but one of them took pity on her and brought her to safety. Pierre de Brézé got her safely abroad, with Exeter and others."

"Thank God she was spared that. Did she talk of me before she left?"

"She called you pretty much what you would expect after she heard the news that you'd gone over to York. After that, not a word about you. She's too proud. And you wouldn't want to hear it if she did."

"I wouldn't mind, actually. I'm fonder of castigating myself than you might think. Having it come from another mouth would be diverting."

"That's the one thing I can't understand. I know you were reaching the end of your tether there at Bamburgh. Sometimes I think I'm coming close to it myself. But how could you abandon her? Or not so much her, since you told me she ended your physical relationship, but her cause. That's the worst of it. Why did you desert us, knowing how badly it would hurt her?"

"I don't know." I put my head in my hands. "I like to think that it wasn't because she did end our physical relationship, but who knows? Maybe I'm the vile creature she thinks I am."

Tom got up and walked toward the window as I sat there in a miserable silence. "It is pleasant here," he ventured.

"It's dreary and dull. Tell Margaret that, it will please her. The men of Northampton tried to kill me, did you know that? If I venture off my estates here someone's liable to try again. And the ones at Edward's court who don't try to murder me won't speak a civil word to me. The only one of the lot who has any use for me is the king himself, and I'm beginning to doubt that too, since he sent me here and seems to have no interest whatsoever in bringing me back to court. Don't even think of becoming a Yorkist, Tom. It's not nearly as amusing as they say it is."

Tom walked back to my side and put his arm around me, and my mind flashed back to a time when I was four and he had consoled me after I'd fallen off my pony.

"When you're ready to come back, Hal, you only have to say so."

Tom stayed at Chirk for the next few days. I would have liked to have introduced him to the fine sport of otter hunting—it was quite the thing for us at Chirk—but under the circumstances, he had to keep within the castle walls and out of the public view. He and my younger brothers and I diced and played cards a great deal. For the rest of his short visit, we avoided the subject of Lancaster and York altogether.

Then, just after dawn a few days later, Tom came to bid me farewell. With him were Edmund and John, dressed in warm cloaks. "You're going over to Lancaster." I glared at Tom. "You talked them into this?"

"No, it was our idea." Edmund looked straight into my eyes. "I love you, Hal. I know you did what you did partly for me, and I'm grateful. But Edward's not my king and never can be. I can't stomach this life anymore."

"And I want to go with Edmund," said John. That was no surprise; John had always trailed behind Edmund the way I had trailed behind Tom growing up.

"Then God be with you."

Edmund started. "You're not going to try to stop us?"

"No. How could I? Throw you into a dudgeon? You must do what you think is right." I handed Tom a purse. "This was going to be for you, but it'll have to do for the three of you now, for it's all I have to spare. But wait." I pulled two rings off my fingers and gave one to Edmund, one to John. "Surely someone will give you some gold for these."

"Hal, you know that anything you give us is going to be used to aid Henry's cause."

"I don't know that, actually. You can give it to the Church, go on a spree, eat yourselves silly on it. I don't need to know what you do with it, and I'd rather not know."

Tom reached for me and locked me in a long embrace. "Go with God, little brother," he said when he finally released me.

I embraced my younger brothers, both in tears. Then I watched as the three of them rode away with just a man apiece accompanying them.

Not long after my brothers left, news floated over from France and drifted slowly into Wales: England and France had entered into a truce, brokered by the Duke of Burgundy. One of the terms was that France would offer no help to Henry and Margaret. And where France went, Scotland soon might follow, especially since Edward had been threatening an invasion. Having been unimpressed by the Scots' military might so far—it was hard to believe that this was the same nation that had won the battle of Bannockburn over a century before—I foresaw that an English-Scottish truce might soon follow. Henry would lose his safe refuge in Scotland. What would he do then? Hole up in Bamburgh? Flee abroad?

But there was a chance that Lancaster's fortunes could be retrieved, even without Scotland and France. The treaty with France would anger some; the money that Edward kept exacting from his subjects would anger others. We held three castles in England; we held Harlech Castle in Wales. We had a friend in my old friend the Count of Charolais. We might have a friend in the Duke of Britt—

We. That was the word I'd used in my thoughts. Not *they*. *We*.

∽

The Lord and I had been on rather distant terms as of late, so it must have surprised Him when, in early November, I spent several hours closeted with my confessor, hitherto one of the most underworked men in Wales. Then I entered the chapel at Chirk and dropped to my knees in earnest prayer, not my most accustomed activity. The sheer novelty of all of this must have lent me favor in the Lord's eyes, for when I finally rose and called two of my most trusted men to me, I felt better than I had in months. Or maybe it was the decision I'd at last taken.

"Go to Joan Hill and give her this," I said, handing one of my men a bag of gold. "Tell her that it is all I can spare, and that I do not know when—if ever—I can send her more. Remind her that if she or Charles ever needs help and no one in our family is in a position to give it, she should contact one of the people I have told her about." I felt my eyes tear when I thought of Joan and my fine little son, but I managed to go on firmly. "Tell her and Charles that I love them, and tell Charles that he will never be absent from his father's thoughts. Tell Joan also that she was right about me and the House of York, much as I hate to admit it. And then go to my mother and tell her that I love her dearly, and am sorry for the trouble that I have brought upon her."

"Yes, my lord."

"Give this to the king," I continued, handing a ring—once my father's—to the second man. "Tell him I have work to do here, and when I finish it, I will join him and serve him for all of my days."

"King Henry, you mean," the man said quietly.

"King Henry, of course. There is no other rightful king of England. I was a fool to ever pretend otherwise."

∽

By late November I had laid all of my plans, made all of my contacts. With a handful of men I rode out of Chirk. I was planning to travel secretly to Newcastle, where my men would seize the castle and the town for Henry. But someone recognized me and sent up the alarm at Durham while I lay abed, so I had to flee in my shirt and ride straight for Alnwick, fifty miles off.

But at last—wearing clothes borrowed from someone at Alnwick—I arrived at Bamburgh. Less than a year ago, I'd been besieged here and had broken faith with the best man I knew.

My brothers were waiting for me at the castle gates. "We had a bet as to how long you'd last as a Yorkist," Edmund said after we had embraced.

"Oh? Who won?"

"I did," said Tom. "John gave you until the New Year. Edmund thought you'd last until Easter. But I didn't think you'd last long at all after we left Chirk."

"I'm glad you were right. Is the king expecting me?"

Tom smiled. "I think he's been expecting you for months now. He never thought you'd desert us for good. But yes, he knows you've arrived here. Come. I'll take you to him."

If there was one castle I knew from top to bottom, it was Bamburgh. But as Tom led me along, I found that I needed his guidance. What would I say to the man I'd treated so shabbily?

King Henry smiled at me when I came through the door.

I fell at the king's feet, sobbing. "Forgive me, your grace. Forgive me." I could hardly speak the words, yet they kept tumbling forth. "I have wronged you in so many ways. I never shall again. If you will only pardon me and let me prove to you that I can be worthy—"

"Rise, Hal." Henry hauled me up as he had that day at Coventry when I'd brawled with York's men. He kissed me on both cheeks. "You are back with me now, and that is all that matters. Let us forget the past." The king looked me straight in the eye. "All of it."

I stiffened. "You know?"

"Yes. Marguerite told me the night before she left for France. It weighed on her mind, poor girl."

"It was all my fault, your grace."

"Really? She said that it was all her fault. I suspect that it was rather both of yours. I have no experience in these matters, but I do believe it is how those things work." Henry half smiled. "I am not that naïve anymore, Hal."

I gripped his hand. "It will never happen again."

"I know. She promised me." He sighed. "She has undergone great hardships for me, more than any man has a right to ask of his queen. And so have you. How can I pass judgment upon the two of you?" He cut me off before I could once again beg his forgiveness. "But no more of this. You look tired and hungry, and you must tell me your adventures of these past few days."

We talked for several hours more until the hour for the king to retire arrived. He smiled at me shyly. "They say you and March shared a bed. I never invited you or your father to do so. Would you do me the honor of sharing mine tonight?"

"Yes, your grace."

"Good." Henry gave me his sweetest smile. "It gets chilly in here at night; I like the company."

A single man prepared the bed, then brought Henry a clean nightshirt and helped him into it as my own page helped me undress. Then we settled into bed together, and the man drew the curtains. They kept the worst of the cold out, but Henry was right: this was a chilly chamber. I remembered Margaret's being more hospitable, but I could hardly say so. Then Henry said, "I do not sleep in the queen's chamber, though it is more comfortable than any of the rest; it is my little way of honoring her until she can return someday. Do you think I'll see her again, Hal?"

"Yes. Of course."

"I was not so sure of it a couple of months ago; things have gone hard with us as of late. But now that you are returned, I feel more confident. Good night, Hal."

I lay in bed beside the king and waited until he fell asleep before I rolled over on my own side, just as I'd done when I shared Edward's bed. This bed was much less comfortable than Edward's, and the furnishings were threadbare in places. But in this bed I had no difficulty in falling asleep, as I had when I was Edward's bedfellow; instead I was dozing within minutes, my conscience clean as a newborn babe's. I was back in the House of Lancaster, home at last.

20

Margaret
January 1464

L ETTERS HAVE COME FOR YOU, YOUR GRACE."
I looked up from the household accounts of Koeur Castle, which no matter where I looked or how I turned the paper screamed the same message: we were poor. "If you bring them yourself, Doctor Morton, they must be ill tidings. Who has deserted us now? Who is putting us off with fair words?"

"Your grace, you must not be so pessimistic."

"It is hard not to be sometimes." I sighed. When I had left England in July, I did so with the knowledge that there was to be a peace conference between England and France, aided by the Duke of Burgundy, which I had done my best to prevent, or at least to postpone, by trying to win over Burgundy. Landing at Sluys, I had sent a man to inform the Duke of Burgundy that I was coming to meet him, and when Burgundy had done his best to put me off, I had left Edward at Bruges and commandeered a humble cart, the type that one might use to take goods to market. From there, accompanied by only three attendants and Pierre de Brézé, I had set off with the intent of intercepting the duke, who out of sheer exhaustion had finally agreed to see me. At St. Pol, he had given me a grand banquet, presented me and my women—none of whom had a change of clothing—with money and jewels, and sent his womenfolk to me to show me hospitality. But he had given me no promises and no aid for my cause, and there'd been no alternative for me but to go back to Bruges, then to make my way to my father's castle at Koeur. The peace conference had gone on without me, and England and France were now officially at peace. If that were not bad enough, we had learned just days before that Scotland and England had entered into a truce, with the promise of further negotiations to come. Peace was breaking out all over, and it was not doing us a bit of good. I glared at the smiling Doctor Morton. "How do you stay so optimistic?"

"I have faith in the Lord, your grace. You might try to cultivate more your-self. But here are your letters. They are to be read in the order in which I shall give them to you."

I opened the first one, from Henry. *My dear, I have seen the letter that you are about to read, and I know you will be pleased at its contents. Henry R.* "This is like one of those boxes within boxes that someone once brought as a gift to my father. Well, let me see the second."

Bishop Morton handed it to me. It bore my name, *Margaret the Queen*, in a hand that was unfamiliar to me. My jaw dropped as I looked at the seal. *Somerset.* "What does this mean?"

"Read it."

Madam, I have returned to the side of the king's highness, and begged and received his forgiveness for all of the wrongs I have done him. I pray that your highness will do me the same gracious favor. And I shall not stray again, but shall live and, if God wills it, die the king's loyal subject.

Your true subject and liege man,

Somerset

"Is this true?"

"It is, your grace. The messenger took the letter from Somerset himself."

I stared at the letter, tears beginning to course down my face. *All of the wrongs*, with *all* slightly underlined. I knew what that, and the formal language of the letter, meant: there would be no more stolen moments between me and Somerset. That suited me well; I had already promised Henry, and the Lord, that I would never wrong my husband again. Hal serving Henry faithfully again was all I wanted, and more than I had ever dared to wish for. With Somerset's youth and military ability, his friendship with the Count of Charolais, his con-tacts in Wales and in the South, our dying cause might gain new life.

And Hal had already gained back his honor.

I turned to Doctor Morton again. "You are right. I must cultivate more faith." I smiled at the letters in my hands. "And I must listen more to my hus-band. He knew all along that Somerset would come back."

21

Henry Beaufort, Duke of Somerset
April 1464 to May 15, 1464

Y ou will forgive me if I do not dwell too much on the last two battles of my life. What man wants to recount another's triumph, when it has cost him all?

We should have won the battle that took place in April near Hedgeley Moor. John Neville, Lord Montagu (I suppose I must call him by his rightful title) was on his way to lead a delegation to York to treat with the Scots, and we had set out to ambush him. We had every hope of succeeding: with the help of Sir Ralph Percy, we'd brought much of Northumberland under our control. But there was a spy in our midst, and when Montagu's men encountered mine, they were ready for us—more than ready. When they killed Ralph Percy, together with his horse, it was if they had ripped the very hearts out of the northerners in our forces, for the Percies were all but kings here. Our line broke, and there was nothing for us to do but to limp back to Bamburgh and to plan our next move.

But "plan" is the wrong word, perhaps, for it implies a choice, of which we had little. We were short of men, supplies, and money; we were dispirited over the loss of Ralph Percy; we knew that Scotland was barred to us from henceforth; we knew that Edward, who was mustering men from thirty counties at Leicester, would soon be heading north with an army to finish us off. I had stirred up some trouble in Wales and elsewhere before I left Chirk, but these disturbances were not enough to distract Edward from his northern progress. Margaret was trying her best to persuade the Duke of Brittany and the Count of Charolais to help us, but beyond worthless words of encouragement and a little money we had been able to get very little aid.

"We can hole up here," I said as my brothers and I paced outside Bamburgh Castle. "Another siege. How long can we hold out? Probably not much longer

than in '62, even without the—er—temptations of last time." My cheeks
burned as I thought of my conduct during the last siege of Bamburgh, and
Tom gave me a consoling pat on the shoulder. "Our only hope would be to
have relief from abroad, because it's sure as hell not coming from Scotland
now. And no one seems inclined to incur Louis's wrath. God, I wish King
Charles were still alive."

"And even if they did send us some men, would they be enough?" Edmund
asked.

I shook my head. "Staying here would be suicide. Slow suicide, but suicide
nonetheless. There won't be terms for any of us this time; we'll be dragged
out and beheaded straightaway. But if we can go south, we have a chance, at
least. If we can make one gain, just one gain, we can lure more men to our
side. And perhaps gain some support from abroad."

"And if that doesn't work?" John said.

"We can get the king safely abroad, at least. And as for the rest of us, well,
Bruges is an attractive city. Or there's always piracy." I grinned. "All four of
us pirating together, how do you think we'd do? The Buccaneering Beauforts.
But that doesn't account for Tom."

"Or there is death," said Edmund.

"Yes, that's at the back of my mind." I stared out at the sea. "Not very far
back at all, actually. But there's no need to dwell upon it."

Near the middle of May, we—including the king—left Bamburgh Castle and
began moving south. I looked back at Bamburgh, where I'd made love to a
queen and shared a bed with a king, and I knew that whatever happened next,
good or ill, I'd miss the place.

By and by we encamped near Hexham, lodging Henry at the more comfortable quarters of Bywell Castle—Bywell Tower, it should have been called, for
that was all that had been completed—some ten miles off. We set up camp near
a stream, called rather uncheerfully the Devil's Water. I was dozing in my tent
at dawn on May 15 when I was shaken awake and told the news: John Neville
was within five miles of our camp.

"How many men?"

"A good six thousand."

We had about four thousand. "How the devil did our scouts miss them?
But never mind that. Go to King Henry and tell him that he must get away."

I turned to my men, still groggy from sleep. "We can't meet Montagu here; it's a death trap. We'll assemble on Swallowship Hill."

We armed quickly, not pausing to break our fast or to say our morning prayers—though we could have done with both—and marched to the crest of Swallowship Hill. Barely had we aligned ourselves there when we saw Montagu's men marching up the hill. There were even more of them than we had expected.

Our archers—of which we had relatively few—did their best to drive them back; they couldn't. We all did our best, God knows, or at least the core of men who were loyal to us did. The rabble, the men who had joined us only for pay, soon broke rank and fled under the weight of the onslaught, but the rest of us fought on until there was absolutely nothing left to fight for, until our chances had crumbled like the clods of dirt beneath my feet. "Save yourselves!" I yelled to my brothers.

For I myself was past saving. I was down, my weapons knocked out of my hands, my sword arm broken, and there were men surrounding me. They were about to dispatch me as they had my father on an equally beautiful May day nine years before. May was not my month...Had they laid hold of my brothers? I whispered the Lord's name, either in prayer or reproach I am not quite sure. Then someone yanked my captors off me. "Are you mad? Save the duke for Lord Montagu. Don't spoil his fun."

Four men, securely bound, were already standing before Montagu when my captors, having stripped me of my armor and bound my hands, haled me into his presence. Three of them—Edmund Fish, Edmund Bradshaw, and Wate Hunt—were my own followers; the fourth, one Black Jack, was more my brother Tom's man than anyone's, having joined him after he helped Margaret flee from Norham. Montagu, who had been looking at these lowly prisoners with unconcealed contempt, brightened visibly when he saw me surrounded by my captors (Sir John Middleton and his men, to give credit where credit is due). "Now, that's more like it. No one's found the other leaders, then?"

"They made off toward those woods, they say. We'll find them."

"Aye, we shall. We'll make a hunting party of it." Montagu turned toward me. "Kneel, Beaufort." Someone forced me to my knees when I did not obey fast enough. "What do you think we're going to do with you?"

Evidently Montagu was the sort of victor who enjoyed asking rhetorical questions. "Hold another tournament in my honor? Marry me to one of your sisters?" I offered.

The Nevilles will not be recorded in the chronicles for their sense of humor. "Hang, draw and quarter you? Or just beheading?"

"You might recall that after our second little get-together at St. Albans, we didn't execute you," I pointed out.

"Yes, I recall that, and it'll do you no good. You were a traitor to King Edward, you might recall."

"No. I was a traitor to King Henry. The rightful king," I added pleasantly.

Montagu drew his foot back and methodically but firmly kicked me in the balls.

"That," he observed as I collapsed groaning to the ground, "is for the Duke of York. And for my father," he added, almost as an afterthought. And this"— he slapped my face with his gauntlet—"is for not knowing when to keep your mouth shut. Get him on a horse, men, when he's able. We'll have the sorry whoreson's head cut off at Hexham marketplace."

Having given himself the gratification just described—I must be honest and say that if our positions had been reversed, I might have similarly indulged myself—Montagu seemed disinclined to abuse me further, perhaps because there was more satisfaction to be had in displaying me as his prize during the short ride into town. They'd found my abandoned standard, and one of my captured men was made to carry it while I rode behind, my hands tied to the pommel and my feet tied to the stirrups. This wasn't conducive to easing the pain in my arm, but I'd not give the Yorkists the pleasure of complaining about it. I tried to fix my mind on the ride I'd taken with Joan and my son the previous July, when the world had been a happier place.

"I'm talking to you, Beaufort." Montagu's irritated voice broke in on my daydream. "Answer my question. Did you ever tumble her? Rumor has it that you did."

"Her? Can you narrow it down a bit?"

"You know what wench I mean. The Frenchwoman you call your queen."

A vulgar question, so typical of a Neville. My great-grandfather and great-grandmother, John of Gaunt and Katherine Swynford, had been adulterous lovers, God knows, but they had not been vulgar about it. "What business is it of yours?"

"Answer, Somerset, or you'll find the headsman has a poor aim."

So now we were up to my ducal title, at least. "Well, then. No." I looked at Montagu wearily. "Does that answer disappoint you? If so, I'm sorry, but it happens to be the truth."

Montagu did indeed look somewhat disappointed, and I wondered if he would have pressed me for details had I told the truth. "You never even tried?"

"No. Neither did she." At least I could go to my death knowing that I had not compromised my lady's honor.

"Did you want to?"

There was no point in lying about this. "Since I first saw her when I was fourteen."

Montagu gave his version of a smile. "So did I."

"How charming. We have something in common after all." We were passing over a rough spot, which jounced my arm, and I could not forbear groaning at the pain.

"You're injured? Where?"

About time he noticed. "My arm. It's broken. In the same place your brother's men broke it at the first battle of St. Albans. Where, since the topic of old grudges came up when you kicked me back there, your brother murdered my father."

Montagu gave me a look that I couldn't read, then turned round to one of his men. "Get the surgeon up here. We need him to put Somerset's arm in a sling."

"That's not necessary," I said. "Almost a waste of time, really."

My captor shrugged. "It'll be a good two hours before everything's ready."

"That long? I'd hoped for sooner. Purgatory or no purgatory, this day can't be over faster to suit me. Speaking of purgatory, I trust I shall be able to confess my sins before I die?"

"Why, of course," Montagu replied, a little huffily. "What do you think I am?"

I wisely kept silent.

We were now in the town, where spectators had gathered to see me being brought in. (News travelled fast here in the North.) Some of the women, I was touched to see, were weeping, and I was able to catch the eye and smile at a few of them. I nodded toward Hexham's abbey, the town's most prominent building. "Is that where you'll take my body?"

"Most likely." Montagu scowled at the crying women, whom he too had noticed. "You weren't expecting Westminster, were you?"

I looked again toward the abbey, a fine old structure that dated back to Saxon times. "No, a man could do worse," I conceded. Maybe some of those weeping women might even bring me some flowers from time to time, and say a prayer for me. Probably no one from my own family or Joan would be able to come up here any time soon. My shoulders sagged as I thought of those

I'd never see again, and for a moment I almost gave Montagu the satisfaction of losing my composure.

Near the abbey stood the jail, which turned out to be my and my fellow prisoners' destination. "Don't worry, you won't be troubled with them long," Montagu explained to the jailer, who was looking nonplussed at this unexpected company. "All five of them are for the headsman."

I pushed forward. "Aren't you going to release them?" Except for Sir Edmund Fish, they weren't even knights; such men who survived a battle were usually relieved of whatever possessions they might have and sent on their way home. "They've done nothing other than fight for me bravely and loyally. Surely that's nothing to die for."

"They're your followers. They're to be an example for anyone else in this part of the country who might be tempted to join your cause, or what's left of it once you're gone. And we'll do the same with the rest of your adherents when we catch them."

I stared at the four men. All I could say was, "I'm sorry."

In our cell, the five of us sat in a dismal little circle, sipping what passed for ale and trying to keep each other's spirits up by making grim conversation. Would the executioner grow in skill as the heads piled up, making it more advantageous to go last, or was it better to go early, while he was still fresh and not tired? How great was our likelihood of getting a competent executioner up here, anyway? Or would the ever-resourceful Montagu provide his own executioner, not trusting to the local facilities? Whose neck would prove the easiest to cut? We bantered as best we could, until a couple of the men turned to prayer and the rest of us grew silent.

I settled, half dozing, against the wall. I wished I had one of Joan's delicious wafers to munch upon; it would bring a smile to my face. I wished I had Joan to hold me one last time and to kiss me good-bye. I wished I could know what the future held for my mother and my brothers and my sisters, and above all, my little son. I wished I could write Charles a letter of fatherly advice and concern; though I was not exactly the best preceptor in the world, at least he would know that he had been in my thoughts. I wished I knew what would become of the king and of the queen. I knew one thing at least: as long as there was breath in Henry and Edward's bodies, Margaret would never stop fighting for them. Margaret... No, with my Maker and I soon to improve our acquaintance, it was best not to think of Margaret as I'd seen her that last afternoon at Bamburgh, lying naked and lovely in my arms. Much better to think of her only as my queen.

Black Jack, of all people, put his head in his hands and started weeping. Relieved at this interruption in my thoughts, which had been taking such a dangerous turn, I put my good arm around him and patted his back until he had finally regained his composure. "She told me that I'd not come to a bad end, if I followed her."

"Who?"

"The queen. She stood there in those woods like a ragged angel, telling me that I should give up my old life, or I'd come to the gallows. And here I am, at the gallows. Or at least the block."

"And she was right," I said. "If you'd kept up your old life, you would have died for a sheep, or a horse, or a jewel. But today you die for a king. And for a queen," I added softly. "A very great lady."

Black Jack pondered this. "That's something."

"It's everything." I heard a rattle of keys. "And it looks as if our time has come."

Sir Edmund Fish, who'd been one of the ones praying, and perhaps weeping as well, cleared his throat. "I wish I could have done a better job for you back there, my lord. I fear that our cause is dead."

"You did the best you could. All of you did." I clapped him on the shoulder as Montagu's men, followed by a priest, came to lead us to the block. I smiled at Fish and the rest of my men, then at the Yorkists as they hustled us out of our cell. "And our cause isn't dead; it won't be as long as one of us somewhere has breath left in his body. It's only resting."

22

Margaret
June 1464 to December 1464

I KNEW IMMEDIATELY FROM DOCTOR MORTON'S EXPRESSION THAT HE HAD nothing to say that I would want to hear. In a low voice that was as equally alien to him as his bleak face, he said, "Your grace, I must prepare you for ill news."

"The king is dead."

"No. That is the one piece of news that is not entirely bad, and it is encouraging only by comparison. King Henry is free still, at least the last that I heard. No one knows his whereabouts. He is a fugitive. We have suffered a great reversal of fortune, however."

I stood up straighter. "Tell me the rest."

"There were two battles." Morton swallowed. "The Duke of Somerset encountered John Neville's men at Hedgeley Moor in late April. Neville was traveling to the Scottish border to meet envoys there, and the duke ambushed him. But the duke was outnumbered and defeated and Lord Ralph Percy was killed. Just a couple of weeks later, Neville surprised Somerset's men near Hexham. The duke was attempting to move south, to force an encounter, I believe, before he was overwhelmed by the forces that Edward was raising. He and his men fought valiantly, but to no avail. More than thirty of our men were captured after the battle and beheaded. They put to death lords, knights, squires—all manner of men. Your yeoman Thomas Hunt. The king's purser Roger Water. Lord Hungerford. Lord Ros. Your friend Black Jack. Somerset, God assoil his soul, was among those men, my lady. He in fact was the first to die."

Katherine Vaux came from behind and held me as Morton's voice blurred on, his litany of loss now barely comprehensible to me. "The duke was put to death at Hexham, in the marketplace, on May 15. They say he died with composure and courage. Lord Ros and Lord Hungerford managed to evade capture for a day or so but were caught and executed two days later at Newcastle. Lord Ros begged to be buried beside the Duke of Somerset at Hexham Abbey and was granted that one favor."

"Edmund and John Beaufort? Do they live?"

"No one knows, your grace. All that can be said is that they were not known to have been among those that Montagu executed. Edward made him the Earl of Northumberland for his services."

I struggled against the sickness that was beginning to overtake me. "Thank you for bringing me this news. Have masses said for the souls of these brave men. I would like to be alone."

Doctor Morton nodded, his eyes full of pity, and left the room. As soon as he was gone, I sank to the ground and wept in Katherine's lap as she stroked my hair. "My poor lady," she said when my sobs had subsided. "You still loved him, didn't you?"

"Yes," I whispered. I raised my eyes to Katherine, and the tears started to stream from them again. "God forgive me, but I did."

My health had been delicate for some days before I learned of Somerset's beheading, and soon after hearing the news I became gravely ill. But for the skill of my father's best physician, who was summoned specially to Koeur Castle to attend me, I might well have died. But he was not a man to submit tamely to losing a patient, and brought me around through sheer willpower, so that by July I was well enough to contemplate just how grim our situation was. It had grown even worse while I was ailing: of the castles we had held in the North, Alnwick and Dustanburgh had surrendered. Only Ralph Grey, in Bamburgh Castle, held out. This time, there had been no effort to starve him out: Edward brought his three great guns to the castle and began firing upon the castle walls. Gravely injured by a falling wall, Grey was hauled to Doncaster and beheaded. By mid-July, only Harlech Castle in Wales still belonged to us. And no one knew where poor Henry was.

Then in October, Doctor Morton again brought me news. "It appears that Edward of England has married."

"Married?" I stared at Doctor Morton, who bore an expression entirely out of keeping with the gravity of his words. A marriage to a foreign princess would bring the possibility of new, or stronger, alliances for Edward, and make it all of the harder for us to get help from anyone. "That is horrid news. To whom?"

"You do remember Jacquetta, Duchess of Bedford, and her many children."

"Yes." I scowled at the thought of the fecund duchess, whose large family had made its peace with Edward after Towton. And why had I heeded her request to stay out of London after the second battle of St. Albans?

"You might remember that she had a lovely daughter, Elizabeth."

"Yes. She gave Somerset her favor at a joust once," I added sadly. "But what does she have to do with this?"

"Everything. Edward thought she was lovely too, it appears. He has married her. In secret, without a word to his councillors. He announced the marriage to his council at Michaelmas."

"A commoner? A secret marriage? Has the man lost his mind?"

"No, I believe he has lost his heart. Evidently she refused to lie with him as his mistress, and he was so smitten that he decided to marry her rather than to give her up. They say Warwick was outraged. And, of course, King Louis is irked, as he was pushing for a match between Edward and Bona of Savoy."

So there would be no French match for Edward, no great European match at all. Thanks to the lust of this young king and to Elizabeth Woodville's unassailable virtue, we were safe from that at least. For the first time in weeks, I smiled. I did more than that: I laughed outright.

"And I have more good news for you," Morton continued, his smile matching my own. "The younger Beauforts are safe in Paris."

A month later, Edmund and John Beaufort were shown into the modest chamber where I received visitors. I embraced both of them in turn. "I cannot tell you how grieved I was by the loss of your brothers. And I cannot tell you how glad I am that you were spared. You were at Hexham, then?"

Edmund's eyes shadowed. "Yes. Hal screamed for us as he was captured to save ourselves, and we did. I knew that he would not survive when he fell into their hands, and he knew it too." He crossed himself. "I can say no more about that day, your grace."

"Don't, then. Only know that I have masses said for Somerset daily. He will soon be reunited with your father in Paradise, which is a thought that has given me great comfort when I think of how I miss him. And I have them said for Lord Ros too."

Edmund smiled his thanks and looked around at the room, which was furnished adequately, thanks to my father, but no more. "I fear that you can ill afford them. They tell me that you are in straitened circumstances here."

"We manage, and my father is as generous as he can be. Don't think for a moment that you are not welcome here. There are always means by which we can economize more than we do."

John spoke up. "We are hoping to take service with the Count of Charolais; I believe he will welcome us for Hal's sake, so we will not be a burden upon you here for long. But there is another recruit to our cause who has come from England. May I bring him here, your grace?"

I nodded, and John left the room. When he returned, it was with a pretty, rather large woman of about two-and-thirty and a small boy, both dressed in black. In the instant I viewed them before they dropped to their knees, it took no keen eye to guess the identity of the lad's father. "This is Joan Hill, your grace, and her son, Charles. He is Hal's son."

"Rise, Mistress Hill," I said. "What brings you abroad?"

"Your grace," Joan stammered. I smiled at her, and she continued awkwardly, "I'm sorry, your grace. I never expected to be in conversation with a queen, I guess. Hal—I mean, my lord Somerset—told me that if anything should happen to him, I should get in touch with some people he knew, and they would help me and Charles. I could have kept him in London after my lord died; it wasn't as if that Edward person was beating down my door trying to seize my boy. He's not the rightful king, but he's not that great a scoundrel that he would go after a little bastard child. What would be the point? But I know my lord wanted my son to acquire more manners and graces than he ever could from living with me, though he was kind enough never to say so. He was always a kind man, my lord was."

I dabbed at my eye. "He was indeed. Go on."

"He wanted our son to be a knight and to marry well, and I thought that was the least I could do for him, to honor his wishes as best I could. So I found the men—some merchants who had been friendly with my lord and my lord's father—and we decided to send my Charles abroad, where he could live with some friends of my lord in Bruges and get a proper upbringing until things got better in England. I didn't know that Sir Edmund and Sir John were alive then, you see, and I didn't want to push myself on their mother or sisters. We were trying to make arrangements when we heard that Hal's brothers were safe and sound, and that they were looking to the same merchant to help them get abroad to safety. So we decided to send my Charles with his uncles, and I decided to go too—I wanted to see him safely settled." Joan blushed. "I did go on, your grace, didn't I? I'm sorry."

"You told me what I wanted to hear, and I am glad to hear it." I beckoned the boy closer. "Come here, Charles. That is a fine name. Do you know I had an uncle named Charles? Well, I did. Do you miss your father, my dear?"

"Yes, mum. He played games with me and took me riding on his 'orse."

"He was as brave as any man could be, and he was very proud to be your father." I patted Charles on the cheek. "Your father was very dear to the king and me, and you will always have friends in us for his sake. Now, will you go with Lady Katherine here for a few minutes?"

Katherine Vaux—big with her second child—led Charles away. I turned back to Joan Hill. "You do not plan to stay abroad?"

Joan sighed. "No, your grace. I think I would stand in Charles's way if I were to stay with him. I don't speak the languages; I'm a bit like a fish out of water here. When I see Charles settled safely in Bruges, I'll go back to my shop in London, and when King Henry is back on the throne, as I pray daily he will be, then maybe my Charles will come back and we can visit."

"I do not want you to return to England unless you can do so safely. If Edward thought you might be spying…"

"The men I know are careful, your grace. They're back and forth between here and England doing their trading; they will bring me back safely." Joan dropped her eyes. "I can't tell you, your grace, how much I cried when that Edward had it told in London how that Neville creature had beheaded my lord. You wouldn't believe that a woman could hold so many tears, even a woman of my size. Him meeting his death is what I dreaded when I heard that he'd gone back to supporting Lancaster. But I knew that supporting York clawed at him, and that his mind at least was at ease when he died. Still, I miss him so very much."

"We all do. I am very glad he has left a part of him behind."

Joan sniffled. "My Charles will grow up to be a fine man, I daresay, and know more than I will ever know. And to think it is all because my lord liked the smell of my wafers and decided to come inside my shop."

"Bring Charles back in," I said to one of my men. "And bring me one of my son's badges."

Charles returned. Like other boys his age, he had the remarkable facility of getting dirty quickly, for he already was a little grimy. He made a neat little bow that Katherine must have taught him just moments before. "Yer grace."

"Look what I have for you. It is a badge. My son's badge of the House of Lancaster. It is the house your father served so bravely. Will you wear it in his honor?"

"Yes, yer grace."

I pinned it on him. "Be a good servant of the House of Lancaster, Charles," I said softly.

"I will," Charles promised me. "It was my father's 'ouse."

23

Edward of Lancaster
July 1465

I WAS COMING IN FROM MY MORNING'S HUNTING, EAGER TO BOAST TO MY mother of my success, for she herself had been a keen hunter when she was younger and always liked to hear of my triumphs. Sometimes she still joined me on the hunt, on those days when she wasn't dictating letters begging someone or the other to help us regain my father's throne or thinking of whom she could enlist in our cause next.

Today, however, she stopped me before I even opened my mouth. "Not now, Edward. There is something I must tell you, and you must be man enough to bear it. Can you promise me that?"

I noticed for the first time that her eyes were red. Had she been crying, like she had the year before when I fell ill and everyone thought for a day or so that I might die? "I promise."

"Your father was captured."

"Is he dead?" I managed to ask.

"No." My mother's eyes clouded over. "He is a prisoner." She clenched her fist. "He was hiding in the North, moving from place to place, but finally someone betrayed him, and he was taken to the Tower." I had the sense that my mother was losing her sense of me as her audience. "The whoresons could not be content with just imprisoning him. They tied his feet to the stirrups, paraded him through London for the crowds to jeer at—and he a king since he was nine months old! My God, such treatment will send him over into madness again! I hope it does; it is better that he be mad than he be miserable and lonely there, mocked by those creatures. I pray he goes mad!"

She dropped to her knees and began weeping, all sense of self-control lost. I had never seen her like that in my life—and I had seen her after she'd lost battles, after she'd been confronted by robbers, after thirty of our men had been executed following Hexham. I wished more than ever that I was not a boy who still had to wait a couple of months for my twelfth birthday, but a man who could come back and claim my kingdom and put my mother back in her palace at Greenwich instead of in a borrowed castle in France. I wished I could take my sword and sweep off all of the heads of the men who were making my mother cry so hard.

But I couldn't do any of these things yet, so I knelt beside her and awkwardly patted her on the back until her sobs subsided. Sitting next to her, I realized for the first time how small she really was: I would soon be taller than she. "Mother, I promise, someday we'll free him. And if he is mad, he'll get better. Just like he did after I was born."

My mother lifted her head and tried to smile. "You have to practice your fighting harder from now on," she said, sniffling. "Your poor father can do nothing now that he is locked up. You are our very last hope now."

⁓

When I left my mother (dry-eyed now, and beginning to dictate more letters), I went to my tutor, Sir John Fortescue, who in better days had been chief justice of the king's bench. This was not a very spacious castle, but because Sir John was a scholar, my mother had allotted him a tiny chamber all to himself. It was crammed with stacks of books and paper, which teetered dangerously upon my arrival but remained bravely upright. "Good day, your grace. You have heard the news?"

"Yes."

"Sad. Very sad. Now, where is the book we were reading? It was here yesterday."

I instantly spotted the great red book he was seeking—it was at the bottom of a particularly unsteady pile by the door—but decided to say nothing. "Sir John, I was wondering if you could tell me something."

"Well, I shall certainly try." Sir John, having given up searching for our book of yesterday, began to extract one from the middle of another pile. It was a delicate process, one that I thought would have required his full concentration, but he said over his shoulder, "Go on."

"Am I a bastard?"

"No," Sir John told the pile of books.

I noticed that he didn't appear to be shocked at the question. He drew his quarry from the pile triumphantly. Only then did he say, "Has someone here been telling you that you are a bastard? Because he has no business in this household if he has."

"No, but I have heard that the Yorkists say that I am."

"They have been claiming that since you were a small child. But there's nothing to it. Your mother the queen has been—how shall I say this—in a unique situation. When a woman takes charge, as she has been forced to do, she breeds enemies, who reach for what weapons they can, and attacking her virtue is the easiest to wield. Of course, it is a doubly useful weapon, for by challenging your legitimacy, they can also challenge your very right to the throne." He opened the book. "Warwick is more responsible for the rumors than anyone, I believe. Now, shall we read?"

"No. Not yet. Do you think they will kill my father?"

"I would think they would have done so immediately if they planned to do so." Fortescue looked at me for a moment or two, then closed the book quietly. "I can see your grace has much on his mind, and quite understandably so. We'll not study today."

"Wait." I looked at the book, *De Re Militari*, by Flavius Vegetius Renatus. "I should like to hear of a battle, but not one that took place in Roman times."

"Which one, my lord?"

"Agincourt," I said. "I want to hear about my grandfather."

24

Margaret
May 1470 to August 1470

FOR THE PAST FEW YEARS, KING EDWARD AND THE EARL OF WARWICK HAD been staging a veritable pageant of quarrels and reconciliation. They argued over foreign policy, over affairs in England, over the king's new Woodville relations, over Warwick's desire to marry his two daughters to Edward's two younger brothers. From my exile at Koeur Castle, I followed this farce with intense interest, for any rift in the relationship between Edward and the man who had helped him to the throne could only be to the good as far as I was concerned. Each time news of the latest falling-out occurred, I hoped that it might create a crack that we in exile could somehow widen to our advantage.

Not even I in my most fond imaginings could have predicted what happened in 1469, however. Under the guise of an uprising by one of his retainers, Warwick began a rebellion against Edward in the North. For good measure, he married his daughter Isabel to Edward's younger brother the Duke of Clarence, who had joined the rebellion. And then he did the most extraordinary thing of all: he took Edward prisoner. Was he going to put Clarence on the throne? Was he going to restore my husband to the throne? No one knew, least of all those of us at Koeur Castle.

Almost as quickly as the whole business started, it was over. Edward, whose presence had been needed to put down an uprising by one of our own followers, was freed, though Warwick first murdered two of the Woodvilles and another person he considered to be an upstart. By the end of 1469, Edward and Warwick appeared to be on polite, if not particularly warm, terms. They even kept Christmas together. Hearing about that, I wondered whether poor Henry, shut in his Tower cell, was following all this and if so, if he was reminded of his ill-fated Loveday.

Yet we had had peace after Loveday for nearly two years: Edward and Warwick's reconciliation was over in just months. By March, it was clear that Warwick was plotting to put his son-in-law, Clarence, on the throne. This time, Edward, who had been taken off guard in 1469, was no laggard: he tried to seize Warwick and Clarence, forcing them to flee England in order to save their lives.

On May 1, 1470, father and son-in-law landed at Honfleur, with their wives—and with Warwick's unmarried younger daughter, Anne. And just days later, King Louis wrote me a letter.

I met Louis on June 22 at the Chateau d'Amboise, one of his favorite residences. Louis kissed my hand, presented me to his queen, and then got down to business. "You were slow to come here."

"I had much to think about before I came." I started when something brushed against my leg. Looking down, I saw that one of Louis's omnipresent dogs was nosing me.

Louis snapped his fingers, and the dog, a long-eared type that I had long coveted myself, lay down. "Well, it is as I told you. Warwick and I have engaged in daily discussions during his visit to me here, and he wishes to restore your husband to the throne. He plans to bring an army to England, and he wishes the Prince of Wales to accompany him. And he wants to marry his daughter Anne to the prince."

"I have heard these things. Indeed, I understand that the marriage is being spoken of as a certainty."

"Because it is eminently sensible and desirable. Why, I believe the idea has even been broached in the past by some of your councillors at Koeur."

"I cannot gainsay it. Nor can I deny that there has been talk among us in the past of an alliance with Warwick."

"Well, then, my dear lady, why stall now that this opportunity is finally in your grasp? Why not bring it to fruition? I do not believe you will ever have such a chance again to restore King Henry to his throne."

"I know."

"Well, then?"

"For one thing, Warwick has insulted my son—and me, for that matter. He has alleged that my son is a bastard."

Louis chuckled. "My dear lady, you are too sensitive. Men engage in such tactics against each other all of the time. It is a mere game to us, though it is a pity when the gentler sex is caught up in it. He is willing, nay, eager, to marry his daughter to your son now. That will speak loudly that he believes him to be legitimate."

"He has destroyed some of the men who were dearest and most loyal to me, such as the elder Duke of Somerset and the Duke of Buckingham."

"And would not they have destroyed him, had they been given the chance? And both men were given honorable burial."

"He has humiliated King Henry by forcing him to ride through the streets of London and to be mocked by the crowd."

"Warwick was acting under Edward's command. When he swears his allegiance to King Henry, he will no doubt pay all proper honor to him."

"What of the Duke of Clarence? He cannot be pleased that Warwick no longer plans to place him on the throne."

"Warwick has seen the disadvantages of replacing Edward with his brother. Men who would not fight for Clarence will fight for King Henry."

"You have an answer for everything," I said testily. "But do you have an answer for this? I simply do not trust the man. Even in those desperate moments when I have thought that an alliance with him was my only hope, I have wondered if it was truly a chance worth taking."

"My dear lady, Warwick and I have talked of these matters at length. I told him that I did not believe that you would be quick to forgive him, and these were some of the points that came up in our conversation. The earl does not expect that the past can be forgotten in just a few days. He is aware that your trust is something that he will have to win, and he proposes to win it by setting your husband safely upon the throne. What have you got to lose by allying with him? It will be his life at stake when he returns to England. If he fails, he will forfeit his life. If he reneges, he will probably forfeit it as well, for I do not doubt that there will be men in your own camp who will not forgive such a betrayal. And his younger daughter will be in your hands. He is trusting you as well."

I said nothing. I thought of the Duke of Somerset being bludgeoned to death by Warwick's men as a dazed Hal looked on. I thought of the Duke of Buckingham, who had tried all of his life to act for the best, being butchered after Warwick suborned Lord Grey to turn traitor. I thought of my gentle husband, feet tied to the stirrups of his horse, being paraded through London for the amusement of the crowd. I thought of my own dear boy, the one comfort of my life, being branded a bastard and I a whore. I thought of the sorry fate of Elizabeth Woodville's father and of her brother John, killed the year before by Warwick simply because he wanted to be rid of them. I thought of the men who had held the Tower for Henry after Northampton, being executed by Warwick, and of Hal and the twenty-nine others who had lost their heads after Towton on the orders of Warwick's brother. Perhaps I could indeed trust Warwick if he felt that acting for me was in his interest, but did I want to trust such a man?

"I cannot give you an answer immediately. I must think upon this."

Louis smiled. "My dear lady, take your time." He made a gesture that encompassed all of the luxurious appointments that surrounded us, which contrasted sharply with my own fading tapestries and battered furniture at Koeur Castle. "You and the prince shall be quite comfortable here while you do. And"—he glanced at his dog, which I must have eyed rather wistfully—"this one's mother is breeding. You shall have your pick of the litter."

"As part of his plan, Warwick wishes you to marry his daughter," I told Edward later that day as we stood on the balcony of my chamber, which overlooked the River Loire. Were we to get on a boat and travel west, it would float us to my father's castle at Angers. "She has just reached her fourteenth year, and Warwick assures King Louis that she is an attractive girl, well grown for her age and accomplished. More about her I cannot tell you."

"What did you say?"

"Nothing yet. I do not know what to say." I stared down at the river as it sparkled in the sun. "I know why King Louis is pressing the match: he wants to isolate Burgundy, which is presently on good terms with England. If he can force King Edward off the throne and put Henry on it, then Henry will ally with France against Burgundy." Charles, the Count of Charolais, had succeeded his father as Duke of Burgundy. To my dismay, he had married King Edward's sister Margaret a couple of years earlier.

"Mother, I can figure that out for myself. I do listen to my tutor."

"Yes, you do. I must remember that you are not a little boy anymore." I sighed. "I should take especially care to do so, because you will be playing an important role in your father's government should this plan succeed. Warwick says your father has been much affected by his arrest and imprisonment. He is not mad as he was before, but he sinks into long silences and forgets things, very simple things. If Warwick can be believed, he may not be capable of running the kingdom on his own, though it may be that being freed from confinement improves his state."

"It was Warwick who paraded him to the Tower."

"Yes. And it may be Warwick who can set him free." I turned from my pretty view of the Loire and into my chamber, where I paced about. "And what of the Beauforts? Any plan to put Henry back on the throne must include them, as much as they have suffered for us. But they are in favor with Burgundy, and they hate Warwick with a mortal passion. Exeter too—he has gone half starved sometimes in exile. He might have made his peace, especially as he is married to King Edward's sister, but he has remained loyal to us. He cannot be forgotten. There are so many others to be considered."

"Does the girl approve of these plans?" She and the rest of Warwick's family were at Valognes in Normandy. Warwick himself had intentionally left Amboise before I arrived, so that Louis and I might conduct our conversation in private.

I smiled. "Since when did men keep us informed of their affairs? It is likely that she is just learning about the proposal now. If she is anything like her father, I daresay the possibility of being Queen of England will appeal to her." I stopped and looked at my son. "So. Does it appeal to you? It all rides on you. You are all but grown, and will, I pray to God, be King of England. I would not have you make a match against your will."

Edward was silent. Had he known women? There were none at Koeur, other than my own ladies, all of whom were around my own age and who had been in my service since I was in my teens. Going to my impoverished court was no attractive prospect to the young and ripe. But Edward did not spend all of his time within the castle walls, and there were certainly places he could have found a woman to dally with had he been so inclined. Was he? If he was, was there a certain sort of woman he preferred? It was disconcerting to realize that there were aspects of my son's life about which I knew nothing.

"You give me a choice, but I don't see where I really have any," he said at last. "If I say no and slink back off to Koeur, what will happen? Warwick will go to England anyway, and put that Clarence on the throne. He's married and will soon have a child. I'll be as far from the throne as I ever was. I'll live the rest of my life as an exile, and perhaps Father will die in prison."

"I said you had a choice. I didn't say it was a palatable one."

"I will marry the girl, Mother. Even if I didn't want to be king—and I do—I couldn't let Father just rot in the Tower, knowing that I had the chance to set him free and let it slide by."

I embraced my son. "You have grown up into the sort of man our house needs."

"Then I shall accompany Warwick to England when he sails?"

I dried my eyes. "That," I said firmly, "is another matter entirely."

Over the next few days, Louis tried to convince me to send my son to England with Warwick, but I did not budge. How easy it would be to dispose of my son on the voyage between here and England: he could be shoved overboard, and who could gainsay Warwick when he claimed that my son, unused to the sea, had lost his footing during a rough crossing? And if my son made it safely to England's shore, what was to keep Warwick from turning him over to King Edward as a captive? King Edward would be most forgiving of Warwick after being handed such a present—and if perchance he was not, Warwick still had a possible rival king in the person of George, Duke of Clarence. Indeed, there had been rumors, probably of Warwick's and Clarence's making, that King Edward himself was a bastard, born when the Duchess of York conceived a passion for a mere commoner. I did not believe the rumor, but having been the victim of such falsehoods myself, I knew well what powerful weapons they could be.

Finally, Henry's half brother, Jasper Tudor, who had attempted to invade Wales on our behalf a couple of years before and who had been living in Louis's household since that time, gave us our solution: he would accompany Warwick to England, and Edward need not come until I was comfortable sending him. I saw the sense in this plan instantly. Jasper Tudor had never shied from a fight, yet had never been captured. Such a man was too sharp and wary to fall into a trap. Better yet, if any treachery were to occur, there would be unrest in Wales, for the half-Welsh Jasper was a popular figure there.

With that difficulty out of the way, Edward and I soon traveled to Angers, where for the first time in years I would meet my enemy face to face. King Louis was there when we arrived. "You have not changed your mind, dear lady?"

"I would hardly be here if I had," I snapped.

Edward was less on edge than I. "Will the Lady Anne be here?"

Louis smiled. "You are eager to see your bride, dear boy? I fear that you must wait a few days more. The countess and her daughters and the Duke of Clarence are still in Normandy, but don't worry. You shall be bedding her in due time."

My son blushed, and so did I.

A clattering of hooves and a blowing of horns indicated an important arrival, who I knew could be none other than the Earl of Warwick. Though the most powerful man in France stood beside me, I could not help but wish that my father and my brother, who were busy with their own military affairs in Provence, were at my side as well.

"Stand still for a moment," Katherine Vaux hissed, and I obeyed. She tucked a stray bit of hair that had escaped my hennin into its place and smoothed my gown. "There. You look splendid."

I sank into my chair of state moments before Warwick was announced. Respectfully, he stood at the door until I motioned him forward. Studying him before he dropped to his knees, I was struck once more at how ordinary a man he looked. He was magnificently dressed—indeed, as Louis scorned elaborate robes, and Edward's and my own clothing showed the poverty we had been living in over the past few years, he was the best dressed person in the chamber—but otherwise there was nothing in his face that one would recall, seeing him in a crowd. "You may speak."

"Your grace"—Warwick addressed the general area of my feet—"I have done great wrongs to you in the past—"

"And to my son."

"And to your son. Your grace, I beg that you put the past behind us and that you allow me to offer you my humble service now."

"You faithfully served the man you seek to remove from the throne now." Beside me, I heard Louis cough in warning, but the sight of Warwick, even this kneeling Warwick, was beginning to revive my old anger. "How do I know that having turned traitor to him, you will not turn traitor to me? How do I know that you are not double dealing now?"

Louis stopped in the middle of a second cough. "My dear lady, we have discussed this—"

"We may have discussed these things, but it is one thing for you to tell me what this man intends, and another for him to tell me himself what he intends. How do I know that he is sincere? How do I know that having struck at my dear friends, he will not strike at them again? How do I know that having humiliated my dear husband once, he will not humiliate him again?" I glared down at Warwick's neck. "Speak!"

"Your grace, Edward of England has done me wrongs, which would be tedious to recount here. Your grace may be assured that I have no intent of reconciling with him. And I have suffered hardships coming here myself, which cannot be forgotten easily. Did your grace know that my first grandson was born to the Duchess of Clarence on our way here?"

"No."

"The birth was premature. He was born, died, and buried at sea, all within an hour's time."

"I am sorry to hear it." It was typical, I thought, that Louis had never mentioned this to me.

"It grieved me very much, the more so as I have never been blessed with a son and never will be. Watching his body being lowered into the sea made me understand, better than I ever have in the past, your grace's love for your own son. Your son by King Henry."

Despite myself, I relaxed slightly in my chair. Louis gave an encouraging cough.

"I well understand your grace's doubts; I would have them too. But I came here prepared to swear an oath that I would serve King Henry, Prince Edward, and your grace, and one thing that can be said of me is that I have not broken a solemn oath." Warwick raised his eyes as far up as he deemed politic. "Your grace, King Henry was generous enough to take the late Duke of Somerset back to his side after the duke deserted him for Edward. Some might have turned the duke away, but King Henry welcomed him, and the duke subsequently died for his cause. I am honest enough to admit that I would rather survive the risk I am about to take, but I am willing to die for the House of Lancaster, just as the duke did, if God ordains it. I can offer no greater proof of my sincerity."

He drooped his head. I was silent for a moment or two. "Very well," I said. "In the king's name, I grant you pardon."

Louis's sigh of relief filled the room as I silently calculated how long I had kept the earl on his knees. Fifteen minutes at least, I decided.

Several days after I had officially forgiven Warwick, we processed to the Church of St. Mary, where the Earl of Warwick swore upon the cross that he would uphold the cause of House of Lancaster. King Louis and his brother, Charles of Guienne, swore that they would uphold Warwick in his task, and I swore that I would henceforth treat Warwick as a faithful subject and would not reproach him for his past deeds. Things moved quickly after that: within days, Warwick, accompanied by the Duke of Clarence, had gone to the coast to see to the assembly of his invasion fleet, and Edward and I were at Amboise, watching as Warwick's womenfolk were ushered into our presence.

The Countess of Warwick, the Duchess of Clarence, and Lady Anne were unmistakably a mother and her daughters. All three were tall and slender, with fair complexions, and the sliver of hair their headdresses revealed was light blond. They each wore the tall, pointed hennins that were the fashion here in

France; in my nervousness, I wondered if the truncated version still held sway in England.

Edward stared at Anne with undisguised appreciation as she and the rest rose at my command. No man in his right mind could have disliked what he saw: dark blue eyes, blooming cheeks, a straight little nose, and kissable lips. Could Anne dislike what she saw? I tried, with great difficulty, to see my son objectively. He had shot up a couple of inches recently and had yet to grow into them, which gave him a certain gawky air, but he had largely been spared the spottiness that troubled so many other boys his age. Dark-haired and dark-eyed like his father, he had a similar facial structure as well, but Henry's mild features had turned sharper, more determined, in his son. It lent his handsome face a stern expression, which softened, however, when he smiled or when he was gaping at a pretty girl, as he was now.

With a start, I realized that I had been so busy with these reflections that I was tardy in greeting my daughter-in-law to be. I smiled quickly. "Welcome, my dear. I am very glad to see you here, as well as your mother and sister."

"Thank you, your grace."

"You left your father the Earl of Warwick well, I hope?"

"Yes, your grace," Anne said

"You had an uneventful journey here, I trust?"

"Yes, your grace."

How long could we go on like this? I truly did not know what to say to the child. Even if she had not been daughter to a man I had hated for so long, my lengthy stay at Koeur, where I seldom saw anyone other than my fellow exiles, my servants, and my French relations, had not improved my ability to carry on an inconsequential conversation. Edward might be scarcely better. He was well-read and well-trained in the art of war, I realized belatedly, but there had been little time or money during our exile to train him in the more gentle arts. Perhaps I should have sent him to my father's court, where he would have learned how to play an instrument, to write verse, to pay the compliments that young ladies expected.

But Edward was the one who rescued us. "Welcome, my lady." He lifted Anne's hand—a dainty one, I saw—to his mouth and kissed it with more savoir-faire than I would have expected. "It is pleasant to see an English rose here in France."

Where in the world had Edward learned this manner of talk? It did not, however, have much of an effect on Anne, who thanked him stiffly.

Unbowed, my son turned to me. "Mother, I would like to speak to my betrothed privately. May we walk out in the garden?"

"Why, of course," I said, wondering what further botanical compliments this would inspire my son to muster and hoping that they proved more successful than the last.

25

Edward of Lancaster
August 1470 to April 1471

"I ALWAYS THOUGHT I WOULD MARRY THE DUKE OF GLOUCESTER," ANNE informed me as soon as we entered the garden at Amboise. Aside from a brief exchange about whether we should go here or to the menagerie (I vetoed the menagerie, feeling that I did not need the competition from Louis's elephant), it was the first thing she had said to me since we had left our mothers' presence.

Gloucester, King Edward's youngest brother, was just a year or so older than me, I recalled. I had no idea what he looked like. "Did you want to marry him?"

Anne shrugged enigmatically and accepted my invitation to sit down on a bench of turf. In a finicky manner that made me wonder how she had survived the miserable voyage from England, during which her sister had given birth, she arranged her skirts around her. "I had grown so accustomed to the idea, I hardly thought about wanting or not wanting. It was just part of my life. But I did like the idea of being a duchess."

"Well, with me you will become Princess of Wales. Then queen."

"If all goes well."

"It's your own father who is arranging all of this. Don't you have faith in him?"

"Of course I do in him, but not necessarily in the rest of you. If this plan fails, I will be exiled at Koeur with you. And then I'll just be a hanger-on among your family."

How could I have wanted to kiss this girl just a few minutes before? "If it comes to that, we'll get an annulment."

Anne considered this for a moment or two, then frowned. "It won't be easy, not with the dispensation we'll be getting. And I'm sure our parents will make us consummate it."

"Horrors," I murmured. "Did you tell your father that you didn't wish to marry me?"

"Goodness, no. One doesn't argue with my father. And he gave me this." She held out her wrist. A sapphire bracelet that could have fed us at Koeur for a month flashed upon it.

"You should have argued. Perhaps he would have given you rubies for the other wrist."

"He did promise me a nice gift on our wedding day," my bride said.

"My mother has some jewels she plans to give you on that day," I said. "They used to be her mother's."

"Poor thing, can she afford it? It is petty to notice those things, but her gown looks as if it is on its last legs. Though she is still a beautiful woman for her age." She studied my clothing. "Your clothing is rather stylish, though."

It was, because Mother always insisted that I be clothed like a prince even when she could no longer afford to clothe herself like a queen. By God, when my father recovered his crown, she would have some new clothes—and jewels to replace the many she had pledged to pay our expenses—even if I had to rip them off the back of this spoiled brat. "Her father has them, actually. He will send them after the dispensation arrives."

"Oh, I see."

I cast around for a topic that wouldn't tempt me to shake this girl. "Do you like France?"

"Well, of course, I have spent much time in Calais, so it isn't entirely new to me, but I suppose Calais doesn't quite count. But no, I don't like it very much. I like the North of England, actually."

"The North? I wouldn't have thought it was your sort of place."

"That shows how little imagination you have. The North is very beautiful in its way. Of course, I spent more time at Warwick Castle than anywhere. I miss it there too."

She did look homesick, and for a moment I felt almost sorry for her. It couldn't be easy, I reminded myself, for this pampered girl of barely fourteen to suddenly find herself in exile. I'd been living that life since age seven, following Palm Sunday Field, short of money and always on someone else's sufferance; though I didn't like that mode of living, I was used to it. "When Father's back on the throne, we'll spend some time in the North," I offered.

"Father," Anne mused, and I tensed, knowing already from this brief encounter that this tone of voice did not bode well. "Edward, I hardly know how to put this, but well, I'll just ask it. You are legitimate, aren't you?"

I could do nothing but sputter, "How dare you insult me—and my mother—like that?"

"Well," said Anne reasonably. "It is rumored, and it is something that I should know for sure. Don't you think? One doesn't want our marriage to be founded on a lie."

"I am legitimate. The rumors you have heard were of your beloved father's own making and for his own purposes. And now, if you'll excuse me, I shall go for a walk on my own. If I stay here one more minute, I would strangle you. And not only would that be against the rules of knighthood, that would spoil everything, wouldn't it?"

"I only asked," Anne called as I stalked away.

Though Anne's and my first interview had been less than successful, I found when I returned that our mothers had gotten on rather better—probably to the countess's credit, for my mother was not the sort of woman who spoke easily to other women, save for those who had served her forever, like Katherine Vaux. With us gone, they'd busied themselves by sewing baby clothes for Queen Charlotte, who had given birth to a son just a few weeks earlier. I'd been one of the godfathers.

When my mother asked later how I had gotten on with Anne, I didn't tell her how unpleasant the experience had been. Almost as if we'd agreed upon it, Anne must not have told her mother either, for when we supped with Louis that evening, the countess was all smiles. Anne and I sat side by side and made polite conversation, and Louis beamed at us paternally.

Under the circumstances, we would have to make the best of each other, I knew, and Anne no doubt knew it too. So we passed our days at Amboise, alternating between bickering and cool civility, while Warwick and Clarence, along with the Earl of Pembroke and Warwick's brother-in-law the Earl of Oxford, attended to their men's business on the coast. They were expected to leave for England any day, but unfavorable winds, and a blockade of La Hogue by Burgundy and England, held them there until more friendly winds scattered the ships pinning them in. At last, on September 9, Warwick's ships pulled out of harbor.

I have never seen any woman pray as much as my mother did that September; we might as well have been living in a nunnery. She fasted too, sometimes several days a week, and I do believe that she would have donned a hair shirt if someone could have been found to make her one. When she wasn't on her knees, she was pacing around the castle, waiting for the messenger who would give us news of our enterprise. The rest of us were scarcely better. Even Louis, who alone among us had no close relation whose life would be forfeit if our invasion failed, was on edge. His greyhounds, who sensed his moods about as well as or better than as any human being, slunk around their business quietly.

By the end of September, we had received an optimistic letter from Warwick, bringing the news that he had landed safely and was gathering support. This was something, but not enough to lure my mother from the altar or strike any comfort into Louis's hounds.

Then, during the first week of October, Louis burst into the solar that had been assigned to our group of refugees. "Where is Queen Margaret?"

"Praying," I said.

"Get her up, get her up!" Katherine Vaux obediently went to the door, and Louis all but shoved her out of it. "Hurry, woman!"

Katherine had barely rushed out of the door when she collided with my mother approaching it, as if lured there by a sixth sense. "Have you news?"

"Yes, I have news. We have succeeded! Without striking a single blow. Warwick has entered London. Edward, knowing that resistance was futile, has fled England. And King Henry sits again upon the throne of England."

"My husband is free?" whispered my mother.

"That's what I said. He was taken from the Tower and lodged in state at the Bishop of London's palace. He is to be recrowned with great ceremony in a few days."

My mother seemed about to faint for a moment. "God be thanked," she muttered as I steadied her. She pulled from my grasp and embraced Anne, toward whom up until now she had been polite, but somewhat distant. "This was all due to your father—and to King Louis," she added politicly. "I am grateful to them beyond words. I should never have doubted them—or the Lord. I thank them for giving me you as a daughter, too, for this could not have otherwise come about."

Anne smiled rather smugly.

"My husband is a man who can do great things," the Countess of Warwick said.

"How does King Henry fare? Did he send a message?"

"Yes, he sent his love to you and the Prince of Wales, and longs to see you soon," Louis said. "He looked rather shabby when they led him out of the Tower, they say, but they put some proper clothes on him, and he looks fine now."

"But how is his mind?"

Louis seemed to find the question largely irrelevant. "Well, it will take him some time to get used to being a free man, and to ruling, again. But in the meantime, Warwick will manage all."

"Where did March go? What will he do?"

Louis blinked as my mother reverted to King Edward's former title. "Seek support from Burgundy, no doubt, as his sister is married to the duke there. But why fret over all of these details today, my dear lady? Surely today should be a time for rejoicing."

"And I do. It is just so sudden." My mother embraced me. "To see you restored to your rank as Prince of Wales gratifies me beyond words. I must go give thanks."

She walked shakily away, led by Katherine Vaux. Anne stared after her before turning her attention to me. "So you and I are now Prince and Princess of Wales," Anne observed. "Or the next best thing in my case, since we have been betrothed." She looked at me with a new interest, then turned to Louis. "When shall we get our dispensation to marry, your grace?"

"Any day now." Louis winked at me.

That afternoon, Anne let me take her to a secluded part of the garden and kiss her, not once but three times—I couldn't help myself, for the girl was quite cuddlesome once she melted a bit. She even kissed me back to some extent. "You really are quite handsome," she observed breathlessly.

Daringly, I laid a hand upon her breast, albeit a breast with several layers of fabric shielding it from my insolent touch. She frowned and backed away. "But not that handsome," she warned, bending and patting one of the ever-present greyhounds, who growled at me. "Why, the dispensation hasn't even arrived yet!"

❧

Every day at Koeur, under the tutelage of some of the knights who shared our exile, I had practiced the arts of war with my companions—most of them boys connected with my grandfather René's court in some way. Louis had arranged for me to keep up this routine at Amboise. I was running against William Vaux in the tiltyard when I saw Anne watching me from a distance, the first time she'd shown much of an interest in my daily activities. I decided not to halt what I was doing, but went on about my practice while she stood watching, though it was disconcerting to have those blue eyes fixed upon me.

"You're skilled," she acknowledged when I, finished for the day and stripped of my armor, walked over to acknowledge her presence. "I used to watch the boys in my father's household practice, and you're as good as any of them. Of course, they were younger."

I had just turned seventeen, an anniversary that had been marked with more jollity than in the past. "Thanks for nothing." I grinned.

"Well, it's just that they left to go back to their homes when they were fifteen or sixteen. You needn't be offended."

"I wasn't. When you've spent your life in exile, being called a bastard and the son of a madman, you either get offended at everything or nothing. I'm more the latter, I suppose."

"I suppose you are still offended by my asking you whether you were a bastard."

"No, though I do find it amusing that now that my father's on the throne again, you no longer seem to care."

"It is not that," Anne said testily. "It is simply that I believed you." She looked at me, and I felt another delicate question coming on. "Edward, how mad is your father?"

I supposed that this was a step up from questioning my legitimacy. "You forget I haven't seen him since I was nine. Back then he never acted like people say madmen act, at least not when I was old enough to notice things. He never spoke gibberish; he could talk to someone just as you and I are talking now. But there was always something very odd about him. Unworldly, you might say. Or even other worldly."

"He's never fought in a battle."

"No. The closest he came was at the first St. Albans, they say, and all he really did there was stand around. That's one reason I've always practiced my fighting skills; a king should fight in battle. My grandfather the fifth Henry did." I hesitated, wondering whether I should confide in my future wife, and took the leap. "When my father was captured, I decided I would do everything I could to be like my grandfather instead of my father, even though I do love him."

Anne didn't make the rude remark I'd dreaded, but simply nodded. "Yes, a king should fight. Your mother would like him to, I'm sure."

"Probably, but she accepts him as he is, and loves him. I think she always has."

"She half scares me," admitted Anne with some trepidation. When no reprimand came from me, she added, "She's always perfectly pleasant to me, but I don't find her easy to be around."

"Yes, I've noticed that you're quiet around her. But she likes you; she's told me so." (I was not strictly telling the truth here, but my mother had never said that she disliked Anne, after all.) "Just talk to her as you do your own mother. She'd probably like it."

"She wouldn't find me impertinent?"

"Not unless you ask her if I'm a bastard."

Anne looked at me warily, then laughed. "Well," she said, "I guess I can try."

"The Bishop of Bayeaux has granted the dispensation," John Morton announced in early December. He held up a document triumphantly. "King Louis's people have read it, and I have read it, and it is sufficient for the Prince of Wales and Lady Anne to marry."

"Here in France?" Anne asked.

"Why, of course," Mother said. "Your father wished you to marry my son once he took England, and I shall keep that promise. We have been waiting only for a proper dispensation."

"I just thought it might be nicer to marry at Westminster Abbey," Anne confessed. "An English royal couple should be married in England. And I always wanted Father to be at my wedding, instead of across the sea." She brightened. "Perhaps we could marry here, and then marry again at Westminster? Then Father could see me married, and my uncles and my aunts. Oh, and King Henry too," she added. "He should be able to see his own son married."

"A second ceremony," my mother mused. Our victory had had a noticeable effect on her appearance; dressed in one of the fine new gowns that Louis had provided for her, she looked no more than thirty, ten years younger than her true age. She smiled. "Why not? The people would enjoy a grand wedding between two such handsome young people, and we could make a great festivity out of it. And King Henry and your father will indeed like to be present. I think that would be an excellent idea, Anne."

The Duchess of Clarence looked up from her embroidery. There was an acidic tone to her voice when she said, "But when shall it be consummated?"

"On their wedding night," my mother said. "It is what the Earl of Warwick wished."

Anne and I simultaneously gulped. For she was without a doubt a virgin, and so was I.

How had I maintained this state at age seventeen? There had not been any women at Koeur except for my mother's ladies and the laundress, all of whom

were unsuitable. Our poverty at Koeur was so well known in the neighbor-
hood there that no woman there would risk getting with a bastard by me or by
any other man there. That left only whores, and even if I could have afforded
one, which was not always the case, there was enough in me of my father—and
of my grandfather the fifth Henry, who'd been a fastidious man—not to wish
to lie with such women. So I had stayed pure, and at Amboise, which Louis
kept isolated from the surrounding town, there had been nothing to threaten
this state, though I probably wouldn't have minded an attack on my virtue.

So it was Anne who would be my first woman—my only one, if I kept my
wedding vows sacred. My father too had been a virgin when he married, and
had by all reports never strayed from my mother's bed. Perhaps I was more
like him than I realized.

On December 13, at Amboise, Anne and I were married. Much of the French
court was present, though Louis's omnipresent greyhounds had been banished
to their kennels for the occasion. As we said our vows, our mothers appeared
to be holding a little competition to see who could shed the most sentimental
tears—much to the disgust of Louis, who was heard to hiss, "Wenches! It is
a wedding, not a funeral!" But Anne, with her long blond hair trailing to the
waist of her rose-colored gown (she'd at first picked a blue, but it turned out
to be too close to the Duke of York's blue to suit a Lancastrian wedding),
looked lovely, and the ladies of the court bestowed approving nods upon me
as well.

There was the usual feast, during which Anne and I picked at our food, the
usual blessing of the marital bed, the usual putting us to bed together. Then
the guests left our bedchamber, and I was alone with my wife.

I reviewed the information I'd received from William Vaux, whose guidance I'd solicited the day before. *Don't pounce on the girl as soon as you get
aroused. Kiss her, play with her a while. Put your hand there, if you're feeling daring
and she's not too nervous; it can help. Go slow. And it never hurts to tell her she's
beautiful, whatever else you do.* I turned to Anne, sitting up straight and alert in
her elaborately embroidered nightshift, her golden hair spilling loose over her
shoulders. "You're beautiful."

"Thank you."

Evidently girls were not told to say, "You're handsome," in these situa-
tions. My nerve broke. "We can put this off if you like," I said. "Maybe until
you're fifteen."

"And disappoint my father? Heavens, no. We must do it tonight." Anne began to untie her shift. "Here. I'll get us started."

I stopped her. "No. *I'll* get us started." I untied her shift and took her into my arms. *Start off cuddling her a little, women like that. Kissing their duckies always seems to work also. And if you're really bold, you can—*

Suddenly William Vaux's voice faded out; I was managing just fine on my own—or as fine, I suppose, as could be expected under the circumstances. Sooner than I had hoped, but not nearly as soon as I had feared, I was lying spent atop Anne. "I didn't hurt you too much, did I?"

"No, not too much," Anne said. I rolled off her, and she curled against me as I ran my hands through her hair. "Really, it wasn't bad at all, considering."

☞

"Paris," said Louis, seeing us off for that city two days after our wedding. "The perfect place for young lovers."

"How would he know?" muttered Anne under her breath so only I could hear—or at least, I hoped only I could hear.

Anne, however, had pitched her voice correctly. Serenely, Louis went on, "You will not forget your promise to us, I trust."

"No, your grace." I had promised to aid him in his cause against Charles, and to urge my father to declare war on Burgundy. "I shall keep it faithfully."

"Good, my dear boy." Louis stepped back and waved our escort forward. "To Paris!"

King Louis having received favorable reports from his ambassadors to England, he and my mother had deemed it safe at last for us to return home. We were to travel to Paris and then to Rouen, where Warwick was to meet us and then escort us to England. It was what my mother had been impatiently awaiting for weeks—yet now, as we left Amboise behind, she looked preoccupied. "What is wrong, Mother?" I asked when the men Louis had sent to escort us were out of earshot.

"Burgundy. Its duke has been good to us in the past—and he was a friend to one I held very dear." An odd expression passed over my mother's face, so fleetingly I wondered if I had imagined it. "I do not like the idea of going to war against him."

"But it is what my father wants as well as King Louis," said Anne.

"Yes, it is what both men want, and I have long known that it was the price of Louis's aiding us to begin with." My mother sighed. "But sometimes it pricks at my conscience nonetheless." She sat silent for a moment or two, then roused herself. "You shall like Paris, Anne. King Louis is right: it is a wonderful city for the young."

"Indeed, madam?" Anne winked at me. The night before, we had had our most satisfactory session of lovemaking to date—and our marriage was only two days old. "Then I think we shall like it very much indeed."

And we did. Louis had ordered the citizens to give us a royal welcome, and not a night went by when there was not some great banquet in our honor, followed by dancing far into the night. We were never too tired, though, to enjoy the majestic bed that graced our chamber at the Louvre, which we put to very good use.

"Will the two of you stop making sheep's eyes at each other and attend to me?" the Duchess of Clarence asked us one afternoon while our mothers were out of the room.

Anne turned guiltily from the window seat in which we had been sitting, rather too close together. "Yes, Isabel?"

"I said that I am leaving France, and that the men George sent to escort me home should be here any day. I am tired of lingering here, and I wish to join my husband. The more so since I have to watch the two of you pawing each other all of the time."

"We do not paw each other," said Anne. "We simply show our affection toward each other."

"Is that what you call it?"

Anne tossed her head as well as a girl with an outsized hennin could. "There's no need to be hateful to me just because you can't be queen now."

I watched this quarrel begin with a certain interested detachment: as I was an only child, fights between siblings were a novelty for me.

Isabel snorted. "And what makes you so sure you will be queen?"

"Why, Father has secured England for us."

"And since when was Father invincible?"

"Isabel!"

"And do you really think the old King Edward is going to give up on England?" Isabel asked. "He has a son there now, in case you don't remember. Do you think he's just going to stay abroad and forget about him? And his daughters as well?"

Elizabeth Woodville had proved a fertile queen, though the first three children she had borne the king all turned out to be girls. In November, though—after taking sanctuary at Westminster for fear of Warwick's intentions—she had at last given birth to a boy, who was named after his exiled father. The French court had found it rather amusing that not only did England have two rival kings, she now had two rival princes bearing the same Christian name. I had failed to see the humor in it myself.

"Father won't let him. After all, he made Edward king to begin with. He can unmake him. He *has* unmade him. Anyway, how can you talk so? Whose side are you on, anyway? Edward, why aren't you saying anything?"

"I—"

Isabel cut me off. "I am on my husband's side, if you must know. In my opinion he has been treated shabbily by both Father and by King Edward. And my place is with him, not wandering through France." In a milder tone, she said, "Besides, I miss England."

"Father will be angry that you've gone to England without waiting for him to escort you there."

"Why should he care, as long as I am escorted as befits my station? As you said yourself, you are the future queen, not me. I am of small importance to him now. And George would not have sent men to take me home without advising him, anyway. I don't understand, though, why the rest of you don't come now." Isabel suddenly appeared to remember my presence. "I should think that you, Edward, would want to see England after you've been gone all of this time. And that you would want to see your father."

I did not miss the malice in her voice. "My lady mother has given her promise to your father and to the King of France that she and I will tarry here until your father arrives, and she keeps her promises. But I am eager to return home, you can be assured of that." I hesitated. "What does the Duke of Clarence say of my father's condition?"

"That he is sane, but that the governing of England is all in my father's hands. I should think you'd want to hurry to England to take up your part in it, if nothing else. After all, you are the heir to the throne." Isabel stood. "I am going to begin packing. You lovebirds can get back to your petting."

"Mother, why are we staying here?" I asked a few days later after Isabel and her escort had left for the coast.

"We must wait for Warwick."

"You keep telling me that, and I don't believe you. Why must we wait for Warwick, really? There are men who would escort us, and who would really want to harm us, anyway?"

"With France on the verge of war with Burgundy, we could be intercepted by Burgundy and seized as hostages."

I shook my head. "Since when have you been so cautious?"

"You are speaking to me rather impertinently, Edward."

"I am next in line to the throne. I am not a child; you have said so yourself. I have a right to know what we are about. When we go to England I will be all but king. Isn't that so? Father is unfit to do anything but the most trivial tasks."

"Who tells you that, and how dare you speak of your father in that manner?"

"You said before you met Warwick that Father might not be capable of running the kingdom on his own, and from what I can gather from what's left unsaid, he's not. And I am sorry, Mother, to speak harshly, but I am seventeen, almost at man's estate. I am too old to be fobbed off with excuses and half-truths."

My mother raised her hand, and for a moment I thought she was going to slap me. Instead she drew her hand back and sank onto a settee, where she began weeping.

"Mother!" I sat beside her. "Don't cry. I'm sorry."

My mother wiped her eyes. "Your father wrote me a letter the other day, in his own hand. All of the others have been written by his clerks. Very loving, but very businesslike and formal. In this one he called me his Marguerite, his Daisy, and begged me to come home. He said he was so lonely, even with everyone treating him with respect again, and that sometimes when they had been pressing too much business on him, he got confused and thought he was in the Tower again. He thought he would be so much better if you and I were there with him. He would not be so forgetful and nervous."

She answered the unspoken question in my eyes. "I told him the truth—or part of it. I do want to see him; I want to take care of him. With my love he will be at peace, even if he never is fit to rule on his own again."

"Then why don't you return to England, Mother? It would make him so happy, and everyone else too."

My mother snorted. "No one in England but Henry wants me in London, or anywhere. That will never change. But that is not why I am in no hurry to return to England."

"Then why?"

My mother stared at her lap. "Because I am terrified that when I do come, something will happen to break my heart."

"That's irrational, Mother," I said sensibly. "You should not be so superstitious."

Mother shrugged. "I know it." She stood and tried to smile. "But nonetheless, I am content to wait until Warwick comes to get us. Aside from my fears, he knows the situation in England and the mood of the people there."

And so we did. We waited, and waited, while others came home. Edmund Beaufort, who'd assumed his brother Henry's title of Duke of Somerset, came home, having been released from the Duke of Burgundy's service. His brother John came home. The Duke of Exeter came home. Everyone who lived in England was coming home, except for my mother and me, England's queen and her Prince of Wales.

Finally, in late February, John, Lord Wenlock, and Sir John Langstrother arrived to fetch us home—Warwick having been too wrapped up in England's affairs to escort us himself. But bad weather had kept us at the port of Harfleur, and when we finally did set sail on March 24, we were constantly knocked back to shore. It was not until April 13 that we at last caught a favorable wind.

While we had waited at Harfleur, however, yet one more person had come home. Edward, with ships paid for by the Duke of Burgundy, had sailed for England. And the winds were in his favor.

26

Edward of Lancaster
April 1471 to May 4, 1471

A NNE'S EYES WIDENED AS WE APPROACHED THE HILLSIDE NEAR CERNE Abbey in Dorset. "I cannot be seeing what I am seeing. Edward? Is it—"

"Yes," I said, gazing at the hillside, which bore a huge chalk figure of a man holding a club. It was not the club, however, that was his most prominent feature, but the appendage that left the figure's gender in no doubt whatsoever.

"I have never seen so crude a sight! So vulgar! How do the monks bear it? Can we ride closer?"

I was ready to oblige when William Vaux galloped up to us. "Your graces, the Duke of Somerset and the Earl of Devon are at the abbey. They rode out from London when they heard that you had embarked from France. It is most urgent that you return to see them immediately."

"Do they have news?"

"Yes." William's eyes glanced at Anne, then fixed and held mine. "They do." He hesitated. "Perhaps I should not be saying this, but it seems cruel to delay saying it. My lady, I have ill news for you. The Earl of Warwick has perished in battle."

"When Edward first arrived in England, he said he only wanted to recover the dukedom of York," Somerset said, staring at the ground. "He was even wearing the prince's badge. He began collecting men to his side, so many that when he reached Coventry and found the Earl of Warwick staying there, he offered him battle. But the earl was waiting for more troops from his brother Montagu, and refused. Edward moved on and proclaimed himself as king. Soon after that, the Duke of Clarence deserted our cause."

"Mother of God," whispered my mother.

Somerset nodded grimly. "It seems that all of his womenfolk—including his wife—had been at work on him." He went on, ignoring Anne's strangled sob. "After that, with Edward all the stronger from the forces that Clarence had raised, he again offered to do battle with the Earl of Warwick. When that failed, he offered Warwick terms. Warwick refused. He had sworn his loyalty to King Henry at Angers, he said, and he would not break his oath."

My mother crossed herself. "I did not trust him, and yet he kept his word," she said sadly. "Forgive me."

Somerset went on wearily. "Just a few days ago, Edward then entered London in great state. The citizens offered him no resistance; indeed, they greeted him joyously."

"Of course they did," my mother said flatly. "They have never been our friends, those vile Londoners. What of the king?"

Somerset reached for my mother's hand. "Edward took King Henry into custody. I am very sorry, your grace, but he is a captive once more."

My mother put her head in her hands. She did not weep, but I saw her shoulders shaking.

"Where were you and Devon?" I asked. "You came from London, Vaux said. Could you have not held it for us?"

"When we heard that your grace and the queen had taken ship, we came to meet you," Somerset said. A flush spread over his handsome face. "We felt it more important to meet you safely than tarry in London, as you are but a small party. And we had small forces in London, and could have been overwhelmed. We felt we could raise more forces in our own dominions."

There was more to it than that, I thought. I'd been but a babe when Somerset's father was killed at St. Albans by Warwick's men, but I knew there was no man Somerset hated more than Warwick. Had Somerset been unable to face the possibility of fighting alongside Warwick? And alongside Warwick's brother John, who'd executed Somerset's brother Henry after Hexham?

"Edward was crowned again at Westminster," Somerset said grimly. "After collecting more men, he rode out of London on April 13 and encamped on a field near Barnet. He even brought King Henry with him, as a captive, to flaunt in Warwick's face."

My mother moaned.

"Yesterday at dawn, his forces encountered those of the Earl of Warwick's. Exeter and Oxford were commanding alongside Warwick. There was a fog, so thick it was difficult to see past your own nose. The Earl of Oxford's men overcame the men led by Lord Hastings, but Oxford's men began pursuing Hastings' men to London until Oxford could get them back into good order.

When he did, they ran into Montagu's men and mistook them for Edward's. There were cries of treason, and that spelled the end; our own forces began attacking each other. Montagu was killed. Oxford is believed to have escaped after the battle; someone saw him and his brothers riding off. Exeter is believed to have fallen in battle, but no one has seen his body. The Earl of Warwick was killed in the rout." Somerset nodded at Anne. In a kinder tone than he had used previously, he said, "Your father fought bravely, your grace."

Anne had not fainted or cried when Vaux gave us the news when we were out on our ride. Since our return to the abbey, she had sat like a stone figure. Now she rose from the stool a monk had brought in for her and pointed straight at my mother, sitting on another stool. "You did this. You killed my father."

"I, girl?" My mother rose.

"Anne—"

"Don't touch me!" Anne struggled to free herself from my grasp. "You did! You tarried in France, enjoying yourself, while we all begged you to return home. But you would have none of it; you had to wait for my father. If you'd come sooner, Somerset and Devon could have been fighting alongside of him instead of bothering with us. You could have left at any time! But you didn't, and you left my father to fight. And you used my father to make your pathetic husband king again. You used your son. You used me, you used all of us. You should rot in hell. I hate you! I hate all of you! I—"

Anne sank senseless upon the ground. For a moment, we did nothing but stare at her motionless figure. Then John Morton stooped beside her. "The Princess of Wales is merely in a swoon," he said, after lifting her wrist. "Your grace, I would ask that you not be too hard upon the girl when she awakes. She is suffering under the shock of extreme grief." He shook his head as I started to reach for my wife. "I would advise leaving her alone for a while, your grace."

My mother said nothing, but sank back upon her stool. John Morton beckoned to Anne's ladies, who followed him as he lifted Anne and carried her off to the tiny chamber we shared at the abbey. "The Lady Anne is right," she said dully when they had left. "I should have left France earlier."

Devon spoke for the first time. "Your grace, you cannot blame yourself for being unable to foretell the future. And you cannot control the winds that blew you here so tardily."

"I failed to march on London after the second battle of St. Albans, and I failed to come from France in time," my mother said. "And now my dear

Henry is a captive once more, and Warwick dead." She rose. "Tomorrow we leave here. I have failed miserably at this man's game of war I have been playing, and I shall play it no more. I will return to my father's lands, and I will beg Edward to allow my husband to return to me there. This comedy is at an end."

"Your grace, you cannot give up!" Somerset caught her by the wrist as she began to walk from the room. "I know our fortunes seem at their lowest, but think! I will not lie to you, your grace. In the absence of the Princess of Wales, I may be honest with you: I have had the utmost difficulty in resigning myself to living under a regime under the Earl of Warwick. I would not be surprised if once Edward was driven out of the country, Warwick would have found some excuse to get rid of me. And there are others like me who mistrust him. With him gone, our cause may well be strengthened, for those who have shied away from it because of Warwick's presence there may now rally to it. And there is something else: Burgundy. Your grace is well aware that I have served him faithfully for some years and that he was a good friend to my late brother Henry, and that Warwick's waging war against him stuck in my craw. With Warwick gone, we can make peace with Burgundy."

Mother shook her head. "I will not play games with fate anymore. Tomorrow my son and I return to my father."

"No, we do not. I am going to stay here." I took my mother by the shoulders, not roughly but firmly. "Mother, I am the Prince of Wales! I am not going to spend my days as a pathetic exile, being pointed out as a curiosity by those around Koeur or wherever we eke out our days. I am going to fight for my rights, and for those of my father. You are right; a woman has no place in these affairs. But I am a man now, and I do. I have not come here to turn tail and head to France without seeing battle."

"The prince is right," Somerset said. "This is our moment to seize. Think of those who have died for our cause. My brothers and my father, Devon's brothers, Oxford's father and brother, the men who fell at Blore Heath and Northampton and Towton and Hexham and Barnet—all of them. They will have died in vain if we give up now."

"And there is Father! Do you really think Edward would allow him to join us in exile? He will spend the rest of his life in the Tower."

"They say that he was ill-clad and unkempt when Warwick first freed him from his long imprisonment," Devon added. "They are bound to treat him wretchedly now."

"We must free him, Mother! All these years, you have never given up fighting for him—and for me. It will throw him into despair if you abandon him now. It may even kill him."

Mother raised her palms. "I cannot stand against all of you," she said quietly. "Stay here and fight, then. And I will stay here alongside you." She gestured toward the direction of Anne's chamber. "Go to your wife, Edward, and give her what comfort you can. And I shall go to my chamber and pray. God knows, we need all of the heavenly assistance we can get."

✍

"Go away." Anne, her chalky face blending in with the coverings of the narrow bed she occupied at Cerne Abbey, spoke in barely audible tones.

"No, Anne. I am your husband." I approached the bed and sat beside it. "Anne, I am very grieved about the death of your father. So are the rest of us."

Anne stared at the ceiling for a long time. Finally, she said, "I never thought it would end so. It had been so easy for him in the past. He demanded what he wanted, and he got it. He seemed invincible to me."

"Yes, I can see where he would." Perhaps I was lucky, in a way, that any illusions I might have had about my own father's invincibility had been shattered so early.

"I don't remember much of what I said out there. The words just poured from my mouth. Is your mother angry at me?"

"No. She is in despair. She wanted to return to France."

"Will we?"

We, she had said. "No. We are going to stay here and fight. Mother gave in."

"And me? Now that my father is dead, you won't want me anymore. What use can I be? Your mother will want to try to marry you to someone whose father can help your cause. She will annul our marriage."

"That's rot." I stroked Anne's golden hair. "You will stay my princess, and when my father runs his course on earth, you will be my queen. I promise you that. Even if my mother does try to part us—and I do not believe she would be so cold as to do so—I will not let her. We will celebrate our marriage at Westminster, just like we talked about." I kissed her gently. "Now go to sleep. I will hold you close as you do."

"And you will keep fighting? Even if your mother doesn't want you to?"

"Yes. It is my duty. To my father, and to myself. And to my mother, even though she doesn't appreciate it at the moment."

Anne managed a very faint smile. "You are like your father in some ways, Edward," she said. "But in many others, you are very like your mother."

∽

While we were still at Cerne, more news arrived: Anne's mother, who as Warwick's countess had required a separate ship for herself and her entourage, had arrived in Portsmouth on the same day that we had arrived at Weymouth—the day of Barnet. Hearing of Warwick's death, she had fled into sanctuary at Beaulieu Abbey.

My own mother, having agreed to remain in England and continue our fight, showed no signs of the doubt and despair that she had shown at Cerne. We traveled to Exeter, where we spent hours each day raising troops and studying maps.

"We have two viable choices: to go to London or to the North, through Wales," Somerset said early on. "I prefer to go north. The Earl of Pembroke has been active for us in Wales, and can bring us a mighty force. And though the Earl of Northumberland has yet to commit to anyone, he is more likely to commit to us now that the Earl of Warwick is deceased." Had my wife not been present, he would have probably said "out of the way."

"Northumberland did nothing to stop Edward from landing, though," I said. "And he owes his freedom and his restored earldom to Edward."

My mother chewed her lip. "We shall go north," she said finally. "If Northumberland didn't stir himself against Edward, at least he hasn't stirred himself in his favor, either. I'll not put my faith in those around London. I'll enter its gates only when I have that Edward's handsome head to put upon its bridge. And his faithless brother Clarence's as well."

Anne nodded vigorously.

∽

On May Day, we arrived at Bristol, where we got not only money and men, but artillery. "Guns," my mother said fondly as our men hauled them into their places among our train. We had about six thousand men now, and that was without the Earl of Pembroke, waiting for us in Wales. It was a far cry from the small entourage we had had when we arrived at Weymouth just three weeks before. "We have needed them so badly. And we shall get even more, perhaps, at Gloucester."

Instead, when we arrived at Gloucester the next morning—having evaded Edward's men, who were been hoping to do battle at with us at Sodbury Hill—its gates were shut fast against us. We had been planning to march through the town and cross the Severn into Wales.

"Whoresons," muttered my mother as we conferred at a distance. It was an unseasonably hot day, and even at this early hour, we were sweating from our long march, Mother no less than the rest of us. She absently patted her weary horse; we had been marching all night after only a brief stop at Berkeley. "We could assault the town. There are men inside those walls who are loyal to us; I know there are! It is simply a matter of clearing off these nuisances here." She glared toward the gates.

"We've no time to waste with that," Somerset said. "Our men are exhausted, and Edward is too close to risk it. We must go around this city and remember its intransigence later, madam."

"I suppose you are right," Mother said. She sighed. "Then we must go via Tewkesbury. Ten miles off, is it? Well, we can do it."

I looked at Anne, who had dismounted like the rest of us and stood beside me. With her travel-stained gown and her glorious hair bundled hastily into the simplest of headdresses, she looked as bedraggled as my mother. At least my mother had experienced these all-night rides before. "Anne? Can you manage this?"

"Of course I can manage it," snapped Anne. She gave me what I had begun to think of as her father's look and stood up straighter, though a minute ago she had looked as if she might fall over. "And if I couldn't, what would it matter? I can hardly rest here."

"I only asked," I said mildly as a weary Somerset gave the signal for our army to resume marching.

By four that afternoon, the tower of the Abbey of St. Mary the Virgin at Tewkesbury appeared in our sight. We had pressed through woods and across stony paths, through narrow lanes overhung with branches. Our footsoldiers could barely limp further; our horses were hobbling. Those of us who were mounted were swaying in the saddle. We could cross the Severn only by ferry at this point, and Edward's men were bound to catch up with us long before we finished doing so. "This is it," I said. "Isn't it?"

"Yes," said Somerset. "We'll be doing battle here." He reached out and took my mother's hand. "The Earl of Pembroke would have to develop wings to get here in time. But we shall do our best here for you, your grace."

"I know you will." Mother's voice was very quiet.

Somerset turned to a couple of his pages. "Take the Queen and the Princess of Wales to the abbey. They can rest there while we make camp."

"The prince—" my mother began, and for an awful moment, I thought that she was going to demand that I go with her and the other women. Instead, she said, "You will come to the abbey later?"

Somerset and I both nodded, and my mother, Anne, the Countess of Devon, and Katherine Vaux rode off.

It did not take us too long to choose our position: at a field in the back of the town and abbey, a difficult place, Somerset said, to assail. We felled a few trees to defend it further, but there was little beyond that we could do. When the cooks had begun to feed the common soldiers, I and our commanders went to the abbey to join the women. "Would you like to see my ancestors' tombs?" Anne asked brightly after we had been served supper by the monks, who seemed less than enthralled at the prospect of the coming battle. "There are quite a few of them here."

I could think of less gloomy pastimes, under the circumstances, but my wife was proud of her ancestors, and it would be good to be in marital harmony before the battle. "Lead away."

From the stained-glass windows in the choir, Anne's Clare ancestors looked down approvingly at us as we examined the tomb of Anne's maternal grand-mother, Isabel le Despenser, countess to an earlier Earl of Warwick. It showed the cadaver of the lady, her arms crossed demurely over her bare chest, her long hair cast backward, with a few industrious worms draped across her ribs. "Interesting," I said.

"I should like something more conventional for myself," admitted Anne. "Do remember that, Edward."

"I will."

Not far from Isabel's tomb was the modest one of Isabel's father, Thomas le Despenser, who Anne told me had been beheaded at a young age for rea-sons that were not at all his fault. Before I could inquire further, she directed my attention to the kneeling effigy of Edward le Despenser, who had died at age thirty-nine, head intact, and then she hustled me to the double tomb of yet another Despenser, Hugh, and his wife, Elizabeth de Montacute. "He died of the plague at age forty-one," Anne said. "In 1349, the first time it hit England."

"Anne, didn't any of these people live past their forties?"

Anne ignored me and led me through the ambulatory to get a better look at Edward le Despenser's chantry, which lay on the other side of the choir. On the way, I passed an elaborate but somewhat out-of-the-way tomb. Its effigy bore what I now recognized instantly as the gold-and-black Despenser arms. "Now, who's this?"

"That," Anne said dismally, "is Hugh le Despenser the younger."

"You mean the one who was hanged, drawn, and quartered? Edward II's favorite? Why, he's the most interesting one of the lot, you know." I glanced at Hugh the younger appreciatively. "Your direct ancestor, is he not? Why, they even castrated him!" My Froissart, which Fortescue had spent so much time reading with me, came back to me. "For being a sodomite with the king," I recited cheerfully.

"You needn't rub it in," Anne snapped. "Come. Let's leave this place. I don't know why I brought you here if you can't even be respectful."

I followed her out dutifully. Lord, I knew I'd gotten her pretty little nose out of joint, but it was worth it to see her look angry for a change, instead of pensive. I caught her hand. "Sweetheart, I was only teasing. After all, my father's a madman, or has been one. So was his mother's father. What's the harm of having a castrated traitor for a distant ancestor?"

Anne scowled. I looked into her blue eyes, and suddenly I could no longer joke. "Anne, if anything goes—wrong—tomorrow, you must promise me something."

"Oh, Edward, don't talk of that, please."

"But we must." Since Anne and I had left France, we had not shared a bed: there had been no opportunity on that wretched voyage to England, and after the news had arrived of the Earl of Warwick's death, there had been no inclination on Anne's part. I had not attempted to press her. Now, in a way, I was relieved that if the worst happened, there would be no child facing an uncertain future. "Anne, you once said you had thought to marry the Duke of Gloucester. If it comes to that, and if doing so will make your life easier, don't feel you have to stay true to my memory. Marry him, or marry whoever else they offer to you, if it's best for you. But only if it is."

"I don't want to think of that! I have already lost my father. And my sister might as well be dead to me, after she talked the Duke of Clarence into deserting Father. And my mother is shut up in sanctuary."

"But you must think of it. Men and women must think of these things before battles; it is the way of the world. Anne, you must promise me that. And you must promise me also that you will be strong. For your father's sake. He would be grieved for you to be weak."

"I promise. For his sake." Anne leaned against my chest. "And for yours. I've come to like you."

I didn't dare ask if she had stronger feelings than that; it would not do to have the word "no" ringing in my ears during a battle. "And I've come to like you too. A very great deal."

We held each other tightly. Finally, Anne pulled back. "I know your mother will be wanting to spend some time with you tonight. I will go sit with the Countess of Devon and Lady Vaux."

"Thank you, Anne."

Anne tapped my nose. "But tomorrow night, I shall have you all to myself."

Mother had been given the abbey's best guest lodging, and she sat there with the Duke of Somerset, his brother, Lord Wenlock, the Earl of Devon, Lord Wenlock, and Sir John Langstrother when I entered. "This will be the command order tomorrow, Edward. Somerset is our chief commander." I nodded; I could live with that. "He shall have the right; Devon the left."

"And the center?"

"You." My mother said quickly, "But not on your own. Lord Wenlock and Sir John shall be there with you, and you must listen to their advice. It is your first battle, remember; they are veterans."

"Thank you, Mother."

"Don't thank me. If I had my way, you would stay with me and Anne. But I know that at your age, and given your position, that cannot be. I cannot even ask these men to keep you safe."

Her voice broke, and Somerset rose. "We shall return to the camp. You will be there, your grace?"

"Yes, I will come before dawn."

Somerset kissed her hand and made his exit. The others followed suit, so that there were only Mother and I left. "You should be going to bed soon, Edward. You will need your rest for tomorrow."

"I know. I won't stay long. You look tired yourself." I looked around the room and saw a set of playing cards, probably furnished by the considerate abbot. "Shall we play a game? And then I'll leave."

Mother nodded and I dealt out the cards. For a half hour or so we played, saying only what needed to be said for purposes of the game. Then Mother said from behind her shield of cards, "Edward. There are two things I must tell you."

For a moment I felt slightly ill. "Yes?"

"You are your father's legitimate son. I know you have heard otherwise. It was slander."

I could not help but feel a sense of relief. "I never doubted it, Mother."

"I am sure you did, but I wanted you to know for certain. You could not possibly have another father; there was no other man in my bed but my husband." She tossed her cards aside—her hand could have easily beat mine, I saw—and looked me in the eye. "The second thing is that after tomorrow, win or lose, I shall take no more part in making decisions for England. I leave it all in your hands, and the men who advise you. I trust you, Edward. You are all I have wanted in a son." She drew a breath. "That is all I wanted to say, except that I love you very dearly, and I want you to be well rested for tomorrow."

"I can take a hint." I stood and embraced my mother. "And you are all I have wanted in a mother."

She shook her head. "Sometimes I wonder if it would not have been better to accept York's Act of Accord," she said sadly. "Perhaps they would have let you be Duke of Lancaster."

"Duke of Lancaster—pfft!" I kissed her on the cheek. "Good night, Mother."

Before dawn, the news we had been expecting came to our camp: Edward was marching in our direction. Like us, he had about six thousand men. With him were his younger brothers.

Doctor Morton celebrated a hasty mass for us the next morning, after which my mother rode up. Last night she'd been constantly near tears: today she sat straight up on her horse, her bearing making the travel-worn clothes on her back look almost fine. "Men, you fight for a noble cause and for noble men today," she said clearly, in a voice that could be understood by all in spite of her French accent, which had grown more pronounced during her exile. "You fight for a crown that has been worn by the House of Lancaster since the time of my husband's grandfather, for a king who has ever loved his country and his people and who has never ceased to remember you in his prayers. And you fight for a prince of spirit and valor who will lead this country to great things. To victory abroad and to peace at home! Huzzah!" My mother raised her fist.

"Huzzah!" To a man, we all raised our swords or fists.

"Fare thee well, gentlemen! May God grant us victory!" My mother waved, turned her horse, and galloped away.

Everything has become a jumble now, between what I heard as reports were brought back to me and what I saw with my own eyes. Arrows and shot—far more shot than we had—raining down on Somerset's men. Somerset, under this deluge, deciding to switch tactics and go on the offensive, leading his men downhill into the heart of Edward's men. Somerset's strategy working for a few minutes, then turning disastrously wrong when Gloucester, unengaged, was able to come to Edward's aid, causing Somerset's men to take the brunt of both forces. Two hundred men-at-arms, hidden by Edward nearby, material-izing like a *deux ex machina* and destroying what was left of Somerset's men. Edward's men, giddy with victory, turning upon my own forces and Devon's.

John Beaufort falling. Wenlock falling. Devon falling. William Vaux fall-ing. I shouting out orders, swinging my battle ax, killing one man, killing another—but always finding that one promptly rose up again to take his place.

I taking a blow to my helmet that made me sink to the ground, dropping my weapon. I looking dazedly up to see three or four men standing above me wearing the insignia of the Black Bull of Clarence, and another man, clearly the superior of the others, wrenching off my helmet and laughing. "Clarence," I muttered.

"Yes, I'm he," Clarence said amicably. He smiled down upon me. "And you're a sorry little bastard whose death will please my brother to no end. What? You have some fight in you left? Make yourselves useful, men! Hold the whoreson."

He lifted his dagger, and even as I struggled, I knew that there would be no St. Crispin's Day for me, no words of love from Anne, no standing before my father and telling him that I had won his crown back for him. Only death in a muddy field and the breaking of my mother's heart that she had feared all along.

27

Margaret
May 4, 1471, to May 21, 1471

From the crest of Holme Hill I watched as my world fell apart. I do not know when I first realized that all was lost. All I remember is that I knew where my son was stationed and that when I saw his standard fall, I sank to my knees and sat there rocking myself. *So this is what it feels like to be mad. It is a relief.*

"The queen must leave," someone said. "It is what was arranged, that she would leave if the battle went against her." Someone hauled me up and lifted me into a litter.

"I fear that the Prince of Wales is dead," I heard myself say, in the impatient voice one uses to point out the obvious. "Someone needs to tell the Princess of Wales."

Those were the last words I remember saying before I lost consciousness.

"Where am I? What day is it?"

"Little Malvern Priory. It is Tuesday." Marie, the Countess of Devon, told me. She wrapped a blanket around me more tightly. "You have had a very bad fever, my dear."

"My son is dead. Isn't he?"

"Yes. He fell in battle."

"Saturday," I recalled. "Who else?"

"Wenlock. And John Beaufort, Vaux, and Whittingham." Marie listed name after name of the men who had shared our exile. Her eyes filled with tears. "Devon." He was the last surviving brother of her late husband, himself executed after Towton. "And yesterday, Edward executed many who had survived and had taken sanctuary in Tewkesbury Abbey. Somerset was chief among them."

"The Lady Anne?"

"She is here with us. She has taken the Prince of Wales's death very much to heart."

"And Katherine is a widow too. I made her match myself." I sat up slowly. "Bring her and the Princess of Wales to me. We should mourn together."

"My lady, there is something you must know. Edward's men have found us. You were too ill to be moved."

"Are you saying we are prisoners now?"

"Yes."

"Tell Edward that I am henceforth at his commandment. On one condition."

"I do not think they will grant any conditions."

"If there is any shred of decency in them, they will grant this one condition. It is a harmless one for them: I wish to see my son's grave."

"Our abbey has been polluted by men's blood," Abbot Strensham informed Anne and I as he led us into the choir, an act that in itself made Anne begin to weep. Next to us, a monk steered Marie and a sobbing Katherine Vaux toward the chapel where William's body lay. "King Edward promised to pardon those who took refuge inside on the day of the battle, but on the Monday next, he changed his mind and dragged them out, killing some who resisted. We tried to protect them against his fury, your grace."

"I know you did." From a distance, I saw a bier. "Is that—"

"Yes, your grace. Because of the presence of those who sought refuge here, and the trial and beheadings afterward, there was no time to bury the dead. We will do that today."

Half supported by the abbot, I slowly approached the sight that no mother should ever have to see. Edward's face was bruised, but not badly, and I could see no signs of injury to his skull. His body was shrouded from the chin down. "What killed him?" The abbot hesitated. "Tell me!"

"He was stabbed in several places," the abbot said softly. "But I believe it was a wound to his throat that was fatal to him." He turned his attention to Anne, who had knelt beside Edward's body and was fingering the shroud as though to pull it back. "Please don't look, your grace."

Anne nodded and laid her cheek against Edward's. "We shall meet in Paradise, my love," she whispered. "It may be a long time before we see each other there. But we shall meet again, and then I shall tell you that I did love you, only that I was shy of saying so."

She kissed him, then rose with the abbot's help. He led her away, weeping afresh, and then I was left alone with my son.

I had yet to shed a tear for him. There was no need; I knew that I would shed many, many in the years to come. "I could not give you an earthly crown, my son, as much as I longed to," I said at last, as I bent to smooth into its place the lock of his dark hair that always went astray, even in death. "But you shall have a heavenly one, and that is far better." I stroked my son's cold cheek. "You were the light of my life."

The abbot approached. "Your grace, I am sorry, but the king's men wish to be off."

I looked at my hands, on which I wore a single jewel: my ruby wedding ring. Through two robberies, exile, infidelity, and poverty, I had always somehow managed to hold onto it. I tugged it off my hand. "Take this and use it to have masses said for the souls of my son and the other dead of Lancaster. My husband will understand."

"For the dead of Lancaster only?"

"Yes. Lancaster." I looked around the abbey, still strewn with the armor of the men who had taken sanctuary there and spotted with their blood. "King Edward can look to the welfare of the dead of York. I am ready, Abbot."

✢

During the years that King Edward and I had fought against each other, we had never met face to face; the last time I had seen him was as an overgrown adolescent at the Loveday jousts. At Coventry, where the Yorkists had stopped on the way to deal with a threat in the North—a threat, alas, that failed to materialize—we finally got the chance to look at each other.

Aching from my long ride in an open chariot—Edward's men refused to allow me to ride my own horse, lest I gallop off to freedom—I knelt slowly before the king as Anne, Katherine, and Marie followed suit. Edward stood gazing down at me as his followers pressed forward to watch me submit to him. After several minutes passed, he said in a voice that had something of his father's in it, "You have caused a great deal of trouble for us all, woman. Do you have anything to say for yourself?"

"Your grace has a newborn son. Would you not do anything in the world to protect his birthright? Everything I have done, I have done for the love of my dear son." I choked back the tears that had chosen this inconvenient time to come at last. "I have nothing to strive for anymore, not with my husband a prisoner like myself. I only ask that you allow us to live our remaining days on earth in quiet and in dignity. And I have another request."

"Go on."

"I ask that you be merciful to these ladies I have with me, the Lady Anne, the Countess of Devon, and Lady Katherine Vaux. They have been loyal wives and, in the case of the Lady Anne, a loyal daughter. She in particular deserves your grace's kindness. She is not yet fifteen, and she did not have a voice in the arrangements that have brought her here."

"The innocent shall not suffer," Edward said, looking at Anne, who to my pleasure did not quake before his gaze. "The Lady Anne shall be given into the care of her sister, the Duchess of Clarence. As for you and the other Frenchwomen, you shall be held in the Tower until suitable arrangements can be made for you. We start back to London tomorrow." His gaze turned back to Anne. "Cousin, forgive a blunt question. Are you with child?"

Anne said coolly, "I believe not. Is that the answer you wished, your grace?"

Edward snapped, "Yes." He gestured toward the four of us women. "Do you have anything more to say to us? No? Then rise."

I painfully hauled myself to my feet and finally got a close look at Edward. He had gained a few inches since the Loveday jousts and was as good-looking now as he had been as a youth, but the years of fighting had put a hardness into his face, as I supposed they had into mine.

Edward had been studying me too. "Amazing," he commented almost genially. "You are much smaller than I remember you being; I would have thought such a troublesome woman would be much larger. Well. You are dismissed."

Under guard, we women spent the evening in Coventry at a merchant's house where I had occasionally lodged in happier days. The next morning, a couple of men wearing the Duke of Clarence's badge were shown into the chamber where we sat breaking our fast, or to be more accurate, pushing our food around. Directing his words to Anne, he said, "My lady, we are here to escort you to your sister the Duchess of Clarence."

"Already?"

"Yes, my lady. The duke considers it unsuitable for you to be traveling with an army, and the king concurs."

"My mother-in-law will be traveling with an army."

"She is a prisoner of the crown. You are not. And that is another reason it is unsuitable for you to remain in her company."

"I have no women attendants now. I cannot travel without women."

"The duke is aware of that, my lady. He has arranged for two widows here in Coventry to attend you until you reach your sister's household." He waved and a couple of middle-aged women, whom I faintly remembered from my own stays in Coventry when their husbands had been alive, stepped forward and curtseyed. "I believe Lady Margaret can tell you that they are most respectable."

I blinked at this new appellation for myself. "Yes," I admitted. "They are of good character."

"Then if there is no further objection, we will be ready to leave as soon as Lady Anne can make herself ready."

"I will be ready shortly," Anne said resignedly, and the men withdrew. She turned to the widows. "Let me take my leave of my mother-in-law." The widows nodded and left the room. Anne turned to me. "Already the Duke of Gloucester is paying attention to me."

"So I noticed last night." He had made a great point of seeing to it that Anne's coffers from Tewkesbury had all arrived and of making certain her supper had been to her satisfaction.

"My Edward said that I should marry him if it would be the best for me."

"It might well be the best for you, to protect your rights in your father's estates. Gloucester was instrumental in defeating us, they say. He will be in favor with his brother the king, perhaps more so than Clarence. You know Gloucester, don't you?"

"Yes, he was in my father's household for a time. I liked him well enough then." She looked at me with fear in her eyes. "Your grace, shall you be executed?"

I shook my head. "I doubt it. It is unprecedented to execute a queen, and I do not think King Edward is strong enough yet to risk setting such a precedent. I hope only that I am allowed to see my husband, at least occasionally. Together we can bear our Edward's loss better than we could separately."

Outside, footsteps paced pointedly. I embraced Anne. "I believe you made my Edward happy in the short time you were together, and you have a place in my heart for that. Whatever the future holds for you, I wish you the best. Go with God, and if you are able, visit Edward's grave when you can."

"I will, your grace. Go with God."

A few minutes later, I watched from my window as my daughter-in-law and her escort left for Clarence's estates. Probably I would never see her again, and yet another earthly tie to my son would be broken.

I had a moment of hope as the king's victorious army headed toward London: a bastard nephew of Warwick, Thomas Neville, was assaulting London with the intent of rescuing Henry from the Tower. But the Tower was in the hands of the Earl of Essex and of Queen Elizabeth's brother Anthony, now Earl Rivers, and King Edward had left it well garrisoned and supplied. By May 18, Thomas Neville had deserted his men, and on May 21, the mayor and aldermen of London were greeting King Edward at Shoreditch. It was time for the king to make a grand entry into the city.

William, Lord Hastings, Edward's chamberlain, saw to the business of ordering the procession: settling arguments between nobles about who got to ride closest to the king, making sure that the artillery that had done so much damage to poor Somerset's men was proudly displayed on its carts, checking that flags were fully unfurled, frowning at the stray page picking his nose. Meanwhile, Edward, wandering amicably up and down the train of people, horses, and carts, chatted with the soldiers and showed off what I had learned during my unwilling travels with him was a remarkable ability to remember names and faces. "All's ready," said Hastings at last.

"Not quite," said Edward. He pointed at my chariot. "See to the Frenchwoman, will you?"

"Your grace—"

"See to her, Hastings, as I ordered you to."

Hastings sighed and nodded to a boy nearby. "Bring me a box—say, this high—from one of the baggage carts." In no time at all, it was produced. "I am sorry, your gr—my lady, but I am going to have to ask you to sit upon this as you ride into London. Stand, please."

I complied and Hastings put the box where I had been sitting, then carefully sat me down upon it. I now towered head and shoulders above Marie and Katherine. "High enough," he commented. He turned his eyes upon my ladies. "Sit close to it and hold it steady so she won't fall."

"You are going to make a spectacle of my lady," Katherine said, her voice trembling. "Have you people no sense of decency? She has lost her only child, she is to be imprisoned—and now you want to display her to this mob to jeer at?"

"The king has not forgotten the indignity of the display of his father's and

brother's heads at York," Hastings said. "He insists upon this." He produced
a bit of cord. "Let me tie your hands behind your back. I won't pull the
knot tight."

"You swine!"

"Hush, Katherine. Let the king have his triumph. It is quite Roman of
him." I clasped my hands behind my back. "My husband bore this. I can too."

Gently, Hastings completed his task. "Courage, my lady," he said softly as
he left to return to his own place. "You've plenty of it, I know."

With a sound of trumpets, the procession began. Marie and Katherine steadied my box as my chariot began to move, lurched to a stop as some confusion
far ahead of us brought our progress to a temporary halt, and began to move
again at a more steady pace as matters were righted once more.

Twenty-six years before, on a fine May day very much like this one, I had
ridden into London as its queen.

I gazed ahead as the procession cleared the city gate and the onlookers began
to jostle each other for a better view. The splendidly clad king and nobles, some
distance ahead of my chariot, caught all eyes, of course, but the knights who
came after them were of little interest, the city officials who followed them of
even less except to their friends. For the crowd, I was therefore a sweet sight.

"There's the Bitch of Anjou!"

"Minus her bastard pup!"

"Not a bad looker, though!"

"Think she'd have you?"

"Why not? All of her pretty boys are dead!"

"She's not blinking an eye. Is she real?"

"One way to find out, ain't there?" A stone whizzed through the air and
clipped me neatly on the cheek.

A horseman, evidently appointed to deal just with this sort of situation,
swung a club in the direction from where the stone had been thrown, giving
me a respite, but every few feet it was the same: the same jests, the same cold
stares, the same clubbing when someone got out of hand. Only the missiles
varied: eggs at one corner, cabbage at another, horse dung at the worst. With
my hands tied I could not wipe my face, and my ladies were too busy holding
my box to assist me either.

At last my chariot diverged from the rest of the procession, which was to go
to St. Paul's for a service of thanksgiving for the king's victory. I was bound
for the Tower.

My chariot had barely stopped moving when Katherine and Marie unbound my hands and took me off my box. I sank into the seat of my chariot as Katherine wiped my face with her skirts as best she could. "It's over, dear," she whispered as my tears began to blend with the filth on my face. "It shall never happen again."

A man stepped forward. With a start, I recognized him as Sir John Dudley, who had served Henry for years. Once he had knelt when he came into my presence. Now he merely inclined his head as he handed me out of the cart, shaking his head with disapproval at the state of my face as if it had been my own idea to hurl horse turds at myself. "My lady, I am constable here and shall be looking after you."

"Shall I be executed?"

"Goodness no, my lady. Who would do that to a woman?"

I was not sure whether this came as a relief or as a disappointment. "Might I see my husband?"

"I have not been given permission to allow you to do that, my lady."

"For God's sake! It is what has kept me sane while that mob jeered at me and threw muck at me, that I might have the comfort of my husband, and him of me. We have not seen each other in years." I felt my lip begin to tremble. "Have you no compassion? Cannot you allow me one small indulgence? I am not asking to be quartered with him; I am not even asking to see him privately. I am only asking that I be allowed to look upon his dear face."

"I cannot arrange it without the king's permission."

"Then get it!" I remembered my position. "*Please.*"

"I will ask the king; I can promise no more. But in the meantime, come. Your chambers in the White Tower have been prepared for you."

It is strange, but despite the deadness in my heart I was still able to observe with some relief that the small comforts of life were not being denied to me. The bed, though narrow and old, looked sturdy and comfortable, and the bedding itself was clean, though faded. A garderobe provided more dignity than I had been used to as of late. The window was low enough for me to see the Thames flowing past. There were truckle beds for my companions, an altar for me to pray at, and an inexpensive book of hours for my devotions. "The queen didn't want you to be uncomfortable, my lady. She remembers that King Henry was good to her own family."

"I wish I could see my husband."

"All in good time. In the meantime, I shall bring you materials with which to tidy yourself."

"Yes, I would not want Henry to see me like this," I admitted. "It would distress him."

With the pots of warm water that Sir John directed be brought up, Katherine and Marie scrubbed me from head to toe, then scrubbed themselves. Cleaner than I had been in weeks and dressed in a fresh nightshift from the coffer I had brought with me from France and had been allowed to keep, I lay on my bed, drew the curtains, and fell asleep, though it was not yet dark.

It was late when the sounds of voices in and around the White Tower half-woke me; Edward's court was lodging here tonight, I recalled dreamily. Poor Henry would find it difficult to sleep; he had always liked quiet…They were bound to let me see him. Weren't they? He had been poorly kept during the last period of his imprisonment, I had been told. I would see to it that his keepers gave him proper attention. I would sew shirts for him, mend his hose, trim his hair as he liked it. We would grow old and die here, no doubt, but at least we would spend our last days together.

Tomorrow, they would let me see him. We would weep over the death of our son, but we would also comfort each other as no one else could. I would see him tomorrow. Tomorrow…

28

Henry VI
May 21, 1471

KING EDWARD'S MEN ALWAYS SAID THAT I WAS A FOOL—A HOLY FOOL, they said, as if this somehow softened the insult. But I was not the simpleton they said I was, for when all of my servants were dismissed the very same day Edward returned in victory to London, I knew what lay in store. I did not believe Edward's men for a moment when they said that it was only a matter of reorganization and that new servants would be assigned to me in the morning. I would not live to see the morning; I was certain of it.

But when night fell and the supper I was served proved to be free of poison, I began to doubt myself, as I always did. Perhaps they were right: I was a fool and I would indeed get new servants in the morning. Perhaps, I thought as I finished my prayers and blew out the candle by my bedside, I would even be allowed to see my dear Marguerite, brought a prisoner to the Tower that afternoon.

Yet not long before midnight I awoke to find a young man standing over me with a large pillow. "Edward?" I said.

"How dare you confuse me with Margaret of Anjou's bastard whelp?"

It was a foolish mistake; I realized immediately. I had seen this young man before: he was Richard, Duke of Gloucester, King Edward's youngest brother. He had been at Barnet, to which I had been taken with Edward's forces as a prisoner. Gloucester was a competent man and a brave one, I had noted in the dispassionate way I had learned to observe things during my long captivity, and a man who was well liked and respected by his own men, but with something else in his character as well, I had sensed. Something that made him well suited for the task that he was about to perform. "I beg your pardon. You are about the same age as my own son, or just a little older. For a moment, in the darkness, I thought you might be him. Tell me, young man. Is my son dead, as they tell me?"

"Yes." For the first time I realized that there were two other men in the room, standing on either side of Gloucester. They were burly, silent men, who watched me with blank faces and crossed arms, and I knew then that there was no point fighting against what was soon to happen, even if I had been inclined to fight.

"God assoil his soul. And do you know what the king will do with my Marguerite?"

"How should I know?" The young man raised the pillow again and brought it down.

"God protect you, my sweet girl," I whispered. "*Pater noster, qui es in caelis, sanctificetur nomen tuum...*"

"Nicely done, if I must say so myself," Gloucester said. He removed the pillow from my face, tucked it under my head, and arranged the sheets neatly around me. "Why, that doddering old fool Dudley might actually believe that he died in his sleep." He chuckled and turned toward the men. "Well, I've done Edward's dirty work tonight, while he frolics in bed with that Woodville wife of his. He has a talent for delegation, I'll say. If he asks, I'll tell him that the worst part of it was having to make conversation with the useless fool."

He turned away, having made the common mistake of thinking that the dead cannot hear, and that God is not watching all. If I could have spoken, I would have told him that. I would have also told him that someday, the Lord would exact a price and that a man, having gained everything he wants, can very easily lose it.

But I could not speak, so I would let him find out those things for himself, in time. Meanwhile, I could look forward to beholding my son's dear face. And in the course of time I would clasp my sweet Marguerite in my arms again and be the strong husband in heaven for her that I never was on earth.

It was Gloucester, not I, who was the fool.

29

Margaret
May 22, 1471

"I AM VERY EMBARRASSED, SIR JOHN. I WAS SO TIRED, I SLEPT VERY LATE today." I gathered my cloak around me to hide my dishabille. "You have asked the king about my seeing Henry?"

"My lady, I am very sorry to tell you this. Your husband was informed of your son's death, and your imprisonment here, as gently as we could. We could not have been more gentle. But the knowledge broke his will to live, and broke his very heart. This morning he was found dead in his chambers."

How many people can say how it feels, the moment when they have lost everything? For the time being, I felt only numbness, and the knowledge dawning at the back of my mind that I should have guessed my husband's fate all along. "I should have known," I said after a pause.

"Should have known what?"

"Should have known that Edward would murder him. It makes perfect sense, now that our son is dead. So. How did he do it? Strangulation? Suffocation? A stab? A blow to his head while he knelt at his prayers? Poison? Did someone at least see to it that he made his confession first?"

"My lady! I told you! The late king died of sheer melancholy."

"My husband has known nothing but sorrow for the last ten years. Am I to think that he could not bear this latest ill news? No. He has his faith; it has sustained him and would have yet." I began to laugh. "Is it not ironic? The one person of all of us who could not bear violence dies a violent death."

"I tell you, it was not a violent death!"

"You lie."

"My lady, this will not do. I was going to offer to let you see him before he was taken from here, but if you persist in these wild accusations, I cannot allow you to do so."

There was no point in arguing further, no point in much of anything any-more. "You will let me see him?"

"Only if you behave yourself and hold your tongue."

"Then I will." I took a breath. "I promise."

"Then make yourself seemly and get your words under control. I will be back in an hour."

"Where are they to bury him?" I asked Sir John as he led me to the Chapel of St. Peter of Vincula. "Here?"

"The king plans to bury him at Chertsey."

I frowned. "Why Chertsey? He had no ties there. He wished to be buried at Westminster by his mother and by other kings. Or why not Eton?" My eyes glistened as I thought of Henry poring over his plans for that school. "That would please him."

"I don't know, my lady. The king specified Chertsey."

"It matters not," I said, crossing myself. "He will be with the Lord soon."

Sir John pushed open the chapel door and led me inside. There, my hus-band, clad in a shroud, but with his face visible, lay on a bier as a priest read psalms over his body. The priest started when he recognized me, but went on chanting as if he had not been interrupted.

The murderers had been tidy; there was no sign of violence visible. Though the years and illness had aged Henry, time had been kinder to him than I would have thought. Only two things had changed greatly: his neatly trimmed hair, which had had a few strands of gray when I last saw him, had turned completely that color, and he had grown a beard. No one had ever told me. "I was his wife for six and twenty years. Might I have a lock of his hair as a remembrance?"

Sir John said nothing, but took out his dagger and lifted a strand of Henry's hair, then cut it. He pulled out a handkerchief and carefully wrapped the hair inside it before giving it to me.

I thanked him. Then, expecting to be stopped, I knelt and kissed my hus-band's cheek, but no one interfered. "Rest in peace, my dear Henry," I said softly, putting my hand on the cheek where my lips had rested. "You will soon meet our son in Paradise, and there you will have the peace you have always longed for." My tears began falling hard. "I meant well, my love," I said. "I truly did. All I wanted was what was right for you and our son. All I did was for your sake."

I turned away, unable to hold back my sobs anymore, and Sir John supported me out of the chapel. His own eyes were wet when he said, "He knows it, my lady."

Part IV

Lady Hope

30

Margaret
August 1482

HENRY DIED MORE THAN ELEVEN YEARS AGO. HE NOW SLEEPS AT CHERTSEY; my son sleeps at Tewkesbury. I grow weaker every day and shall soon join them in death. The thought makes me smile.

I spent over four more years in England after Henry and Edward died. My time in the Tower was short: I was moved first to Windsor and then to Wallingford, where the dowager Duchess of Suffolk, who had mothered me when I came as a seasick fifteen-year-old to England, could visit me from time to time and mother me once more.

Then in 1475, Edward mounted a great invasion of France. With Burgundy's aid (the quarrel of 1471 having been mended for now), he would win back all that my Henry had lost; the fall of Normandy, of Gascony, would soon be nothing more than a bad memory. But Burgundy proved an unenthusiastic ally, and in the end my cousin Louis did not have to raise a finger against Edward: only to give him and his leading nobles handsome pensions. There was yet another part to the bargain: for fifty thousand crowns, I was ransomed. So in January 1476, I sailed from England for the very last time, as "Margaret, lately called queen."

At least, I thought as I gazed back at the land I'd first entered while borne in my dear Suffolk's arms, I'd left England standing upright.

⁓

There was a rub to Louis's generosity, of course; I'd never thought it would be otherwise. In repayment for his ransoming me, and in repayment for the costs he had incurred in helping me to recover my husband's throne—the small matter that helping me had furthered his own ambitions seemed to have slipped my cousin's mind—I was required to renounce my rights of inheritance to my father's dominions. It suited me; I had no heir of my body, only the memory of my beautiful boy. So I took the pension that Louis offered me—I found it amusing that both I and King Edward were his pensioners now—and settled in my father's manor at Reculée. I seldom saw my aged father himself. Having himself suffered somewhat from Louis's sharp dealing, he had elected to spend his declining years in comfort at Provence. Though I was welcome at his court, I, clad in the black I had worn since 1471, a moth in a house of butterflies, was ill suited to its gaiety.

I had been at Reculée for about four years when my father died, which thanks to the renunciation Louis had forced me to sign left me with no home. Father in a burst of practicality had arranged, however, for me to go to the home of François de la Vignole, a family friend, and so I live now as a guest at his chateau at Dampierre.

Who of us is left from those bloody days in England? My cousin Marie returned to France after Tewkesbury and remarried, but my dear Katherine Vaux stayed by my side; she remains with me today, and if there is a hand other than hers that I am holding as I die, I shall be sorely surprised.

The Duke of Exeter was not killed at Barnet, as we had thought: he lay on the field, stripped and left for dead, until a servant found him and carried him off to a surgeon, then to sanctuary at Westminster. But Edward removed him from sanctuary and imprisoned him in the Tower. He was no longer the wild young man of my own youth: during the short time he and I were both prisoners there, Sir John would allow him to visit me and play a game of chess or cards. He was freed to join the great invasion of 1475, but drowned on the anticlimactic voyage back. Some say he fell overboard after quarreling with some drunken soldiers; others say that King Edward, always eager to lose one of the House of Lancaster, had him pushed.

The Duke of Clarence, the sorry turncoat, never ceased to plot against Edward, who solved his Clarence problems in 1478 by locking him in the Tower, then having him privately executed. My daughter-in-law Anne married the Duke of Gloucester, by all accounts a loyal and dutiful brother, rewarded as such by King Edward. I wonder if Anne ever thinks of my own Edward. She has a son by that name; he was named for the king, of course, but I like to think that he might have been named for a Prince of Wales too.

I like to think a lot of things; it is my main occupation these days. Yet I do not think so much of the past but of the future: the day that I shall see my dear ones in Paradise.

I am poor, I suppose, but a queen with no court needs very, very little. Yet as little as I have to leave, Louis keeps himself very well informed about my state of health. Once this would have infuriated me; now, as I prepare to leave behind the folly of this world, it rather amuses me.

My last will is ready. It is short: I ask Louis to pay any debts that the sale of my few goods is insufficient to pay, and I ask to be buried at the cathedral at Angers where my mother and my father already lie. I make no provision for a tomb, as this would no doubt strain Louis's already meager generosity to the breaking point.

There is no tomb for my husband either, no effigy of him in his royal robes. His grave is indicated only by a simple marker, but that does not stop the people from flocking to Chertsey Abbey to be healed of their afflictions, for many now regard my Henry as a saint. Edward does his best to discourage these visits, they say, but the visitors come nonetheless. It must give Henry great pleasure to have them all, more pleasure, probably, than he ever had from his crown. "You will visit Henry when you go back to England?" I ask Katherine as she straightens my pillow.

"You know I will."

"I know; I ask you at least once a day. And you will visit my Edward when you visit your William at Tewkesbury."

"Yes, my dear."

"He would be nine-and-twenty come this October." I finger the rosary I keep in my hand at nearly all times, then take Katherine's hand. "And your William would be five and forty. Sometimes I forget your own loss when I dwell upon my own, Katherine. Forgive me for that."

"I do, my dear. Come. I can tell from your face that you are in great pain today. Shall I give you some poppy juice?"

"No. Let us do some letters. That distracts me."

For the past few days, Katherine and I have been busy sorting the papers I have kept over the years: I reading over them one last time, Katherine then feeding them into the fire that burns low even on this August day, for I chill easily. They are harmless mementoes—the poem dear Suffolk gave to me, an old lesson of my son's, a prayer composed by my husband, an inquiry from my father about whether one of his dwarfs might cheer me up in my exile—but I do not want Louis's agents putting their inquisitive hands upon them, the little treasures of a bereaved and dying woman. Katherine picks up one from the pile and smiles. "Ah. I have always wondered if you kept this."

I unfold it and feel a pang as I stare at Hal's letter to me. With his own hand, he had written this and sprinkled the sand on the ink when it was finished. *I shall not stray again, but shall live and, if God wills it, die the king's loyal subject.* Though I have trained myself to think of Hal only in the most chaste and correct manner imaginable, I cannot forbear from giving the letter a kiss before I hand it to Katherine. I shake my head as the flames consume the letter. "My Beauforts were brave men." I think of Hal abandoning the comforts of Chirk Castle to face almost certain death in service of our cause. "And he was the bravest of them all."

We spend an hour or so reading and burning, a task which in my state of health exhausts me so that I soon drift off. When I awake, the sun is low in the sky. "A new letter arrived while you were asleep," Katherine says, coming to my bedside.

"From whom? Louis? If so, tell him I am not quite dead yet." Already he has written to my friend Jeanne Chabot, Madame de Montsoreau, demanding that she give him, my heir, the dogs I have sent to her in gratitude to the kindnesses she has shown me during my illness. She in turn has written to inform me that she had no choice but to comply, but she has secretly kept one bitch puppy, named Margaret, which Jeanne hopes will breed. At least one Margaret may have descendants.

I manage a snicker. "Perhaps we can put some paint on my face and parade me in my chariot around town as having made a recovery? That will no doubt cast Louis into great gloom for a day or so."

"The letter is not from him. It is from the Earl of Pembroke."

Having escaped from Edward just in time after the debacle of 1471, Henry's half brother, Jasper Tudor, Earl of Pembroke, is now in exile at the court of Brittany. He sends me his respects from time to time, though it has been a long time since I have received one of his missives. Pembroke was accompanied in his exile by his nephew, Henry Tudor, the son of that Margaret Beaufort who had given birth at such an early age. I still think of him as a boy, although he must now be well into his twenties. "Well, then, let me read it."

Katherine hands me the letter. "It is addressed to the Queen of England."

Madam, I have heard that you are very ill, perhaps even dying.

I hope the reports are wrong; I pray that they are. But if they are correct, I want your highness to know that the cause of the House of Lancaster, for which you fought so long and so hard, will remain alive in my heart, and in that of

my nephew Henry and his mother, until the end of our days. You will never be
forgotten, madam.

Your true subject and liege man,
Pembroke.

I smile at this masterpiece of wistful thinking. Its sentiments about me are kind, but what of the cause of the House of Lancaster? Jasper and his nephew are near-penniless exiles. The Earl of Oxford, having waged a nearly one-man war against the House of York since escaping from Barnet, has been captured at last and is now a prisoner, held fast in dreary Hammes Castle near Calais. It will take a miracle to restore Lancastrian rule to England—and a rule by whom?

Yet as I approach death, I am in a state of mind to remember that miracles do happen, and not only at my husband's grave. My uncle Charles's throne had been saved for him by a peasant girl, after all. Who knows what the Lord can do when so inclined? "Thank him for his good wishes. Now read to me a while, so I can sleep again."

"From your Book of Hours?"

"No. My father's *Book of the Love-Smitten Heart*. Let me look at it first."

Katherine obeys. I leaf through the book, looking for the words that Jasper Tudor's letter has so oddly brought to mind. "Read from here," I command.

During his last years, my aged father had completed a manuscript he had been working on for two decades, a tale of a knight named Heart who goes in quest of Sweet Mercy. He never sent it to me during his lifetime, as I had let it be known that I had no patience with such tales, but after my father's death in 1480, my stepmother had sent an illuminated copy to me. Slowly turning the pages out of curiosity, I had been startled to find a picture of a woman, past her youth but still pretty, with dark blond hair and a crown on her head. There was no better likeness of me, or at least of me when I had been twenty years younger.

Her name was Lady Hope. Tears streaming down my face, I had read the words she speaks to the hero:

> You shall have sorrows in profusion
> So often it will be unjust,
> For Love by custom so apportions
> His rewards and afflictions
> Whether deserved or not:

He cares little who wins or loses.
Into the Forest of Long Awaiting
You shall enter, so I say, and
Shall drink from the Fountain of Fortune,
Which is not the same for all men.

Had Father had me in mind when he wrote those words? I will never know, but Jasper Tudor's letter has brought them home to me. I settle back against my pillow, listening to Katherine read:

But guard you well, I pray you,
From the Path of Madness,
For by this way you would arrive
At the manor wherein dwells Despair.
If, by chance, you should enter within,
I shall tell you what you should do:
Keep me then in memory,
And this will grant victory to you,
And you can soon retrace your road
To the Path of Joyful Thought.
Through which you shall find Mercy.
But your heart shall then be overcast,
For before this conquest
You shall receive many blows upon your head
From Harsh Discord and Refusal,
Who will quite overcome you.
If Despair comes upon you,
Joy will no longer remain within you:
So be you ever mindful of me
Who bears Hope as name.

"I will be, Father," I whisper. "Thank you. I can sleep now."

Epilogue

Katherine Vaux
June 23, 1509

I T IS PLEASANT BEING AN OLD LADY. TAKE THIS PROCESSION BEFORE THE DAY
of the royal coronation, for instance. I have been asked to ride in Queen
Catherine's train, but at my age I feel the heat as keenly as the cold, and I know
that were I to take part, I would be prostrate for a week. "I would be honored
to attend the queen, your grace," I tell young King Henry. Not quite eighteen,
he is tall, handsome, and genial like his grandfather, that fourth Edward. "But
my health will not allow it. I must miss this occasion, I fear."

"Well," Henry rumbles. "We shall miss you. But why should you miss the
procession? You may watch in comfort with my grandmother."

So on the day of the procession, I do not sit in a litter with the sun beating
down upon my poor old head, nor do I sit in my chambers waiting to hear a
description of the day's festivities from my son and daughter, who are in the
procession themselves: Nicholas as one of King Henry's knights, Jane as one
of Queen Catherine's ladies. Instead, I sit on the upper floor of a hired house
in Cheapside alongside Margaret Beaufort, Countess of Richmond, and watch
the procession from the comfort of a well-cushioned chair.

The king's thirteen-year-old sister, the Lady Mary, is with us as well.
My daughter, Jane Guildford, has virtually raised this beautiful girl, who
has made it known that when her time comes to marry, she will not budge
out of England without her Mother Guildford in her train. "Have you ever
seen such a sight?" she breathes as she leans far out the window. She speaks
merely of the banners that festoon the street: the procession itself has not
even begun.

"It will be but more splendid when it starts, but you will not improve the
occasion if you fall out the window," I said. You see? A younger woman could
never say that to a princess.

The Lady Mary obediently takes a somewhat less precarious stance. "You were at my mother's coronation, weren't you, Lady Vaux?"

"Indeed I was. And I was at the coronation of my lady Margaret of Anjou as well."

Mary's face lights up with curiosity, for Margaret of Anjou is little more than a name to her, the wars of the last century the abstract stuff of her tutors' lectures. This girl has grown up in an England of peace and prosperity, an England where her father the king died quietly in his bed and where her brother Henry has no one trying to push him off his new throne. For her, Wakefield, St. Albans, Towton, Hexham, Barnet, and Tewkesbury are simply the names of English towns. "That's right. You served her, didn't you, Lady Vaux?"

"Until her dying day."

My lady, so thin and shrunken that I could have carried her from room to room, died in my arms on a hot day in August 1482. She had been in great pain for days, and sometimes I saw that it made her sob into her pillow when she thought no one was watching, but never did I hear her complain or fret. "Rest in peace, my brave lady," I said as she at last gave up fighting for her last breath while her small household stood by weeping. "All those who loved you are waiting in Paradise, and they have missed you sorely."

I saw Margaret buried in dignity near her parents at Angers, and then what was there for me in France without my lady? Though William had died under attainder, his estates forfeit to the crown, I had been allowed two manors in England, and my children were living there, so it was to England that I returned. It was ruled, and ruled well, I had to admit, by King Edward.

And then just months after my return to England, King Edward, not yet one-and-forty but given to overindulgence and not the fine figure he'd cut at Tewkesbury, died after a chill that went to his lungs. He had survived my own dear lady by just eight months. As all of Europe watched, amazed, Edward's younger brother, the Duke of Gloucester, the one all had thought most loyal, snatched the throne from his brother's twelve-year-old son, Edward V. Just over two years later, this Gloucester, calling himself Richard III, having destroyed his brother's friends and relations and his brother's sons, destroyed himself. For on August 22, 1485, nearly three years to the day after my lady breathed her last in Dampierre, the impoverished, exiled Henry Tudor, aided by the Earl of Oxford, defeated and killed Richard III in a battle no one had thought Henry would win. Sharing his victory on the field that day were my son and Charles Somerset, the son of my lady's beloved Hal.

A few months later, the houses of Lancaster and York were at last joined as the new king, Henry VII, married Edward's oldest daughter, Elizabeth of York. With their union ended my own family's poverty, for the Tudors did not forget the friends of Henry VI—or of his queen. Within weeks of Henry VII's victory, Nicholas was restored to my husband's lands, and he and my daughter were called to court. And now with the death of Henry VII, they will be serving this handsome new King Henry and his queen, both of whom have clearly captured the Londoners' hearts.

"Was Queen Margaret as pretty as Queen Catherine when she processed through London?"

Prettier, I must admit, but this is not something even the license of the old will allow me to say aloud. "She was beautiful. Her blond hair was combed down around her shoulders, and she was dressed in white damask powdered with gold. And she loved her king and loved the idea of bringing peace to England through her marriage, so she glowed with happiness and pride."

Mary gives a romantic sigh.

And twenty-six years later, they paraded her through the streets like a common whore while the crowd threw dung at her, days after she had lost her only child. Needless to say, I do not voice this addendum aloud. But perhaps Margaret Beaufort guesses my thoughts, for she says sternly, "Fortune is fickle. Remember that, Mary."

"Yes, Grandmother," Mary says dutifully, and pokes her neck out the window again. "Harry is coming!"

The king, preceded by the great-grandson of the Duke of Buckingham who died at Northampton, is indeed coming down Cheapside, splendidly clad in red velvet and cloth of gold. But for all of his magnificence, he is, after all, only Mary's brother, and she soon draws in her head again.

Then, at last, comes the sight that Mary and every other young girl in London has been waiting to see: Queen Catherine, a princess of the House of Aragon. Shimmering in white, her auburn hair flowing loose, she is smiling and waving to the crowd as she passes down the broad lane of Cheapside, her entire life before her. And then I see in my mind's eye the lovely French princess who rode down this same street four-and-sixty years ago, and a tear rolls down my wrinkled cheek.

Author's Note

KATHERINE VAUX WAS STILL ALIVE ON JUNE 28, 1509, WHEN THE YOUNG Henry VIII granted her an annuity, though I have taken artistic license in having her watch his pre-coronation procession in the company of Margaret Beaufort and Mary Tudor (who did indeed watch it from a hired house in Cheapside). The date of Katherine's death is unknown, but she first appears in Margaret's records as one of her damsels in 1452 and must have been at least well into her sixties when she died. Katherine was survived by her children, Nicholas and Jane. Nicholas served both Henry VII and Henry VIII militarily and administratively and was made Lieutenant of Guînes. Jane is best known as the aged "Mother Guildford" who accompanied Henry VIII's sister Mary Tudor to her marriage to the ailing French king Louis XII. The king, believing that the overprotective Jane was interfering with his fun with his young bride, sent Jane home, where she received a large annuity from Henry VIII as consolation.

Charles Somerset, the natural son of Henry Beaufort, fought for Henry VII at the Battle of Bosworth. (He was originally named Charles Beaufort and took the name Somerset when Henry VII became king; I declined to bore the reader with this detail.) He served Henry VII and Henry VIII as a soldier, a diplomat, and an administrator; the magnificence of Henry VIII's famous Field of the Cloth of Gold was largely a product of Charles's organizational flair. Somerset was made the Earl of Worcester by Henry VIII in 1514. The present-day Dukes of Beaufort are his descendants.

Joan Hill, Henry Beaufort's mistress and Charles's mother, was still living in 1493, when Henry VII granted her an annuity, but nothing else seems to be known about her. I have therefore invented the details of her background.

John Fortescue and John Morton each made their peace with Edward IV after Tewkesbury. Fortescue died in 1479, having written several influential treatises on political theory. John Morton was made Bishop of Ely during Edward IV's reign. He was heavily involved in efforts to remove Richard III from power and became Archbishop of Canterbury during Henry VII's reign.

The tombs of Margaret of Anjou's parents in Angers Cathedral were destroyed during the French Revolution, although René's skeletal remains were found in his coffin and photographed in 1895. Margaret's remains were not located. A plaque inside the cathedral commemorates her and her family. Edward of Lancaster's approximate resting place is marked by a plaque in the choir of Tewkesbury Abbey.

Not long after Henry VI's burial in Chertsey, pilgrims begin to flock to his tomb, and a number of miracles were soon attributed to the late king's intervention, In 1484, Richard III ordered that Henry VI's body be reburied in St. George's Chapel at Windsor Castle, where it rests today. Various motives have been given for this decision, such as remorse for his alleged role in the king's death, a desire to associate himself with the cult of sainthood that had grown up around Henry, or a wish to benefit the chapel, which could hope to reap profits from pilgrim visits. Later, Henry VII attempted to have Henry VI canonized, but his efforts to do so did not outlive his own reign.

In *The Queen of Last Hopes* I have taken one great historical liberty: that of making Henry Beaufort, Duke of Somerset, the lover of Margaret of Anjou. It was rumored in 1461 that Margaret had poisoned her husband and intended to "unite with" Somerset, but otherwise there is no indication of a romantic relationship between the pair at that or at any other time, and the gossip that Margaret poisoned Henry was clearly false. As my novel progressed, though, I found the characters gravitating in the direction of an affair, and it seemed to me that if Margaret could have ever been tempted into adultery, Henry Beaufort, whom contemporaries found handsome and charismatic, was the one man who could have done so, especially after he eliminated Margaret's enemy the Duke of York at Wakefield. Nonetheless, the relationship that I portray between the two of them here is the product of my imagination. Henry Beaufort did abruptly abandon the Lancastrian cause, then return to it a year later at the cost of his life. During his brief career as a Yorkist, he jousted wearing "a sorry hat of straw."

I do want to emphasize also that there is no historical basis, other than contemporary gossip and Yorkist propaganda, to support the claim that Edward of Lancaster was illegitimate. Henry VI spent the time during which Edward would have been conceived at Margaret's manor of Greenwich. He was sane at the time of his son's conception and during the period that Margaret's pregnancy would have first become readily apparent. During this time, he showed himself to be pleased with Margaret: he granted an annuity to the man who brought him news of the pregnancy, spent two hundred pounds on a girdle known as a demiceint for the queen, and gave her a generous grant of land. Presented with his child following his recovery from madness, he is recorded in a private letter to John Paston as having held up his hands and thanked God. None of this suggests that he believed the child to be another man's.

One source, however, has been cited by those who have taken at face value the rumors of Edward's illegitimacy. Prospero di Camulio, the Milanese ambassador in France, reported to the Duke of Milan on March 27, 1461, that Henry had remarked that Edward of Lancaster "must be the son of the Holy Spirit." What writers who latch onto this tasty morsel of hearsay almost never quote is the rest of Camulio's sentence: "but these may only be the words of common fanatics, such as they have at present in that island." Certainly the timing of this gossip, circulating just weeks after Edward IV had taken the throne—and more than seven years after Edward of Lancaster's birth—should make us suspicious, as it did Camulio. Sexual slander has long been used against women who take power, and the Yorkists missed no opportunity to smear Margaret's reputation as she took an increasingly active role in English affairs.

Margaret did indeed take eight years following her marriage to conceive her only child, which has been viewed by some as evidence that some man other than Henry had to have been the father. Given that we know nothing of Margaret's gynecological history and that there is no indication that Henry was unable to function in bed prior to his madness, however, it seems most fair that we give the couple—and Edward of Lancaster—the benefit of the doubt.

Those who are familiar with Shakespeare's plays will recall that the Bard presents Suffolk and Margaret as being lovers. There is no historical basis for this portrayal of the pair; the first reference to such a relationship is by the sixteenth-century chronicler Edward Hall, and that is merely in the form of a throwaway description of Suffolk as the "queen's darling." Though for dramatic purposes I allowed rumors about Suffolk's and Margaret's relationship to circulate in 1450, there is no indication that such rumors actually were current at that time.

Was Henry VI murdered? The official account of the events of 1471 reported that he died of "pure displeasure and melancholy," but other contemporary sources attribute his death to human hands, as do most modern historians. The involvement of Richard, Duke of Gloucester in Henry's death was hinted at by the chronicler Warkworth, and the Tudors elaborated upon the story with gusto, but there is no proof that Richard was in fact the killer. Any order to murder the defeated king, however, would have been given by Edward IV, and his loyal youngest brother would have been a reasonable choice for the task.

Henry VI's mental state after he recovered from his stupor of 1453 to 1454 is difficult to assess. He does not seem to have ever been completely incapacitated again, but he apparently was dependent on others to make major decisions and might well have been quite fragile. His injury at the first Battle of St. Albans, his capture by the Yorkists after the Battle of Northampton, and his imprisonment from 1465 onward cannot have helped him mentally, but objective accounts of his condition after 1454 are hard to come by. Notably, when Henry was restored to his throne in 1470, it seems to have been taken for granted by all concerned that he would be a mere figurehead.

Whether the Duke of Suffolk's murder was the spontaneous act of the seamen who happened across his ship, or whether more powerful forces were behind the killing, is unknown. As Roger Virgoe pointed out in an article, "The Death of William de la Pole, Duke of Suffolk," Henry VI's government seems to have believed that York or his agents were behind the murder of the duke and the other unrest during 1450, and an indictment against some of the men accused of the murder makes reference to "another person then outside the kingdom" whom the defendants intended to make king. Certainly it is possible that Margaret viewed York as the instigator of the violent events of 1450.

Though Margaret's two encounters with robbers after Northampton and after Norham may seem like one too many, each is attested to by contemporary chronicles, with some variations as to time and place. A man named only as "Black Jack" was executed with Henry Beaufort following the Battle of Hexham, but his identification as one of the men who robbed Margaret after the failed siege of Norham is my invention, as none of the robbers in that episode are named in the chronicles. Margaret's shipwreck was also widely recounted by her contemporaries.

There is debate as to the age of the chalk figure of the Cerne Giant, the "rude man" that Edward and Anne see while staying at Cerne Abbey. Though some claim that that the figure could date back to ancient times, there is no written reference to it before 1694. It seemed a shame, however, to deprive Edward and Anne of seeing it.

The letters from Henry Beaufort and Jasper Tudor to Margaret are fictitious; the letter of William de la Pole to his son is genuine and can be found in the Paston letters. The poems in the novel are also authentic (albeit with modernized spelling), although there is some question as to whether Suffolk wrote the poem attributed to him and as to whether René of Anjou was the author of "Regnault and Jehanneton." René was certainly the author of *Le Livre du Cuers d'Amours Espris* (translated into English by Stephanie Gibbs and Kathryn Karczewska as *The Book of the Love-Smitten Heart*), which, as Margaret says, includes in its exquisite illuminations a depiction of Lady Hope, who wears a crown. There is no evidence that René intended this figure to represent his daughter Margaret, but it is pleasant to think that he might have meant it as a fatherly tribute to his daughter's indomitable spirit.

Andrew Trollope was killed at Towton, but the story of Henry Beaufort cutting his throat to spare him from a lingering death is my invention. I have followed the suggestion of C. A. J. Armstrong in his article "Politics and the Battle of St. Albans" that Edmund Beaufort, Duke of Somerset, was targeted for assassination by the Duke of York and his followers rather than simply happening to die in battle.

Some readers may object that I have understated the atrocities perpetrated by Margaret's army on its march south from Wakefield. As B. M. Cron has noted, however, the stories that the Lancastrian army pillaged, plundered, razed, and raped its way toward London are "strong on rhetoric but short on detail"; they are also strongly rooted in Yorkist propaganda and in southern prejudice against the "northern men" of Margaret's army. Hard evidence of the havoc that such large-scale destruction would have wreaked is markedly lacking, as Cron pointed out. Significantly, it was Margaret's failure to be ruthless enough—her refusal to march into London after the second battle of St. Albans—that proved to be her undoing in 1461.

Margaret has been much condemned for her role in the executions of Bonville and Kyriell following the second Battle of St. Albans, but it is likely that she regarded the men as traitors to Henry VI, whom they had once served, and therefore deserving of death. Margaret was not present at the battle of Wakefield, contrary to the account by the chronicler Hall, who also depicts the seventeen-year-old Earl of Rutland, most likely slain during the rout, as a pathetic, unarmed twelve-year-old murdered in cold blood. If bloodthirstiness is measured in terms of executions, Margaret's record pales beside those of the Yorkist commanders: Edward IV is said to have ordered the deaths of more than forty men on the field after Towton; John Neville executed thirty men after Hexham; and Warwick ordered seven men from the Tower to be executed following the Battle of Northampton, despite the fact that the men condemned to death had been holding the Tower on behalf of Henry VI, whom the Yorkists still recognized as king at the time. Edward IV executed a dozen men after the Battle of Tewkesbury after breaking a promise that they would be pardoned. Few of those who have condemned Margaret as cruel and merciless, however, have criticized these killings by her male counterparts.

This brings us in closing to the question of Margaret's reputation. Smeared first by the Yorkists, then by the Tudors, Margaret has found few defenders until recently, when historians began to reassess her actions and to untangle the historical Margaret from the crazed she-wolf depicted by Shakespeare. Even so, popular culture has lagged behind, and she continues to be depicted unsympathetically by many popular historians and by historical novelists, who grudgingly admit her courage but who condemn her for embroiling the country in civil war on behalf of a losing cause. Yet the Yorkist claim to the throne was far from undisputed, and men of the time were often prepared to resort to violence to uphold their rights: It hardly seems reasonable to expect Margaret and her supporters to have sat back quietly while the boy they and many others regarded as the rightful heir to the throne was shoved aside in favor of York and his progeny. Had Margaret won her dogged fight for the rights of her son and her husband and succeeded in perpetuating the Lancastrian dynasty through her son, she might well be remembered as a heroine. As it is, her cause almost succeeded, and had she lived for just three more years, she would at least have had the satisfaction of seeing her husband's nephew, Henry Tudor, take the throne as Henry VII.

Further Reading

J. J. Bagley, *Margaret of Anjou, Queen of England*. London: Herbert Jenkins, Ltd, 1948. This is outdated in some respects, but is probably the best of the older biographies of Margaret.

Juliet Barker, *Conquest: The English Kingdom of France 1417–1450*. London: Little, Brown, 2009.

Helen Castor, *She-Wolves: The Women Who Ruled England Before Elizabeth*. London: Faber and Faber, 2010.

B. M. Cron, "Margaret of Anjou and the Lancastrian March on London, 1461." *The Ricardian* (December 1999).

Diana Dunn, "Margaret of Anjou, Queen Consort of Henry VI: A Reassessment of Her Role, 1445–53." In Rowena Archer, ed., *Crown, Government and People in the Fifteenth Century*. New York: St. Martin's Press, 1995.

Diana Dunn, "The Queen at War: The Role of Margaret of Anjou in the Wars of the Roses." In Diana Dunn, ed., *War and Society in Medieval and Early Modern Britain*. Liverpool: Liverpool University Press, 2000.

John Gillingham, *The Wars of the Roses*. Baton Rouge: Louisiana State University Press, 1981.

Anthony Goodman, *The Wars of the Roses*. New York: Dorset Press, 1981.

R. A. Griffiths, *The Reign of King Henry VI*. Gloucestershire: Sutton, 2004 (paperback edition).

Michael Hicks, *The Wars of the Roses*. New Haven and London: Yale University Press, 2010.

Michael Hicks, *Warwick the Kingmaker*. Oxford: Blackwell Publishers, 2002.

P. A. Johnson, *Duke Richard of York: 1411–1460*. Oxford: Oxford University Press, 1988.

Margaret Kekewich, *The Good King: René of Anjou and Fifteenth Century Europe*. London: Palgrave Macmillan, 2008.

J. L. Laynesmith, *The Last Medieval Queens*. Oxford: Oxford University Press, 2005 (paperback edition).

Helen Maurer, *Margaret of Anjou: Queenship and Power in Late Medieval England*. Woodbridge: The Boydell Press, 2003.

A. J. Pollard, *Warwick the Kingmaker: Politics, Power and Fame*. London and New York: Hambledon Continuum, 2007.

Charles Ross, *Edward IV*. New Haven and London: Yale University Press, 1997.

Cora Scofield, *The Life and Reign of Edward the Fourth*. London: Frank Cass & Co. Ltd, 1967 (reprint of 1923 edition).

Bertram Wolffe, *Henry VI*. New Haven and London: Yale University Press, 2001.

An Excerpt From The Stolen Crown

IT WAS ON A FINE SEPTEMBER MORNING IN 1464 THAT THE KING MARRIED MY sister, although I couldn't tell a soul about it, and in truth I wasn't supposed to know myself.

I found out the secret when, just after dawn, my older sister kicked me in her sleep. As Joan was a compulsive kicker and I was well used to such awakenings, I normally would have gone back to sleep, but something made me sit up instead and listen. There appeared to be more life in our manor house at Grafton than usual, a sense of something extra going on besides the usual servants arising.

Disentangling my legs from my sister's—not only did she kick me, she encroached upon my half of the bed, though she claimed it was purely accidental—I climbed out of bed, took my night robe off its peg, draped it over my shoulders, tucked my favorite doll under my arm for company, and quietly made my way downstairs. Sure enough, there were sounds coming from the chapel—a highly unusual occurrence, for these days my family was in no position to keep its own chaplain. I pulled upon the heavy door.

Inside were a priest, my mother, two gentlewomen of my mother's acquaintance, a good-natured-looking man whom I guessed to be in his thirties, my sister Elizabeth, and a rather young man—the last two kneeling by the altar. It was obvious even to my six-year-old self that I had interrupted a wedding, but why on earth was my sister getting married at dawn, with none of the family present but Mother? And why was everyone—even the bride and groom—in everyday clothes? Why, the groom might have been going out for a day's hunting, so casually was he dressed.

As I stood there, at a loss for words and sensing that I had somehow done a Bad Thing, the groom turned and stood, making me gasp. He was tall—well over six feet—and dazzlingly handsome, with hair of a rich brown. Small, sallow, and of middling appearance, I was none of those things, and I averted my eyes as if caught gazing into the sun. "Well, now. Who is this young lady?"

"Katherine, sir," I managed.

"Kate," the groom said as I thrilled from my head to my toes. How did this man know that I loved to be called "Kate," only Mother insisted on the more dignified "Katherine"? He turned to my sister. "I've changed my mind, I'm afraid. *This* will be my new bride."

"She's a trifle young for you," said my sister a little tensely. (She was, I could not help but notice, several years older than the groom.)

"Oh, maybe a bit," the man conceded. He smiled. "Some other lucky man will have little Kate, then. Lady Kate? Can you keep a great secret?"

"You had better," my mother warned.

"I know Kate will," the man said reassuringly. He looked down—a long way down—straight into my eyes. "Kate, I am getting ready to marry your sister. But it is a great secret. No one can know until I announce it personally."

"Your family would not approve?" I ventured, as he was being so confiding.

"Indeed no."

"That is a pity."

"But they will come to understand in time." He cleared his throat and looked thoughtful for a moment, then appeared to make up his mind. "But there are other reasons why there are difficulties just now. I suppose you have not seen our King Edward yet, Kate?"

"No."

"Have you heard much of him?"

I was delighted by his question, for it gave me the opportunity to demonstrate what a good Yorkist I was, a great necessity in our family, since it was not so terribly long ago that Papa and my brothers Anthony and Richard had fought for the House of Lancaster. Having gone over to what now all agreed heartily to be the right side, Papa had sternly informed us children that we should always speak well of the House of York. As with all of my father's advice, I had heeded it dutifully, but I seldom had the chance to put it into practice, for all of my brothers and sisters, being older and much wiser, were naturally much better Yorkists, and never made a mistake I could correct. "No," I admitted. "But I hear he is very brave. And very handsome."

The second man laughed, a sound that made the chapel echo. He was well over a decade older than the groom and less handsome, though his ruddy face was a pleasant one. "Ned, there's a fine courtier for you! Shall I?"

The younger man nodded, and the older man reached in a purse and drew out a fine gold chain, then handed it to me. (Later, I was to learn that he always kept one or two on his person, in case of emergencies.) "There's a reward for your loyalty, Lady Kate."

"Thank you," I said vacantly, staring at the chain. It was lovely, and even to my inexpert eyes looked frightfully expensive. Was my sister marrying a highwayman?

The younger man laughed at my expression. "You see, Kate, *I* am the king. And I have come here to marry your sister."

There were any number of dignified and proper responses I could have made to this announcement. I, of course, made none of them. My mouth gaped open, most unattractively I fear. "*You?*" I asked. "*Her?*"

"Me. Her." The king nodded. "She will make a lovely queen, don't you think?"

"Yes," I admitted feebly. Bessie was indeed lovely; sometimes I thought that she and my brother Anthony had taken so much beauty for themselves that there was not enough left for the other ten of us children, especially me.

"But you must keep this a secret, Kate, as I have said. You will promise?"

"On my life!"

"Good girl," the king said. He grinned. "Or I would be obliged to put you in my Tower as a lesson, you know."

My previous promise was empty compared to the one I made now. "I swear and hope to die if I break my promise," I vowed, kneeling and making the sign of the cross for good measure. I might have gone further and prostrated myself had Bessie not interrupted.

"Time passes. Ned, I know the child will not tell. Can we please resume the ceremony?"

Acknowledgments

MY WORK IN WRITING AND RESEARCHING THIS NOVEL HAS BEEN MADE more pleasant by a number of people. I would like to especially thank Lesley Boatwright, who translated a long passage of Latin for me, and Kathryn Warner, who helped me with several questions about medieval French. As with my last novel, I greatly benefited from the publications and other resources of the Richard III Society.

A special thanks goes to all of those who have discussed Margaret of Anjou and her contemporaries with me on my blog and on Facebook. Your interest in Margaret's story, and your sympathy for the triumphs and tribulations of a long-dead medieval queen and her allies, have kept me going through many a rough patch.

I would like to thank my former editor, Sara Kase, and my current editor, Shana Drehs, for their encouragement, as well as my agent, Nicholas Croce. Regan Fisher gave my manuscript a sound proofreading.

Finally, I must thank the usual suspects: my parents, Charles and Barbara Higginbotham; my husband, Don Coomes; and my children, Thad and Bethany. Having made my thanks, I look forward to seeing how many more bookcases I can slip into the house between the writing of this and the completion of my next novel.

Reading Group Guide

By Susan Higginbotham

1. Fifteen-year-old Margaret is instructed by her uncle King Charles to urge Henry VI to cede Maine to the French. Should she have refused to do so? Could she have? Would her refusal have changed anything, or would Henry VI have likely made the disastrous decision to cede Maine on his own?

2. Though many people share the blame for the reversals in France, William de la Pole bears the brunt of popular anger and is brutally murdered for his role in the disaster. Can you think of examples of such scapegoating today?

3. Margaret suspects that the Duke of York is behind Suffolk's murder, Cade's rebellion, and the rumors of her adultery, and she also believes that York would have murdered Henry VI in order to attain the crown sooner rather than later. Do you believe that her suspicions were justified? Had she been less suspicious, do you think York would have ultimately claimed the throne?

4. Many events contribute to the outbreak of civil war—the English losses in France, Henry's temporary insanity and weakness as a ruler, Margaret's unpopularity as a Frenchwoman, the Duke of York's belief that his claim to the throne is better than Henry VI's. Do you think any one of these factors was determinative, or was it simply a fatal combination of circumstances? Do you believe war could have been averted?

5. William de la Pole's four brothers all die serving in the war in France, while all of the Beaufort brothers and their half brother Tom die fighting for Margaret's cause. Can a war over territorial rights, like the Hundred Years War, or a dynastic struggle, like the Wars of the Roses here, be worth wiping out entire families in fighting? What about a war against clear-cut tyranny like Hitler and the Third Reich?

6. Facing the risk that her own son might die in battle, Margaret wonders at Tewkesbury whether it might have better to accept York's Act of Accord. Should she have? Would you have as a ruler and a mother?

7. Henry VI never leads men into battle, but he faces shipwreck and his own death calmly. What are the various types of courage people display in this novel? Are some sorts of courage more admirable than others?

8. During his imprisonment, William de la Pole takes some comfort in reading poetry, and Margaret at the end of her life finds consolation in her father's verses. Are there literary works that you turn to in times of trouble?

9. Margaret is the target of malicious gossip when she begins to assert herself on behalf of her son. Over five hundred years later, character assassination is still a prominent—and often effective—feature in politics. Can you see this situation ever changing?

10. Hal begins his attempts to seduce Margaret shortly after he defeats his enemy and Margaret's, the Duke of York, in battle. Margaret does not succumb until she is on her own in Rouen. What does their timing say about them?

11. During an unguarded moment, Margaret dreams of a simpler life as Hal's duchess. Do you believe that she would have been happier as an ordinary wife and mother instead of as a queen? What about Henry VI? Do you believe he would have been happier as a private person?

12. Margaret tells Pierre de Brézé that she loves both Henry and Hal, and Hal himself professes his love to both Margaret and Joan. Do you believe it is

possible to truly romantically love two people at the same time? Can you see yourself doing so?

13. Hal Beaufort's sudden betrayal of Henry and Margaret benefits not only Hal personally, but also his imprisoned brother Edmund and his young son. His decision to return to Henry VI, though it eases his conscience, jeopardizes not only his own life, but also the security of those he loves. Would you have made the same decisions he made?

14. Henry VI readily forgives both Margaret and Hal for their adultery, as he forgives many of the wrongs done to him throughout the novel. Other characters, like Hal after his father's murder at St. Albans, carry grudges that determine many of their subsequent actions. Can one be too forgiving or too vengeful, or does it depend entirely on circumstances? Is there a middle ground between the two?

15. The love affair between Margaret and Hal Beaufort is the author's invention, albeit with some foundation in contemporary gossip. How far do you think a historical novelist should go in fictionalizing history? In filling in gaps in history?

16. Just as Margaret is married to further peace between England and France, Anne Neville is married to further the political alliance between her father and Margaret. Both accept their roles without protest. Are they mere pawns, or something more? What of their husbands, who also enter into their marriages for political rather than personal reasons?

17. York's son Edmund and Margaret's son Edward, each aged seventeen, fight and die in battle. Edward IV claims the throne for himself and leads his army to victory when he is not yet nineteen. Margaret leaves France to marry when she is fifteen. Do you believe that modern-day adolescents would be capable of taking on the same tasks as their medieval counterparts did?

18. At the beginning of the novel, Margaret says that as a woman, she had no role in the negotiations over Maine and wanted none. As the novel

progresses, however, she takes on more and more power until her role and Henry's are virtually reversed. Do you think she wanted such power? Did you believe her when she told her son before Tewkesbury that she would give up her leadership role to him?

19. Edward IV orders the murder of Henry VI, thereby removing a figure that Lancastrian loyalists could rally around. Can a political murder be justified if it results in peace for many? If you were in Edward IV's position, could you have ordered such a murder? Do you believe that such a murder would be acceptable today?

20. Margaret reflects that in a kinder world, she and Cecily of York might have become friends. Could the same be said for others in the novel? Can friendship flourish in the midst of a power struggle?

21. When the exiled Jasper Tudor writes to the dying Margaret, the Lancastrian cause seems hopeless to Margaret. Three years later, Jasper's optimism is justified when his nephew Henry becomes king and founds the Tudor dynasty. Would you have been able to keep hope alive in exile?

About the Author

Tim Broyer

SUSAN HIGGINBOTHAM LIVES WITH HER family in North Carolina and has worked as an attorney and as an editor. Her first two historical novels, *The Traitor's Wife* and *Hugh and Bess*, were republished by Sourcebooks in 2009; *The Traitor's Wife* won the gold medal for historical/military fiction in the 2008 Independent Publisher Book Awards. Her third novel, *The Stolen Crown*, was published in 2010. More about Susan's novels and the historical background to them can be found on her website, www.susanhigginbotham.com, and on her blog, Medieval Woman.

The Traitor's Wife
SUSAN HIGGINBOTHAM

From the bedchamber to the battlefield, through treachery and fidelity, one woman is imprisoned by the secrets of the crown.

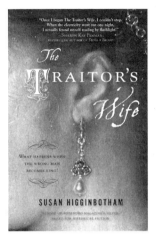

It is an age where passion reigns and treachery runs as thick as blood. Young Eleanor has two men in her life: her uncle King Edward II, and her husband Hugh le Despenser, a mere knight but the newfound favorite of the king. She has no desire to meddle in royal affairs—she wishes for a serene, simple life with her family. But as political unrest sweeps the land, Eleanor, sharply intelligent yet blindly naïve, becomes the only woman each man can trust.

Fiercely devoted to both her husband and her king, Eleanor holds the secret that could destroy all of England—and discovers the choices no woman should have to make.

"Conveys emotions and relationships quite poignantly…entertaining historical fiction."

—*Kirkus Discoveries*

"Higginbotham's talents lie not only in her capacity for detailed genealogical research of the period, but also in her skill in bringing these historical figures to life with passion, a wonderful sense of humor, honor, and love."

—*Historical Novels Review Online*

$14.99 U.S./$15.99 CAN ~ 978-1-4022-1787-6

Hugh and Bess
SUSAN HIGGINBOTHAM

*An unforgettable novel of young love set in
fourteenth-century England.*

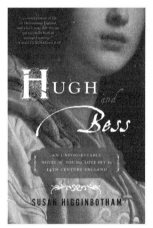

When forced to marry Hugh le Despenser, the son and grandson of disgraced traitors, Bess de Montacute, just thirteen years old, is appalled at his less-than-desirable past. Meanwhile, Hugh must give up the woman he loves in order to marry the reluctant Bess. Far apart in age and haunted by the past, can Hugh and Bess somehow make their marriage work?

Just as walls break down and love begins to grow, the merciless plague endangers all whom the couple holds dear, threatening the life and love they have built.

Award-winning author Susan Higginbotham's impeccable research will delight avid historical fiction readers, while her enchanting characters brought to life will be sure to capture every reader's heart.

"Following in the footsteps of Jean Plaidy and Norah Lofts...filled with a gentle, dry, very subtle sense of humor."

—Dear Author

$14.99 U.S./$18.99 CAN/£7.99 UK ~ 978-1-4022-1527-8

The Stolen Crown
SUSAN HIGGINBOTHAM

It was a secret marriage…one that changed the fate of England forever.

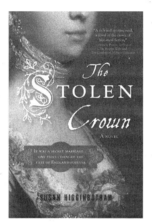

In 1464, six-year-old Katherine Woodville, daughter of a duchess who has married a knight of modest means, awakes to find her gorgeous older sister, Elizabeth, in the midst of a secret marriage to King Edward IV. It changes everything—for Kate and for England.

Then King Edward dies unexpectedly. Richard III, Duke of Gloucester, is named protector of Edward and Elizabeth's two young princes, but Richard's own ambitions for the crown interfere with his duties…

Lancastrians against Yorkists: greed, power, murder, and war. As the story unfolds through the unique perspective of Kate Woodville, it soon becomes apparent that not everyone is wholly evil—or wholly good.

"A rich and riveting read, a jewel in the crown of historical fiction."
—Brandy Purdy, author of *The Boleyn Wife* and *The Confession of Piers Gaveston*

$14.99 U.S./$17.99 CAN/£7.99 UK ~ 978-1-4022-3766-9